# A CRUISE FOR SOUS

---

## A KENNEDY REEVES MYSTERY

# MJ MAC

Paperback Edition 2022

ISBN: 979-8-9870479-3-4


e-book Edition 2022

ISBN: 979-8-9870479-2-7

*To Dan, for believing.*

# Sunny Dayz Cruise Line

# THE HELIO

## *ITINERARY*

**DAY 1:  DEPART PORT CANAVERAL, FLORIDA, USA**

**DAY 2:  AT SEA**

**DAY 3:  COSTA MAYA, MEXICO**

**DAY 4:  COZUMEL, MEXICO**

**DAY 5:  AT SEA**

**DAY 6:  ARRIVE AT PORT CANAVERAL, FLORIDA, USA**

# Sunny Dayz Cruise Line

## THE HELIO

### DAY ONE

DEPARTURE FROM PORT CANAVERAL, FLORIDA, USA

BOARDING BEGINS AT 2:00 P.M.

Kennedy Reeves, cruise director for the *Helio*, stood in the empty lobby. It amazed her how, in the course of a day, the ship could go from a beehive of activity to eerily quiet and then swarming again with passengers. She looked down at her watch, thankful there were a few hours before she would greet the next group of passengers. Moments before, her radio had squawked, alerting her that the holiday decorations and stage props were on their way to the pier. Kennedy had been put in charge of the ship's holiday decorations when her boss, Alfred, explained that the decorating company, which usually turned the *Helio* into a floating winter wonderland, had not been contracted to do the work this year. "Budget cuts," he sighed. "But it's only a few trees and some things for the outlets, and I'm sure you know where everything goes."

As Kennedy's eyes traveled around the lobby, she saw Rosemary Flores, the executive housekeeper, shaking her finger at her nephew and right hand, Mer Thane, as they stood in the middle of a large seating area at the far end of the lobby. Near the guest services desk, Franklin Blaas, the ship's chief engineer, was standing on a ladder shining his flashlight above the ceiling tile.

"Mer!" Rosemary barked in her thick Filipino accent. "This lobby is a disaster! You told me you were ready for my inspection." She ran her hand across a side table and held it up for him to see. "Just look at this dust." Mer's thick black bangs hung in his face as he bowed his head to hide the smile on his face. They both knew there was no dust on Rosemary's hand. Rosemary stalked over to a large grouping of tropical plants near the seating area and scanned it with her laser eyes. She pointed at a long green leaf and frowned. "Just as I expected, these leaves have so much dust I could write my name on them."

Mer smiled mischievously and raised his head to look at her. "Auntie, let me put the disgraceful leaves together; then you would have enough to write a letter." Rosemary laughed at Mer's fast response. "Insolent boy," she clucked her tongue. "I should use them to write to my sister to tell her how disrespectful her son is, but instead, I will supervise you as you prepare the VIP cabins. You will be responsible for them on this trip. It is the *one thing* you do well." She looked at Mer with love. "It must be the lessons I am forced to give you."

Kennedy walked over to Franklin, who was coming down from the ladder. "Everything okay?" she asked.

"Faulty light," he said, looking down at her. "Don't worry. We'll have it fixed before the passengers arrive." He stepped off the last rung and spoke to the man holding the ladder. "Replace the socket and let me know if that fixes the problem." He gestured for Kennedy to follow him. "Explain to me again why the *Solana* team couldn't build four mini kitchens for whatever this harebrained idea the corporate office dreamed up this time." He ran a hand through his thick white hair.

Kennedy cocked her head and shrugged. "You and I got the same information. The cruise line is partnering with the Classic Style Network, which is hosting a chef's competition on the cruise. They are sending someone from the network and corporate office to oversee things. We'll be in the background doing our regular jobs. I think they wanted us because the *Solana* team is still very new." She gave him a mischievous look. "Plus, they knew you would *love* to figure out the logistics to design and build the competition set."

Franklin closed his eyes and pinched the bridge of his nose. "I need to retire," he groused. He pulled a piece of paper from his pocket and unfolded it for her to see. "I'm doing the best I can on this thing," he said, putting on his glasses. "Besides this sketch and a list of equipment, I wasn't given much to go on. The equipment is coming up now. Getting enough power out there was the biggest problem. I had to run a lot of lines to get this on the putting green, and it looks like a snake pit. This whole thing reminds me of our first cruise. No information from the corporate office—what a surprise," he said gruffly.

Kennedy visibly shuddered at the memory of their cruise a few months earlier. "Please don't remind me. I want to put that whole terrible cruise in a bottle and throw it into the ocean," she sighed. "Although, that would be littering."

"Speaking of lack of information, did your holiday décor and stage props arrive, oh Queen of Christmas?"

Kennedy rolled her eyes. "I was on my way down to the pier. I just received a message that it was on its way. I hope Ali has a couple of extra storage lockers. Like you, all I got was a list of what was coming. You, at least, had a sketch of what they wanted. Alfred sent me a note telling me it was just a few trees and I'd know where to put them." She made a face. "Honestly, I never paid attention to the holiday decorations. I was too busy concentrating on the shows and making sure Santa showed up where and when he was supposed to." She hit her forehead with the palm of her hand. "Oh no," she sighed.

"What?"

"I forgot to—" She stopped speaking, scrutinizing her friend, who had snow-white hair, a beard, and a pair of silver-rimmed eyeglasses perched on the end of his nose.

"Why are you looking at me like that?" Franklin asked warily.

"Do you realize you could double for Santa? White hair, tall, handsome." She fluttered her eyelashes at him. "Oh, please say yes, Franklin! It's for five measly minutes during the holiday show, and you would be so much better than a crew member wearing a wig and pillows.”

“ABSOLUTELY NOT!” Franklin thundered and glared at her.

“Please?” she pleaded. “It’s for one song, and you don’t have to do anything but sit in the sleigh and slide across the stage. The reindeer will dance around you, and you wave your hands to the audience. That’s it, I promise.”

Franklin furrowed his brow. “I’ll think about it,” he said grouchily, holding up his finger when she began to clap her hands together. “No promises, and I’m only a backup plan. You need to find someone on the crew to do it. And don’t you dare breathe a word of this to Rosemary. I am not going to play Santa for her housekeeping party!” He took his glasses off and folded up the piece of paper he had been holding, stuffing both back into his front shirt pocket. “I’ve got work to do,” he growled.

“So, you’ll do it?” she asked hopefully.

“I’ll think about it!” he snarled and stomped off, muttering as he walked away.

Rosemary and Mer walked over to Kennedy, and the three watched Franklin leave the lobby.

“What happened to Mr. Jolly Pants?” Mer asked, looking at Kennedy.

Kennedy placed a hand over her mouth; her eyes were full of merriment. "I poked the bear but can't say anything else."

"Come on, Kennedy, it's not like he would stay mad at you for long," Mer said. "Besides, there are no secrets on the ship. Everybody knows everything about everyone," he chuckled.

"Okay, but this stays between us." She motioned them to come closer. "I asked him if he would play Santa for one song in the holiday show instead of getting one of the crew to do it. He first said no, but I might be able to convince him."

Rosemary chuckled softly. "Good luck, but I doubt he will. Years ago, he agreed to fill in when the regular Santa became seasick." She looked around to make sure no one else could hear her. "But there was an incident, and Franklin swore off ever playing Santa again. The cruise director at the time had planned an after-hours party in what is now Longitudes Lounge." Rosemary closed her eyes, remembering the story. "Back then, it was called the Siren's Song, and the nicest thing I can say about the bar is that everything in there went into a dumpster when it was renovated." Kennedy and Mer exchanged stares.

"It couldn't have been *that* bad, Rosemary," Kennedy said.

Rosemary gave her a knowing look. "Close your eyes and picture a giant aquarium filled with enormous pieces of neon-colored coral, King Neptune's throne, and fish floating in the air on invisible fishing line. Even the tables were made to look like pieces of coral. Now add blue lighting."

Kennedy's eyes flew open. "Oh, wow! If my imagination is even close, it was awful."

"You're getting the picture, and the uniforms were even worse. But back to my story. As I said, the cruise director had planned an adults-only holiday party in the bar. She wanted Santa to sit on Neptune's throne to oversee the merriment." She took a deep breath and tucked a stray lock of black and silver hair behind her ear. "Unfortunately, one woman on the cruise had been chasing and propositioning Franklin all over the ship, and she had heard he would be in the Siren's Song as Santa." She shook her head. "Poor Franklin came into the bar, hollered out a hearty 'ho-ho-ho,' and sat on Neptune's throne. Then, according to Luke, who was new to the team, the woman began to walk seductively but drunkenly over to Franklin with a red feather boa. When she got to Franklin, she took off the boa, wrapped it around his neck, and plopped herself onto his lap. He was mortified. He couldn't push her off because she was a guest, but he didn't want her on his lap. Then she began to whisper in his ear, and whatever she said made him turn as red as the Santa suit he was wearing. After a few minutes, Luke rescued him by announcing that Santa had to deliver more presents, but not before the woman pulled her cabin key out of her cleavage and gave it to him in front of everyone. Franklin didn't know what to do, so he stood up, shook his finger at her, and walked out of the bar waving to the crowd. He hid in his office for the rest of the cruise, terrified that she would find him."

Kennedy wondered how this story had stayed under wraps for so long, but before she could ask, Rosemary looked intently at Kennedy and Mer. "You cannot tell this to anyone. Franklin would be furious with me if he knew I told you the story."

"My lips are sealed," Kennedy replied, running her fingers across her lips. "He might change his mind," she mused.

"If I were you, I would find someone else to play Santa," Rosemary said sternly.

"I can do it, Kennedy!" Mer put his hands on his hips and shook his slight frame. "Ho-ho-ho, I'm Santa Claus."

Kennedy and Rosemary exchanged a look and began laughing at his impersonation. "Mer, thank you for volunteering. If I can't convince Franklin, you are at the top of the list." She looked at her watch. "I've got to go down to the pier to check on my delivery." She took a deep breath. "I hope things go smoothly with the change to our itinerary."

"That's the great thing about housekeeping," Mer said. "It doesn't matter where we go; it's always the same—clean, clean, clean."

Rosemary glared at him and pointed to the tropical plants they had been previously standing by. "And you can't even get *that* right!"

Kennedy walked down to the pier and saw her best friend, Mila Casimir, the ship's spa director, signing for a shipment of supplies. "Where's Anna Marie?" she asked. Anna Marie, the spa's receptionist, was in charge of ordering and receiving the products used and sold in the spa.

"I thought it would be nice to take a turn," Mila replied, looking up from her clipboard. "She's so good at juggling everything from the passengers to the staff. I thought I would give her a break. Besides, it's exciting to get all of this." She smiled impishly and winked at Kennedy. "It makes me think I've been shopping." Mila's long brown hair began whipping around as a sudden gust of wind kicked up. When the wind stopped, her face was covered with hair, making it hard to see her features. "It never fails," she moaned, clawing her hair away from her face. "The minute I step outside, Mother Nature decides to blow like a hurricane, and while I think I have that sexy windblown look, in reality, I look like a hairy goblin." She bent her head down, took the long mass of hair in her hands, and pulled it into a high ponytail.

"Well," Kennedy said thoughtfully with a smirk, "maybe not a hairy goblin, but you do remind me of an English sheepdog or one of those Highland cows."

Mila flipped her head back and straightened up. "Really? A Highland cow or an English sheepdog? I was hoping for something more regal, like, an Afghan hound."

Kennedy heard a horn beeping, and someone shouted her name. She looked around and saw Billy Higgins, one of the *Helio's* bellmen, waving his arms at her. "Hey, Kennedy," he hollered, "the stuff arrived." He jerked his thumb behind him. "Do you want to look at what is here before we start loading it? Did you find somewhere to put everything?"

Mila looked at Kennedy quizzically. "Holiday décor and stage props," Kennedy said. The two women watched uneasily as Billy began raising and lowering the forks. "I'd better go. I'm suddenly extremely nervous about Billy driving a forklift."

"I can understand," Mila said dryly. "I've seen him push a bell cart." She smiled at Kennedy. "In fact, I'm going to get my stuff on board before you two get anywhere near the loading area. Catch up later?"

"Sure," Kennedy said and watched Billy spin the forklift in circles. She left Mila and walked briskly over to him. "Billy, remind me again how you learned to operate a forklift?"

He grinned and pressed the stop button. "When we were shut down." He saw Kennedy's puzzled face. "I worked in a warehouse store and became the forklift guy. I spent most of my time moving stuff from place to place, but the best part was learning the cool tricks these things can do."

Kennedy started to ask about "cool forklift tricks" but changed her mind. "Billy, we need to get the boxes inside, but I want it done a certain way. Can we look at what we received? Did they give you a list?"

Billy nodded and pressed a button on the panel as the forklift sputtered to life. "Hop on, Kennedy. I'll take you over there."

Kennedy eyed the forklift uneasily. "I think I'll walk, but no more tricks. Remember, safety first."

Billy raised his hand to his temple in a salute. "I'll meet you there."

Kennedy picked her way across the pier and stopped to wave to the storeroom manager, Ali Asad, who was keeping a close eye on the deliveries. Ali raised his hand in response but quickly looked back down at his clipboard. While the more prominent cruise lines had the luxury of tractor-trailer deliveries brought directly to their loading docks, the small Sunny Dayz fleet had to use a more labor-intensive method. Their tractor-trailers were parked further away, and storeroom crew members dressed in white coveralls and blue baseball caps offloaded the provisions to forklifts which would be driven down the pier to the ship. When they arrived at the ship's loading area, a second team would move the pallets and boxes on board, dividing them between the various freezers, refrigerators, lockers, and storerooms.

The provisions area was enormous and took up most of the lower deck. Ali ran his department with a keen eye and a pocket watch. Hours earlier, he and his team had transported the passengers' luggage to the cruise terminal. Deliveries began arriving as the luggage left, and as soon as the provisions were loaded, it was time to take delivery of the baggage for the next cruise. It was in moments like this, as she watched the ballet of loading provisions between arrivals and departures, that Kennedy would take a step back and appreciate how each person's job was a piece of the puzzle that made the ship run like clockwork.

Omar Meier, the director of security, walked up to her as she surveyed the busy pier. "Looking for something special?" he asked. He pointed to the boxes of produce waiting to be inspected by Chef Ano and Chef Michèle. "I would recommend a date; they are one of my favorites. They have a way of being versatile and mysterious at the same time, like you." He smiled broadly, and his white teeth flashed brightly against his olive-toned skin. Kennedy and Omar's friendship had developed into something more during the last six months, which was challenging as life on the ship often felt like living in a fishbowl.

"I'm afraid I don't know much about dates, Mr. Meier. Unfortunately, we don't get to go on any," she said playfully at the double entendre. "And how did you know I would be down here?"

"I meant this kind of date." He pulled a plastic bag out of his pocket and placed what looked like a large, plump raisin in her hand. Omar smiled widely as she looked warily at the wrinkled fruit. "*And,* as director of security, I make it a point to know your whereabouts." Kennedy blushed. "Although I was surprised to see you on the video screen walking the pier on an embarkation day. Usually, you tell me that you have a million things to do before the passengers arrive." She opened her mouth to speak, and he popped the date into her mouth. She had seen dates, but they were a complete mystery to her. Her mother, Lolly, would have called them forbidden fruit as they were high in sugar and calories. As she sunk her teeth into the chewy mass, caramel and cinnamon flavors swirled around in her mouth. Then, swallowing and closing her eyes, she sighed. "I take it that this date met with your approval?" Omar asked, seeing the smile on her face.

"Why have I never eaten them before?" she asked, opening her eyes in wonder.

"You hadn't met me yet," he winked. "So, I'll ask again, why are you down here?"

She put her hands on her hips. "Oh? Our esteemed director of security doesn't know everything? I'm shocked." Omar furrowed his brow. "Remember? I'm in charge of decorating the ship for the holidays." She pointed to her clipboard. "I want to make sure I have this organized perfectly. Somehow, I managed to schedule the holiday decorating for the same night we are putting on a new show, which only leaves a few hours to transform the ship into holiday headquarters."

Omar saluted her mockingly. "Private Meier, reporting for duty, General Reeves."

Kennedy burst into laughter and shook her head. "You don't want to be anywhere near the holiday décor. All that glitter on your dark suit would make you twinkle like a star in the night sky. We'll be okay. We can divide and conquer between the cast, spa, housekeeping, and maintenance staff." She looked in the direction of Billy and the mountain of boxes around him. "Alfred said it was only a few trees, but I think he misrepresented things."

"Kennedy, what do you know about this cooking competition? And the change of the cruise itinerary?" Omar asked, changing the subject.

Kennedy explained to Omar, as she had to Franklin, that they had all received the same information. The *Helio* and the *Solana* would change routes for one cruise. "It has something to do with the partnership between Classic Style Network and the cruise line," she said. "I told Franklin I wondered if corporate made the switch because the *Solana* team is still very new. It will be a nice change of scenery."

"I suppose it doesn't matter to me what the scenery is. I seem to be focused on only one thing lately." He looked intensely at her.

Kennedy was seldom at a loss for words, but she was suddenly tongue-tied. She was about to reply when she was distracted by Billy and Ali waving frantically at her. "I have to go, Omar," she said with reluctance. "It seems like something's wrong." Omar turned and saw the two men waving anxiously. "Either the delivery or Billy is upsetting Ali."

"Or both," Omar said and swept his arms to the side so she could leave. She got halfway to where Billy and Ali stood and wondered if Omar was watching her. She looked over her shoulder, trying to look nonchalant, and blushed when she heard Omar let out a hearty laugh.

"Kennedy," Ali said in a clipped tone when she arrived, "would you please explain this to me?" He waved at the mountain of large boxes. "And why is Billy driving one of my forklifts?" He looked down at his clipboard. "None of this is on my list of arrivals."

Kennedy swallowed. "This is all my fault," she said quickly. "I got a note from Alfred in the corporate office last week that the holiday décor would be delivered this morning." She looked at him apologetically. "I was so busy on the last cruise trying to find additional activities for the passengers because of the rain that I never got a chance to come down and talk to you. When I realized I had messed up, I didn't want to make things harder on your team, so I asked Billy if he would help me."

"I am a certified forklift operator, sir," Billy said proudly, straightening his shoulders. "I have my license in my wallet if you want to see it."

Ali looked from Billy to the pile of boxes and then back at Kennedy. "There's a lot of boxes here, Kennedy."

Kennedy looked at Ali anxiously and twisted her hands. "Could I store it in the cages down by the security cells? That's where I keep the props for the stage shows and the things I use for passenger events. There is one huge cage that is empty, and the one beside it, too. Please, Ali?"

Ali sighed and ran a hand through his thinning hair. "You can have the lockers for a few weeks until the holidays are over. I'll manage. Do you and Billy need help?"

Billy tripped over one of the forks, crashed into several boxes, and fell to the ground. Kennedy looked at him as he struggled to get up. "I'm okay!" he said, holding up his arm.

Kennedy whispered behind her hand to Ali, "Yes, we need help if you don't mind. I'd feel better if we had someone with more experience to load things. Billy can organize the lockers with me." Ali bobbed his head, and Kennedy called over to Billy and explained the plan. "I'd rather have you help me organize the lockers," she said. "When it is time for us to decorate, I'm going to rely heavily on your help to tell everyone where things go." Billy smiled, basking in Kennedy's words.

Ali whistled loudly to three members of his crew and walked toward them. Kennedy had a knack for making people feel good. A few months earlier, she had pulled together an outrageous impromptu diva show. The performance had been memorable, and many passengers still asked which night the diva show would take place. But what Ali remembered was how Kennedy made every member of the ship feel vital to the event and took the time to thank everyone during the next cruise for their hard work. She was unlike many others he had worked with in the past, and he was glad he had returned to the *Helio* after the shutdown.

Billy and Kennedy stood in front of the empty storage lockers. The chain-link paneled lockers were approximately fifteen feet high and twenty feet wide, with two doors at the front. Kennedy was thoughtful as she looked at the space. She mentally pictured what she wanted to do. "If we stack the trees around the perimeter of this locker and put another row on top, we should be fine. The large boxes that make up the ornament arch for the lobby will have to go in the center. We can fill in the boxes of ornaments, bags of snow, and other items where we can." She turned to Billy. "Oh, and there will be a large tree and Santa's sleigh we won't use immediately. They are props for the holiday show."

Billy looked at the empty lockers and slowly shook his head. "There was a lot of stuff out there," he said. "Are you sure it will fit?"

Kennedy looked at the empty lockers and then at Billy. "I hope so. We should think about this like a giant 3-D puzzle and use every inch of space. Ali doesn't have any other lockers, and the only other open spaces down here are the security cells.”

“But we don’t use them that often,” he began, but before Kennedy could respond, Ali and his team had arrived with the first load.

Kennedy looked at the line of boxes behind them and took a deep breath. “Okay, let’s get started.”

Kennedy and Billy got into a good rhythm, and the locker’s organization was falling into place. When the fourth load of boxes arrived, Billy saw Kennedy look at her watch. “I can handle this,” he said, grinning. “I know you have a lot to do before the passengers arrive. All I need to do is change my clothes and be ready with the bell cart.”

Kennedy looked up, her face sparkling with glitter. “Really? You are a lifesaver!” She brushed herself off and stepped out of the locker. “I think I’ll take the stairs,” she said, pointing to the back staircase near them. “It will be quicker than taking the freight elevator today.” She opened the door, looked up at the stairwell, and began climbing the stairs. When she finally reached her cabin fifteen minutes later, she was sweating and out of breath. She dropped into a chair and gulped the bottle of water on the desk. *I’m counting those stairs as my exercise for today*, she thought.

She reached for another bottle of water and pressed a button on her computer to wake it up. While she waited for the welcome screen, she glanced at the calendar on the wall. The *Helio* team had been on a much longer contract than usual, and everyone was tired and ready to take some time off. She wondered what Omar had planned. She had tried asking him questions about his personal life, but he would always dance around the subject.

Her computer screen came on, and she looked at her messages. A few were from Alfred, and one contained photos of previous holiday cruises to give her a better idea of where the decorations should go. In his note, he thanked her again for agreeing to manage the holiday installation. *It's not like I had a choice, Alfred. And what happened to "it's just a couple of trees?"* She took a few minutes to review the photos and began making a list.

Alfred's second message was a recap of the switch of routes, the culinary competition, and the partnership between the cruise line and the network. The Classic Style Network started as a monthly magazine five years ago. They had recently branched out as a regional television network, and it was rapidly gaining popularity. The partnership and the competition had been the brainchild of Winnifred Wallace in the corporate office. Sunny Dayz had paid a sizable fee for advertising and was underwriting the competition in hopes the investment would bring increased bookings and future opportunities to host the network's shows on their ships. Winnifred, Alfred reassured Kennedy, would be on board to oversee everything for the competition. Kennedy would only need to take care of the guests and put up the holiday decorations.

Kennedy saw the manifest in her messages and opened the document, perusing the VIP travelers. Monique Patrick, a freelance travel journalist, was on board to write about the competition. Unfortunately, there were no other notes, and Kennedy put a star by her name so she could look her up. Next, Kennedy scanned the manifest and saw the names of three of the four competing chefs and the show's producer, Deuce Dawson. She wished she had the fourth chef's name but only saw the letters TBD.

Kennedy's eyes continued down the list and saw VIP VIP VIP written in bold red letters next to the name Emily Abbott. There was a note that an additional message about Mrs. Abbott would come from Alfred, and Kennedy wondered if it was the same Emily Abbott who sat on the cruise line's board of directors. She was pleasantly surprised to see three other names under the VIP code on the manifest. Her friend David Stearns, a frequent cruiser with ties to a popular Florida nightclub called Club Diva, would be on the cruise. David, a travel writer, was on board to write about the spa. She looked forward to catching up with him. Several months earlier, while on the inaugural cruise for the *Helio*,

John, Club Diva's owner, along with David and their friends, had hit upon an unusual but lucrative idea, and she wondered how it was working out.

The last two names on the VIP list surprised Kennedy, and she was curious to know what had happened in their lives since their previous cruise. Jones and Terri Butler, the founders of the fast-food restaurant Buck-A-Cluck, had booked the Owner's Suite. Kennedy smiled as their faces popped into her head. Selling their multi-million-dollar chain of restaurants to a conglomerate earlier in the year, they had taken a cruise to celebrate and unwind after the sale. Jones had negotiated a deal tough enough to make Kennedy's father, an attorney for a bank, mention the sale one night at dinner. Kennedy was surprised months later when she met them on the cruise. The colorful couple wore jaw-dropping outfits to dinner each night and were hard to forget. Kennedy looked forward to seeing them. However, she was a little surprised that she had not heard from them directly. After an unfortunate event on their first *Helio* cruise, Mr. and Mrs. Butler decided they only wanted to work with Kennedy for any future cruises. She remembered that they were beginning the renovation of their home, Tara, a palatial estate in Mississippi, and had requested the name of the decorator who had designed their stateroom—the Owner's Suite.

The Owner's Suite was not for the faint of heart, and the Butlers had fallen in love with the design the moment they set foot in it. The cabin, designed by the wife of a board member who claimed to have a natural flair for decorating, looked as if Elvis Presley and Hugh Hefner had created a set of rooms that expressed their inner fantasies. Kennedy shuddered as she pictured the cabin's living room: the zebra-striped carpet, the gold and white filigree wallpaper, and the custom-made round ivory couch that looked like it belonged in a casino lobby.

Kennedy shook her head to remove the image of the suite from her mind and turned her attention back to her computer screen. She clicked on the message from Alfred. As she read it, cold sweat began forming on her neck. Alfred asked how Chef Michèle felt about being one of the judges for the competition. Alfred explained that the network believed having the ship's executive chef as a judge would give the contest more authenticity. Kennedy was bewildered. She was sure that Michèle had not been asked as he would have blown up at the suggestion and would have vented about it during one of their daily meetings. Kennedy took a deep breath and picked up the telephone. She knew she should have the conversation in person, but she had too many other things to do before the morning leadership meeting. Taking a deep breath, she dialed the number for the galley. "Chef? It's Kennedy. I know you are busy, but I need to share some information. And I need you to remember that I am the messenger." After she disconnected a few moments later, she could still hear the angry chef cursing in French. She turned back to her computer to read the rest of Alfred's message:

MONIQUE PATRICK: Freelance journalist and travel blogger. She also owns a boutique travel agency. She is a friend of Winnifred Wallace from corporate, who is the brains behind this collaboration. Monique is writing about the competition (she's made separate arrangements with the network on this). According to Winnie, she might write an article about the cruise line, but nothing is confirmed. Winnie will handle anything Monique needs.

DAVID STEARNS: Travel writer. You know who he is. We've partnered with him to write about the spa. Please let Mila know to comp all services.

DEUCE DAWSON: Food and beverage producer for Classic Style Network. Deuce is also bringing his technical guy, Art. Would you make sure Bert is available to help him with whatever he needs? Art will be running the cameras, video loop, etc.

Kennedy pulled a fresh sheet of paper from her clipboard and began to take notes to share with the group at their morning staff meeting. If so much was riding on the competition, why were they just now hearing about the details? She blew out a large breath. *Probably like a lot of other things we found out about later.* She looked back at her computer and the message.

COMPETITION CHEFS: I won't bore you with this. Winnie will oversee them. I understand there was a minor glitch with one of the competitors, and the network selected an alternate chef.

The cold sweat that had formed on Kennedy's neck now reached around and popped out on her forehead as she read the next paragraph.

EMILY ABBOTT: Board member. She's also the great-granddaughter of our founder and best friend of Vera Jameson, whom you have taken care of many times. After learning about what happened earlier this year, Mrs. Abbott has decided to take a more active role in the company. She will be the third judge for the competition. Mrs. Abbott has expressed that she wants the same experiences Mrs. Jameson has on her cruises. If Mrs. Jameson got it, ensure Mrs. Abbott also gets it. The captain has been informed that she will be at his table each night for dinner. Kennedy, I know you will take excellent care of her. We need her to bring back a glowing review of her cruise.

Kennedy began to roll her shoulders and put a warm hand on the back of her neck, now damp with sweat. *No problem, Alfred: transform the ship into a holiday wonderland, journalists, the great-granddaughter of the company's founder, a culinary competition, and a national marketing campaign. No stress at all. What else?*

Then she read Alfred's last paragraph.

Oh, could you get some competition together so a passenger can win a Sun Trophy? Mrs. Abbott saw a replica in my office, and I explained what it was. She was shocked we get so much social media chatter about it. The winners of Seventies Night a few months ago gave us a lot of attention. I'm sure you have something in your back pocket. Make that Kennedy magic happen!

After Kennedy finished reading her messages, she left her room and walked to the conference room on deck five. The senior staff met formally twice on embarkation days and daily when the ship was underway. The short meetings allowed them to share information quickly and efficiently. In his last message, Alfred said he wanted to speak with all of them this morning. When she arrived, several members of the team were already in conversation, and Chef Michèle glared at her. "Sorry," she mouthed to him as she took a seat.

"Have we figured out who is playing Santa for the employee party this year? I hear that Kennedy is also looking for someone to play the big guy for her holiday show," Mila said mischievously, looking at Franklin with a smile.

Rosemary tapped a finger on her chin. "Goodness, if we only knew someone tall, with white hair and a luxurious beard." She sighed. "What a distinguished and handsome Santa."

"NO!" Franklin thundered. "The matter is closed. Kennedy knows to find someone else because it won't be me."

"But, Santa," Mila pouted and fluttered her long eyelashes.

Franklin scowled at the two women who were holding back giggles. He shook his finger at them. "You are both the reason why Santa has a naughty list." He turned away from Rosemary and Mila and faced Omar, who was sitting across from him. Omar's eyes were dancing with amusement from the needling Franklin was receiving. "Omar," he said in a serious tone, "we need to figure out how many cameras are broken. Have you had a chance to walk the ship? We could have them fixed when the ship goes in for deep cleaning and maintenance."

Omar shook his head. "I'm not finished. Several in the lower storage level and staff areas are broken, and none of the stairwell cameras work. I will have a complete list by the time we return to Port Canaveral." He grimaced. "I'm embarrassed I allowed this to go on this long. The safety of our passengers and staff cannot be an afterthought."

"Don't be too hard on yourself," Franklin said softly. "We didn't have much time to turn things around when we returned a few months ago. We—"

Omar cut him off, "It was my responsibility. I should have caught it."

Kennedy looked around the room. Everyone was present. She got up from her seat and turned on the television at the head of the table. "Well, if everyone is ready, let's see how much we can get done before Alfred comes on. I just read a message from him, and there is a lot of information we didn't know." She turned toward Ano and smiled warmly. "But first, I'd like to welcome Chef Ano to the group today. There has been a slight change of plans, and Chef Michèle will be one of the judges for the competition. Ano will join us for our daily meetings."

Michèle snorted and crossed his arms. "This competition is ridiculous. Chefs are competing to be on a television show. What has the culinary world come to?" He shook his head. "Being a chef is demanding work. It is certainly not about being pretty or doing tricks for television viewers. It's about creating dishes that are pleasing to the eye and the palate."

Luke snickered. "And that's why you are a judge and not one of the competitors, Michèle. You just aren't pretty enough."

"Spending my time doing silly taste tests is ridiculous when I need to be in my kitchen. Things could very well fall apart."

"Aw, Chef, maybe you are worried things will run smoother without you, and we will like Ano better than you." Luke chuckled and cocked his head. "Although that wouldn't be too hard, you aren't likable." He turned to Tony, the dining room manager. "And you might get to relax during the dinner service instead of worrying about when he might erupt."

Tony looked nervously at Michèle. "That's not true, Chef." He laughed nervously and looked at the others around the table. "I only freak out when Michèle's eyes bulge out of his head, and he's walking toward me. If he's yelling, it only means he's annoyed with me."

Franklin joined in on the pileup against the ship's executive chef. "He yells at me all the time. It must mean he loves me!" He let out a hearty laugh.

Chef Michèle's eyes widened, and his nostrils began to flare. "I will not put up with this nonsense, Kennedy." He pushed back in his chair and slapped his large hand down on the table. "Ano, come!" Ano began to get up.

"Chef, Ano, please sit down. The boys are sorry," Kennedy said placatingly. "Aren't you?" She gave Franklin, Tony, and Luke a stern look and turned back to the large, dark chef. "Look, I know being a judge got sprung on you and isn't what you like to do, but the network values the opinion of a chef of your caliber." Kennedy looked at the others. "Let's go around the room quickly, and then I'll share what I learned this morning." She turned to Rosemary. "Would you start us off?"

"Certainly, all VIP cabins are ready for my inspection, and Mer will be in charge of them on this cruise." She crossed her arms and gave a firm nod. "I am entrusting him with this new responsibility."

"That will be the day. Rosemary will never be flexible enough to trust someone, even Mer," Franklin muttered quietly.

Rosemary turned and frowned at him. "Ask any member of the housekeeping team. I'm flexible as long as things are done the right way—my way."

The others gave their updates, and Mila was the last to speak. "Kennedy, is there anything we should know about the competition and the VIPs? We haven't heard much."

Kennedy shared what she had learned from Alfred's messages. As she spoke, the faces of those around the table tightened.

"As far as the VIPs," Kennedy continued, "we have Winnifred Wallace from the corporate office, Emily Abbott, who sits on the board—"

"*The* Emily Abbott?" Franklin interrupted, "as in, one of the great-granddaughters?" He had been with the company the longest and knew its history.

Kennedy nodded, and the group groaned in unison. "The other VIPs are the competing chefs, the representative from Classic Style Network, two journalists, and our favorite couple, Jones and Terri Butler."

"Well, dinner should be entertaining," Tony quipped.

Omar spoke up, "Kennedy, do we know anything about these journalists?"

"One is a friend of our corporate marketing person, and the other," she turned to Mila, "is David Stearns, our friend from Club Diva. He's here to write about Oaza. Isn't that exciting?"

"Thank goodness it's David," Mila said, relieved.

"I'm sure he will come to the spa as soon as he arrives. So please save a few appointments for him each day if you don't mind. Oh, and Alfred said to comp his services."

"Got it!" Mila said, jotting her information down. "I'll speak with Anna Marie. She has a crush on him, so it won't be too difficult for her to find a few openings. And I'll need to bring up a case of champagne for him. He drinks it like water."

Kennedy looked around the table. "One last thing before Alfred gets on. I'm sure you will be excited to learn that the holiday décor arrived and is currently in the storage lockers next to the holding cells."

"Mila, do you feel like taking a trip down memory lane?" Luke teased playfully.

Mila cut her eyes at him. "I will remind you that I was never down there," she said primly. "Omar made sure I was confined to the luxury of my cabin, thank you." She motioned to Kennedy. "Please continue."

"Operation Elf will take place on day three of the cruise. I need as many volunteers as possible. We'll meet in the main dining room after the passengers have finished dinner." She looked at her clipboard. "There's more set up than I expected, but I've mapped out a plan, and I think we can be done in a few hours and still have time for a little holiday cheer and a couple of hours of sleep." She looked around the room and added mischievously, "I even have some surprises planned!"

"Does it include a short, red, fur-trimmed Mrs. Claus costume?" Luke asked. "I bet Omar would be an exceptionally good boy if you wore something like that!"

Omar blushed, and Kennedy looked at Luke as if he had lost his mind. "N-n-no," she stammered.

Tony took a roll of antacids from his pocket and put one in his mouth. He was an anxious man, and anything out of the ordinary sent him into a tailspin. "Kennedy," he said worriedly, "with all these VIPs, who do I seat where? Can we talk after the meeting?" A grimace crossed his face. "I need to stand up. The stress is starting to make my back hurt."

Kennedy looked at Tony, and her heart went out to him. He was a perfectionist and would make himself sick with worry over the dining room's seating chart. "Of course," she said gently, "as soon as the meeting is over."

Tony looked at her gratefully and mopped his forehead with a handkerchief. He suddenly grabbed his lower back. "Spasm," he yelped.

Suddenly Alfred's face appeared on the screen, and it jerked around while he adjusted his camera. "Good morning," he smiled at the camera nervously. Kennedy noticed Alfred did not look well. His normally tan complexion was pale and waxy. "I'm sure you are extremely excited to be the team who will bring our little cruise line to the viewers of the Classic Style Network. We are counting on all of you to make our 'Sous Cruise,' " he made quotation marks with his fingers, "a recipe for success." The group let out a collective groan at his pun.

Michèle spluttered, "Alfred, the company is not really calling this the Sous Cruise, are they?"

Alfred's brows knit together. "Yes, it is, Chef Michèle. Our marketing team came up with the idea, and the network loved it! Is there something objectionable to the name?"

Michèle studied the papers on the table in front of him. "No, not at all," he answered. "It's an unusual play on words." He silently wondered if someone on the marketing team had gone through a list of words that rhymed with the word cruise to develop this marketing ploy. This was the same group that had named the company's signature cocktail, the SunRumbrella, after an afternoon of drinking.

Alfred coughed and took a drink of water. "Franklin, how is the set coming on the pool deck? Did the equipment arrive?"

Franklin counted to five before he answered. "Yes, sir. We are in the process of completing the installation." He cleared his throat. "I moved the location from the pool area to the putting green. The putting green is not used much and allows for a seated audience."

Alfred looked surprised. "Great idea! We assumed the pool would be the most popular area on the ship, but this is much better." He looked down and scribbled something on a piece of paper. "Kennedy, I received some distressing news and need to discuss a matter with you. Would you like me to tell you now or call you later?"

Kennedy was caught off guard and stuttered, "N-n-now is fine, Alfred, unless you are firing me."

"Fire you? Heavens no! We need you to run point on the competition. Unfortunately, Winnifred Wallace, who was coming from the corporate office to manage things from our end, was in a car accident last night and is in the hospital." There was a collective gasp from the group.

"Is she okay, Alfred? What do you mean by run point? I don't have any of the information," she said anxiously.

"Winnie will be fine, and I'll send everything over to you," he blinked his eyes rapidly. "Really, the competition should run itself. Franklin has built the set, Michèle's team will take care of the food, Deuce Dawson will oversee the competition, and the judges will select a winner." He gave a brittle chuckle.

Kennedy's mind was whirling. "Other than the competition, are there other things the chefs will do? Your email mentioned interviews with Winnifred's associate, Monique. Are there excursions planned for them?" Kennedy's pen was poised over her clipboard.

The group watched Alfred's Adam's apple bob up and down as he paged through his notes. "Ah yes," he pointed at the sheaf of papers on his desk. "They each have an interview, as do the judges, but you can schedule those after everyone arrives, and the network has set up the group excursions." He looked up from his notes. "You won't have to do much, Kennedy. Just babysit the competition. I'll send you the information I have. For your peace of mind, maybe you could put an itinerary together for everyone." He rubbed his hands together. "Okay, next, Omar, I am glad you are here. We have a special request of you."

"Yes, sir, how may I be of assistance?"

"As you probably know, Emily Abbott, one of the board members and a family member, has requested that she dine with you. She is a close friend of Vera Jameson's, and after hearing about Vera's last cruise, Mrs. Abbott has insisted that you escort her for all evening activities on board." He looked at his notes and then back at the camera. "I'm sorry, Omar. I know you detest this sort of thing, and I wouldn't ask, but it's out of my hands."

Franklin, Luke, Tony, and Michèle looked down and began to snicker. Their snickers became chortling laughter, and suddenly the four men could not control themselves. Franklin looked up, wiping the tears from his face, "Couldn't happen to a nicer guy, Alfred." He looked at Omar. "I suddenly feel the need to fix as many cameras as I can before tonight. I want to capture every moment!"

Alfred continued, "Mrs. Abbott will also be one of the judges for the competition along with Deuce Dawson and, as you know, Chef Michèle." He looked down again at his notes. "Mila, please have some spots open for Mrs. Abbott. She has followed the spa transition and was impressed by your revenue report at the last board meeting. Your numbers are climbing steadily, as you projected. She may be your key to renovating other spas on our ships."

He cleared his throat again. "There are two other items I need to discuss. First, are any of you willing to extend your contract for a few weeks? I know you are long overdue for time off, but I need to ask. We are still struggling to fill positions. Kennedy, would you please check with the cast? I don't need an answer today, but please see if anyone is willing to extend." Everyone at the table exchanged uneasy glances. It had been a challenging contract, and they were ready for a break. "And for my second piece of news, we are contemplating restarting our Alaskan cruises. I am looking for volunteers to work a soft cruise on the *Malina* in May. The cruise will be by invitation only." He looked up at the camera. "Mila, it might be a good idea for you to see the spa. I'm told it only needs a few upgrades and could be done quickly in preparation for the following year's cruise season."

Mila bobbed her head vigorously. "I'm in, Alfred. The only thing I like more than making people relaxed is making money!"

"Okay, kids," Alfred said, looking visibly relieved. Some of the color had come back to his face. "I'm signing off. Remember, you are my dream team!" He gave the camera two thumbs up. "Think about the contract extensions and Alaska, and let's talk soon!" And suddenly Alfred's face was gone, leaving a blank screen.

"Wow," a stunned Kennedy said, slumping in her seat.

Twenty minutes later, Kennedy and Tony were looking at the seating chart. The competing chefs would sit at a table in the middle of the dining room, and Kennedy would introduce them after the captain made his welcome toast. They also decided to put Mr. and Mrs. Butler in the same area as their outfits would undoubtedly cause the passengers to chatter. Tony and Kennedy chuckled at the memory of the Butlers' first dining experience on the *Helio*. They had arrived late for the Captain's Dinner, which started with the traditional parade of servers. However, when the doors opened and the spotlight turned on, it was Mr. and Mrs. Butler, not the servers, who stood there blinding the passengers as the harsh light bounced off the sea of rhinestones on Terri's denim ballgown.

Kennedy giggled. "You must admit, it was unforgettable, and we are still talking about it six months later."

Having solved Tony's dining room seating crisis, she left the conference room to check on Billy and the holiday décor. She also needed to find Bert, the ship's photographer. She did not relish telling him he would need to help the network's audio-visual guy while on board.

The freight elevator let her off at the lower level, and she maneuvered her way around the pallets of liquor and racks of canned goods waiting to be housed in the various areas of the hold. As she walked down the corridor, the door to one of the walk-in freezers opened, and arctic air swirled around her ankles, causing her to shiver. She wound her way around and finally reached the lockers where Billy was working. *I should take the back steps next time. It will be a lot quicker.* Billy looked serious as he lifted and placed a large rectangular box against the chain-link cage.

"Hi, Kennedy!" Billy wiped his forehead with the sleeve of his shirt. "We are almost done. There are a ton of decorations! It reminds me of Mrs. Jameson and her luggage," he grinned.

"Did everything on the list get here?" Kennedy asked.

Billy stepped out and joined her in the corridor. "I think so. I put a checkmark beside every item when I put them inside. Since this is the biggest cage, I put most of the decorations in here and the stage props in the other locker. The only one I couldn't fit was the sleigh, so it's in here." He pointed to the double stack of boxes lining the chain-link cage. "The lobby trees are on that wall, and the dining room trees are over there." He patted the top of another stack of boxes. "These are the ornaments that hang from the ceiling in the lobby." He stepped over to the other storage locker. "In here are the stage props, bags of snow, and the boxes of extra ornaments." Billy looked at Kennedy anxiously. "I thought there would be more of those."

Kennedy looked in amazement at the lockers, and she turned and gave him a wide smile. "Billy, this is more than I could have hoped for, and as far as the ornaments, they are just extras. The trees inside the boxes are already decorated. The ornaments are wired on, so they won't fall off, which is good if we hit a storm like the last cruise."

Billy looked at her open-mouthed. "I should tell my mom about wiring on the ornaments. Every year it's the same thing, the cat climbs up the tree and knocks the ornaments off until he gets to the top. Then he cries as it sways back and forth until someone rescues him. I did have a question, though."

"What's that?"

"Well, when I was lifting and moving the boxes around, I never heard anything moving inside the boxes. Is that okay? Shouldn't I have heard the branches scratching against the cardboard? That's what I hear when I am helping my mom."

Kennedy grinned. "The company we get the trees from fills the boxes with packing material, and the trees are wrapped in plastic, so it's added insurance with wiring the ornaments on—nothing moves around. Once you take the trees out of the box, theoretically, all you have to do is fluff the branches."

"Whew, I was worried for a moment when I couldn't hear anything."

Kennedy walked into the largest locker, noticing that Billy had made a small path inside. Getting things out would be easier than she had envisioned. She turned to him, "Billy, you did a terrific job. How did you know to do it this way?"

Color rose to his cheeks. "Once I saw what we had and what you wanted, it was easy. And now, I have a place to go if I need to hide." He pointed to the middle of the large locker. "No one would see me with these boxes stacked around the sides."

"I think I'll be the one who needs the hiding place. Something tells me this cruise may not go as smoothly as it looks on paper." Kennedy looked down at her watch. She still had things to attend to before the passengers began to arrive. Kennedy stepped out into the corridor and walked toward the door that led to the back staircase. She didn't want to waste time going through the maze to get back to the freight elevator. "Thanks again, Billy, and don't forget to meet me on the lobby floor," she called out over her shoulder. "We've got some VIPs I need you to help me take care of."

Billy groaned and called out after her. "Please tell me it isn't Mrs. Jameson."

"Nope, her best friend!" She giggled, seeing Billy's gaping mouth, and opened the stairwell door.

While Kennedy was below with Billy and the holiday decorations, Chef Michèle and Ano were in the galley preparing for dinner. Michèle was in a horrible mood taking out his frustrations on a pile of pork cutlets.

"I don't have time for this!" Michèle growled as he swung the mallet and brought it down with a bang. "I have kitchens to run, staff to oversee, menus to—"

Ano walked over. "Chef, if I may?" He placed his hand on the mallet that had just violently landed on the pink meat. "This poor piece of pork has done nothing to make you angry."

Michèle glared at him and begrudgingly handed him the mallet. If anyone else had taken the utensil from Michèle, he would have brought it down on their head, but there was an unbreakable bond between the two men.

Long before Michèle had been the executive chef of the *Helio*, he had been a cook on a cargo ship, and Ano had been a timid teen washing dishes. One afternoon, Michèle looked up to see Ano mimicking Michèle's hands as he chopped vegetables. Michèle was mystified; no one had ever watched him as intently as the young dishwasher. The next day, curious to see if the young man was watching him again, he began deboning several fish that had just been caught and would be a part of the chowder he was preparing for dinner. Ano's eyes widened as he watched Michèle wrap his finger around the fish's tail and pull it while he made quick sawing motions with his knife to remove the skin. "Why do you mimic my hands? Are you making fun of me?" Michèle called out in his thick Haitian accent. He put his knife down and walked over to where Ano stood at the sink.

Ano was terrified. The thickly built chef with blue-black skin and a bullet-like head terrified the diminutive teen who stood on a milk crate at the sink. "N-n-no, Chef," he squeaked. "I mimic your hands to learn how to be a chef like you." He looked dejectedly at the pile of dirty plates. "Now I am the lowest of the kitchen, the dishwasher." He raised his eyes to meet Michèle's and straightened his shoulders. "But someday, I hope to be a great chef like you." He looked down at the soapy water. "I apologize if I have offended you."

Michèle was speechless. He had never been called a great chef. He had been on his way to becoming one, but that changed one violent night. Now, he was just another vagabond on a cargo ship searching for a better life.

Michèle had begun his culinary education at his grandmother's knee. From her, he learned how to use spices to enhance the flavors of their simple meals. When he was older, he got a job in a hotel kitchen in the city, starting as a dishwasher and working his way up the line. Much like Ano, Michèle learned by mimicking those around him who had formal training. He worked long hours and took on more responsibilities, and after a few years, he was promoted to sous chef. Word spread about the talented sous chef, and soon locals and tourists filled the hotel's dining room. Then tragedy struck when political upheaval in the government turned deadly, and Michèle watched as rioters burned the hotel to the ground. Michèle walked in a daze through the smoky streets the next morning. He did not want to return to his village, where his only prospect was hot, sweaty work in the fields. The only alternative was to leave Haiti. With only a few dollars in his pocket, he knew he would have to work on one of the cargo ships in exchange for passage. He wandered the docks looking for work and found a ship needing a cook for the crew. He quickly signed on, not knowing what the future held.

Michèle saw in Ano a hunger to learn. "Follow me," he said and walked over to a large cutting board. He placed his chef's knife gently in Ano's hand, molding his hand around it. "This is my knife, and I am giving it to you. Your knife is your best friend. Be good to it, and it will be good to you." From that moment, an unlikely bond formed between the two men. Each day Ano washed dishes looking forward to the time when the galley would be quiet and he could stand beside Michèle to learn. When one of the kitchen helpers left, Michèle asked the captain to allow Ano to have the job. And a few years later, when Michèle joined the cruise line, Ano went with him.

The kitchens on the *Helio* ran smoothly due to Ano's diligence and quiet ways. Ano and Michèle would plan the menus, but it was Ano who took care of the ordering and scheduling so that Michèle could be the star. He dreamed of having his own kitchen but felt he owed too much to Michèle to leave him.

"Chef, why does this competition bother you so much? It's for a television show and has nothing to do with what we do here on the ship."

Michèle sighed deeply. "These television chefs are pretty people who look good on camera and follow a script." He gestured around the galley. "They don't understand or remember what happens in here. When they get in their fancy television kitchen, the preparation has been done. They smile and wave to the audience, make witty remarks, stir something, taste the food, and smile for the camera." He waved a spoon around. "I'll bet you twenty dollars that not one of them will step foot in here during the entire cruise." He shook his head. "And then there is that ridiculous name for the cruise. You should be offended!"

Ano smiled and shrugged his shoulders. "Chef, the words rhyme. People who know what a sous chef does will chuckle. I did."

Michèle blew a large breath out of his nose and motioned to a pile of meat. "Well, then get to it! I can't wait on you all day to finish flattening those pork cutlets.

Kennedy had taken the stairs from the lower hold to her room to get her computer. She wanted to be somewhere she wouldn't be distracted while she reviewed the file Alfred was sending over. Her eyes scanned the screen, and she began to make notes. Meeting with the man from the network, Deuce Dawson, was high on the list. Winnifred Wallace's notes called for the competition to be broadcast daily on the network's morning show. While they could do that when the ship was in port, Kennedy was unsure about the rounds that would take place on the two sea days. The competitions might have to be taped and sent back to the network, but she would confirm with the ship's audio-visual team. She also realized there were no promotional materials now, as Winnifred had planned to bring them with her, so she would need to add that information to the daily newsletter and announcements. Kennedy twiddled her pencil between her fingers. She didn't want to add to her list of things to do, but she wondered if the chefs would teach a cooking class or do a Q&A session. It would give the passengers a special connection to the competition and the chefs.

As Kennedy read further down in the file, she saw Winnifred had intended for the competition to move to various locations on the ship. *We can't do that, but we could move the production into the theater for the last two days.* It would take a lot of convincing on her part to get Franklin to do it.

Halfway through her list, she heard a tap on the door, and Mila walked in. "I had a feeling I would find you here." She handed her a cup of coffee. "From my private stash," she added, and Kennedy took it gratefully. Mila looked at the balled-up papers on the table. "How bad is it?"

Kennedy bit her lips together. "I have a handle on most of it. I just can't figure out why Alfred didn't send someone else from the corporate office."

Mila let out a little laugh. "Because he knew you would handle it! Got a problem? Call 1-800-K-E-N-N-E-D-Y."

Kennedy picked up one of the balled-up pieces of paper and threw it at Mila. "Thanks a lot! I'm going to have to ask Chris and the AV guys for some unexpected favors."

Mila grinned. "Bribe them with haircuts. They look like mangy dogs. I think they are cutting their hair using nail clippers and a soup bowl."

Kennedy pressed her head back into her chair and looked at the ceiling. "You are the best, and I adore you."

"I know." Mila gave a little sigh and shrugged her shoulders. "Talented, smart, funny, beautiful..." She trailed off and made a face at Kennedy. "Why do I hang out with you again?"

Kennedy tapped her temple. "Guilt over the fact I recently got clobbered in the head trying to prove your innocence?"

Mila cocked her head. "Meh. Weren't you just being nosy? And I will point out that *it did* jumpstart things with Omar. So, proving my innocence was just a sidebar."

Kennedy began rubbing her eyes. "I'm thinking of a word that rhymes with how my eyes are feeling right now." She removed her fingers and threw another balled-up piece of paper at Mila. "Go! I have a million things to do."

An hour before the passengers were due to arrive, Kennedy found Bert, the ship's photographer, red-faced and sweating in the lobby as he struggled to put up the backdrop the corporate office had sent over.

"I'm so glad to see you!" Kennedy sang out, walking over to help him.

He narrowed his eyes at her and stopped what he was doing. "Why?" he asked, breathing hard and holding the base of the backdrop while Kennedy pulled the screen up and hooked it onto the top of the pole.

"I need help. This chef's competition got thrown into my lap because the corporate person isn't coming. She was in a car accident and is in the hospital."

"And that affects me how?"

"Well, first, I need you to take the network's AV guy, Art, under your wing. Show him where things are, help him get set up, and be there for him during the competitions."

Bert held out his hands. "Kennedy, I don't have time to babysit anyone. The corporate office already has me sending them my photos whenever someone stands in front of this thing." He pointed at the backdrop, which featured a giant stockpot with two crossed knives. Above the knives was a banner that read, "Classic Style Network's Sous Cruise."

"Bert…"

He crossed his arms and rolled his eyes. "Oh, all right," he sighed. "I'll show this Art guy around and be on standby, but if he's a real AV guy, he'll know what to do."

"That's the team spirit I'm looking for, and why don't you meet Art before you decide you don't like him? Give him a chance, huh?"

Forty-five minutes later, the passengers began to arrive, and with it, the butterflies Kennedy always felt. She enjoyed greeting the passengers and helping them get settled on the ship. She noticed a woman in a yellow floral print dress walk purposefully through the lobby, causing several people to stop and stare. The woman looked like a runway model, with high cheekbones, mocha-colored skin, and close-cropped hair. Her regal look would make someone remember her long after she passed by.

She walked up to Kennedy. "I'm Monique Patrick. I should be on your VIP list."

Kennedy remembered the name and smiled. "Welcome to the *Helio*, Ms. Patrick. I'm Kennedy Reeves, the ship's cruise director. We are certainly happy to have you on board. I understand you are an accomplished travel writer." She saw Billy over Monique's shoulder, struggling with her carry-on luggage.

Monique gave Kennedy a patient smile. "It's a gift, and I've turned it into a business." She waved her hand dismissively. "People will go somewhere on vacation simply because I wrote about having been there. The big travel networks are always asking me for something. I'm using this trip to gather information for several articles and a tour I plan to host." Monique sniffed. "If I have a suitable time on this cruise and receive excellent service, my readers will flock to book cruises on this ship in particular. I'm sure the cruise line will want to express their thanks when they see an uptick in their profits."

Kennedy felt a mild warning bell go off in her head. "All our passengers receive excellent service while on the *Helio*, Ms. Patrick."

Monique looked around the lobby. "Now, where is Winnifred? We were supposed to discuss the interviews and a few other matters. The network was thrilled when I offered to write the article, and from the background work I gathered so far, the article should be," she paused, "noteworthy."

"Ms. Wallace will not be on the cruise," Kennedy said hesitantly.

"And may I ask why not?" Monique asked, piqued.

"She was in a car accident and will not be able to join us. If you will tell me—"

Monique cut her off by holding up her hand. "Then *you* will need to set up these interviews. I have a specific order I want them in." She rummaged in her tote bag, pulled out a file, and handed a piece of paper to Kennedy. "As Winnifred won't be here, it will be your job to make these people understand this is not an option. I want to start this afternoon with the ship's executive chef, whom I understand is one of the judges."

Kennedy opened her mouth to speak. Interviewing Chef Michèle today was a terrible idea as he was already irritated and would be preparing for the Captain's Dinner.

"Ms. Patrick—" she began, but Monique cut her off a second time.

"I'll interview him in the main dining room unless there is a better place to do it." Kennedy scribbled a note on her clipboard about Chef Michèle's interview and wondered how on Earth she would explain it to him. "I'll let you know the location for the others once I have walked around the ship." Her eyes roamed around the lobby. "Is the ship going into drydock soon for renovations? Surely with this partnership, the cruise line understands they should invest some money in their public spaces, if only to increase bookings. I can see I will have my work cut out for me when describing the ship. I hope my cabin is less dated than what I have seen so far." She turned her attention back to Kennedy. "The other article I am gathering information on is about cruising in this new age. I discussed the angle I wanted to take with Winnifred, and she liked it. I want to let the readers have a peek behind the curtain. To meet the people who work on the ship. Winnifred said I would have full access to everyone on the *Helio*. According to Winnifred, there are some interesting characters on your ship, including your spa director whose family ran a circus in Europe and someone who spent time in jail."

The mild warning bells that had been going off in Kennedy's head earlier were now a clanging fire alarm. Kennedy chose her words carefully. Alfred had not mentioned this, and there had been nothing in the file about interviewing any of them. "Ms. Patrick, I don't know if we will be able to accommodate your request. With the competition, it is a busy cruise. I will check with our team to see if anyone would like to give an interview. As we are in the public eye for months at a time, we hold on dearly to our privacy." She held out her hand with her palm up. "In the meantime, Billy will show you to your cabin." She turned and looked at Billy. "Cabin 701, please." She turned back to Monique. "I'll begin to work on the interview schedule as soon as possible, Ms. Patrick, after all of our passengers are settled."

Billy began to walk toward the elevators, and Monique followed him. She was disappointed that Kennedy had not jumped at the idea of interviewing the staff. Winnifred understood Monique's angle for the article and had excitedly blurted out some information she shouldn't have. The next day Winnifred called Monique and explained that she would need to speak with certain members of the corporate office and the *Helio* team before Monique could proceed.

"Good Lord, woman, who allowed Cruella on the ship?" Kennedy whirled around and yelped. David Stearns: travel writer, friend, backstage mother, and diva impersonator, stood before her, and Kennedy threw her arms around him.

"You have no idea how excited I am to see you!" Kennedy said happily. "You look fabulous as always!" David always looked like he had just stepped out of a catalog. Today he was wearing a navy-blue silk shirt with white polka dots and a pair of white linen slacks. A guidebook and travel writer, David wrote beautifully descriptive pieces about the hidden gems of the south. Elegant hotels in Atlanta, Charleston, Hilton Head, Savannah, Nashville, New Orleans, and Palm Beach carried his guidebooks for their clientele.

He stood back and looked at Kennedy, turning her head from side to side. "I was given explicit instructions to report on how you look and the status of your love life. I'm also to remind you that your presence is demanded for the New Year's Eve show if you aren't working."

Kennedy frowned. "I'll be here. But how is the club?"

David's smile could have lit up an airport runway. "Club Diva is going like gangbusters. John wheelbarrows money to the bank each morning wearing his rhinestone sunglasses. This little brunch idea of his is a goldmine. And everyone is working at the club now except for Don, who is there on and off. He had to find a bigger warehouse in Florida because his online sales are going through the roof!" He took a breath. "Now, suppose you tell me why Monique Patrick is on the cruise?" He whispered, "Rumor in the writing industry is whatever she doesn't dig up, she makes up!"

Kennedy took a deep breath. "She's writing two pieces. One about the chef's competition and a potential one on cruising."

"Be careful," he said in a low tone. "Don't let any of the staff or crew speak to her. She will skewer them."

"Noted. Before I forget, you are in Cabin 915, and Anna Marie is expecting you in the spa. She's held some appointments open for you." She grinned. "Only you could land writing an article about spa treatments on a cruise ship."

"The sacrifices I make for the reading public," he said theatrically, placing his hand on his forehead. "Now, I must go and see the darling Anna Marie. Catch up soon?" And in a blink, he was gone, jogging up the steps to the spa.

Kennedy noticed Billy coming out of the elevators as he made a beeline for her. "Kennedy, that woman is worse than ten Mrs. Jameson's," he said in a loud voice, causing several passengers to turn and look at him.

Kennedy grabbed his sleeve and pulled him aside. "Billy, remember our training classes," she said with a fake smile. "We use quiet voices in public spaces, and no matter how challenging a guest can be, we never speak about them in public. Now, what did Ms. Patrick say?"

Billy blew out a breath and lowered his voice. "She had plenty to say, but you would have been proud of me," he said in a rush. "I kept to the script. I talked about the amenities available, the events happening, and how exciting it was that the Classic Style Network was hosting the competition. But she interrupted me and told me she would pay big money for any stories I had about the staff, 'The more scandalous they are, the more money I will pay,' she said." He was panting. "Then we got to her cabin, and I held the door open for her to go inside. She walked in and said, 'Wow...what a dump! And they want me to promote this?' " He gave Kennedy a confused look. "She's in a nice stateroom, Kennedy. I don't understand."

Kennedy put a reassuring hand on Billy's arm. She was thankful he had taken the refresher training she had just given to heart. "You did great, Billy. You stuck to the script and came to me with her comments. I'll take care of things from here. Mrs. Abbott should be arriving soon. Would you go down to the terminal and keep an eye out for her?"

Billy raised his hand and saluted. "I'm on it!"

The clanging bells going off in Kennedy's head now became screaming sirens. She would make everyone aware of Monique's intentions when they met after the ship departed.

"Excuse me, Kennedy," one of the junior staff members walked up to her. "I need some help. Mr. and Mrs. Bain are unhappy with their cabin." Kennedy listened to the couple who demanded to know why their ocean-view cabin was looking at a pier. She explained that as soon as the ship left port, they would be able to see the ocean, but until they left Port Canaveral, their view would be of the pier. She suggested they stop by the pool bar for a SunRumbrella and walk the promenade, as it would allow them to see a full view of the ship.

As she was turning around to face the oncoming passengers, a man walked up to her.

"Are you in charge?"

Kennedy looked at one of the most ruggedly handsome men she had ever seen. He looked as if he would be equally comfortable wearing a leather jacket riding a motorcycle down the Pacific Highway or in a tuxedo at a gala. His thick shoulder-length, curly hair was iron gray, which complemented the thin, gold-framed glasses he was pulling down from on top of his head.

"How may I be of assistance?"

"I am Deuce Dawson from Classic Style Network. I am looking for Kennedy Reeves. Could you please direct me to her? I was told she would be in the lobby," he said in a well-modulated voice.

"I'm Kennedy," she said, putting out her hand. "Welcome aboard, Mr. Dawson. We are excited to have you here."

He shook her hand. "I got a call this morning telling me you will be overseeing things for the competition, and I'd like to discuss the details with you. This competition must go flawlessly, and this change has me very anxious."

Kennedy gave him a gracious smile. "I understand, Mr. Dawson. I learned of the change late this morning, but I am confident we will pull this off. Could we meet after you have gotten settled into your cabin?"

When Deuce didn't answer her, Kennedy realized he was looking over her shoulder, scanning the lobby. "I wonder where Art is?" he muttered to himself. "We got separated in the terminal. I thought we would see each other by now."

"Mr. Dawson," Kennedy said gently, "there are several changes we need to make to accommodate the competition." Kennedy saw a wave of relief wash over his face as a woman with short, wavy, red hair entered the lobby. She had a small video camera at her eye, and seeing Deuce through the lens, she lowered it and waved. Then, as she walked toward him, she suddenly tripped and landed face-down on the lobby floor. Kennedy and Deuce quickly ran over to help her up.

"Well, Miss Coordinated strikes again," she laughed as Deuce helped her to her feet. Kennedy handed her the camera and bag that had flown out of her hands when she fell.

"Let me guess." Deuce mimicked her holding his fingers in a square. "There was this epic shot, and—"

"Well, there was," she said stubbornly. "I'm only thinking of footage for the show. It can't all be about cooking. There *are* other things, you know." She smiled at him impishly.

"Kennedy Reeves, may I please introduce you to Art, my AV goddess."

"It's Artura," she said sheepishly. "But people butcher it, so I go by Art."

Kennedy grinned. "I can sympathize. My sister and I both have boy names, and the first day of school was always awkward. The girl sitting at the desk didn't match the boy's name."

Art began to laugh hard, and she suddenly snorted. "That was not very ladylike. I apologize," she said, embarrassed.

Deuce rolled his eyes and sighed. "And now you can see and hear why she's behind the camera." He smiled warmly at Art. "But she's the only person I trust when I am in front of it." He turned his eyes to Kennedy. "Art needs to meet with the team she will direct for the competition."

Kennedy bit her lip. She had not wanted to have this conversation in the middle of the lobby. "Why don't we step over here." She motioned for them to follow her. She took a deep breath and plunged forward. "I'm afraid there have been some assumptions and some miscommunications." She shared her information about the live streams and the set locations. Deuce and Art exchanged looks as she spoke, and his face went from purple to a pale gray. Art put a hand on his forearm to calm him. "My suggestion," Kennedy said, "is that we tape the competitions on our sea days and send the footage back to your network."

Deuce was shaking his head. "No. The plan was to announce the winner live during the morning show."

"But Mr. Dawson, we won't be able to do a live feed that day. We will be in the middle of the ocean. But I have an idea if you are open to it. Our last show is holiday themed. Would you be willing to flip-flop the themes on days four and five? You could announce the winner to the passengers first. It may even make them loyal viewers because of the personal connection. Then you could announce the new host chef to the network the next morning when we arrive back in Port Canaveral."

Deuce pinched the bridge of his nose and winced. Art looked nervously from Kennedy to Deuce. Kennedy spoke again, "I am sorry to cause you such frustration. I know how important this competition is for both companies, but you need to understand the reality of doing this competition on the ship. Why don't you look at the set and see what you think? We can meet as soon as we are underway. I promise, Mr. Dawson, we will make this work. This competition is as important to us as it is to you," she said earnestly.

Deuce nodded slowly. "Okay," he said with resignation, "I suppose I will have to trust you since we will be working together. We can meet later."

Kennedy waved to Bert, who had been staring at the small group from where he stood by the photo area. Kennedy turned to Art. "I want to introduce you to Bert, our ship's photographer. I've asked him to lend you a hand during the competition."

Bert walked over, never taking his eyes from the perky redhead in the black T-shirt and fishing vest. "H-h-hi," he said shyly, extending his hand. "I'm B-B-Bert."

"Hi Bert, I'm Art. It's a shame my parents didn't name me Ernestine; we could have been Ernie and Bert!" Art began laughing at her joke and then snorted. "Sorry. That joke just came out, and my nose thought it was funny." She raised her eyebrows at Kennedy. "Sometimes my mouth says things before my brain catches up."

Bert stood rooted in place. "Earth to Bert, hello Bert?" Kennedy poked his shoulder, "Hello?" He shook his head quickly but kept his gaze on Art. "Bert, I know you are busy taking our embarkation photos, but would you mind taking Art under your wing? Show her where things are on the ship?"

Bert nodded slowly but remained mute. It was as if he had lost the power of speech. Art cocked her head and looked at Bert. "Is that okay, Bert? I don't want to be a pest. Maybe you could show me the competition area, too?"

There was an awkward silence, and Deuce cleared his throat and began searching his inside coat pocket. "I think the information about my cabin is in here."

Kennedy gestured to the elevators. "Mr. Dawson, you are in Cabin 926. The competition set is also on that deck. Look for the putting green. Art, you are in Cabin 817. And please don't worry; I promise we will make this a successful competition, Mr. Dawson."

He placed his glasses back on top of his head. "Thank you. Since we will be working so closely together, you should call me Deuce." He shook her hand again, and he and Art walked to the elevators to find their cabins.

Kennedy was encouraged that her introduction to the network's producer had gone well and turned around to see who else she could help in the lobby. She saw Billy walking a few steps behind a very tall woman with short, ash-blonde hair. He caught Kennedy's eye and pointed at the woman vigorously. "It's her," he mouthed. Emily Abbott wore a leopard print blouse and a black, form-fitted skirt. The black scarf around her neck completed her ensemble. She peered over the heads of the others in the lobby and locked eyes on Kennedy. When the woman and Billy reached Kennedy, she said graciously, "I would know you anywhere. You must be Kennedy Reeves. Vera has talked about you so much; I feel as if I know you."

Kennedy shook her hand. "Welcome aboard, Mrs. Abbott. We are delighted you are joining us on this cruise."

Emily waved her hand, which was curiously unadorned. Unlike Vera Jameson, Emily did not wear any rings or bracelets. She gave Kennedy a little smile. "Let's be honest. I bet you groaned when Alfred announced I would be on the ship."

Kennedy's eyes twinkled. "Well, if we are being honest, I didn't exactly groan, but I was nervous. Is this your first cruise on the *Helio*?"

"Well, yes," Emily answered. "It's my very first cruise, which I am sure sounds strange as we own the cruise line. I'm more of a land lover. However, after hearing Vera go on about you and the others, I decided I needed to meet you, especially after that dreadful business a few months ago. So, when the partnership with the network was announced, I decided I would experience a cruise on the best ship in the fleet." She looked around the lobby wistfully. "My great-grandfather built this cruise line, and I'm embarrassed to say I don't know anything about it." Emily reached into her purse and pulled out a small notebook. "Now, I have a few requests."

Kennedy pulled out her pen and flipped over a piece of paper on her clipboard. "First, am I in the same cabin Vera normally books? She's always bragging that you upgrade her to the best cabin."

"Yes, ma'am," Kennedy answered. "Stateroom 802, and Billy," she motioned for him to step forward, "will personally escort you to it."

Emily frowned. "Didn't Vera have someone else escort her to her cabin the last time? She kept calling him the silver fox."

Kennedy chuckled. "Unfortunately, Mr. Blaas is unavailable right now. I am certain he will be sorry he could not escort you, but I will make a point of introducing the two of you."

"Very well. Regarding dinner, I would like to have dinner with…" She looked down at the notebook, "Mr. Meier, the director of security?" She huffed. "Honestly, Vera will not shut up about the man. I believe she has a crush on him, which is foolish at our age." She mimicked Vera's voice and put her nose in the air. "He has European charm, Emmy. You wouldn't understand." She gave Kennedy a wry look. "I lived in Europe for over twenty years, and I know how charming European men can be."

Kennedy giggled at Emily's impersonation of Vera. "Mr. Meier is looking forward to escorting you to dinner tonight. The captain has asked that you dine at his table each night, which is far more than Mrs. Jameson ever received." She whispered confidentially, "On the last cruise, he only had her at his table one night as a favor to me."

Emily beamed and slapped her thigh. "That will set the old girl off!"

"May I ask how the two of you met? If I remember right, Mrs. Jameson mentioned you two were best friends in college."

Emily laughed out loud. "We didn't start that way." She saw the curious look on Kennedy's face. "Neither of us fit in at our sorority. I'm not sure if you've noticed, but I'm tall and ox-like. And Vera is…" she hesitated. "I suppose challenging is the nicest word that comes to mind. The sorority paired the two outcasts together, and somehow, we became best friends. I can go without talking to her for months, and one telephone call melts the time away."

Kennedy understood what Mrs. Abbott was saying. She and Mila were similar in that respect. "I'm proud of Vera," Emily said. "She's taken a small humdrum chain of funeral homes and turned it into an empire. Did you know she's contemplating destination funerals?"

"Destination funerals?" Kennedy squeaked.

Emily chuckled. "I don't know the details, but she mentioned it on the phone before I left today. It will be another one of her brilliant ideas. She has the Midas touch." She frowned. "It's a shame she has no one to share her accomplishments with. She and her husband," she rolled her eyes at Kennedy, "—what a bore that man was—never had children. But then again, could you imagine Vera as a mother?" She shuddered. "She mentioned that her niece was working for her and was receiving pressure to take her nephew under her wing. Honestly, you and your team are more of a family to her than the ones she is related to." Emily cleared her throat. "Now, I understand that you are taking charge of the competition.

Kennedy nodded. "I learned about it this morning. The first challenge seems unique."

Emily's eyes sparkled with excitement. "I came up with that one! My grandparents had all the dining books from the ships in their library, and I loved reading them. That's where my love of history and travel came from."

Kennedy was confused. "Dining books?"

Emily explained, "In the late 1800s and early 1900s, hotels would have a book with the dining room menu pasted in it. The general manager would make notations about guests staying in the hotel or special events. My great-grandfather worked for a hotel as a young man, and one of his jobs was to paste the menu into the book each day. When he started our company years later, he kept the tradition. There were entries about celebrities, storms, and a near mutiny."

Kennedy was enchanted. "I hope we can speak more about the books. They seem fascinating. In the meantime, would you like to have your photo taken by our ship's photographer? We can then have Billy escort you to your suite."

"Billy?" Emily whirled around. "Oh, my goodness, young man, I am terribly sorry. I have been chatting up a storm with Kennedy, and I completely forgot about you."

Billy grinned, and Kennedy mouthed a silent thank you to him as she escorted Mrs. Abbott over to Bert. Then, after Bert took her photo, Billy whisked her away to the elevator.

While watching Mrs. Abbott get on the elevator, she suddenly felt a pair of cool, slender hands fall over her eyes. "Guess who?" a man's voice said with a slow southern drawl. The hands flew away, and Jones Butler stood in front of her. Terri quickly danced around Kennedy to stand beside her husband.

"I bet you are surprised to see us!" Terri said breathlessly.

"Mr. and Mrs. Butler, how are you? I was shocked to see you on the VIP list. I thought you were busy remodeling the estate and couldn't get away for at least a year." She narrowed her eyes at Jones and pointed a finger at the cigar in his mouth, clearing her throat.

Jones took the cigar out and smiled weakly. "Shucks, Kennedy, I just forgot. I promise it's not lit." He stuffed the cigar into the pocket of his denim jacket.

"There's Bert!" Terri said in her breathy voice. "Jonesy, I'll be back," she called over her shoulder. Jones and Kennedy watched Terri's filmy, green, jungle-print dress flow behind her as she quickly made her way across the lobby to the photo area. Bert was snapping photos of a mother, father, and three children and did not see Terri walk up behind him. She placed her hands over Bert's eyes and squealed in his ear. "Guess who?" Bert turned bright red. He knew only one person with that voice.

"Mrs. B-B-Butler," he stammered. "I didn't know you would be on this cruise." He stared at her and saw dollar signs dancing in his future. On the last cruise, Mr. Butler had bought every photograph Bert took of Terri and booked him for a private photo shoot. Terri waited patiently for Bert to finish taking the photos of the family, and when they left, she took her place in front of the backdrop and began posing as Bert pressed the button on his camera.

Monique Patrick entered the lobby, scanning the room for Kennedy, who was engaged in a conversation with a thin man with a graying black pompadour. He wore a rhinestone-studded denim suit, and each time the man moved, the lights from above bounced off the rhinestones, creating a kaleidoscope of dancing beams around him. Monique noticed that while he spoke with Kennedy, his eyes never left the woman posing for the ship's photographer. Monique knew at once there was a story that went with the couple. They were too vibrant.

"How is the renovation going?" Kennedy asked.

Jones made a face. "Well, it's like this, Kennedy. Our contractor says there are just not enough hours in the day to do what we want as quickly as we want. There are issues with the foundation, the plastering, and the wiring, and to top it off," he pointed his hand at Terri, "Sweetsie keeps changing her mind about things." He sighed. "I thought a little R&R would be helpful, plus we need to check out some of the details of our cabin. I think it's one way, Sweetsie thinks it's another, and to not fight about it, I figured it was easier to book a cruise and find out who was right. We do have our suite, right?"

Kennedy nodded. "Of course, Mr. Butler, your cabin is just waiting for you to open the door."

Terri bounced over to Jones and Kennedy. "I sure surprised Bert," she grinned. "Kennedy, you look wonderful. I, however, am a hot mess." She blew out a breath of air into her caramel-colored bangs causing them to float in the air. "Renovating a house is exhausting work. There are so many decisions, and I am terrified of making the wrong choice. Whenever I change my mind, the contractor adds three weeks to the schedule." She looked at Jones. "Did you tell Kennedy why we are here?"

"Yes, but I still think I'm right."

Terri rolled her eyes at her husband and then turned to Kennedy. "We'll find out soon enough. I keep telling him the bathtub is in the center of the bathroom and is gold," Terri said with a touch of exasperation to Kennedy. "He thinks it is beside the shower and is black. I can't wait to show him he's wrong." Kennedy caught a sly smile on Jones's face. Something told her he knew precisely where the bathtub sat and what color it was.

"I'm sure you two are eager to get to your suite and get situated," Kennedy said. "Do you remember where it is?"

Terri saluted her. "Yes, ma'am. I remember where my *mustard station* is, too, just in case."

Kennedy burst out laughing. On their first cruise, Terri had confused the words muster and mustard and couldn't figure out why they would need to get condiments if there was an emergency on the ship.

"Before you go, I did have one thing to share." They looked at her with interest. "As you are special VIPs, Tony, our dining room manager, has selected one of our premier tables in the dining room for you."

"That rascal," Jones said with a grin. "He remembers Terri's outfits!"

Kennedy bit back a smile. Tony had been traumatized with worry each time the Butlers entered the dining room. "I'd like to ask a small favor. As you know, Tony can be very anxious." They nodded their heads, grinning. "He's under some stress because a lot will be happening tonight at the Captain's Dinner. Would it be possible for you to arrive a little earlier than normal? We are introducing the competing chefs tonight in addition to the parade of servers."

Jones poked Terri's side. "I think she's trying to tell us to be on time because we caused a spectacle at the last Captain's Dinner."

Terri blushed, and Jones chuckled. "We'll be on time, Kennedy, and on that note, I think we'll make our way to our cabin and get settled in. Sweetsie will need a few hours to figure out how she will dazzle the dining room tonight."

While Kennedy and the Butlers were talking, Monique glided over to Bert. "I forgot to have my photo taken when I got on board," she said, placing money in the pocket of his camera bag. Monique posed in front of the backdrop. "Who's that?" she pointed her head toward the Butlers.

Bert snapped a few more shots of Monique. "A couple who cruised with us not too long ago."

"They must have a lot of money if they can afford to cruise that often," Monique mused.

"They're loaded, but I'm surprised they are back so soon. Mr. Butler's last cruise wasn't as relaxing as he had hoped."

Monique's ears perked up. "Oh? What happened?" she asked casually as she stepped away from the backdrop.

Bert made a zipping motion across his lips. "I'm sorry, we aren't supposed to talk about the passengers."

Monique smiled darkly, "I understand, confidentiality and all. When will the photos be ready?" she asked.

"They'll be here in the morning," Bert said in a bored tone. "You can write down the numbers of the ones you want, and I'll have them printed for you." Monique nodded distractedly and stared as Jones and Terry Butler made their way to the elevators.

A petite woman with a bouncy brown ponytail entered the lobby from the gangway wearing a zebra-striped jumpsuit and high heels. She held her camera up in the air taking photographs of herself from different angles. In some photos, she pouted her lips, and in others, she gave a wide smile. She saw Bert and decided he must work for the ship. "Hi, there, I'm Lola Cobb, one of the chefs for the cooking competition. I need to check in with someone. Do you happen to know who I should speak to, handsome?" Bert became flustered. He was not used to women calling him handsome. His mother had never even called him that. Instead, she would lick her thumb, try to control his cowlick, and say he had unique qualities that the right woman would appreciate someday. He pointed to Kennedy, who had just finished helping another passenger.

"S-s-she can."

"Thank you!" The tiny brunette winked at him dramatically. "Make sure to cheer for me. I'm the Lovely Lola, and I intend to win this competition, hands down!" She turned on her heel and walked quickly to where Kennedy was standing. "Hi, I'm Lola Cobb, one of the chefs for the cooking competition, and that man over there," she hooked her thumb behind her, "said you would be the person I should check in with."

Kennedy looked down at the petite woman with the high ponytail. "Ms. Cobb, you must be my chef to be named. Welcome to the *Helio*." Kennedy looked down at her clipboard and ran a finger down the list. "You are in Cabin 626, which is up one deck. There have been a few changes to the competition timetables, and we will get that information to you immediately."

"Great!" She turned to leave but then turned back to Kennedy. "Are the photos over there free? My followers love to see my pictures."

Kennedy was momentarily confused. "Your followers?"

"My clients and the people who follow me on social media. They love to see what I'm doing: flying off in a private jet to cook for someone famous, making something delicious in a fancy kitchen, or setting up for a big party." Kennedy was captivated by the confidence the young woman exuded. Lola pointed at Bert. "I'll ask my new friend Bert to snap some pictures of me with his camera and mine. Thanks for your help!" Before Kennedy could say another word, Lola was on her way back to the photo area.

Kennedy watched as the young woman handed her camera to Bert and began posing. "Bert, I've learned how to make the perfect pose every time I need to take a photo. The camera loves me." She placed one hand on her hip and one by her ear. "I call this one the pin-up girl. It reminds me of the actresses in the forties. My male followers love this pose the most." She struck another pose and chattered. "Bert, we are a good team, and you'll be taking lots of photographs of me when I win the competition."

"When you win what competition?" a man's voice asked. He had been listening to their conversation. He looked her up and down. "The Miss Wannabe Pageant? You can't be talking about the chef's competition. Because I've already got it locked," he pointed his index finger at her, pretending it was a gun, "loaded, and in the bag. The competition is just sizzle for them to market the program." He grinned devilishly. "I can win this thing on my good looks alone, as the ladies will tune in to see me. Right now, you are proving my point. You can't take your eyes off me."

He took Lola's hand and led her out of the photo area. Then he motioned to Bert for Lola's camera. "I believe it's time to allow this nice man," he looked at Bert's nametag, "Bert, to take photos of the real winner." He gave Bert and Lola a toothy smile and placed Lola's camera in her hands. Then, he took his place in front of the backdrop. "I'm Chef Tristan Colon." He crossed one arm across his waist, and the other cupped his chin. "And I cook…as good as I look."

Lola shook herself out of her daze when she saw Bert's flash go off. The man who had removed her from the photo area was like many others she had run into over the years. They exuded charm and charisma but only for their benefit. "Tristan," she called out sweetly, "I'm not sure if you know this, but trash pickup is tomorrow, and you should be ready and at the curb."

Tristan coughed at the comment Lola directed at him. He turned opposite to allow Bert to take a few more photos with his signature pose and smiled roguishly at Lola. "I was going to give you a nasty look, but I see you already have one."

"If laughter is the best medicine, your face must be curing the world!" Lola retorted and rolled her eyes.

"Keep looking back there; you might find a brain!" He snickered.

"Aargh!" Lola gave Tristan a murderous look and stormed off. He laughed and tipped Bert. "That was the most enjoyable photo shoot I ever had."

Kennedy walked over to see what had caused the tiny chef to walk away upset. "Good afternoon. Is everything okay?"

Tristan chuckled. "I apologize for causing a problem, but she should understand that there is only room for the star." He held out his hand, "I'm Chef Tristan Colon, the soon-to-be host chef of the Casual Living Network's new cooking show. You can tell people you've met me."

"Welcome aboard, Chef Colon, I'm Kennedy Reeves, cruise director for the *Helio*, and I don't think we've had the contest yet."

"Oh, rest assured, I will win," he said and struck what he had decided would be his signature pose. He gave Kennedy an appraising look. "And I cook as good as I look." Then, he straightened up and gave her a wink. "I have the whole package: the style, the looks, the brains," he pointed to his forearm, "and the tats."

Kennedy raised her eyebrows. "I didn't realize that tattoos were a requirement for chefs."

"All the cool ones have them."

"Well, Chef Colon, let's get you to your cabin," she looked down at her clipboard. "Cabin 704. Just take the elevators to deck seven and follow the signs. But, before you go—"

"Yes, I'm single," he gave her a toothy grin.

Kennedy was taken aback at the man's boldness. "That's good to know, Chef Colon, but I was going to say that we've had some changes to the competition itinerary, and we will get the information to you at once. Is there anything else I can help you with?" she asked.

"Would you like to escort me to my cabin personally? Check the firmness of the mattress?"

Kennedy gave him a tight smile. "I'm sorry, but I am still greeting our other passengers. I'm sure that you will be able to find your cabin easily. We have plenty of signs."

"Maybe next time," he said and strolled toward the elevators.

"Wow," Kennedy said to herself, bewildered at the man's arrogance. After meeting the first two chefs, she wondered about the other two still due to arrive.

A tall, slender man wearing a dark blue Panama hat stood in the lobby and looked around. He went first to the guest services desk and showed them the papers in his hand. The agent at the desk pointed out Kennedy, and he walked over to her. "Good afternoon," he said, taking off his hat and revealing a bald head. "Have you ever had a perfect stranger tell you that you are beautiful?"

Kennedy groaned inwardly but smiled. "No, I can't say I have."

"Well, now you have." He stuck out his hand and took her proffered one. "Chef Miles White, and now we are no longer strangers," he bent down to kiss her hand and peered at her nametag. "Kennedy Reeves, I would like to tell you again how beautiful you are."

Kennedy gave an awkward laugh. "Do you pick up many women with that line?"

Miles chuckled good-naturedly. "I'll admit, it's been a while since I tried it out. I don't go out on dates often."

"You might want to find some new lines," she suggested. "That one was terrible."

"Miss Reeves, I wonder if I could trouble you, I need to meet with the ship's doctor as soon as possible."

Kennedy was concerned, but professionalism kept her from asking him what was wrong. "I'd be happy to call him for you. Would you prefer to meet him in the ship's medical office or your cabin?"

"My cabin would be better, but I'm afraid I don't know which one I am in." He waved the packet of papers in his hand and searched for his glasses, padding his jacket pockets.

Kennedy softened. He was older than she had first thought. "Chef Miles, you are in Cabin 757, and I see you have an additional cabin across the hall."

Miles looked pained. "I should have canceled that reservation." Kennedy gave him a puzzled look. "My mother was supposed to be on the ship with me. But unfortunately, she passed away a few weeks ago," he explained. "She and I were joined at the hip until she died."

Kennedy wasn't sure what to say. She knew of men like Miles, and while her mother tried valiantly to make sure Kennedy dated every available bachelor in Charleston, she made sure to steer her clear of any man who still lived with his mother. "Men like that, Kennedy, will never put you first. You will either be a third wheel or become his other mother."

Miles turned his hat in his hand. "I'm sorry. I didn't mean to make you feel awkward. I'm still learning how to adjust to life without her."

Bert walked up. "Excuse me, Kennedy, have any other chefs come through? I want to send those photos to corporate before we leave."

"Bert, this is Chef Miles White. He just arrived." She turned to Miles. "We'd be grateful if you would allow Bert to take some photographs."

"How grateful?" Miles asked, smiling devilishly at Kennedy.

Kennedy was stunned. This could not be happening in the space of a few minutes. "I-I-I'm not sure it would be prudent for me to favor one chef over another."

He waved her off and chuckled. "I just wanted to see you stammer again. It's very charming." He placed his hat back on his head and gave Kennedy a wink. "So long, my perfect, beautiful stranger. I hope to see you soon." He turned to Bert. "Let's go!"

Kennedy offered him a weak smile and hoped she wouldn't have to dodge him for the entire cruise. She stepped over to the guest services desk and picked up the house phone. "Doctor Craig? It's Kennedy. Our passenger in Cabin 757 needs to meet with you in his cabin, please." She paused. "No, sir, I'm not sure what it is about, only that he requested to meet with you in person."

"Excuse me," a woman said softly, walking over to Kennedy as she hung up the phone. "Can you help me? I'm afraid I don't know what to do."

Kennedy turned to find a woman with straight shoulder-length black hair and soft brown eyes beside her. A jagged scar running from her cheek to her chin marred her delicate features. "Hello," Kennedy said, extending her hand. "I'm Kennedy Reeves, your cruise director."

Before Kennedy could say another word, Deuce Dawson walked quickly through the lobby and over to where Kennedy stood with the woman. "Jordan! You made it!" He turned to Kennedy. "I was just coming over to see if all of the chefs had arrived."

"They have. Do you two know each other?"

Deuce bobbed his head from side to side. "Not well. We only met a few weeks ago when I was in St. Augustine. Jordan's one of the brightest new chefs I have ever met. After tasting her melitzanosalata and moussaka, I demanded to meet whoever had made the dish."

"I was terrified something was wrong with his meal," Jordan offered quietly.

Deuce beamed. "I offered her a spot in the competition right there. It took some explaining to her executive chef," he paused, "and to her, but I felt she had to have the chance to compete."

"May I get a photo?" Bert asked.

Before the others could say yes, Jordan, wild-eyed like a frightened rabbit looking for an escape route, cried out, "NO!"

Bert jumped back. "I'm sorry," he said, startled. His eyes darted to Kennedy.

Jordan was embarrassed as three sets of eyes stared at her. "I'm sorry, I didn't mean to yell. I'm just nervous about the competition and being on a ship. I've never been on one before."

"Let's get you to your cabin and through the safety drill," Kennedy said kindly. "Perhaps you will feel better then."

"Would it be possible to walk through the galley?" Jordan asked hesitantly. "I always feel a sense of peace when I am in a kitchen."

Kennedy was thoughtful. "I'll ask our executive chef." She silently prayed he would be in a good mood when she asked him.

Jordan, relieved, turned to Bert. "I am sorry I yelled. A photographer hounded me long ago, and I'm still a little wary." Bert nodded, and he and Kennedy shared a quizzical look.

Kennedy offered Jordan a wide smile. "Jordan, you are in Cabin 662, and the easiest way to get there is to take the stairs." Jordan thanked her and made her way to the staircase.

"I think I can relax for a minute, knowing all my chefs are now on board. I'll see you in a little while on the set, Kennedy," Deuce said and walked toward the elevator.

Kennedy breathed a sigh of relief and looked around. The lobby was almost empty as the passengers settled in their cabins or toured the ship. She decided she could safely leave when she heard a group of male voices standing between the gangway and the lobby.

"Maybe we go this way?"

"Nah, it's gotta be that way."

"None of you know where you are going. We need to find a map."

"I don't need a nap!"

"Map! Nobody said anything about a nap, Pop!"

Four men entered the lobby looking lost, and Kennedy walked up to them. "Gentlemen, can I help you find something?"

"An angel of mercy, come to rescue us." A slender man in a wheelchair rolled slowly toward her. "And she has a nametag which means she is in charge." He held out his hand to her. "We are the Gents of Breezy Bayou and are here to surprise our friend Chef Lola Cobb. I am Marshall, the president of her official fan club."

"Wow!" Kennedy said with surprise. "I didn't know our competitors had fan clubs. She's fortunate to have you here and to cheer her on." Marshall reminded her of a wizened elf with his curly white hair, which framed his head like a cotton ball, and his too-large glasses that magnified his eyes.

"I'm Larry," a stocky man with an ascot said. He waved to the others. "And this is Karl, Paulie, and..." He looked around. "Where's Eddie?"

"Probably trying to find the machine room," Paulie offered dryly. His eyes ran around the lobby. Paulie's silver and black hair was combed back from his head, and he ran his hand through it absentmindedly. His sad brown eyes did not match the smirk on his lips. Looking at both, Kennedy wondered which feature was the real man: the eyes or the mouth. "He'll tell anyone willing to listen that he singlehandedly ran every ship he was on in the Coast Guard." He looked over Kennedy's shoulder. "My compliments to your housekeeping team, this space positively gleams, which is difficult with the amount of foot traffic you have come through."

"You'll have to forgive Paulie," Larry interrupted. "He's a former hotel guy and can't seem to break himself from doing inspections."

"Thank you, Mr. Restaurant," Paulie said snidely. He stopped scanning the lobby and turned his eyes on Larry first and then Kennedy. "We don't go to restaurants anymore because this one," he pointed at Larry with his thumb, "spends the entire meal instructing the staff."

"I apologize, miss." The fourth man of the group was tall and lanky with weathered features. He extended his hand to Kennedy. "I'm Karl, and you've met my father, Marshall," he gestured at the man in the wheelchair. "You'll have to forgive us. We don't get out with respectable people these days. We seem to forget when there is a beautiful lady in our presence."

"Not me!" Marshall said, chortling, "I'm single and ready to mingle if you are, hot stuff." He patted his chest. "You may not see it now, but inside this old man is a young one dying to get out and show you a fun time."

Kennedy laughed graciously. "I'm sorry, Marshall, but the cruise line has a strict policy, no love affairs with the passengers."

"Rats! How are shipboard romances supposed to happen if you aren't allowed to have them?" He waggled his eyebrows at her. "We could be sneaky, toots. We could meet in clandestine spots. I'll bet a girl like you knows where they all are."

"Pop, that's enough," Karl interrupted. "Please apologize, or I'll have you confined to your cabin." He looked at Kennedy. "I can do that, right?"

Kennedy smiled. Karl and Marshall reminded her of Dolly and Laura, a mother and daughter who often cruised with them. "I believe the last of your group has arrived."

"Eddie, where were you?" Paulie asked.

A barrel-chested man with a gray flattop strode up. Had his friends not mentioned his career, Kennedy would have immediately guessed he was a former military man comfortable with the sea. "Sorry, I got caught up looking at the ship. She may be an old gal, but she is a beauty!"

"Only man I know that gets more excited about looking at a ship than a woman," Marshall said sadly, shaking his head.

"Except for Lola," Larry smirked, and Eddie blushed a deep shade of scarlet.

"Now that you are all here, welcome aboard the *Helio*. I'm Kennedy, the cruise director for the old gal. How may I assist you?"

"Help us find Lola!" Marshall shouted and raised a spindly arm in the air. "As president of her fan club, I demand we find her first."

"Please excuse my father, Ms. Reeves. He packed his swim trunks and teeth, but as you can tell, he forgot to pack his manners. We should find our cabins," he looked meaningfully at his father. "Maybe by then, I will have decided whether you will be allowed out of your room."

"Do you know what time the competition begins?" Marshall asked excitedly. "We want to make sure to be front and center for Lola. She's perfect for the new show. I'm sure you've met her, right?"

Kennedy nodded. "I met her briefly, and I'm sure she will be thrilled to know her fan club is on board. Information about the competition will be on your cabin televisions and in your daily newsletter." She looked at her watch. "However, as we are about to depart Port Canaveral, we can't leave until you have gone through the safety drills in your cabin."

"I think that's a polite way of saying we need to get a move on it," Eddie said to the others. Kennedy consulted her clipboard and showed them how to get to their cabins.

"Remember my offer, toots," Marshall called out as he wheeled toward the elevator, "I'm loaded and single!"

"Pop!" Kennedy heard Karl admonish his father as the doors to the elevator closed, and as they did, she wondered what it would be like to have the Ladies from Harmony Lakes on the same ship with these gentlemen. Dolly and Marshall would be an act to watch. She looked down at her watch. There was still much to be done and standing in an empty lobby was not one of them.

Monique Patrick went up to the pool deck. She frowned when she stepped off the elevator and walked through the double doors leading outside. Not a single seat was open, and the railing was a wall of bodies as passengers stood looking out at the ocean, chatting amiably, and sipping on complimentary drinks. Looking at the passengers, she wondered if she had been dropped into a floating retirement village. Spying the steps to the promenade deck, she climbed them and was pleased to discover fewer people. She found an empty table with a single chair and sat down. Monique reached into her tote bag and pulled out her notebook. She wanted to write down her initial impressions of the cruise. After seeing the ship's age and the passengers' demographics, she would need to adjust her descriptions. Phrases such as casual, relaxed atmosphere and comfortable, informal travel ran through her mind. She could punch up the article by writing about the newly renovated spa, which could be a possible segue into the spa director's unusual background.

Monique crossed her leg and bounced her foot up and down as she wrote what else she needed to accomplish on the trip. Her thoughts drifted to the article she had discussed with Winnifred Wallace. She wondered why the staff and crew had chosen this lifestyle, what they did on their time off, and their favorite things to do in port. She was sure they had connections, and that kind of insider information would be pure gold for her concierge tours. She thought about Kennedy's reaction to her request to interview the personnel. She hadn't decided how she would write the piece about the competing chefs. Common sense told her to write something light to garner more work from the network and a nice paycheck; however, her darker side wanted to write an exposé under her pseudonym and collect a fat check from a gossip magazine. *What was it George Orwell said? "Journalism is printing what someone else does not want printed, everything else is public relations."*

When Terri and Jones Butler came up the steps to walk the promenade, Monique's brain shifted gears as she remembered her conversation with the ship's photographer. She had been disappointed when he clammed up so quickly. She wondered what Bert meant when he said the cruise had not been relaxing for the man. If she had some of the details, she could figure out if it was worth pursuing. The key was to find someone who would remember the couple. *Who are the friendliest people on the ship? Who would have the time to talk?* She stuffed her notebook into her tote bag so it wouldn't blow away and walked over to the railing overlooking the pool bar. She saw a bartender laughing with a group of passengers, and her brain snapped to attention. *Bartenders! They are a natural source of gossip.* The problem was finding the right bar to test her theory.

The pool bar was too noisy and busy and would require shouting. Monique walked back to the table and picked up her bag. She wondered if there was a quiet lounge on the ship where she could chat up a bartender. She had only taken a few steps when she saw a directory pointing out the locations of all the lounges on the ship. *Well, it appears the universe is telling you, Monique, to be like Dorothy and follow the yellow brick road.*

As Monique was making her way to the Vantage Point Lounge, the ship's horn blew, and Kennedy, standing on the pool deck, announced the ship's departure over the public address system. She smiled as she watched the passengers hurry to the railings. Kennedy firmly believed that saying bon voyage allowed them to reset their brains and escape the demands of their everyday lives. She saw Omar and waved cheerfully. He was talking on his phone intently, and his face was a storm of emotions as he paced and gesticulated. She felt a flicker of concern. Omar was not one to allow his feelings to be seen and never near a guest.

The conference room was abuzz with chatter when Kennedy entered and took her seat. She rapped on the table. "All right, everyone, settle down. We've got fifteen minutes to get through a lot of information." She handed Michèle a file. "Information about the competition." She turned to Franklin. "Would you start us off?"

"All well in maintenance and engineering."

Kennedy looked at the executive housekeeper. "Rosemary?"

"Housekeeping's good. Any comments from the VIP cabins?"

"Silence so far. The only person unhappy with their cabin was Monique Patrick, who felt she should have had a more opulent room."

Kennedy turned to Tony. "Ready for tonight?"

Tony patted his jacket pocket. "Server's parade, the captain's toast, and a full roll of antacids. Are you going to introduce the chefs and talk about the competition after the captain's toast?"

"That's still the plan. I'm meeting with the network's producer in a little while. If there is a change, I'll let you know." She looked around the room. "Where is Luke?"

"He was in the Vantage Point Lounge when I was putting more CO2 in the soda guns," Franklin answered. "I don't think he will be here. He was already chatting up one of the passengers. I don't know how he does it, he seems to be a magnet for beautiful women, and she was stunning."

If looks could kill, the glare Rosemary was giving Franklin would have had him wrapped in a piece of sailcloth and tossed overboard. Franklin saw everyone staring at him.

"What?" he asked and saw Tony dart his eyes at Rosemary. "Oh."

"Hmph," Rosemary retorted. She crossed her arms and scowled at him. Mila stifled back a snort while Tony fished around noisily in his pocket for his antacids.

"It appears that Rosemary doesn't need a mood ring to tell you how she is feeling, my friend." Mila patted Franklin on the shoulder.

"What did she look like?" Kennedy asked, and from Franklin's description, Kennedy felt a mild twinge of concern. Luke was a known lady's man, and his stories became more colorful and livelier the more he tried to impress a woman. Kennedy worried this could be a time the player might be played. She would make a point to talk to Luke about Monique as soon as possible. Mila finished updating the group, and it was Kennedy's turn to speak again.

"The journalist writing about the competition, Monique Patrick, who I believe is the woman Franklin saw in the Vantage Point Lounge with Luke, wants to interview the staff and crew for an article about cruising. She claims she discussed this with Winnifred Wallace from corporate and received the green light, but there was nothing in the notes from Alfred."

"Why does she want to do this?" Franklin asked.

Kennedy saw looks of apprehension on the faces of those around the table. "She claims she wants to write an article that," she held her fingers up in the air, 'lets the readers have a peek behind the curtain.' I explained this was a busy cruise but told her I would ask." She looked at Mila. "She mentioned you by name, Mila. Ms. Patrick also offered Billy cash for any stories he would share with her." The group was grim. Kennedy turned to Chef Michèle. "Chef, as I told you earlier today, you will be interviewed by Ms. Patrick, and I'm afraid it is this afternoon."

"But Kennedy, that is in the middle of my preparations for the Captain's Dinner. And this is very last minute." He shook his head back and forth. "No, it's unacceptable. I cannot accommodate her."

Kennedy held up her hand. "I know, and I'm sorry. But you always complain that no one ever pays attention to the culinary team. So, here's your chance to be the peacock we know you to be. Ms. Patrick will meet you in the dining room at five o'clock for your interview. That should give you plenty of time to work on being nice." There was laughter around the room except for Chef Michèle and Ano, although Kennedy thought she saw Ano's slim shoulders shake a little.

"Chef Michèle, one of the competitors made a request." She watched Michèle's eyes narrow. "Chef Jordan has never been on a ship and is anxious. Would it be possible for her to walk through the galley? She said being in a kitchen gave her a sense of calm."

Chef Michèle began to bluster, but Ano interrupted him, "Kennedy, I will accompany her. Have her come during Chef's interview."

Kennedy smiled, "Chef Ano, thank you. I'll leave her a message."

Michèle gave Ano a venomous look. "Make sure she doesn't touch anything," he said curtly. "She may say she is a chef, but I won't believe it until I see her knife skills with my own eyes." He folded his arms and nodded his head once.

"Chef, do you even consider Ano a chef yet?" Franklin asked, chuckling.

Michèle snorted. "He's a baby chef!" He looked at Ano with pride. "But he'll do."

Kennedy looked at Omar. "Omar, anything for the group?" He did not reply. He sat there staring at his phone. "Hello? *Helio* to Omar. Come in, Omar?"

"OMAR!" Franklin and Michèle bellowed in unison.

"What?" Omar's phone flew up and landed on the table with a crack.

"Kennedy asked if you had anything for the group," Franklin said. Omar gave a quick shake of his head but did not speak.

"Okay, anything else?" Kennedy asked. The others shook their heads and wondered about their director of security. His lack of attention during the meeting was odd, and his not paying attention to Kennedy was even stranger. "Chef, I am meeting Mr. Dawson on the set in thirty minutes. Would you care to join me? I want to introduce you."

Michèle nodded. "I have questions as well. How am I supposed to judge these competitors? What do we know about these chefs? I didn't know about judging this competition until you called me, and now I am being forced to give a ridiculous interview."

Kennedy had a feeling Michèle's grumbling was bluster for his nervousness. He was scowling. "Don't glower like that," she giggled. "You look like an ogre."

"I *am* an ogre!" Michèle hollered and stood up. "A horrible, mean, nasty ogre. Ask any member of my team." He walked out of the room, cursing in French.

The others filed out, and Kennedy touched Omar's sleeve as he was about to follow Rosemary. "Is something wrong?"

"No, everything is fine. I'm sorry I was not paying attention during the meeting. Please excuse me. I have some matters to attend to." He left the room quickly, never once looking at her.

Kennedy slipped into the Solstice Theater, where the cast had gathered to walk through the evening's entertainment. Tonight's show was a tribute to the musical and movie *Footloose*. Kennedy had been apprehensive about the show, but the team talked her into it after explaining they felt bored and stale doing the same productions each week. She empathized with them. The corporate office had extended their contracts several times, and they were mentally exhausted. She didn't feel that now would be the best time to bring up Alfred's request for another extension. She saw Chris and the other members of the ship's audio-visual team standing by the entry doors. "Just the gentlemen I was looking for," she grinned.

Chris looked around. "Gentlemen?" He whispered theatrically behind his hand, "You can always tell when she wants something."

She gave Chris a wry smile. "I need some help with the chef's competition. Could you meet me on the putting green? It seems the corporate office didn't consider some things."

Chris rolled his eyes. "Now, there is a shocker. We finished the video footage you wanted for the holiday show, so we have some time on our hands. You are going to flip when you see it."

"I always love what you guys do. Without you, the shows don't have that extra pop."

"Oh, man," Skip, one of the technicians, said. "She is laying it on thick. Whatever she wants must be huge."

"Well, it's big enough that Mila offered to throw in free haircuts."

"And I just got a new soup bowl and nail clippers!" Skip retorted.

"So, here we are," Bert said as he and Art picked their way around the putting green, which was now a culinary set. The ship's audio-visual team was milling around looking at the setup, and Bert introduced them to her.

Art looked intently at the layout. "The set is so…so…"

"Flat?" Bert offered.

"Exactly. Putting cameras in front of each cooking station will make it look like an elementary school production and block the audience's view." She walked around one of the kitchens. "I wish we had met about it before I got here. Deuce and I had been told the ship was managing this. An overhead option would have been good to have," she sighed. "Have you ever made one?" He shook his head, and she continued, "They are fairly simple to make. You can take a quick trip to the hardware store and get everything you need." She looked out at the ocean. "Wishful thinking on my part. I'm sure we don't have the capabilities to make them."

"Capabilities to make what?" Franklin's deep voice interrupted, startling Art and making her fall backward.

Franklin reached out a hand to help the tiny redhead onto her feet.

"An overhead rig for each competition station," Art answered, brushing herself off. "It gives the audience a bird's-eye view of what the chefs are doing."

"Can you draw me what you would need?" Franklin asked, patting his pockets for a piece of paper. Art had piqued his interest, and he was always ready to tackle a challenge.

Art pulled a small notepad out of her jacket pocket and sketched out a simple overhead rig. Franklin looked at the drawing. "We could use some pipe and clamp it to the workstation with a floor flange. Let me look around the maintenance shop to see what we can come up with to make these overhead contraptions."

Deuce walked up to the set just as Kennedy and Chef Michèle arrived. It was perfect timing as Kennedy could introduce everyone at the same time.

"First things first." Deuce looked at the cooking stations and then at Art. "How are we going to get different camera angles?"

"Franklin and I will build some overhead rigs, and I'll run them during each competition." She turned to Chris and Skip. "If you could help me with the camera work and hook up some large televisions for the audience, I can direct you." She turned her head to Deuce. "We will keep it simple on the live feed days, but on days we are taping the show, Bert and I can edit the footage and send it back to the network. They can tweak and air what they want." Deuce had an anxious look on his face. "I've got this, boss. Have I ever let you down?"

Deuce shook his head, stunned at Art's quick assessment of the situation and how she would manage it. "No, you haven't." He ran a hand through his gray curls. "And you are sure about this?"

Art grinned, her eyes twinkling. "Relax." She looked at the others, who were nodding their heads. "Now, we're going over there to figure out the details."

Franklin spoke up, "I'm going to head to the shop. Bert, would you mind bringing Art down?"

Emily Abbot was standing at the edge of the set. "Hello?" she called out and began walking toward them. She wobbled as she stepped into a sea of cables and wires. Franklin, who had been leaving, quickly went over to her and held out his hand. "My goodness, you are a handsome man," she said and clamped her hand over her mouth. "I am so sorry," she said to a blushing Franklin. "I forgot to wear my filter. Words just come out on their own sometimes."

"Good afternoon, Mrs. Abbott," he said as he led her through the maze of cables. "I'm Franklin Blaas. I'm sorry about the mess." He pointed at the sea of cables. "We'll have it cleaned up and taped down soon."

Emily smiled. "Oh, I know who you are. My friend, Vera, calls you the silver fox, but she failed to mention how wonderfully tall you are. We tall girls seldom get to meet a man bigger than us." She gazed at Franklin. "I wonder if I should ask Kennedy to change my dining partner for tonight," she smiled wickedly. "You might prove to be more interesting."

Franklin chuckled. "I wouldn't want to take away Mr. Meier's opportunity to escort you to the Captain's Dinner; however, if you find him disappointing, please let Kennedy know. I'm not only taller, but I am light on my feet." He handed her off to Kennedy.

"Gracious," Emily said under her breath after Franklin left. She looked at the group. "I'm sorry to barge in uninvited. I wanted to see where the competition would take place. I hope I didn't interrupt anything."

Kennedy made introductions. "Deuce, since we are all together, perhaps we could go to our conference room to talk. I think everyone has questions."

Emily clapped her hands together. "What a splendid idea. I want to make sure I am judging this competition correctly." Deuce nodded, and the group took the elevator down to deck five.

They settled around the conference table, and Chef Michèle was the first to speak as he sat down in a chair. "The competition themes are quite interesting. The first round should make them put on their thinking caps. I had never heard of dining books until Kennedy gave me the file. Now I understand why I was asked to send my menus to the corporate office for so many years." He turned to Emily. "I am certainly glad I was not a chef on one of your great-grandfather's ships. Our modern conveniences make serving our passengers much easier."

Emily nodded as she took her seat. "It had to have been difficult. So, I was thrilled when the network wanted to go forward with the first theme."

Kennedy looked at her watch. "Unfortunately, our time with Chef Michèle is limited. He has an interview soon." She began to pass out notepads and pens.

"Ah, the first victim," Deuce chuckled and put his glasses on.

"Mr. Dawson," Michèle began, "could you explain how we will judge the candidates? The way I would judge them is quite different from Mrs. Abbott."

Emily looked anxiously at Deuce. "I agree. I am not as versed as the two of you. I wonder if I should be one of the judges. I only have a kitchen in my house because it came with it."

"But we do need you as a judge, Mrs. Abbott," Deuce insisted. "You bring fresh eyes and a unique perspective to the food. Because Michèle and I have run kitchens, we demand perfection and can come off as bullies." He peered over his glasses at Emily. "I believe you will be able to keep us in check."

"You were a chef?" Emily asked.

Deuce smiled sadly. "In another lifetime." The room became uncomfortably quiet, and Chef Michèle cleared his throat.

"I understand this competition is sous chefs competing against each other. Do we know for a fact they are all sous?"

Deuce shook his head. "I believe two are not. One is a personal chef, and one runs a small family-owned restaurant." Michèle nodded, understanding what Deuce was implying. "Now, as you know, there are four rounds, and each round has one winner. We will assign each chef points based on taste, behavior during the round, cleanliness, presentation, and creativity."

"I'm sorry, Deuce," Emily interrupted. "Behavior? How do we judge their behavior?"

Deuce folded his hands together. "We will watch and listen as they prepare the food. For example, are they stressed? Perhaps they did not think through their dish completely. Are they overly confident? They may have ignored the challenge or made something ordinary. Boldness has a place in the competition, a chef who correctly executes an inventive dish is someone to pay attention to, but a chef who is cocky is a warning sign. Sticking to one style of cooking is another red flag. We need our winner to be versatile."

"I would think cleanliness is another key part of this competition," Michèle offered. "A chef with a messy cooking station would probably have sloppy kitchen habits or little regard for their peers or customers."

"Or," Deuce added, "lacks confidence in the dish they have prepared."

Emily was scribbling down notes. "I'm not sure I'll be able to catch all of this," she said worriedly.

Deuce patted her hand. "Mrs. Abbott, I don't want you to worry. I want you to have fun. Our television viewers don't want to see the judges stressed. They want to see us enjoying ourselves while we find the host chef for the new television show." He gave her a conspiratorial wink. "*But* I do want the competing chefs to sweat."

Michèle stood up, looking at his watch. "I apologize for leaving, but I need to check on the kitchen before this interview." He bowed to Mrs. Abbott and nodded to Deuce. "I feel much better about this competition and look forward to working with you."

After Michèle left, Kennedy updated Deuce and Emily with some of the changes she had come up with to allow the passengers to engage more with the competition. "Ballot boxes are a better idea than online voting. It's more exciting to see someone physically casting their ballot. You wonder whose name they wrote on the piece of paper. We could also have Bert and Art interview passengers to learn who they picked and why. These snippets can be sent back to the network with the footage, and we can post the daily tallies in the newsletter for the passengers."

Deuce nodded and looked at Emily. "It's a clever idea. It builds anticipation and gives a "man on the street" feel." He turned back to Kennedy. "What else?"

"I'd like to see the chefs host some cooking demonstrations. It would allow the passengers a personal bond with the chefs, which television viewers would not get, and may make them lifelong viewers because of that connection." She saw Deuce's agreement and plowed on. "The original intent was to host each competition in a different location so viewers could see different areas of the ship, and while it looks good on paper, we don't have the manpower to reset each day." She saw Deuce's mouth tighten. "I would like to propose that Art film the chefs on a behind-the-scenes tour."

"That is a marvelous idea, Kennedy!" Emily said.

"There is one last piece of business. I mentioned earlier that I would like to flip-flop the last two competitions and host them in the main theater. Our last show is holiday themed. So, we could host the competition, and while the judges deliberate, the cast would perform the holiday show. It would give you plenty of time to decide and build anticipation without the passengers losing interest."

"Let me discuss this with Art, but as long as you can pull this off, I'm okay with it," Deuce said and turned to Emily. "What do you think?"

Emily looked at Kennedy and then at Deuce. "I believe Kennedy has made limoncello out of lemons."

"Chef Michèle, thank you for taking the time to meet with me today," Monique said as she and Michèle took their seats at a table in the dining room. "I know you are a busy man."

Michèle nodded and crossed his arms. "Yes, we are preparing for the Captain's Dinner tonight," he said with a clipped tone.

Monique smiled widely, trying to thaw the chill she felt from the executive chef. "Let's start with something easy. Will you share with me the day-to-day operations of running the *Helio's* kitchens? How do you feed everyone? How many kitchens are there?"

Michèle visibly relaxed. He often answered this question for the passengers. He walked Monique through his day, which started very early in the morning as they prepared for the meals they would cook, the mid-afternoon tasting, and the late-night paperwork. He became animated as he spoke, sharing with Monique that the ship had three smaller restaurants in addition to the main dining room and the staff and crew dining area. "Anything eaten on this ship has been prepared by my team," he said.

"Goodness, I suppose I didn't look at it that way."

"There are no other options in the middle of the sea," he gave a hearty laugh.

"How do you keep it all organized so you don't run out of food?" she asked, writing down her question.

"It's not difficult," the big man answered. "Our trips are short, and we have set menus and a regular grocery list which will be loaded onto the ship when we return to Port Canaveral. In addition, we keep a pantry of items for anyone with food allergies. I am fortunate to have my staff, especially Ano, my sous chef. He is my right and left hand."

"Tell me about your staff. They seem to be very dear to you."

Michèle's chest swelled. "My team is the backbone of this ship, and we work very hard to keep our passengers and the people working on the ship fed and happy.

Monique was thoughtful. "What would you say your staff appreciates most about you?"

Michèle looked down at the floor and then up at Monique. "I would say that I am a teacher. Not everyone has the benefit of having a formal culinary education, but if there is a hunger, I can teach them."

"Some chefs have been likened to tyrants. Have you ever been called one?"

Michèle's face turned dark red. "No, I have not," he blustered. "Did someone say something to you?"

Monique was startled by his tone and put a star by that question. *I must have touched a nerve.*

"Next question," he barked.

"What is your favorite kitchen tool, Michèle?" Monique had a mischievous look on her face. It was an interview tactic she used when the subject got defensive.

He looked at her puzzled, and a wide grin appeared. "A spoon."

Monique had poised her pen over her notebook to write down Michèle's answer, and she put it down when she heard his answer. "A spoon?" she repeated.

Michèle gave her a wide smile. "I must taste everything that goes out of our kitchens to ensure it is perfect for our guests. As I said earlier, we have a mid-afternoon sampling, and I taste every snack, soup, appetizer, salad, side dish, main dish, and dessert. If it does not taste perfect to me, I cannot serve it to our guests."

"Next question, what is your favorite time in the kitchen?"

Michèle was quick to answer. "Oh, that is easy," he said. "During the dinner rush in the main dining room. I am the conductor, and my staff the instruments. Together we make a culinary symphony."

"That would be something to see," Monique said, grinning.

"You should come and watch. It will make you appreciate what happens when you go out for a meal."

Monique looked down at her notebook. "Michèle, what do you do when you are not on the ship?"

Michèle began to get comfortable again. The interview was going well. "Believe it or not, I spend a lot of my time trying new recipes to see if they are right for the ship. If I find something new, I must first decide if it can be made easily for a thousand people." He waved his arm around the dining room to make his point.

"What is something people think happens in a ship's dining room that is a misconception?"

He answered quickly. "Fire." He moved his finger back and forth. "Big no-no. We had a consultant a few months ago who kept making references to tableside flambés. If he had been aware of ship protocols, he would have known open flames are against the rules."

Monique cocked her head. "Was it difficult having a consultant on board? Did they point out mistakes that you and your staff were making?"

"He was an imbecile, but I will never have to cross paths with him again." There was a frigid tone in the chef's answer.

Monique realized she had stepped on another sensitive subject and put a star beside the question on her notepad. "Tell me about your training. How did you become an executive chef?"

The friendliness and animation Michèle possessed earlier vanished entirely. "Please be assured that I have been trained and educated properly for my job." He looked at his watch. "I'm sorry, Ms. Patrick, but I must wrap up our time together. There are still final preparations for dinner to be made."

Monique looked at the remaining list of questions she still wanted to ask. Finally, she decided on an easy one to regain some footing with the chef. The promise of being allowed to sit in the galley while he held court was enticing.

Monique smiled coyly. "One last question?" He sighed heavily and crossed his arms. "What is your favorite ingredient to cook with?"

Michèle let out a deep laugh. "Oranges."

"Oranges?" She shook her head. "You have given me many unusual answers this afternoon. What do you do other than peel and eat an orange or drink a glass of juice?"

"You can use every part of the orange when cooking. My favorite thing is to make a vinaigrette with oranges for fish. It gives it a unique taste leaving a swirl of sweetness and tartness in the mouth at the same time."

"Is that your way of telling me to order the fish tonight?" she asked playfully.

Michèle stood up and offered Monique his hand. "*That* will be up to you, Ms. Patrick."

The main dining room looked lovely for the Captain's Dinner, and the formal attire the passengers wore gave the evening an air of romance. Kennedy always felt this first dinner set the tone for the cruise. There had been some good ones and some disastrous ones, and she hoped tonight's event would go flawlessly. She was speaking with the couple who had been initially upset with the view from their cabin when she saw Emily Abbott gliding across the room on Omar's arm. They made a striking pair as they walked to the captain's table. In a red silk jumpsuit, Emily caught the attention of more than one table. Kennedy felt a twinge in her heart. She and Omar had not spoken since his curt response earlier in the day, and as she walked back to the podium, she reminded herself not to read into his behavior.

"Good evening Mrs. Abbott," the captain said in his deep voice as he stood by his table. "I apologize for not being available to welcome you aboard when you arrived. We are all excited about the partnership with the network."

"Thank you, Captain," she nodded, and they took their seats. "I am certain you had more important things to do than greet an old woman. I am excited about the partnership as well. It opens many possibilities for the company."

"I trust Mr. Meier took you out for cocktails before dinner?"

"Oh, yes!" She laid her hand on Omar's forearm. "Omar is ensuring I experience everything my friend Vera Jameson gets on her cruises, and I plan to have stories to make her green with envy." She turned to Omar. "She seems to believe you two have a special connection."

Omar blushed and looked at his plate. "I found Mrs. Jameson to be a unique woman who is not afraid to take a chance."

"At our age, Omar," Emily chuckled, "not much can go wrong when we take a chance." She looked around the dining room. "Although I miss being a young woman with all their advantages."

The corners of Omar's lips rose. "I see it another way. It is the younger women who are at a disadvantage. They wear their youth on the surface like a cheap trinket, whereas mature women wear their confidence like a costly jewel."

"My goodness, Mr. Meier," the captain said. "You are quite the poet tonight. I think you should make the toast this evening."

Omar chuckled. "No, sir, I just happen to be in good company."

The captain cleared his throat. "Mrs. Abbott, I'm not sure if you are aware, but we begin the Captain's Dinner on the *Helio* with our parade of servers."

Emily cocked her head. "A parade?"

He explained how the servers would parade through the dining room, weaving around the tables carrying trays with domed covers while they danced to the music. "Think of it as the pregame show for tonight's theater production." He took a sip of water. "The passengers love it, and I have never seen it done on any other cruise line." He made a face. "We had a consultant who—"

"Don't remind me of that debacle," Emily interrupted. "We should have trusted all of you, not some stranger."

The captain smiled awkwardly. "Like any other storm, we survived with only a few bruises." He explained that after the salad course, he would introduce some of the officers and staff and offer his toast for the cruise. "After the toast, I'll introduce you…" Suddenly, he was distracted by a couple at the podium. "Good Lord, I was not aware they were on board."

"Who?" Omar asked and chuckled when he saw where the captain was looking. "Oh yes, Mr. and Mrs. Butler are with us again. I'm surprised Kennedy didn't tell you."

"I suppose I should be grateful she isn't wearing a denim dress and a rhinestone dog collar," the captain chuckled. "Although *that dress* was a bit tamer than what she is wearing tonight. What do you suppose that is? A formal loincloth?"

"Kennedy!" David whispered loudly as she walked past his table. She stopped and bent down. "John will be crushed he was not here to see *that*!" He pointed his head in the direction of the podium. "I don't think I have the right words to describe it."

"What?" She looked and saw the Butlers standing at the entrance to the dining room. "Oh, my goodness, I've got to go!"

Terri's zebra-print gown glittered in the lights. "Mr. and Mrs. Butler," Kennedy said quickly, "you both look lovely. May I escort you to your table?" All eyes in the dining room followed them as they walked to the table in the middle of the room. "That is a very daring dress, Mrs. Butler. You are the only person I know that could pull it off." Terri glowed at Kennedy's compliment.

"Oooh, will you look at her!" Marshall adjusted his glasses as Terri and Jones walked by. "There goes my next wife!"

"Pop, I'm sure the man walking behind her is her husband," Karl said. "And I'm not sure I'm up for a stepmother dressed like that."

"I wonder where Lola is?" Paulie craned his neck, looking around the dining room.

"They might be announcing them after the captain's toast," Larry said, turning over the fork in his hand to see who made it.

"As soon as one of you see her let me know," Marshall said. "I want to make sure she knows we are here. And we want to do everything we can to ensure she wins."

"Have you all realized that if she wins, she will no longer cook for us?" Eddie asked thoughtfully. "No more of Lola's special pot roast or pork loin wrapped in bacon with risotto before our poker games."

"No more chicken pot pies or meatballs," Paulie sighed. "They were better than my mother's." The table fell silent as the men suddenly understood what they might be losing.

"I guess we didn't think about it," Marshall said quietly.

"We were just excited she got the call," Karl added morosely.

After Kennedy seated Mr. and Mrs. Butler at their table, she stopped back at the table where David was sitting and saw Deuce Dawson had joined him. Deuce looked around the dining room and then at the empty table near his. "Where are my chefs?" he asked worriedly. "I don't mean to sound like a nervous mother, but Jordan is the only one I have met."

"They are outside waiting for me to introduce them after the captain makes his toast. It will create some excitement when the passengers see the empty table in the middle of the dining room. Relax, Mr. Dawson, we have this under control."

"It's under control? Was there some concern? Now *that* would have made for an interesting start to the article," Monique purred as she slid into her seat. She was a study in understated elegance in a cream-colored gown and gold hoop earrings. Deuce looked at Kennedy questioningly.

"All is well, Ms. Patrick," Kennedy said brightly. "Mr. Dawson, please meet Monique Patrick. She is writing about the competition for the network. Monique, Mr. Dawson is the—"

"I know all about Mr. Dawson," Monique gave Deuce a sly smile.

"Excuse me?" Deuce said with some surprise.

"The network sent over your bio, Mr. Dawson, although there were a few holes. Perhaps we can chat soon. We have an interview, don't we?" She turned from Deuce back to Kennedy. "Kennedy," Monique pointed her finger at the Butlers, "who is the couple over there? They made quite an entrance, and the staff appears to know them."

Kennedy smiled calmly. "Some returning passengers. Our staff enjoys reconnecting with our encore guests. Now, as you know Mr. Dawson, may I introduce you to David Stearns, who is here writing about our spa, Oaza."

Monique raised her eyebrows at David but didn't say anything. Instead, she turned her attention back to Deuce. "You were a chef before you became a producer for the network, weren't you?"

Deuce looked warily at Monique. "Yes," he answered slowly. "I was, but I am here now on behalf of the network as we host a competition and celebrate the partnership between the network and cruise line."

Sensing Deuce's cautiousness, Kennedy interrupted, "Mr. Dawson, we are about to start dinner. Do you know where Art is? I thought she would be joining you tonight." She pointed at the empty chair at the table.

Deuce waved his hand. "Bert asked her to go to someplace called Longitudes. I was surprised she accepted. There is a lot to do before tomorrow morning's competition."

"Kennedy," David spoke up. "I believe someone's trying to get your attention."

Tony was making an exaggerated face and pointing at his watch. She walked over to the captain and whispered to him. He nodded, and the house lights dimmed as the music began to play through the speakers, and the servers began their parade through the dining room. Kennedy slipped out to make sure the four chefs were ready for their entrance. "Hi, everyone," she said brightly. "It's good to see you all again. Have you met?"

Miles was the first to speak. "We were just making introductions."

Kennedy opened the door a crack and motioned for Tony to come out. "The captain is finishing his toast. Tony will open the door for you. When I introduce you, follow the spotlight to your table, which is the empty one in the middle of the room."

Kennedy quickly slipped into her place behind the captain. "Before I turn the microphone over to Kennedy. I want to introduce you to a special guest we are honored to have on this cruise, Mrs. Emily Abbott, the great-granddaughter of our founder and a member of our board of directors. I want to offer a toast to her, as without her great-grandfather, none of us would be here tonight." Emily blushed as the captain and the passengers raised their glasses to her.

The captain handed the microphone to Kennedy. "Thank you, sir. As you may be aware, this is a special time for our cruise line as we begin our partnership with the Classic Style Network." There was polite applause from the audience. "As we embark on this exciting collaboration, a culinary competition to find the host chef for their new show, *Classic Flavors*, will take place over the next few days, and you will have a ringside seat to watch the chefs battle it out. So, without further ado, please allow me to introduce you to our competitors," she paused for a moment, and Tony opened the doors. "Chef Miles White from Gainesville, Florida." Miles walked through the doors and was momentarily blinded by the spotlight. He raised his hand to the diners, followed the spotlight to the table, and sat down. Tristan was next, followed by Lola. When Lola walked through the room, there was a cacophony of whistles and hollering as she waved enthusiastically to the passengers blowing kisses as she walked by them.

"Seems like Lola has a personal cheering section. Were we allowed to have people we knew on the cruise?" Miles asked in a whisper to Tristan.

"I would have had several tables full of fans if we had. I have a following." Tristan scowled.

Once Jordan, blushing furiously, reached her seat, the room settled down, and Kennedy began to speak again, "The chefs will be competing each day on the pool deck. I'm sure many of you were disappointed to learn four mini-kitchens have overtaken the putting green, but I believe this live-action contest will be more exciting than any of your golf games." The audience tittered. "The daily newsletter will give you information about the competition and opportunities to meet the chefs. Seating is limited, so make sure you get there early." She picked up a clear acrylic box. "Each day, you will have the chance to vote for your favorite chef, and," she looked around the room mischievously, "your friends and family back home may see you as we will be filming interviews with some of you about your favorite chef." Finally, she took a breath, "I see the captain is giving me the wrap-it-up sign. I wish you good night, bon appétit, and welcome to the *Helio*." Kennedy turned the microphone off, and the house lights went back up as the servers brought out the main course.

Now that they were all seated and dinner was underway, the four chefs began to relax. "Tristan, where do you work?" Miles asked.

"At one of the best restaurants in Jacksonville, probably in the top five for the state. I'm the sous chef but more like the star," Tristan replied smugly. "The food is okay, but the main attraction is me. I like to visit with the guests. It's better than being in the hot kitchen."

"Wow," Lola said slowly. "I never met someone who was a legend in their own mind, but here you are in the flesh."

"What about you, Miles? Where is your restaurant?" Jordan asked quietly.

Miles nodded. "In Gainesville. I was a partner with my mother until she passed away a few weeks ago. She was our executive chef, and I was her sous. So, everything I learned about cooking came from her." He grinned. "As soon as I could walk, she had me working in the kitchen."

"Oh, so you're a mama's boy," Tristan snickered. "I guess you finally cut the apron strings."

Lola and Jordan looked at Tristan in horror. "Good grief, Tristan, were you raised by wolves?" Lola admonished him.

"I was just kidding. Miles knows it," Tristan blustered, embarrassed.

The table was silent. "Are either of you going to ask Jordan or me about our backgrounds?" Lola asked.

Tristan chuckled. "I'm not sure I care. This competition will come down to Miles and me." He pointed a thumb at Jordan. "She's too shy to be on television, and you are… well, can you see over the stove, or do you need a step stool?"

"Careful, Tristan. Even a tiny tornado can do a great deal of damage," Miles chided.

"No, seriously, she doesn't have the chef personality." Lola opened her mouth to say something, but Tristan continued, "You have plenty of personality. Trust me. I saw it earlier today. You obviously know how to work a room, but do you know your way around the kitchen?"

Lola bristled. "I'm a very successful personal chef. I cook for some very important people if you must know."

"Name two," Tristan demanded.

"I can't," Lola said primly. "Strict non-disclosure agreements." She waved her hand as if shooing away a fly. "When they need me, they send a jet."

"A jet?" Tristan scoffed. "Sure."

"Mmhmm. It's all on my social media page if you are interested." Lola looked like a cat who had swallowed a canary.

"How did you get in the competition if you are a personal chef and not a sous chef?" Tristan challenged her.

"They never asked, and the tryout wasn't difficult. Maybe it was for you, Tristan?" She took a drink of water. "I heard another chef had to forfeit their spot for some reason. I wonder which of us was the backup."

Miles sighed. He was already tired of the bickering between Lola and Tristan. "Does it matter? The four of us are here now, and we'll get a lot of exposure which will mean more money for our restaurants."

"Yeah, but only one of us will walk away with a new cooking show, and I'm pretty sure it will be me." Tristan sat back in his chair and put his hands behind his head.

Miles turned to Jordan. "Jordan, tell us about your background."

"Yeah, I want to know if you are a sous chef, unlike little Miss Personal Chef," Tristan rolled his eyes at Lola.

Lola could not resist antagonizing him. "Looking for your brain, Tristan?"

"Did you find yours?" he retorted.

Jordan and Miles exchanged a look.

"I worked as a cook in a diner out west for many years," Jordan said, answering Miles's question. "I don't have a formal culinary education like any of you," she looked down at her hands, "but I learned as I went. I hocked my wedding ring to buy my first set of knives. I moved to St. Augustine a year ago."

"What's the name of the restaurant? Who is the chef? I know every executive chef between Jacksonville and St. Augustine." Tristan's questions came out like a machine gun.

"I am a sous chef, Tristan," Jordan replied evenly. "The executive chef is Kendall Ash, and for your information, Mr. Dawson asked me to compete."

Tristan's eyes narrowed. "Oh, so, you already have an in with Deuce Dawson. Isn't that convenient?"

"Tristan, lay off. It doesn't matter how we got here." Miles turned his attention back to Jordan. "How did you know you wanted to be a chef?"

Jordan's face glowed. "It's my calling. I love that moment you walk into the kitchen and turn the lights on. The possibilities for the day are endless."

Miles nodded, understanding what she meant.

"Wait," Tristan interrupted, "you come in first?" He brayed, "I roll in when I feel like it. There are plenty of people at my restaurant to take care of the little things. I'm more center stage and less back of the house."

Miles glared at Tristan. "Jordan, you said Deuce asked you to compete. So, why do it if you are happy at your restaurant?"

Jordan shrugged. "You cannot grow by staying in your comfort zone. So, even if I don't win, I hope to learn something from each of you. A new technique or recipe, a way to better myself."

Tristan pointed at the scar on her face. "Maybe Lola can start by helping you with some makeup to camouflage *that*. The camera will certainly pick up on it." He pointed to her arm. "And I hope you have a long sleeve jacket because even with the tattoo, the one on your arm is pretty gruesome."

Jordan self-consciously touched the puckered skin that went from her cheek to her chin. "Excuse me," she said, looking down. "I can't…I need to leave." She got up quickly and left the dining room.

"Tristan, you can be such an ass," Lola said, looking at him in disgust.

"If you can't take the heat, stay out of the kitchen," Tristan called out, laughing in Jordan's wake.

"Was that really necessary?" Miles glared at Tristan.

Tristan shrugged. "All in the spirit of competition."

Deuce caught the commotion at the chef's table from the corner of his eye and saw Jordan walking quickly out of the room. Monique followed his stare. "Looks like someone over there drew first blood, Mr. Dawson," she purred.

Deuce whipped around. "Don't make a mountain out of a molehill, Ms. Patrick. Not everything is fodder for a story."

"Oh, that is where you are wrong, Mr. Dawson," Monique said with amusement.

Back at the chef's table, Miles looked around the room, feeling awkward after Jordan's abrupt departure. He saw an older man in a wheelchair pointing frantically at Lola.

"Lola," Miles chuckled, "I believe someone is trying to get your attention."

"Really?" She smiled and followed his gaze. "Ohhh," she said slowly and blew out a breath. "I didn't see that coming."

"See what coming?" Tristan asked, twisting his head to look around. His eyes found the table of men waving at Lola. "Some of your famous financial types? What a joke."

"Shouldn't you go over and say hello, Lola?" Miles asked gently. "They seem harmless."

"Oh, it's fine," Lola quickly recovered and blew kisses to the table. "Some of my daily clients. I didn't know they would be here. I suppose I should say hello." She looked at Miles and Tristan. "I'll see you on the battlefield tomorrow." She wiggled her fingers. "Good night, grandpa. Good night, troll." She gave Tristan a scathing look and left the table.

"Good night, princess," Tristan said, smiling.

"Princess?" Lola glared at Tristan and put a hand on her hip. "If you haven't figured it out yet, I'm the queen." She strutted to the table of older men who had been trying to get her attention. "Oh, my goodness, this is such a surprise. How are you? I can't believe you are here," she called out loudly.

"She's cute in a savage pixie way," Tristan said, watching her walk away. "She'll try to seduce me at some point; most women do. Jordan's not bad if you can get past the scar. But it's a pretty big turn-off. The network will want someone good-looking for this show, someone to make the ladies tune in." He began to shovel food into his mouth. "The food tonight is okay. I don't know about you, but how often do you get to sit down and eat? Most of the time, I'm sitting on a milk crate or a five-gallon bucket eating something someone sent back. From what I see," he repeated, "this competition is down to you and me, buddy. Honestly, I'll most likely be the ultimate winner, but, hey..." he suddenly stopped talking. "Miles?" Miles didn't respond. He was sitting very still, and his eyes were closed. Tristan could see them moving rapidly back and forth. *Whoa, is he so old he can't stay awake through dinner?*

"Lola," Miles woke with a start.

"Dude, Lola's gone, and she was right to call you grandpa. You've been asleep."

Miles bristled. "I wasn't sleeping. I was thinking with my eyes closed."

Tristan grinned. "Whatever you need to tell yourself. At least you weren't snoring. Is it past your bedtime, gramps? Your restaurant must only have an early bird dinner so you can get home before the sun goes down. Do you serve decaf coffee with dessert?"

"If you must know," Miles said in a low tone, "I have narcolepsy, but I take medication to control it."

"Whoa, my grandfather had that. He'd fall asleep in the middle of talking. It must be an old person's disease. Do you fall asleep when you are cooking? That would be a bummer to burn someone's dinner because you fell asleep."

Miles was already sorry that he had confided in Tristan. "It's a medical condition, like diabetes or poor vision. And yes, I fall asleep at strange times, when I'm doing an ordinary task or in the middle of a conversation." He looked at his folded hands. "It's why I never cut the apron strings, as you kindly pointed out. I ran the kitchen, and my mother kept an eye on me. She kept everyone safe that way."

"Safe?" Tristan asked warily. "Is there something we should be worried about?"

Miles shook his head. "I take medication and stick to a strict schedule. Before my diagnosis, my mom would find me asleep over an open flame or in the walk-in freezer."

Tristan stared at Miles. "Dude, *that* is messed up. What kind of strict schedule are you on?"

"Lifestyle changes more than anything," Miles explained. "No drinking or smoking, and definitely no large meals." He pointed to his plate, which was still quite full. "I also exercise a lot. It really helps." He looked at his watch.

"In fact, I should find the gym." He rose from the table. "I'll see you at the competition tomorrow morning."

Tristan watched Miles leave. The wheels were turning in his head. If Miles could fall asleep in the middle of a live television show, the producer would be wary of making him the winner. With any luck, Miles would have an episode in front of Deuce Dawson. Lola was a flake, and Jordan was a scared rabbit. Tristan smiled widely and put his hands behind his head, realizing he would not have to work as hard to win as he had thought.

When Bert and Art had been in the maintenance shop scrounging for things to make the overhead rigs, Bert had shyly suggested going to Longitudes, the bar on the lower deck, for dinner. The bar was not popular with passengers due to its location and, therefore, was one of Bert's favorite spots on the ship.

She walked in and climbed onto the stool beside his. She looked around. "My kind of place," she grinned. "A little seedy, and my clothes fit in. I'm not a dress-up kind of girl." She looked at the bartender. "May I have a frozen strawberry margarita?"

"Y-y-you look perfect to me," Bert stammered.

"I hope I'm not taking you away from your work. It was nice of you to invite me down here."

Bert shook his head. "The passengers won't notice if the photos I took before the Captain's Dinner go up a few hours later. Tomorrow is a sea day. So, most of them will sleep in."

The bartender came over with Art's drink. Bert raised his beer glass in the air. "Cheers," he said, and they clinked glasses. Art took a sip, and as she did, her strawberry margarita spilled down the front of her white shirt.

"It's official," she sighed. "I should never wear anything white," Art looked down at the red splotch with amusement. "You can dress me up, but you can't take me out. Another story to add to my collection of clumsiest moments." She dabbed at the stain.

Bert laughed. "I understand. I got a black eye once from playing ping pong."

Art held up her hand. "Dislocated my finger coming down the rope in gym class." She looked at him. "And what was the point of that? I have never needed to climb up or down a rope."

The bartender came over to take their order, and they both ordered a cheeseburger, medium well with pickles on the side.

"You too?" Art asked incredulously. "Do you know about the pickle war?"

Bert looked at Art strangely. "I'm getting an image in my head of people using pickles as swords. En garde!" He held up an imaginary pickle and began swishing it in her face.

Art joined in the merriment and waved her hand, trying to control her laughter. She told him the story of the pickle war and how a simple recipe became a scandal. "Jealousy, betrayal, and drama—all for the lowly pickle."

Bert was dumbfounded. "I'm going to have to give pickles more respect now," he said. "How did you find out about it?"

Art shrugged her shoulders. "I love weird facts. That one was on a day-of-the-month trivia calendar, and I wanted to know the whole story. I spend a lot of time waiting for people, and researching oddities helps to pass the time. I'm weird."

Bert shook his head. "Not to me. So, you are a klutz and into weird trivia. What else? Any strange collections?"

Art cocked her head. "I have an assortment of crutches, slings, and a knee scooter, with a bike basket." The bartender placed two burgers in front of them. They were quiet as they started to eat. "What about you?" she asked, taking a large bite of her cheeseburger. There was a smear of ketchup on the side of her mouth, and Bert stared at it.

"I'm pretty clumsy, too. Being a klutz helped me make my first friend on board," he said sheepishly.

"Oh?"

"My camera strap got hung up on a stair handrail, and I was beginning to pass out when Kennedy came along. I don't want to think about what might have happened if she hadn't been there. She said my face was purple."

Art put her hand up to her mouth to hide her laugh. "I'm sorry. It's not funny, but now I'm getting a mental picture, and it's comical. Purple is not your color."

He pointed to his front tooth. "The great slip and slide incident in college. I knocked it out."

She pointed at one of hers. "Face-plant onto the sidewalk on my way to a blind date. I called later to explain why I didn't show up, but I never heard back from the guy, which was too bad. I don't get to go on dates very often."

Bert picked up his napkin and gently wiped the ketchup from her cheek. "His loss," he said sincerely.

"Oh, I am so embarrassed," she said, turning red. "How long was that there?"

"H-h-how did you get involved behind the camera?" he asked, changing the subject.

Art shrugged. "My dad was an amateur videographer, and there were always cameras around the house. My older sister and her friends would put on these outrageous skits, and while I wasn't cool enough to be in their dramas, they would allow me to film them. And telling them what to do was fun. When I got older, my dad took me along to help." She rolled her eyes. "A lot of weddings, community theater, and church pageants." She took another bite of her burger. "My dad filmed our high school football games for the coach. One day he had the flu, and I showed up on the sidelines with his camera and told the coach I was filling in. I must have done a decent job because I was on the sidelines for the next three years. In college, I took every side gig I could, filming and editing. After graduating, I worked for a company that provided audio-visual services for hotels. That was where I learned how to improvise." She took a sip of her margarita. "That's me in a nutshell."

"And now you have a gig with Classic Style," Bert said, amazed. "Live television, traveling. I bet your family is proud of you."

She grinned. "My dad is, but my mom wishes I did something more," she held her fingers up in the air, "ladylike. But I love what I do, especially when it involves coming up with something on the fly."

"You'll find plenty of opportunities for that on the *Helio*," Bert said and took a bite of his hamburger.

Monique made her way to the Vantage Point Lounge after dinner. As she walked, she pondered what she had observed during dinner. She was beginning to form thoughts about the competing chefs based on their body language when they entered the dining room. The woman in the outlandish zebra print dress flashed through her mind. She wished Kennedy had not been so vague. She placed her hand on the door handle to the lounge, hoping the handsome bartender she met earlier would be there. He had told her to ask for Luke if she needed anything, and she supposed she did. Information.

Luke looked up from polishing a glass when he felt the breeze from the door opening. As the beverage manager, he worked in all the lounges. After flirting with Monique earlier in the day, Luke gave the regular bartender the night off, hoping she would be back. He grinned when he saw her, and she gave him a cool look from the side of her eye. She strolled to the end of the bar, knowing he was staring at her. The cream-colored dress flattered her dark skin, and her gold hoop earrings sparkled in the lights. "Good evening,

Monique. I hoped you would come back. What may I get you?"

She gave him a slow smile. "A French 75, please." He gave her a quick nod and turned his back to her, grabbing what he would need to make the bubbly cocktail. "I saw the most intriguing couple tonight at dinner. I believe Kennedy said they were regulars," she said casually while Luke had his back turned. "The Butlers?"

# **MONIQUE'S FRENCH 75**

1 OUNCE GIN

½ OUNCE FRESH LEMON JUICE

½ OUNCE SIMPLE SYRUP

3 OUNCES CHAMPAGNE

LEMON TWIST

COMBINE GIN, LEMON JUICE, AND SIMPLE SYRUP IN A SHAKER WITH ICE AND SHAKE UNTIL WELL-CHILLED. STRAIN INTO A CHAMPAGNE FLUTE. TOP WITH CHAMPAGNE. GARNISH WITH A LEMON TWIST.

Luke chuckled as he turned around. "What did her dress look like tonight? She always likes to make an entrance."

"So, you know them?" He nodded and poured gin, lemon juice, and syrup into the shaker. "A zebra-striped, one-shoulder loincloth," she answered. "I'm not sure what you would call it, but it wasn't haute couture."

Luke shoveled ice into a cocktail shaker and put the cap on top. He gave a soft snicker. "Well, that's better than the last cruise," he said, and Monique raised an eyebrow at him, silently begging him to continue. "On the last cruise, she was in a denim and rhinestone gown that blinded everyone in the room." He chuckled at the memory. "It was one of those moments you never forget." He stopped shaking the metal bottle and was thoughtful. "But then again, she always wears something to make people look. I suppose if you are as rich as they are, you want to be noticed."

"Rich? As in millionaires?" she asked.

He motioned with his thumb to say more and poured the contents of the shaker into the champagne glass. He knelt and took out a split of champagne. "He's the man behind the Buck-A-Cluck franchise. Sold it a few months ago." He poured the champagne into the glass and added a curling piece of lemon peel. "They came onto the ship after the sale to celebrate and relax." He pushed the glass toward Monique. "Unfortunately, halfway through the cruise, he found something which undid all that relaxation."

"What happened?" Monique breathed. She was having a tough time keeping the excitement from her voice. The ship's photographer had alluded to something and then clammed up.

"Let's just say I doubt he will ever go in a sauna again."

"A sauna?" Monique folded her hands together and propped her chin on them. She knew this was one of her better poses.

Luke leaned forward. "He found a body," he whispered and held his finger up to his lips.

Monique sat up straight. "A body?" she whispered back.

Luke held a finger up to his lips again. He saw two couples come in and sit down at the opposite end of the bar. "Let me take care of them, and I'll tell you the whole story." He winked at her and walked down the length of the bar. Monique brought the champagne flute to her lips, tasting the tart, bubbly cocktail. She had to figure out how to meet the couple. Being new money, they probably had not learned to be cautious about speaking to strangers. Monique could steer the conversation and pull out the information she wanted before they knew what had happened. The bar was filling up. Luke hurried over to her. "Sorry, I'm getting a rush here since dinner is over, but would you stay? I love seeing you sitting here."

"Perhaps," she gave him a dazzling smile. "What's it like to work on a cruise ship? Is it as exciting as it sounds?"

Luke grinned as he made cocktails in front of her. He was enjoying her attention. "It can be," he said. "You meet interesting people. Some of my coworkers have crazy backgrounds. That is what draws us to life on the ship. We don't fit in on land."

"What's Mila's story? The marketing lady from your corporate office mentioned she grew up in a circus. It sounds interesting" She waved her hand. "Kennedy was going to tell me earlier today, but she got busy."

Luke was surprised. Kennedy was friendly but not chatty, especially with passengers, but if she was going to tell Monique, Luke thought it would be okay to share Mila's story. He pointed at her. "Don't move. I'll be right back."

"Excuse me," an older man with black and silver hair asked. "Are you the man with the famous five martini trick?"

Luke looked up and straightened his shoulders, smiling. He knew what was coming next. "I am."

"I'm Paulie, and these are my friends Karl, Marshall, Eddie, and Larry. We hear you can make five martinis at once, and I am willing to bet fifty dollars you can't."

"Gentlemen," Luke held his hands out in front of him, "I assure you I can, but we don't need to place a bet."

Paulie cocked his head and looked at Luke. "Afraid to lose face in front of this beautiful woman?" He motioned to Monique and placed a bill on the bar. President Ulysses Grant stared up at Luke.

Luke shrugged. "Okay."

Monique laughed and clapped her hands. "I've seen the three-martini trick in New York, but never five."

Luke dried his hands on a towel. "Okay, friends, prepare to be amazed." He began to assemble what he needed. "Would you prefer olives or lemon peel?"

"Your call." Paulie laughed and looked back at the crowd, who began gathering to watch. Setting the glasses carefully in a pyramid, Luke placed an olive in the three bottom glasses and a lemon twist in the top two. He shoveled ice into the five mixing glasses and picked up two bottles. Streams of clear liquid poured out of the bottles theatrically. He looked around the bar making sure that all eyes were on him as he made a tower with the mixing glasses and placed a small silver strainer on top of the last one. He smiled and began shaking the column of glasses. As the tension mounted, Luke carefully tilted the glasses pouring the icy contents into each of the five martini glasses in front of the crowd, who cheered and clapped as they were each filled. Smiling devilishly, Luke took the top two martini glasses from the pyramid and placed them in front of Paulie.

"Paulie, *that* is my five-martini trick." He pushed the three remaining glasses in front of the stunned man. Then, he picked up the bill and handed it back to Paulie. "I'm not going to take your money."

Paulie shook his head in amazement. "No. A bet's a bet, and I lost." He looked from the martini glasses to Luke. "I still can't believe what I saw. How did you do it?"

Luke began wiping the counter with a towel. "Too much free time on my hands a long time ago." He put out his hand to shake Paulie's. "By the way, I'm Luke. Who told you about the trick?

"The chief engineer, tall guy, white hair. He said you wouldn't be able to do it."

Luke smiled. "I'll have to thank him later." The crowd began talking loudly, and suddenly the bar was a crush of people ordering drinks.

Monique slid off her barstool. "I'm going to go," she hollered over the din. "You will be too busy to spend any more time with me." She put out her hand. "Good night, Luke. It was a pleasure seeing you again."

He took her hand and kissed it. "I hope I get to see more of you."

"You will. We have a conversation to finish." She winked and left the bar.

Larry watched the exchange between Luke and Monique. "Gentlemen, I think we ruined something for our friend Luke. The responsible thing for us to do is to keep him busy and tip him well to make it up to him."

"Good evening, and welcome to the Solstice Theater!" Kennedy said into her microphone as she walked onto the stage. "On some of our cruises, we have a 1980s dance party on the stage, and it's a lot of fun. Our passengers get dressed up in neon and acid-washed jeans. Of course, there is big hair. The cast and I thought we would take things a step further. A time when you could…"

Suddenly the lights went out, the curtains opened, and a fast-paced drumbeat came out of the speakers, followed by a bass guitar. Kyle, one of the male cast members, slid across the stage on his knees and belted, "Tonight I gotta cut loose, footloose!" Several women in the audience screamed in excitement.

Kennedy watched the show's first few minutes from backstage to ensure things were going well and then left to prepare for her after-hours show in the Lunar Lounge. She was in her cabin staring at the sizable rhinestone bracelet in her hand when a knock on her door startled her. She smiled, thinking it was Omar, and her face fell when she opened the door to find Mila.

"Not who you were expecting?" Mila asked. "I wanted to check on you. I know a lot got added to your plate today. I saw your message about the back of the house tour, good idea."

Kennedy motioned for Mila to come inside. "I can manage the extra work. It's Omar. He's acting so strangely. I wanted to talk to him about the tour but couldn't find him." She threw the bracelet she was holding on the bed.

Mila sat down on the chair at the desk. "He was a million miles away at the meeting. Do you know why?"

Kennedy shook her head. She told Mila how his behavior had changed rapidly from when they had been on the pier and the phone call she had seen him on before the ship left Port Canaveral. She shrugged her shoulders and began fluffing her hair in the mirror. "Well, the show must go on. Are you coming tonight?"

"Probably not. I adore you, but I've seen it before, and I need to catch up on some paperwork."

Kennedy grinned and looked at Mila through the mirror. "You should stop by. Tonight's show has new material. Family holidays: the good, the bad, and the eye-rolling."

"Does your mother understand that the holidays are a time of good cheer?" Mila asked.

Kennedy picked up her long red gloves and her bracelet. "To Lolly, good cheer is something you fake until the guests leave."

Kennedy stood waiting for Vitor, the pianist in the Lunar Lounge, to finish his set. She saw Omar walk in with Emily Abbott and settle her at a table with Deuce Dawson. He whispered something in Emily's ear and then left the lounge. Kennedy watched him go and suddenly felt off her game. "Get it together," she whispered and took a deep breath. Vitor finished his song, and she walked over to the piano, clapping. "Isn't Vitor wonderful, ladies and gentlemen? Let's give him another big hand and pat yourselves on the back. I'm sure all that singing made you thirsty, and our servers are coming around with a glass of champagne for you. While they are passing those out, I'd like to welcome you to our little after-hours show." She walked across the stage and noticed Lola sitting with her fan club, and Tristan at a tall cocktail table, alone.

"How exciting is it that we have a cooking competition on this cruise? I envy those who can cook. To me, cookbooks are a lot like romance novels," she looked around the room and deadpanned, "unrealistic!" Kennedy paced back and forth on the stage. "My mother, Lolly, is a gifted cook. She can whip up a three-course meal out of thin air." She tilted her head to the side. "I'm lucky if I can put milk and cereal in a bowl and have it come out right." She walked over and leaned on the piano. "My mother once suggested I try cooking with wine. After the third glass, I couldn't remember why I was in the kitchen." There were a few laughs from the audience, but the joke fell flat, and Kennedy knew it.

David walked into the lounge during Kennedy's opening and winced. He saw Mila standing in the back and went to stand beside her. "She's off tonight." Mila gave him a worried look and bit her lip.

Kennedy knew she was dying onstage. So, she decided to pull a standby from an old show, as it always got a laugh. "Now that everyone has a drink, I'd like to propose a toast," she paused, "to your livers." She held her glass high.

"I've seen some of you at the pool bar already," she said sarcastically, "and your livers *are not* on vacation." The audience laughed, and both David and Mila felt relieved.

"Thank goodness," Mila whispered.

Kennedy, feeling some of her confidence come back, looked at the crowd. "So, we are entering the holiday season, or as I like to call it: the calm before the storm." The audience tittered. "Last year was the first time I was home with my family for the holidays since I began working on the ship." Kennedy began to pace again. "Let's just say the tree was not the only thing lit each night."

She took a sip of champagne. "How many of you receive a themed holiday card? The photo where everyone looks super cute." There was light applause. "Yeah, those are super awkward, especially when you are a single adult. My sister picked the theme this year, and she decided on rustic. Country chic is apparently in fashion these days." Kennedy cleared her throat and imitated her sister's haughty tone, "Kennedy, it will be fun! We'll take the photo in front of a barn and wear flannel shirts and jeans." Kennedy looked at the audience. "Ladies and gentlemen, my family doesn't do rustic. My mother believes rustic is a hotel without room service." The audience began to laugh. "I reminded my sister, also known as Willie the Perfect, that the only barn our mother had ever been to was Pottery Barn, and going there required a bottle of wine afterward. But, somehow, she talked my mother into it. I never thought I would see the day when my mother was wearing denim and flannel." She began walking back and forth again. "So, we arrive at the location, and my mother gets out of the car looking like she has smelled some horrible odor. The photographer lines us up with the decrepit barn in the background. My mother is standing in the center with my father and brother on either side of her. The dog is sitting in front of my father, not moving because every few seconds, my father would give him another treat. My sister, Willie the Perfect, and her perfect family are beside my father, and I am on the opposite side, next to my brother. Everyone is supposed to be looking adoringly at our mother." She let out a deep sigh. "And when does the photographer snap the photo? The moment I start sneezing. We took several more, but each time something happened—the dog was scratching his ear, Willie the Perfect needed to fix her false eyelashes, or a breeze blew a strand of my mother's hair out of place." Kennedy walked to the side of the small stage. "Skip, can we put the picture up?" And as she said those words, the Reeves holiday card appeared on the screen. Kennedy walked over to it and pointed at her image. "I give you the world's most awkward face." The audience began laughing hysterically. The photo showed Kennedy with a contorted look on her face, her hair flying in multiple directions, and her arms outstretched as if she were holding back a gale-force wind. She looked at the photo once more and then at the audience. "I didn't know about the photo until my mother had mailed out five hundred of them to her closest friends, and a friend of mine called laughing hysterically after seeing it at their mother's house and sent me a picture of the card." She placed the microphone back into the stand. "I, of course, marched over to my mother's house and told her it was one of the most humiliating moments of my life." Kennedy put her hand up in the air. "I swear this is true. My mother peered over her glasses and said dryly, 'Really, Kennedy? I can think of so many more.' " The audience roared with laughter and clapped. Kennedy began to feel better. "Okay, as I now have you all laughing, let's talk about the awkward holiday dinner." She sat back down on the stool.

"Whew," Mila whispered to David, "it looks like she's recovered. Are you going to stick around?"

David shook his head. "No, I'm going to hit the casino." He pointed his head at Kennedy, "I'm glad she seems to be on firmer ground. Her opening was as stiff as my Aunt Beatrice, and she's dead."

"I'll say. Are we still on for tomorrow?" Mila whispered.

"Looking forward to it, doll!"

After the show, Emily Abbott came up to tell Kennedy how much she had enjoyed the performance. "Do we do this on all the ships?"

Kennedy blushed. "No, ma'am, we had paid entertainers until a few years ago when there were budget cuts. Alfred asked me to come up with some shows. We have the comedy show, a few passenger gameshows, and an improv night using the cast. We seem to keep everyone entertained."

"Keep up the good work." Emily tried to stifle a yawn. "My apologies. It's been a full day." She nodded her head at Omar, who was standing at the entry. "My escort awaits."

Kennedy turned to look at Omar, and he quickly averted his eyes. Kennedy bade Emily good night and walked through the lounge, where she saw Tristan talking to Deuce.

"I'm heading to the casino," Tristan announced. "I feel a lucky streak coming on. I hear there are hot tables and hot women in there." He pointed his head in Lola's direction as she left with a group of older gentlemen. "Did you know some passengers are only on this cruise because Lola is on it? It doesn't seem fair to the rest of us that she has her fan club on board. If I had known we could do that, I would have had plenty of people on the ship."

Deuce crossed his arms. "Whether a passenger booked this cruise because of Ms. Cobb or any other competitor is none of my concern. Whoever wins this competition must be able to handle themselves in the kitchen," he gave Tristan a stern look, "and in the spotlight."

Kennedy picked up her radio and said, "Ten." Soon after, Rosemary, Franklin, and Mila joined her on the promenade deck. "I was worried about you for a few minutes," Mila said, bumping her friend's shoulder with her own.

"You and me both," Kennedy said. She looked around the deck. "Has anyone seen Omar?" Before anyone could answer, a beaming Chef Michèle and Ano walked up.

"I guess you had a good interview?" Kennedy asked.

Michèle puffed out his chest. "I had her eating out of my hand. My charming personality enchanted her."

"Good grief," Franklin rolled his eyes. "I didn't think it possible, but somehow his head is bigger than it was before. Do I need to take the kitchen doors off the hinges so you can walk in and out? You should be careful walking down the kitchen line in case your gigantic head hits a pot."

Kennedy cleared her throat. "There's been a change of plan for tomorrow, and I've sent everyone a message with the details. We've added a behind-the-scenes tour for Mrs. Abbott and the chefs, and we'll be filming the tour for some footage for the network. So please, everyone, be on your best behavior." She looked at Michèle and Franklin, "You two especially."

"On that note, I'm going to call it a night so I can get my beauty sleep," Franklin said, patting his hair. "Come on, Rosemary, I'll walk you to your cabin."

"We must go as well," Chef Michèle said. "Ano and I need to prep for tomorrow's competition. But first, we'll let Luke know about the tour." He grinned at Kennedy. "Tomorrow's theme will be attention-grabbing."

Kennedy raised her shoulders. "It looks hard, but I'm the girl who can barely boil water."

"Do you know what I need to pull together for your impromptu cooking demonstration? Ano saw your note."

"Honestly, I haven't asked the chefs yet, but I'll speak with them as soon as possible."

Michèle nodded, and he and Ano left quickly. They still had much to do before the morning arrived.

Kennedy and Mila decided to take another lap around the promenade deck. Mila suddenly elbowed Kennedy in the ribs. "Do you see what I see? I didn't know the chefs had loved ones on the cruise."

While Kennedy had not been shocked to see Lola with the Gents from Breezy Bayou at dinner, she was astonished to see her in a fierce lip lock with one of them in the moonlight. "I think we should make an about-face Mila," she whispered.

"Karl, I can't begin to tell you how happy I am to see you," Lola said as she snuggled into his arms. "How will we keep this quiet while we are on board? Your dad and the others don't know about us yet."

Karl grinned and looked around the deck. "We'll just have to find moments like this," he said. "But how are you? And why were you ignoring us earlier in the dining room? I thought my dad would have a heart attack trying to get your attention. The guys and I spent a lot of money to book the last few cabins to cheer you on."

Lola fluttered her eyelashes and brushed his arm playfully. "Oh, Karl, I didn't have my contacts in." She pulled away from him. "Honestly, I was so shocked and happy to see you that I was afraid I would give us away."

"Well, we're together now, and that's all that matters." He kissed her forehead and pulled her to him.

"Karl," Lola said in a muffled voice, "with the last-minute call from the network…oh, never mind," she broke off.

"What?" Karl asked, pulling back to look down at her.

"No, it's fine, don't worry," she said quietly, looking down at her hands entwined in his.

"Lola, honey, what is it? You can tell me. We don't have any secrets between us."

"Well, the thing is," she hesitated for a moment, "I'm embarrassed to ask this, but here goes. Can I borrow some money? I don't need much. I didn't get to stop by the bank on my way to the ship, and buying new outfits maxed out my credit cards. So, I'm broke until I get back to Port Canaveral."

Karl pulled out his money clip. "Of course, honey, what's mine is yours." He pulled off several bills and folded them into her hand.

Lola looked at the money and then into Karl's eyes. "I don't deserve you," she kissed his cheek and pushed him away playfully. "You should get back before the others notice you are missing."

"But I'd much rather be with you," he said, reaching to pull her back into his arms.

Lola danced away. "No can do! I need to get ready for tomorrow's competition. I can't tell you how much better

I feel having my number one fan there to cheer me on, even if it is in secret."

"Not for much longer, I hope," Karl replied.

"We'll figure it out after the competition," she said and squeezed his hand. "I promise." She blew him a kiss and left him.

Karl watched her shadowed figure depart. He hadn't thought he could fall in love again after his wife died, but there he was, like a lovestruck adolescent. Lately, his feelings had been a lot like a teenager's: happy, sad, excited, and hopeful all at the same time. He thought back to the moment he had met Lola. Paulie had raved at one of their weekly poker games about the new private chef he had found. He explained that the chef, a woman, delivered gourmet meals to his house once a week. Every dish Lola made was out of this world. He also shared that she could cater their poker nights if they were interested. Naturally, their faces perked up at the thought of a home-cooked meal instead of the soggy sandwiches someone would bring from the grocery store. The following week, when Karl had stopped by to check on his father, he found a pretty, petite brunette looking inside the refrigerator. Marshall, with a fat grin on his face, sat at the kitchen table eating a piece of cinnamon cake. "Excuse me? Who are you? Pop, what's going on?"

The young woman wiped off her hands and extended one to him. "Hi," she said with a perky voice, "I'm Lola Cobb, your dad's private chef. You must be Karl. Your sweet daddy has told me all about you!"

Karl looked from Lola to his father and then back at her. "When did this start?"

Marshall sat in his wheelchair, engrossed in the pastry in front of him. He looked up at his son, his eyes magnified by his glasses. "Son, you have to try her cinnamon cake. It is out of this world."

Karl was hesitant but took the piece of cake Lola offered him out of good manners. When he took the first bite, he was unprepared for the tastes swirling across his tongue. He thought he had eaten something like it before but couldn't remember where.

"Well?" she asked, and he was momentarily distracted by a fat, dark brown curl on her cheek.

"I believe we have a new chef for not only ourselves, Pop, but for our weekly poker matches." Karl looked at Lola. "If you are available, of course."

Lola beamed. "If the others are as charming as your dad and as handsome as you, the answer is most definitely yes."

From that moment, Karl could not get Lola out of his head. He rearranged his schedule so he could be at his father's house when she dropped off his weekly meals. Marshall complained about the constant visits. "I'm not an invalid, you know," he said once when Karl arrived moments before Lola. "I never saw you this much until Lola started cooking for me." On poker night, Karl would try to arrive early to help the pretty chef unload her boxes or help in the kitchen, but she would smile and shoo him out with a hand on her hip, explaining she had it under control. While it hurt Karl's feelings, he was intrigued by her independence. Attendance at poker night went up as word spread about the pretty young chef and her excellent meals.

# Sunny Dayz Cruise Line

## THE HELIO

### DAY TWO

### AT SEA

Kennedy stepped into the galley early the following morning. The smells and sounds of a busy kitchen greeted her. "Good morning, Kennedy," Chef Ano said brightly, looking up from the paperwork he had spread out on the stainless-steel counter. "The coffee is fresh."

Kennedy poured a cup from the large urn and raised the steaming cup to Ano in a toast. "You have saved the morning once again, my friend." Ano nodded and went back to his paperwork. She looked at her clipboard with the day's events. After the behind-the-scenes tour, the chefs would have their first competition. Monique Patrick was interviewing Tristan and Lola after today's competition, and Kennedy wanted to ask Miles and Jordan if they would put on a demonstration for the passengers. As she made her way to the pool deck, she saw the staff already preparing for a long day at sea. Rosemary's team was wiping down the tables and chairs and placing fluffy blue towels around the pool area. Kennedy spied Franklin and a few of his team by the competition area setting up the overhead camera frames he and Art had constructed. "Hi, handsome," Kennedy chirped. "Is this going to work out?"

Franklin huffed into his mustache. "It's not as good as I want it to be, but it will have to do for now. We can tweak it if we need to." He shook his head. "That little girl is something else. She knows her way around a shop and isn't afraid to speak up."

Kennedy laughed. "I'm shocked you allowed her in your lair."

Now it was Franklin's turn to laugh. "I invited her, but I didn't think she'd take it over. Before I knew she was down there, she'd started opening drawers and cabinets, pulling things out, and had a plan."

Kennedy bit her lower lip. "Have you seen Omar?"

Franklin shook his head. "Not yet, but I'm sure you'll see him at our nine o'clock."

Kennedy made a face. "Okay, I'll see you in a little bit," she said glumly.

"Come here," he said and opened his arms to hug her. "It will all be fine. He probably has something on his mind. Maybe it's the security cameras and realizing that so many were broken." Then, he turned her around and pointed her in the opposite direction. "Now, go find out what Mrs. Abbott is writing in her notebook. After our last group of corporate visitors, I'm still a little wary."

Kennedy whispered thanks and squeezed his big hand.

Emily Abbott looked up as Kennedy approached her. "Good morning, Kennedy. How goes the world this morning?"

Kennedy sat down beside her. "All is well so far. Is everything okay, Mrs. Abbott? It's rather early to be up here."

Emily waved her hand. "I thought we dispensed with that Mrs. Abbott thing."

Kennedy blushed. "Sorry, old habits die hard. But what brings you out here so early? We have a few hours before the tour and the competition."

"Quite honestly, I'm nervous," Emily answered. "I thought I would come out here to get familiar with the set and where I would sit. I enjoy the early morning hours; it allows me to collect my thoughts and plan my day. It drove Vera crazy in college. While I was up with the sun, Vera would pull a pillow over her face to block it out. I often suspected she was part vampire."

Kennedy grinned. She couldn't picture Vera Jameson as a college co-ed, but the image of Vera in a black satin cape, her arms spread out and smiling devilishly to show her pointed incisors, made her giggle. "I didn't get to ask last night. Did you enjoy the Captain's Dinner?"

Emily's eyes crinkled. "Omar is amusing. He has a dry wit and kept me in stitches all night. And the woman in the zebra print dress, the Butlers, my goodness, but they are a colorful couple." She placed her hand on top of Kennedy's.

"He shared what happened a few months ago in greater detail. I had no idea you were almost killed. And I wish I had seen the impromptu diva show you put on. The captain bragged about how you pulled it together. Of course, Vera told me about it, but I thought she was exaggerating. It sounds like you pulled a rather large rabbit out of a tiny hat."

Kennedy smiled at the memory. Putting on that show had been a tremendous coup, professionally and personally. "We have a wonderful team here on the ship, Mrs. Abbott, and we row the boat together."

Emily looked around the deck. "You can certainly tell this is a happy ship, Kennedy, the staff seems content, and yet you have all been on this ship for several months without any breaks. The maintenance team has been working on the set. People are setting up games; even the bartenders are already getting prepared. This trip is opening my eyes to how fortunate we are to have such dedicated employees. I am embarrassed to say I took it all for granted."

Kennedy noticed the time. "I wish I could stay and chat, but I have a few more things to do before our morning staff meeting. But I'll meet you here for the tour at ten." Kennedy stood up and made her way around the pool deck. She saw Lola's fan club playing cards at one of the tables. "Good morning, gentlemen. Are you ready for today's events?" she asked.

"Good morning, good-looking." Marshall looked up at her. "How about helping me decide which card to throw at these monkeys?"

"My goodness, I wish I could, Marshall, but I need to get to a meeting. I'm afraid I would not be any help at all." She fluttered her eyelashes exaggeratedly. Then, she leaned over his shoulder and pointed at one. "But if I were you, I would put that one down."

"Have you seen our friend Lola?" Eddie asked. "We wanted to wish her luck today in the competition."

"Not yet, but I'm sure she is around. There aren't too many places to hide on the ship. Enjoy your card game!" She waved at the five men and walked away.

"She's a sharp one, that girl. If I were twenty years younger, I'd carry her off this ship and marry her," Marshall said.

Eddie chuckled. "She's a sea rat, Marshall. Too much time on land would make her unhappy. Not that you could make anyone happy, old man."

"For that remark, I will take Kennedy's advice. I was going to be nice, but you are already insulting me, and it isn't even nine yet." He threw down a card, and Eddie groaned.

Kennedy took the back staircase and entered the main dining room through a hidden door. She saw Monique standing at the Butlers' table.

"Hi, I'm Monique Patrick, I saw you two last night at dinner, and I had to come over and say hello," Monique said brightly. "Your dress was one of a kind."

"Please, join us," Jones said good-naturedly and gestured to the empty chair at their table.

"Oh, I shouldn't," Monique said coyly. "I only wanted to say hello. I travel a great deal and have never seen anyone with as much style as the two of you."

"Why do you travel so much?" Jones basked in the compliment and took a drink of coffee.

"I own a concierge travel agency and do some travel writing," Monique answered.

"Oh, my goodness," Terri said breathlessly and jumped up. "You must join us. Jones and I are always trying to plan our next vacation, especially now that we have the time. We would love to get your ideas of places to go."

"Well, if you are sure I'm not interrupting anything," Monique said and sat down. "Someone on the staff told me you are regulars on the *Helio*. You must have a comfortable lifestyle to be able to do that."

Terri giggled. "Well, we aren't exactly regulars, but we've become pretty close to the staff, especially Kennedy, the cruise director."

"That must get you some great perks. As soon as Kennedy seated you at dinner last night, I noticed your server was placing your drinks on the table. I had to wait for what felt like hours to get mine."

"I guess it's one of our VIP perks. Kennedy takes care of us personally," Jones bragged. "And after our last cruise…well, they bend over backward for us." Jones chuckled. Monique looked at him as if she didn't understand. "You see, on the last cruise, I went into the sauna, and I found a—"

"Jones!" Terri interrupted. "We aren't supposed to talk about *it*, remember?"

"Oh, please don't say anything else. I don't want you to get into trouble," Monique said quietly.

"Tell us about your travel company," Terri said brightly, changing the subject. "Jones and I have talked about going on a safari with those cute tents. It looks so romantic in the movies."

Monique talked about the tours she had hosted and saw a flash of interest in both of their eyes when she shared the advantage of using her agency. "It's so much better if you have a guide like me who can get you into areas the average traveler does not know about or isn't allowed to go."

"Excuse me," Terri stood up. "I'm going to get more juice." She gave Jones a warning look and put her finger to her lips.

An uncomfortable silence descended after Terri left, and Jones and Monique concentrated on their coffee, making small talk. Monique's practice had been to ebb back and forth when interviewing someone about an uncomfortable subject. If you went in for the kill too early, people clammed up. She also knew the Butlers would talk more once she lured them into a sense of security. Terri rejoined the table.

"Mr. Butler," Monique said, "please forgive me, but haven't I seen you before? You said you were a businessman; may I ask what you do? I'm certain I have seen you somewhere, but I can't place where."

"Well, heck, Monique, I'm the Buck-A-Cluck guy," he said, breaking into a wide grin and slapping the table. "I was all over the daytime news shows and a few magazines when I sold the company earlier this year. So, I bet that is where you saw me."

"What are you doing now?" Monique asked.

"Too much! Between consulting for the company that bought me out and renovating our little place in Mississippi, I am busier than ever."

"What made you come on this cruise? Were you interested in the competition?"

Terri giggled. "We didn't know about the competition. We needed to settle a bet." Monique looked at her curiously, and Terri continued. "As Jonesy said, we're redoing our house in Mississippi, and there were a few details we couldn't remember. He thought it was one way, and I thought it was another. You see, parts of the new house will look exactly like our cabin here on the ship." Terri saw Monique's expression. "Oh, you must see our cabin," she squealed, causing Monique to wince inwardly. "It is simply amazing. It's the Owner's Suite."

"I want to hear all about it," Monique purred. She knew she had them in the palm of her hand. Terri and Jones took turns describing their cabin, getting more animated and relaxed as they spoke with Monique. "Terri, Jones, I must see your stateroom. It sounds like the Taj Mahal compared to my little cabin," she said and switched gears. "Have you been to the spa yet? I hear they recently renovated it, and it's supposed to be very luxurious.

Jones nodded his head. "And where I found a body," he said. "Right there in the sauna."

"Jones!" Terri whispered harshly.

"You found a *body* in the sauna?" Monique exclaimed. "Was it an elderly person?"

"Nope, he was a young guy. You see, we had been riding horses, and I told Terri I felt like I smelled like a stable and wanted to sweat it out." Jones made a gesture like he was opening a door. "I opened the door, and there he was. Just thinking about it still gives me the creeps." He gave a slight shudder.

"Jones, we aren't supposed to talk about *it*," Terri said through clenched teeth. She moved her eyes at Monique. "She's a R-E-P-O-R-T-E-R."

"Oh, don't worry," Monique said soothingly, looking at Terri's anxious face. "I'm not a reporter. I'm a travel writer. When I interviewed one of the senior staff members, they told me about what happened."

"See, it's fine, Sweetsie," Jones said. "Nothing to worry about." He squeezed Terri's hand and turned back to Monique. "Anyway, after I found the dead guy, they fell all over themselves, giving us free cruises and spa treatments if we kept it all under wraps." He gestured to Terri. "Tell her about the show they put on that night to keep everyone distracted." He slapped the table. "It was a hoot, all of those men dressed up like famous female rock stars."

"You mean they had drag performers?" Monique asked, and the more they talked, the more excited she became. This interview was like taking candy from a baby.

Terri's head bounced up and down. "You were sitting with one of them last night, David. He came out in this darling little costume: a spiky white wig, black leather ball cap, and these amazing black sequined jogging pants. I had to get some as soon as I got home. Let me tell you, he was amazing. They all were."

Monique was spellbound. First, she had confirmed the information about the dead body found on the ship, and now she had been given an unexpected gift. David Stearns was a drag performer. "Why did they do the show? Were they scheduled to perform? I don't understand."

"Well," Terri's eyes were glowing. "They are friends of Kennedy's and are always on her cruises. After Jonesy found the," she looked around and whispered, "B-O-D-Y, they closed the spa. And when that happened, people started to talk." She looked solemnly at Monique. "The dead guy was some bigwig from the company. They needed to distract the passengers, and what better way than to throw a big old drag queen show."

Monique was fascinated but decided to change gears; she didn't want to press her luck. She remembered the cryptic comment Chef Michèle had made during his interview and felt it was connected to the story the Butlers were telling her. "Tell me about the excursions you are taking. As a travel writer, I'm always interested to see what people like to do when the ship docks."

Kennedy entered the conference room and found Omar sitting alone. He looked up from the pad of paper in front of him, but the slow smile she usually received was not there. He gave her a curt nod and turned his attention back to the notepad. "Good morning," she said quietly. "I haven't seen much of you lately. How was dinner with Mrs. Abbott last night?"

"Quite enjoyable," he said in his accented English. "Another remarkable woman, and she is quite the history buff. Although I have traveled extensively, I never took an interest in the history of the places I visited. However, upon hearing her descriptions, I want to revisit them."

Kennedy was about to say more, but the door burst open. Mila, Franklin, Rosemary, Michèle, Ano, and Luke walked in and took their seats noisily. Kennedy stood up and handed Rosemary a stack of papers. "Take one and pass it around. Today will be busy. The sheet of paper coming around is the schedule for the tour. Are we all set?"

Omar, Michèle, and Ano all nodded. "Michèle and Ano will meet you on the competition set and help you get everyone down the service elevators to the lower levels. I'll meet you down there. We'll show off the storage areas and then go to housekeeping," Omar answered.

"I'll take them to the shop," Franklin said, "and hand them off to Ano in the prep kitchens."

"And after they see the magic of the kitchens, we'll send them to the bridge," Michèle said. "Make sure it's a beehive of activity in there," he whispered to Ano.

"We need to keep the tour to a maximum of ninety minutes," Kennedy said. "And don't forget Art will be taping, so please make sure to walk your areas before we start. Remind staff to tuck in their shirts, pick up stray pieces of—"

"We've got it," Omar snapped.

The room went dead silent, and eyes darted in all directions as uneasy glances were exchanged. Franklin decided to try to break the heavy tension that had filled the room. "Any opinions on the chefs yet?" he asked.

Ano spoke up, "Chef Jordan is quiet and shy. She came into the galley yesterday. She didn't say much, but you could tell that being in the kitchen made her happy. Yet, there is a heavy aura of sadness that surrounds her." Michèle looked at him strangely.

"An aura?" Michèle scoffed. "You need to go do some food prep if you are going to talk like that."

"Have you met the younger guy?" Luke asked. "I think his name is Tristan. Quite the ladies' man. He came into the bar and chatted with every woman, showing them his tattoos. He told anyone in earshot he would be the network's new host chef. He even borrowed a pen from me to sign a cocktail napkin and told a woman his autograph would be worth something soon."

"Ugh," Mila groaned, "people like that annoy me."

Tony stood up and stretched his back, twisting his torso back and forth. "My money is on Lola. She's the fiery one and knows how to work a room. Have you seen how those old guys follow her around like a pack of puppies? And she's got that long brown hair and those high heels," he trailed off.

Franklin spoke up, "Omar, what did you think of her?"

"Lola is an attractive woman," he answered slowly. "I can see—" but before he could finish his sentence, Kennedy noisily pushed away from the table, stood up, and grabbed her clipboard, trying to get out of the conference room.

"I believe we have more to do than to sit around and discuss the attributes of the chefs," she said stiffly. "I know I do." She glared at Omar and yanked the door open.

"Wow…" Luke said, still looking at the door Kennedy had just exited. "What's wrong with her?"

"Nothing a little communication wouldn't fix." Mila looked pointedly at Omar.

"What?" He raised his eyebrows and his hands. "What are you talking about?"

Franklin shook his head. "Buddy, for a former detective, you are lousy with clues. Especially when they are sitting in front of you." He stood up. "If you will excuse me, I need to make sure the shop and my guys look presentable for the tour." Franklin pulled Rosemary's chair out from behind the table. "I'm just glad it isn't me this time," he whispered loudly to her.

Kennedy made a beeline for the dining room, searching for the Butlers. She hoped she could get to them before they shared too much with Monique. "Kennedy!" Jones hollered across the dining room. He motioned for her, and Kennedy was thankful to see they were alone.

"And how are the two of you this morning? You look rested," she said, sitting down.

"Sleeping in that bed is like rocking in a cradle," Jones grinned. "Sweetsie and I feel at home when we are here."

"Well, I'm glad to hear that. I saw one of the other passengers chatting with you. I'm so happy you are making friends on this trip."

"Passenger?" Terri trilled. "Oh, you mean Monique? She is so easy to talk to and nice. Did you know she's a travel writer and has a travel agency? She's going to help us with a safari."

Kennedy looked surprised. "A safari? That's great news." She felt relieved that the conversation had been about the Butlers' future travel plans and nothing else.

"Monique said she was writing about the ship and asked us a few questions since we have taken two cruises back-to-back," Jones drawled. "She said one of you told her to talk to us about our experiences on the ship. That was okay, wasn't it?"

"Of course," Kennedy answered, praying they hadn't said too much.

"She was so friendly, too. She said she had seen us at dinner last night and loved Terri's dress."

Terri nodded her head vigorously. "She asked us what excursions we were taking, too. She wants to get our impressions and add them to her article. It's so exciting," Terri squeezed her shoulders inward.

"I'm sure you told her about your cabin. It is one of a kind," Kennedy said.

Terri giggled. "Oh, yes! We've invited her to stop by and see it." Terri took a sip of her juice. "Oh, and we told her about David and the diva show." Kennedy closed her eyes.

"Kennedy, I did mention to her that they did the show because of the…you know," Jones said.

Kennedy groaned inwardly. "Jones, did you go into detail?"

He shook his head. "Not exactly. I told her I found a body in the sauna, and it was some corporate bigwig. I didn't say a name or anything. Monique said a senior member of the staff had already told her about it and suggested she talk with us to get the real story."

Kennedy smiled tightly. "If she has any other questions, let's ask her to come to me, okay?" She looked down at her watch. "Now, before I go, have you two made plans for today? Will you be at the cooking competition?"

"We wouldn't miss it!" Jones said excitedly. "We love those shows! We even bet on who we think will win and what the drama will be."

A thought occurred to her, and she cocked her head. "Would the two of you like to come on a private behind-the-scenes tour of the ship?"

Jones's eyes lit up like a Christmas tree. "Would we ever! Since our last trip, Sweetsie and I have had a hundred questions."

Kennedy smiled to herself. She had inadvertently found a way to keep the Butlers busy and away from Monique. "Meet me by the chef's competition set in thirty minutes," she said.

Terri yelped. "Yikes! I've got to find something to wear! Jonesy, let's go," she said, standing quickly and pulling Jones's hand.

Jones gave Kennedy a helpless look as Terri pulled him through the dining room. "My wife, the fashionista," he sighed.

There was a knock at Miles's cabin door, and he opened it to find Dr. Craig. "I wanted to give you your medication. I wasn't sure what time you took it." He handed Miles a brown bottle and syringe. "There isn't much in there, only the dose for today. I have the other bottle locked up. I did a little reading on your condition. The fresh air and the gym should help to keep you on track."

"Thanks, Doc," Miles said, taking the bottle. "I usually take this later in the day, but it will be safe in my room."

Dr. Craig hesitated. "I can lock it up in the office. I'd hate for it to get into the wrong hands. It *is* a controlled substance."

Miles shook his head. "I don't think that's necessary. No one knows about my condition or the medication, and I have asked housekeeping not to come into my room. Why don't I come by the infirmary every day to pick up my dosage?"

"That will work," Dr. Craig said. "And Miles, if you need anything, just ring the operator and ask for me."

Miles was stepping into the shower when he heard another knock at the door. "Doc," he shouted, pulling a towel around himself, "I'm—" He opened the bathroom door and saw Tristan saunter in.

"Do you greet everyone as Doc? Is it a throwback to your generation?" Miles stood there dumbfounded as he watched Tristan looking around the cabin.

"How did you get into my room?"

Tristan shrugged. "I knocked, the door opened, and I came in. I thought we could walk down together for the tour. Kind of a waste of time if you ask me, but whatever. I figure they need video footage."

"Look, Tristan, I was getting into the shower. Why don't I meet you there?"

Tristan plopped onto the chair at the desk. "I'll wait here for you," he shrugged. "The way they have things scheduled, there is nothing else to do."

Miles felt uncomfortable having Tristan in his cabin, but the manners instilled by his mother required Miles to treat Tristan as a guest. "Make yourself at home, I guess. I'll be right out." He walked into the bathroom and shut the door.

When Tristan heard the water turn on, he stood up and looked around the room. It was a perfect opportunity to snoop and get some intel on his competition. He opened the closet doors. A row of starched, white chef's jackets hung on a rod beside his other clothes. The nightstand yielded only gym shorts, T-shirts, and a hooded sweatshirt. He heard the water turn off and quickly sat at the desk chair. His eyes played across the surface, noticing a small brown bottle and syringe. He picked up the bottle and read the words beside the skull and crossbones. *Where have I heard the name sodium oxybate?*

Miles came out of the bathroom, and Tristan flinched. "Jumpy?" Miles asked, scanning the room. Nothing appeared to be out of place.

"Nah, just ready to kick some culinary butt," Tristan said enthusiastically. He jumped up from the chair and began to punch the air like a boxer.

Kennedy looked around at the group assembled in front of the competition set. "Good morning, everyone. I hope you are all rested after our first night on board." There was a collective nod of heads. "We are delighted to be hosting the competition and look forward to seeing which of you will be the winner and host chef of the network's new show." Kennedy watched the body language of the four chefs. Tristan puffed out his chest and lifted his chin. In her high heels and ankle socks, Lola placed a hand on her cocked hip, and Miles straightened his shoulders, making him seem even taller. Jordan stood quietly, listening to Kennedy, but her eyes scanned the competition space. "On behalf of the staff and crew of the *Helio*, good luck." There was quiet clapping, and Deuce took Kennedy's place in front of the group. Kennedy walked to the rear so she could lead the tour when they turned around.

Deuce cleared his throat. "Good morning. As you are all aware, I am Deuce Dawson, the food producer for the network and one of the judges for the competition. First, I want to introduce you to our other judges. Mrs. Emily Abbott, who represents the Sunny Dayz Cruise Line." Emily stepped forward and shook each of the chef's hands. "Our other judge is Michèle Josef, the executive chef for the *Helio*." Michèle stepped forward and gave each chef a quick nod. Kennedy saw that Michèle had chosen a stern scowl to accompany his starched chef's coat. Ano leaned over to her. "The serious face, he's trying to scare them," he whispered, making Kennedy giggle.

"Chef Ano Keoki, the ship's sous chef, is in the back and will be on the sidelines during the competition." The group turned around and saw a hand waving in the air. Deuce spoke again and pointed at the competition set. "As you can see, the competition will take place in front of an audience. We will do live feeds with the network on the days we are in port. On the days we are at sea, we will tape the competition and send it back to the network. The camera will catch everything you say and do, so please watch your language, especially when we are filming live." He stared at the four chefs and then stepped back. "I invite you to choose your station and get acquainted with the layout. The setup will be the same when we move the show inside for the last two competitions." The four chefs moved quickly.

"Your job is to impress me," Deuce continued as the chefs poked around their stations, "not only with your ability to prepare exemplary dishes but to handle yourselves on camera in a professional and friendly manner. I believe Kennedy has spoken with you about the additional cooking demonstrations for the passengers. Your audience presence and how you act with a rival chef as a team will factor into your scores." As Kennedy, Deuce, and Michèle had predicted, Tristan and Lola took the center stations. Each station was U-shaped, with a six-foot section facing the audience. Behind each station was a small convection oven and cooktop. Between the stations stood racks with cutting boards, measuring cups and spoons, blenders, ice cream makers, and other kitchen utensils.

"Excuse me, is it possible to raise the camera above my station?" Miles asked, coming out from behind his cooking station. "I keep bumping it with my head. I'm not sure if you noticed, but I'm slightly taller than Lola."

"Of course," Art spoke up. "I'm Art. I'll be directing the show. Bert, the ship's photographer, will take still shots during the competition." Bert, red-faced, reluctantly raised his hand. "A few words of advice, act as naturally as you can. I know it's hard having cameras capture your every move, but if you can concentrate on your cooking, you won't see them." She pointed at the cameras stationed around the set. "Don't be nervous if you see me walking around with my handheld camera. It will allow me to give the viewers different angles."

"Just make sure you get my good side," Tristan laughed. "Although I guess all of my sides are good."

"Tristan, you should throw away that bewitched mirror you have hanging at home. It's telling you lies," Lola said, smiling into her camera. She took a snapshot of herself at her station.

Deuce cleared his throat again. "You are being judged for your culinary skills and behavior," he looked meaningfully at Lola, "on and off camera." Lola got the hint and slipped her camera into her pocket.

"I have a question," Miles said. "When the judges taste our dishes, will the cameras be on them or us?"

Art nodded. "Great question. Both. Facial expressions are key. It's a real moment to capture their expression as they taste what you have made and how you hope they feel about the dish."

Deuce began to pace in front of the stations. "Speaking of the judges. You will receive points for presentation, taste, creativity, and cleanliness. Some of you may be entertaining ideas of how to sabotage your fellow competitors. While those antics get ratings and fans for some shows," he stopped in front of Tristan and narrowed his eyes,

"I will not tolerate the behavior. I will deduct points from the total score of anyone caught doing so." Deuce motioned for Emily to step forward. "The first competition is based on menus from the Sunny Dayz Cruise Line in the early 1900s. Mrs. Abbott, will you please explain?"

Emily stepped forward. "As you may or may not know, eating at the turn of the century was quite different than it is now. Dinner was an event that could take several hours. There could even be dancing between courses. Our cruise line has bound books holding every menu for each ship in our line since we began sailing. My great-grandfather enjoyed food, and you could tell by his waistline." She handed each chef a piece of paper. Kennedy and the others watched as the chefs read the menu they held in their hands. Lola rocked back and forth from one foot to another, Jordan mouthed words silently, Miles pulled out a pair of reading glasses from his pocket, and Tristan looked at the paper and then tossed it on the countertop. "We thought it was appropriate for the first competition to pay respect to the first chefs on the cruise line."

Deuce began speaking, "You will prepare three items from this menu, and you may put your spin on the dishes that you concoct."

*THE ROJA*

**DINNER SELECTIONS**

**OCTOBER 3, 1908**

**SOUPS**

Consommé, Shrimp Bisque, Puree of Tomato

**HOR D'OEUVRES**

Olives, Tomato Mayonnaise, Angels on Horseback

**ENTREES**

Filet of Beef à la Bordelaise, Striped Bass à la Cardinal, Ham with Champagne Sauce
Short Ribs of Beef, Broiled Quail à la Americane, Red Snapper à la Creole
Roast Chicken with Bread Sauce, Lamb with Mint Sauce

**VEGETABLES**

Haricots Verts, Chef's Choice Tomatoes, Broiled Asparagus, Collards with Bacon
Duchesse Potatoes, Pommes Souffle

**SALADS**

Lobster Salad, Waldorf Salad, Ambrosia, Salad Panache, Perfection Salad

**DESSERT**

St. Honoré Cake, Turkish Sherbet Sorbet, Chocolate Surprise, Charlotte Russe
Lemon Ice Cream, Chef's Choice Sorbet, Pineapple Water Ice

Miles spoke up in awe. "Mrs. Abbott, this is rather extensive. Your great-grandfather's chefs would prepare from this menu each night?"

Emily nodded. "The menu may have changed a little each day, but this was the basic framework. Remember, sea voyages took longer, and diners would try different combinations."

"It's not *that* bad," Tristan scoffed. "My menu is twice that large."

Jordan raised her hand, and Deuce pointed a finger at her. "How will we know what to make if we don't know what is in the pantry and coolers?"

"We gave Chef Ano a grocery list, and I am satisfied you will have plenty to work with." Deuce looked at each chef and saw apprehension on their faces.

Lola had been searching her station for something while Deuce spoke and had grown frustrated. "Where are the knives? I see cutting boards but no knives."

The other three chefs looked at her strangely. "You didn't bring your knives?" Miles asked. "I don't go home without mine, and it's my restaurant."

Tristan snickered. "Well, well, well, isn't this interesting? Little Miss Private Chef doesn't have her knives. Are you so fancy that you have a set everywhere you go?"

Lola, embarrassed, scrambled for a response. She drew herself up. "I assumed we would have the same knives to keep the playing field level." She glared at Tristan. "And to answer your question, yes, my clients have a set of my preferred knives in their kitchens."

Michèle snapped his fingers to get Ano's attention. "Pull a set of knives together for Ms. Cobb. There are several in the supply cabinet." Ano nodded once and took off.

Michèle wondered what kind of chef would leave their knives at home.

Deuce looked down at his watch. "Are there any other questions?" He looked around and saw the four chefs still looking at the paper in their hands. "No? Kennedy, I believe we can start the tour now."

"We thought it would be fun for the show's viewers and you to get a first-hand look at some areas passengers don't normally see." She looked around and saw Terri and Jones Butler walking up. "I've invited two of our regular passengers, Mr. and Mrs. Butler, to join us." Kennedy took half of the group, including Art, on the first freight elevator. The other group would follow with Chef Michèle and Bert. "Art, you will want to turn your camera on and be at the front as the doors open." She could sense a few of the people in her elevator were getting nervous as they descended. "It's perfectly normal to feel a little claustrophobic as we go down, but I promise what you are about to see will leave you speechless." Finally, the elevator doors opened, and they stepped out. "Welcome to the heart of the ship," Kennedy said proudly. They stood there in wonder. The area was a beehive of activity. A few moments later, the second elevator arrived, and an olive-skinned man with a dark receding hairline walked up. "May I please introduce the maestro of the provisions deck, Mr. Ali Asad?"

"Good morning, everyone," Ali said nervously, running his hand through his wiry black and gray hair. "Welcome. As you can see," he pointed around the warehouse-like area, "the provisions deck has cold storage, freezers, rooms for dry goods, and storage lockers." He clasped his hands behind his back and began to walk. Suddenly, he stopped and pointed at the floor. "Please stay on this side of the corridor as we move forward. We have lanes of traffic and must follow them to prevent any accidents. Sometimes a person cannot see over a tall cart, and we don't want anyone to get hurt." Ali walked the group through freezers of meat, poultry, and seafood and then through the cold storage areas that held the ship's dairy products and other foods that needed to be kept cold or thawing out. Next, they walked through the storage rooms containing produce and dry goods.

"I had no idea this was how it worked," Kennedy overheard Emily say to Deuce in astonishment, her eyes wide with wonder.

"This is some great footage," Art whispered to Bert. "Who knew that people could still be surprised?"

"Now, *this* is the room I'm talking about!" Tristan exclaimed as they passed a wire cage filled from floor to ceiling with liquor. Noticing the padlock was not locked, Tristan pulled the plywood door open and walked in. "Just put me in here, and I'll play pirate for the day." He took a bottle of rum from the cardboard box beside him and lifted his foot onto one of the boxes.

Ali cleared his throat and stepped inside. "If you don't mind, I ask that no one touch anything. Every item is logged in and out for inventory purposes." He gave an uncomfortable grin. "When you run out, there is no grocery store around the corner."

"And security is always watching," Omar said with a voice of authority, coming up from behind. He nodded at the group and walked quickly into the liquor room. "Good day, everyone, I am Omar Meier, and I," he took the bottle of rum from Tristan's hand, "oversee the security of the ship." He held his arm out so Ali and Tristan could rejoin the group in the corridor. "Our beverage manager was getting a hand truck which is why the door was not secure," he told Ali, who let out a nervous sigh of relief. He had been worried when he saw the door open. Omar continued, "Now if you will follow me, I will show you the other areas we have down here."

He showed them the vast storage lockers with paper goods, cleaning supplies, and linen. And when he came to a section of lockers Kennedy used, he grinned and waved his hand at them. "These lockers are used for our cruise director's shoe collection." He winked at her.

"That's not true, Omar!" Kennedy blushed. "It's where I keep the props for the shows, party favors, decorations, and games," she explained.

"If you weren't aware, Kennedy is our ambassador of fun." Omar winked again at a bewildered Kennedy.

Jones Butler piped up, "Are there more ways to get up and down to this space than just the service elevators? I'd hate to think you might need to look for something in a storage locker only to get stuck waiting on the elevators while they make deliveries. It wouldn't be a constructive use of an employee's time."

Kennedy laughed and pointed to a door at the end of the hallway. "We have plenty of staircases throughout the deck, Mr. Butler, and I use them precisely for that reason."

Kennedy motioned to a set of larger lockers. "Mr. Asad was kind enough to loan me a few other lockers for something special."

"More shoes, Kennedy?" Jones quipped.

She pulled the handle on the door of the largest of the two lockers open, and they looked inside the storage unit. "No, holiday decorations. We will turn the ship into a winter wonderland during this cruise."

"It's packed!" Jones looked inside the locker and whistled. "There must be over a hundred boxes in there."

Kennedy gave him a weak smile. She and the team had a herculean task in front of them.

"Is this area always under surveillance?" Miles asked, looking around. "I don't see any security guards."

"Yeah, anyone could waltz down here and take what they wanted," Tristan added.

Ali bristled at the remarks. "We've never had a problem with anyone down here who wasn't authorized."

"Omar," Kennedy interrupted, "would you like to show them where we take people if they don't follow the rules?" She tipped her head toward Tristan.

He gave the group a solemn look. "Ladies and gentlemen, if you will follow me, please." He led them further down the corridor and stopped. On one side of the aisle was a glass cubicle, and on the other were two jail cells. "These are our holding cells. We have only had to use them once, and I hope it stays that way." The group was quiet, stunned into silence by the harsh reality that a crime could occur on the ship. He turned around. "Now, let us go and see the ship's housekeeping and laundry areas," he said brightly.

"Are you getting all of this?" Deuce whispered to Art, who nodded and put her camera back on her shoulder as Omar walked down the hallway.

The somber mood quickly lifted once they left the holding cells. The group watched as pallets of beer and wine passed carts of dirty tablecloths and napkins on their way to the laundry. Groups of women and men laughed and called out to one another. Emily was thoughtful as she walked along. She was stunned at what she had seen and the number of people working. She attended the board meetings and read the bottom lines on the financials, but she had never thought about the person who washed the sheets, put the towels by the pool, or deveined the shrimp.

They went from the housekeeping department to the food prep area. Michèle beamed when he saw Deuce smiling at the efficiency in the prep kitchen. Next, Kennedy led the group to Franklin, who was waiting for them at the entrance of the maintenance shop. When they entered, Emily's nose picked up the familiar scent of machine oil. The smell carried her back to her childhood when she would tag along with her grandfather to the shipyard. She remembered standing beside one of the anchors sitting on the pier. Looking up at it, she felt like a tiny ant beside a giant.

Kennedy was thankful Franklin had put up yellow caution tape to keep everyone close to the center of the space. She had worried someone might bump into something in the shop and get dirty or hurt.

Emily motioned to Franklin, and he walked over to her. "Is this your office?" she asked, looking through the window. The room was littered with papers, binders, rolled-up plans, and tools.

Franklin blushed. "Yes, ma'am, I'm afraid I am not much of an office person."

"I'm told my great-grandfather wasn't either. I think he would have liked you, Franklin. I know I do."

"Thank you, ma'am." He turned to the others. "Now, we will go up to the bridge."

Kennedy could tell the group's initial excitement was beginning to wane. After the captain pointed out various instruments and allowed everyone to walk around, Kennedy clapped her hands together. "Okay, everyone, I believe we have bothered the captain long enough, and he does need to make sure we stay on course." They left the bridge and gathered again on the deck.

Deuce looked at his watch. "We will reconvene in two hours on the competition set. Good luck."

"Chef Jordan and Chef Miles, if you would stay behind for a moment, I need to get a list of what you will need for the cooking demonstration," Kennedy said and then reminded Lola and Tristan about their interviews. "Chef Tristan, Monique Patrick will meet you at the judges' table after today's match. Chef Lola, you are an hour later. Monique suggested the promenade deck for your interview."

"Thank goodness I'll have time to change and freshen up." She looked at Tristan and fluffed her hair. "I guess this is one time it is age before beauty."

Tristan laughed. "Just remember, doll, Beauty was a horse who ended up in the glue factory."

Two hours later, Kennedy was standing on the former putting green in front of the four cooking stations. She was thrilled to see that every seat in the viewing area was filled, and people were standing in the back and above on the promenade deck looking down at the set. She turned on her microphone to welcome the audience. "Good afternoon, and welcome to the first of four competitions to find the host chef for the Classic Style Network's new television show, *Classic Flavors*. Our chefs are vying not only for the chance to become the host chef for *Classic Flavors* but will also receive a cash prize and the opportunity to coauthor the network's first cookbook. Let's meet our competitors." The four chefs were waiting off to the side.

"Ladies and gentlemen, allow me to introduce Chef Miles White from Gainesville, Florida." There was polite clapping, and Miles nodded to the crowd and walked briskly to his station. Dressed in a traditional white chef's jacket and checkered pants, Miles had a black skull cap over his bald head. When he stood in front of his station and crossed his arms, holding a knife in each hand, he looked both comical and fierce. "Miles owns and operates Vivian's, a landmark restaurant in the city. Vivian's is known for their steaks and freshly made pasta."

She walked over to the next station. "Next, please give a warm *Helio* welcome to Chef Tristan Colon from Jacksonville, Florida." Tristan strutted across the stage and stopped in the center. He tipped the black derby hat he wore down his arm, and the crowd cheered wildly. He then went into his signature pose, crossing the arm that held the hat across his waist and cupping his chin, giving the audience a sexy smile. As Kennedy explained to the audience that Tristan was the sous chef of Jacksonville's sexiest restaurant, Swank, he rolled the sleeves of his black denim chef's jacket up.

Lola had been checking her lipstick in a small mirror and snapped it shut when she heard Kennedy call her name. "Let's welcome Chef Lola Cobb from Orlando." Kennedy sucked in her breath when she saw Lola walk across the stage wearing a noticeably short white kimono-style chef's jacket, a floppy chef's hat, and high heels. The jacket came to mid-thigh, and she struck her signature pin-up girl pose when she reached her station. She blew kisses to the crowd and the cameras. The audience was rowdy thanks to her fan club and her short jacket, and Lola played to them. Kennedy continued her introduction, "Lola is a private chef who loves to find new ways to wow her clients."

"Way to go, Lola, you've got these guys beat!" Marshall yelled out in a thin, reedy voice.

"Show them who's the queen of the kitchen, honey," Paulie hollered and then gave a wolf whistle.

Kennedy had to wait for Lola to throw one final kiss to the crowd before she could announce Jordan. "And last, but certainly not least, please welcome Chef Jordan Nima from the beautiful city of St. Augustine." Jordan had pulled her hair back into a tight bun and wore a light gray chef's jacket with buttons on the side. She walked quickly to her station, and her wave to the audience went unseen as many passengers still had their eyes on Lola. "Chef Nima is the sous chef for one of St. Augustine's most charming and romantic restaurants in the city center. Her specialty is Middle Eastern cuisine."

Kennedy turned to where the judges were sitting. "Now, it is my pleasure to introduce the Classic Style Network's culinary producer and executive producer of *Classic Flavors*, Mr. Deuce Dawson." The audience applauded politely, and the four chefs went to stand inside their kitchens as Deuce walked to the center of the stage. Kennedy handed him the microphone.

"Today's competition is exciting as it directly ties to the Sunny Dayz Cruise Line." Deuce held up a piece of paper in his hand. "When you took your seat, you found a copy of the original dinner menu from the *Roja* on October 3, 1908. The *Roja* was one of the first cruise ships in the Sunny Dayz fleet." An image of the menu flashed on the large screens. "You'll see several things you may recognize, some you won't, and others which have changed over the years. Our chefs have one hour to prepare three items from this menu and will receive points based on taste, creativity, and presentation." Deuce looked at the four competitors. "Chefs, are you prepared to start?" They nodded. "Please start the clock." A large clock flashed on one of the monitors. "Begin!" he shouted.

Lola, Tristan, and Miles sprinted to the four refrigerators while Jordan turned on the small convection oven behind her station. She quickly gathered a few tools from the racks and took them to her kitchen.

"That was smart," Larry whispered behind his hand to Paulie. He pointed at Jordan. "She knew the others would be fighting over food. So instead of wasting her time, she set up her station and preheated her oven. She must have a fairly good idea of what will be in the coolers after the others have taken their items."

"What do you think Lola will make?" Paulie whispered and pointed at the menu in his hand. None of this looks like anything she would cook for us." Larry shrugged slowly.

"You go, Lola, you can do it!" Eddie hollered. "Elbow those guys out of the way if you need to."

Lola frantically opened the first cooler door, which contained the meat and fish. She grabbed a large piece of snapper and then went over to where the fresh vegetables were kept and took two tomatoes and a green pepper, clutching them against her chest. When she arrived at her station, she dumped them on the counter and ran back to get chocolate bars, cocoa powder, and powdered sugar. She put the chocolate bars in the small refrigerator at her station and looked around at what she had taken. She suddenly realized she had forgotten something and ran back to the coolers. She opened the first door and, not finding what she wanted, quickly went to the next one and, not finding what she wanted there, jerked the door of the third cooler open. Lola jogged over to Ano. "Where is the Caesar salad dressing?" she whispered.

Ano shook his head. "That would be something prepared from scratch."

"Crap, okay, never mind," she whispered quickly and walked back to her station. Art kept the camera trained on her. Lola put her hand on her hip, thinking. Suddenly her eyes lit up, and she quickly took off her high heels and chef's hat. "I'll be right back, y'all," she said to the crowd. Deuce was perplexed and motioned for Art to follow her. Lola ran to the pool bar. Luke was pouring a bottle of rum into a large container. Lola banged on the counter. "I need some margarita mix, pronto," she said, out of breath.

"What?" Luke asked.

Lola used her arms to boost herself up and snatched a bottle of margarita mix. As she ran out of the bar, she hollered, "Thank you!" Art had not expected one of the chefs to go rogue in the first round of the competition. She hoped other stations would air the mad dash after Classic Style showed it on their morning show.

Lola came flying back to her station and stopped to put on her high heels and hat and wash her hands. "I'm back! Did you miss me?" She banged down the bottle of margarita mix, and the crowd cheered.

"You've got this, hot stuff!" she heard Marshall call out, his voice getting hoarse.

When Miles had seen the menu, he had been apprehensive until he saw the striped bass dish. He sent up a quick prayer of thanks to his mother. Vivian believed there was no one better in the kitchen than the great Julia Child. Believing French cooking methods were superior to others, she had insisted Miles train under a French chef. He quickly grabbed a piece of fish, some shrimp, and a lobster tail from the cooler, confident he could replicate the classic sauce. He put a pot of water on to boil. He had seen Lola leave and return with the margarita mix and couldn't figure out how she planned to use it. As soon as the water reached a rolling boil, he quickly popped two large tomatoes into the water. Deuce and Michèle had been watching Miles intently and looked at one another. Michèle wrote on his notepad, *"Should we ask if anyone else knows what concasse is? Extra points?"* Deuce nodded.

Jordan had decided to lean on her heritage for the first competition. She knew it would not earn her any points for creativity, but she felt, for the first round, she should concentrate on taste, presentation, and completing the dishes in the allotted time. Jordan walked quickly over to Ano. "Are there any roses on the ship?" she asked.

Ano walked over to Deuce. "She is asking for a rose. May I get one from the dining room?" Deuce nodded reluctantly. He had not disqualified Lola for running to the bar, so he could not prohibit another chef from requesting something not found in the pantry or coolers. He only hoped she was not using it for presentation. As Ano jogged away, the passengers craned their necks to see where he was going. Jordan returned to her station, turned her oven temperature down, and put a small saucepan of water on to boil. She decided to make the mint sauce for the lamb while she waited for Ano to return.

"Chefs, you are at the forty-minute mark," Deuce said.

Lola was making whipped cream at her station. "Isn't this beautiful?" she said to the audience, lifting a large dollop out of the bowl for them to see. She popped the bowl into the under-counter refrigerator and pulled out the chocolate bars. She broke one in half, smeared frosting over it, and placed the next piece of chocolate perpendicular to the first piece, beginning to form a box. She took the whipped cream out of the refrigerator and scooped it into the chocolate box.

"Did you see her put the powdered sugar in the whipped cream?" Larry asked Paulie.

Paulie shook his head. "I didn't see her make the whipped cream. I was too busy watching the two guys."

Tristan was frying bacon at his station. "Hey, Miles," he hollered, "did you see a bacon stretcher?"

Miles paused and chuckled. "No, I didn't, but Chef Michèle may have one, especially for the number of people he has to feed."

Tristan snickered and turned to Lola. "Lola, do you have bacon stretchers in your important client's fancy kitchens?"

Lola put her knife down and stared at Tristan. Then, she placed her hands on her hips. "Well, of course, I do. Every kitchen I cook in has one," she said smugly.

Miles and Tristan began to snicker.

"What was that about?" Eddie asked Larry, who was pinching the bridge of his nose.

Larry whispered behind his hand. "There is no such thing as a bacon stretcher. Lola's comment tells Miles and Tristan she isn't as skilled as they are. Chefs will try to find any weakness, and if they catch someone in a lie, they will tease them mercilessly."

"Well, that's a bunch of bull," Paulie said indignantly. "Perhaps after the competition, we should chat with them and explain things."

Larry remained quiet. He thought Lola was in over her head. Sometimes things she said didn't always add up. While she could take care of the poker parties and the simple meals she brought them, he had long felt things were not as they appeared.

Ano returned and handed a rose to Jordan, causing several audience members to make catcalls. "Thank you,

Chef," Jordan whispered, blushing, and placed the rose beside a mortar and pestle.

Tristan took the bacon pieces out of the frying pan, patted them dry, and turned the burner off under the frying pan. He would use the same pan to sear the steak. Walking over to the produce bin, he selected a pineapple, took it back to his station, and cut it into large chunks sliding the pieces into a blender with sugar, water, and ice. After it had become a swirl of pale-yellow liquid, he poured the mixture into the tabletop ice cream freezer he had taken earlier.

"Chefs, twenty minutes," Deuce called out.

When Miles heard Deuce, he quickly chopped the cooked shrimp and lobster and then turned to the piece of fish on the counter, drizzling olive oil over it. Next, Miles picked up an egg, held it to his cheek, and popped it in a glass of water.

"Pay attention to Chef Miles," Michèle whispered to Emily. "He is making mayonnaise." He wrote something on his notepad.

The four chefs were working frantically. Deuce could see the concentration on each face. Jordan and Miles seemed to be the most relaxed of the competitors. Both had done their prep work early to be ready to plate their dishes at the end. On the other hand, Tristan and Lola were in panic mode.

"Ten minutes!" Deuce called out.

"ARRRGHHHH," Tristan hollered as he slid four slices of bread into the oven and turned the temperature dial wildly. "Time for the steaks," he said out loud. Tristan looked at his simmering mushroom sauce and turned on the burner under the pan he had used earlier for the bacon. He opened the ice cream freezer and made a face. The mixture was not freezing, and Tristan had a moment of panic. "I've got this made in the shade," he said loud enough for everyone to hear. "How are things going over there, Lola?"

Lola was looking intently at the menu, her lips mouthing words. She smacked her head with her hand and hurried to the refrigerator and then to the pantry shelves. "Just fine, Tristan," she sang out as she walked back to her station, arms full. "How are things with you, buddy?"

"Awesome! Just like me!"

Deuce called out the five-minute mark, and the stations suddenly became a blur of activity. "Two minutes, chefs!" Deuce said a few minutes later.

"Dude, we've got it!" Tristan hollered. "Ouch," he shouted, shaking his hand as he took the toast out of the oven.

"You know the old saying, Tristan, if you can't stand the heat," Lola snickered and turned around to pull her dish out of the oven. She placed a piece on each plate and added a mélange of roasted tomatoes, peppers, and onions.

"Ten, nine, eight, seven," the audience chanted as the clock ran out.

"And time. Chefs, please step away from your stations," Deuce said as Art and Bert walked up quickly to capture images of the dishes before Ano took them to the judges. The aromas were enticing, and suddenly the studio audience realized how hungry they were.

Michèle motioned for Ano. "Radio the kitchen as soon as you can. We need snacks on the pool deck right away. Watching and smelling the food has made the passengers hungry even though they just ate." Ano gave him a quick nod and went to Miles's station to take his dishes to the judges' table.

"Chef Miles, will you please step forward and explain what you have created and how it ties to the original menu?" Deuce asked.

Miles came out from behind his station and stood before the judges. "Chef, I have prepared a starter of shrimp bisque, a lobster salad, and sea bass à la Cardinal for the main course."

The three judges began tasting Miles's dishes. Emily sipped the peach-colored soup. "Chef, the bisque is both elegant and rich. Well done." She put her spoon down.

"Chef, please tell me about the sea bass. How did you prepare it, and how does it replicate the original recipe?" Deuce asked.

Miles smiled. "At that time, most chefs trained in the classic French methods, and my mother forced me to attend a French culinary school. A chef at that time would have made a cardinal sauce with butter, white wine, cream, tomato concasse."

"Stop right there," Michèle barked. "While it is clear that you know what concasse is, do any of our other chefs know the definition?"

Tristan and Lola looked at each other and shrugged their shoulders. "Guess I missed that on my vocabulary test," Tristan said, snickering.

"I have not made a tomato concasse, but it is the process of blanching, seeding, and rough chopping fresh tomatoes," Jordan said nervously.

Michèle nodded at her answer and smiled at her. "Miles will receive three extra points for using a traditional French method in his dish, and Jordan will receive one point for knowing what the term means," he said. "Chef Jordan, I would suggest you try making a concasse. It gives a dish freshness you would not find in a can of tomatoes or diced tomatoes."

"Thank you, Chef Miles," Deuce said. The audience applauded, and Miles gave him a curt nod and stepped back behind his station.

"Chef Tristan, you are next. Please share what you have prepared for the judges to taste."

Tristan crossed his arms and looked at the judges. "I have prepared angels on horseback, beef Bordelaise, and a pineapple ice."

"You should be standing before the judges when addressing them," Deuce snapped. Tristan winked at the audience as he strolled over.

Emily took a bite of the oysters and grabbed her napkin. "Chef Colon, did you intend the oysters to be raw?"

Tristan turned red and stammered. "T-t-that's how we serve them at Swank." Then recovering his bravado, he continued, "It makes them more of an aphrodisiac."

"Thank goodness I don't need that," Emily said wryly, causing the audience to titter.

"Please walk us through your beef Bordelaise. I'd like to know why you chose that dish." Deuce said.

"Many of the steak dishes at Swank are my recipes. I guess you could say steak is my passion," he paused and tilted his head, "other than the ladies, of course," he gave the crowd a big wink.

Michèle spoke up, "Chef Colon, the sauce for the steak is good. It takes an otherwise ordinary piece of meat to another level. Could you explain to our audience why it can be better to cook a steak in a pan than on a grill?"

Tristan stared blankly at Michèle. "So, the meat doesn't dry out?" he said unsurely.

"Is that a question or an answer?" Deuce asked.

Emily looked at the soupy mixture in the bowl in front of her. Deuce took a sip and shook his head. "Thank you, Chef Colon. You may return to your station," Deuce said dismissively. "Chef Cobb," he barked, "I'm looking forward to hearing your explanation of why you needed to go to the pool bar."

"She probably thought she would need a drink after dealing with you. I know I do." Tristan murmured under his breath.

"Did you say something, Chef Colon?" Deuce asked sharply. Tristan looked down at the floor. "Well, Miss Cobb?"

Lola stood before the judges. She heard a whistle and turned to wave at Marshall and the others. "Thanks, guys!" She sent them a theatric kiss and turned back to the judges. "My fan club is here."

"Yes, we are aware," Deuce said with a hint of exasperation. "Now, please explain what you have prepared."

She motioned to the Bloody Mary in front of each of them. The presentation was beautiful. Each glass had a skewer with shrimp, olives, a cheese cube, and a pickle. Emily took a sip and coughed. Lola explained to the judges that she had substituted the drink for the soup course. "Chef Cobb, you will receive points for your creativity, although you may want to think about a less spicy version."

"Well, my boys do like them hot, don't y'all?" she said and put her hands on her hips. The audience roared, and Eddie whistled.

"That's why we call you hot stuff!" Marshall hollered to her.

Deuce had not counted on a bantering audience, and he didn't want their commentary to detract from the seriousness of the competition. He pointed at the main dish. "I assume your main course is what made you run off the set?"

"Well, I wanted to make my Caesar snapper, but when I couldn't find the salad dressing, I asked Ano—"

Deuce cut her off, "Chef Ano."

She rolled her eyes in exasperation. "*Chef Ano*," she said with emphasis, "where the Caesar salad dressing was and when he told me there wasn't any, I decided to do a lime marinade, and that's when margarita mix popped into my head."

Deuce and the others warily tasted the snapper. "It's interesting and is a unique use of the margarita mix," Emily said, trying to be kind.

Deuce put his fork down, and it clattered loudly on the plate. He waved his hand at the last dish, a six-sided box made from chocolate bars. The top of the box had a dollop of whipped cream and a strawberry. Lola explained this was her take on chocolate surprise. Deuce lifted the lid and peered inside, only to find it filled with whipped cream. He poked a finger inside, tasted it, made a face, and held up his hand to prevent the others from tasting it. Larry sighed when he saw Deuce's expression. "I fear the surprise is that Chef Cobb forgot to add powdered sugar to the whipped cream." Lola turned bright red. Deuce told her she could return to her station but not before she gave a big wave to the audience, who clapped and cheered enthusiastically for her.

"Now it is time to see and taste what our last chef made," Deuce said. "Chef Jordan?" Jordan walked over to the judges, placed her hands behind her back, and gave a quick nod.

"I have prepared rosemary lemon olives, lamb with mint sauce, and Turkish sharbat. I roasted the olives with lemon, garlic, and olive oil. In 1908, the olives would have been served in brine, but I feel my interpretation is more flavorful."

The three judges speared the olives and put them in their mouths. The first bite gave you the nutty taste of the rosemary; the next highlighted the brightness of the lemon.

"Let's discuss the lamb," Deuce said crisply.

"This is my mother's recipe using only Dijon mustard and mint. The sauce is a simple combination of red wine, mint, beef broth, and shallots."

The judges took bites, scribbled notes on their pads, and passed their comments back and forth. Finally, Deuce looked at the other two judges, who nodded, "Chef Jordan, please present your last dish."

Jordan took a deep breath. Her last dish had been a risk. "I again paid homage to my mother." She gestured to the glasses in front of each of the judges. "In your glass is sharbat, a Turkish drink made from rose petals, sugar, lemon juice, and water." She paused, seeing Emily sniff her glass. "It is more aromatic if left in the refrigerator for a few hours."

Deuce took a sip of the drink and put his glass down. "You are fortunate your mother was a gifted culinarian and teacher." He stood and faced the audience. "The judges will leave to confer for a few minutes to decide who will win today's competition."

Kennedy walked across the set and shared that a cooking demonstration would occur later in the day with Chefs Miles and Jordan.

Marshall, Karl, Larry, Paulie, and Eddie made a beeline for Lola. "You did great, honey," Paulie said, hugging her from the side.

"And don't worry about the powdered sugar. I bet chefs make that mistake a lot," Eddie said to her.

"And they loved the Bloody Mary," Larry offered. "Good thinking on your feet."

Lola gave them a weak smile. "Thanks. And thank you so much for being here. It's nice to know I have some friends on board." Karl stood on Lola's other side, wishing he could take her in his arms and tell her how proud he was of her, but he settled for squeezing her shoulder.

They were interrupted by Deuce Dawson, who had returned to the microphone. "Ladies and gentlemen, if you will take your seats, we are ready to announce our winner." Taking a cue from Miles and Jordan, Tristan and Lola stood in front of their stations. "Today's competition was difficult. Our chefs were in an unfamiliar environment and had the challenge of recreating dishes from the early 1900s. There were some difficulties, but overall, I am impressed with their adaptability. I am, however, disappointed no one went out of their comfort zone except Chef Lola."

"Way to go, Lola!" Eddie shouted, whistling.

"The scores are as follows. Chef Jordan, please step forward." Jordan took two steps and looked at Deuce. "Chef Jordan, you have received nineteen points: eighteen for your dishes and one extra point for answering the question earlier today about concasse."

"Thank you, Chef," Jordan said quietly and stepped back. She was disappointed in her score but understood the reason.

"Chef Cobb, please step forward." Lola moved forward and curtsied. "Chef Cobb, you have received seven points. Your fish was overcooked and tasted like someone made a margarita in an aquarium. I don't think we need to discuss your chocolate surprise again." Lola blinked back tears and stepped back.

"Those dirty rats. What the heck do those judges know about Lola? She's a great cook," Paulie spat out.

Larry was more practical. "They know quite a bit. It's a serious competition, and she had some hiccups."

"Chef Tristan," Tristan stepped forward, smiling widely at the audience. "Chef Tristan, you also received seven points. Your oysters were raw, and your pineapple ice tasted like a flat soft drink. However, your Bordelaise sauce was not terrible. Your flip answers to questions were telling. Perhaps you should hit the books instead of practicing hat tricks and poses."

Tristan stepped back and muttered.

"Was there something you wanted to say, Chef?" Deuce asked.

"No," Tristan said, glaring at Deuce.

"No, what?" Deuce raised his eyebrow.

"No, Chef."

Deuce turned his attention to Miles. "Chef Miles, please step forward. You have received a score of twenty-three points. Your dishes were well thought out, stayed on point, and were executed correctly. Your use of fresh mayonnaise and the concasse was impressive. You should thank your mother for forcing you to learn the French methods."

"Thank you, Chef," Miles said, trying to hide his smile.

Kennedy stepped forward and spoke into her microphone. "Ladies and gentlemen, let's give a big hand to our chefs and our judges. What an exciting start to our competition."

The audience was leaving, and Bert, who had stationed himself on one side, began walking toward the center of the set. Suddenly he tripped, flying across a row of deck chairs. Kennedy and Omar were on opposite sides of the seating area and saw him fall. Kennedy began to rush over to help Bert, but Omar called out her name and pointed. She smiled, realizing why Omar had stopped her. He walked over to Kennedy. "It appears that Bert has an admirer," he said, seeing Art come to Bert's aid.

"You should have seen them yesterday. I thought I was back in junior high school."

"It is good when people can find someone they are comfortable with," Omar said and clasped his hands behind his back. He gave her a quick nod. "I will see you later."

Monique was seated at the judges' table, waiting for Tristan. When he reached her, he took off his chef's jacket and placed his knife kit on the table. Monique could not help but notice the well-formed definition of the man's body. Tristan knew she was watching him. Most women did, and he smirked. "On the upside, if the competition doesn't work out, you could take up modeling," Monique said as he put on a T-shirt.

He flexed his biceps and winked at her. "Go ahead, Monique, feel those guns. You know you are impressed."

Monique laughed softly and sat back in her chair. "Thank you, but I'll decline. Something tells me I should keep my wits about me while interviewing you and not become distracted." She cocked her head. "I'm sure there are stories behind those," she pointed at his arms which had dozens of tattoos.

He flexed them for her. "There are, but if we talked about them, we wouldn't have a chance to talk about me," he said, grinning.

Monique shook her head inwardly at Tristan's overinflated ego. She continued to stare at the tattoos. Something didn't look right, but she couldn't place her finger on it. Tristan pulled the chair around to face her. "So, Tristan, let's talk about your background and history. I understand you and another couple had a restaurant in Panama City, but your affair with your partner's wife caused the restaurant to close. Was the affair worth losing your restaurant?"

Tristan was stunned. He had thought *he* would run the interview and flirt his way through it as he had for so many others. "W-w-well, that's not exactly how it happened." He sat down in the chair.

"Oh? Your former partner lost his restaurant, his life savings, and his wife, and you are no longer with the restaurant, are you?"

"Monique, Monique, Monique, there are two sides to every story." Tristan gave her a devastating smile.

"What's your side?" She arched an eyebrow and crossed a shapely leg. Tristan was distracted by the movement. "I wonder how the network executives of a family-oriented television station would feel about this type of scandal."

Tristan leaned forward in his chair. "Monique, let's cut to the chase instead of discussing dirty laundry. We both know I will be the winner of this competition. So, here is your chance to get the first interview."

"You didn't do very well today, Tristan. Why would you believe you will be the ultimate winner?"

Tristan squirmed but covered it by putting his hands behind his head. He leaned back in his chair. "You don't know how these competitions work," he said smugly. "I *had* to throw things today. The winner has to look like the underdog. That way, it becomes a comeback story. It's all a game, Monique. Trust me, I know how this will play out, and why wouldn't they want someone like me?"

"I guess since you know so much, I should play my cards right and ask you questions more befitting the new face of the show."

"That's more like it," he said, rocking in his chair. "Fire away."

"You are the sous chef for a popular restaurant in downtown Jacksonville. They said you had been there for two years."

"Yes," he said slowly. "When did you contact them? The lady who deals with the human resources stuff was going on vacation. It's a good thing you caught her."

Monique looked at her notes and flipped back a few pages. "Two weeks ago. These days you can't get anything more out of those offices other than a start and end date and if the person is still employed. Is there a problem?"

"No," Tristan shook his head, "no problem at all."

Monique was puzzled but decided to let it go. "Let's talk about something fun. What ingredient do you like to cook with the best?"

"Well, I like them all, of course." He paused and looked at her. "But I love butter."

"Butter?" Monique asked, surprised, "Why?"

Tristan leaned forward. "It's sexy," he said, grinning slowly. "It's like suntan oil on a beautiful body."

Monique mentally shook her head. The man thought he could disarm her with his fraternity boy charm. "Interesting," Monique said as she wrote down his answer. "Okay, next question." Monique went through the perfunctory questions: Tristan's family, what it was like to work at Jacksonville's hottest restaurant, and his personal life, which he very eagerly shared. He had even been bold enough to ask her for a date when they returned to Florida. When she asked what culinary school he had attended, he deflected the question explaining it wouldn't be fair to divulge the information as they would be inundated with applications after he won the competition.

"Are we about done?" Tristan asked. He was getting bored.

"Just about." She had one last question and was curious how he would answer it. "What do you think of your fellow competitors?" she asked.

"Oh, wow!" He jumped up and began throwing punches in the air. "I was hoping you would ask that! Where did they find those people?" Monique cocked her head to the right to encourage him. "Miles is a tool. All that snooty talk about French cooking and his dearly departed mama." He stopped moving around and looked at Monique. "But he has a secret he doesn't want to get out." Monique was silent. "He's got some condition that makes him fall asleep all the time; my grandfather had the same thing. Miles told me he's fallen asleep when he's been cooking and once over an open flame. It makes you wonder what would happen if he fell asleep on the show." Tristan continued talking, "Jordan is quiet and moody; the scar on her face would be cool on a guy, but it makes her pretty unattractive. Viewers would notice it." He gave her a wide smile. "Let's face it; she's not television material like me."

"What about Chef Lola? She seems to have quite a fan club on board," Monique asked.

Tristan put his hands on his hips and made a face. "Princess Private Chef? Let me tell you a secret, Monique. She's not a real chef."

Monique cocked her head puzzled. "What do you mean?"

"I can just tell," he said flippantly. "And you have to wonder if any of those old guys are her sugar daddy. Maybe they all are."

"Any comments on the judges?" she asked.

Tristan made a zipper motion with his fingers across his lips. "I have opinions, but as Deuce and I will be working side by side when I am host, it wouldn't be appropriate."

"Okay, one last question. Your bio states that you were the sous chef for a celebrity-studded event. But a source told me you were a line cook. Nothing wrong with that, but I want to have my facts straight."

Tristan's neck began to turn red. "N-n-nope, definitely the sous chef," he stammered. He began shadowboxing again to distract her. "Monique, have you not realized I am the real deal?"

Monique chuckled inside and stood up, holding out her hand. "I guess you are, and I apologize if I got things wrong, you know how it can be when you are getting background information."

Tristan smiled, showing her his white teeth. "It's okay, Monique. I'm glad I could set the story straight, especially as this will be a big story for you. You'll be the first to get the inside scoop for television's next hottest chef."

Anna Marie, the spa's receptionist, beamed when she saw David Stearns walk in. "Mr. Stearns, it is so wonderful to see you again. How are you?" she asked cheerfully.

He gave the slightly plump, freckle-faced young woman an easy smile. "Anna Marie, it's good to see you, too. The boys at Club Diva are envious that I am here, and they aren't. But this is a working trip. I'm doing an article on the spa."

Anna Marie grinned. "Mila told me. It's so exciting." She looked at her computer and then back at him. "You are booked for a Swedish massage today. You are going to love it!"

"You had me at massage." He lowered his voice. "I assume the drill is the same?"

"Yes, sir." She came around the desk and began escorting him toward the locker rooms. "I'll see you in the lounge. May I get you something to drink? Some cucumber water?"

"Is there any champagne?" David asked hopefully. "Just to help me start to relax."

Anna Marie giggled. "Mila brought a whole case up and wrote your name on the box."

"Chef Lola, thank you so much for agreeing to meet me here. Aren't the views fantastic?" Lola looked around and only saw water. She shrugged, shook Monique's hand, and sat down. "I am afraid I am not as prepared for our interview as I like to be. Unfortunately, the network neglected to send your bio over. I understand you were a last-minute replacement."

Lola pushed her curls back from her face. "Why does anyone have to know that? I'm here now. I barely had time to post a note to tell my clients I would be unavailable for a few days."

"Did I hear correctly that a group of your regular clients is on this cruise? I think I saw them cheering for you at the competition—a group of older men."

Lola fluttered her eyelashes and placed a hand on her chest. "I was simply flabbergasted when those dear boys showed up to support me." She giggled. "I guess I won't have to worry about them eating for the next few days."

"I had a moment to check out your social media pages. There are fascinating pictures of you on private planes and yachts and several of you posing in some stunning kitchens. Who are some of the people you have cooked for? They seem to be very wealthy."

Lola bit her lips together and shook her head. "I wish I could, Monique, but I can't. I sign non-disclosure agreements with my clients," she winked at Monique, "but they always send a private plane for me."

Monique put a checkmark in her notebook beside that question. It would remind her to go back and review the photos Lola had posted. Monique furrowed her brow. "So, in addition to cooking for famous people, you also make individual meals for clients. Does that make it an upscale delivery service? Do they know they are all getting the same thing?"

Lola put a finger to her lips. "Shhhh, don't say anything. I rotate fifty different dishes, and they haven't caught on yet."

Monique was stunned. "Fifty? When do you have time to sleep?"

Lola tossed her long brown curls. "Oh, a girl can have her secrets, can't she, Monique? I can't give away everything, you know?"

The two women discussed Lola's choice between becoming a private chef over a restaurant chef, and Lola explained the darker side of the culinary world, which was an angle Monique had not considered. When Monique asked about Lola's schooling, she was surprised at Lola's honesty when she revealed she didn't have a formal culinary education. "I watch tons of cooking shows, read recipe books like novels, and practice a lot."

"What makes you different from the other chefs, Lola?" Monique asked.

Lola smiled. "I'm a bit of a maverick because I didn't go to a fancy school. I learned on my own. And the others like to stay in their little boxes." She giggled. "Did you see Deuce's face when I ran to the bar to get the margarita mix?"

Monique laughed, remembering the thunderstorm that crossed the producer's face when the pretty chef took off her shoes and ran to the bar. "What about the other chefs? What do you think about them?"

Lola shrugged her shoulders. "Miles and Jordan are cool."

"And Tristan?" Monique asked.

Lola rolled her eyes. "Tristan is like every guy I ever met in a bar—arrogant, empty, and sad. I'm willing to bet the line cooks do ninety percent of his job. He may be pretty," she tapped her temple, "but he's no rocket scientist."

A laugh escaped Monique's lips. Lola had summed Tristan up in three simple words, and she agreed. Monique was sure the arrogant chef would take a victory lap before giving credit to anyone else.

"Okay, next question, what is your favorite ingredient?"

"Hmmm, let me think about that." She was quiet for a moment, and a grin came across her face. "Ketchup."

"Ketchup?"

"Yep! I keep a bottle or two in my emergency bag when I go on-site to cook. It's the jack of all trades in the condiment world. You can use it as a marinade for meat, make a sauce, and put it on vegetables before roasting them. Heck, you can even clean brass with it."

Monique wrote down Lola's answer. "Lola, I've got one more question, but it's personal."

"Okay," Lola said warily.

"Because you are so short, do you have problems in kitchens?"

Lola burst out with laughter. "Nope, but it's why I always wear heels, and they make me look good! I might be five-foot-two, but my attitude is six-foot tall!"

While Monique was interviewing Lola one deck above, the passengers began taking their seats for the cooking demonstration.

"I'm nervous," Jordan said. Chris placed the wireless mic on her lapel. "I've never done anything like this before."

"No time like the present," Miles said, coming up behind her. Jordan and Kennedy both caught a whiff of scotch on his breath.

Miles put his arm around her shoulders. "You need to get used to this, Jordan. If you win the competition, you will be on camera constantly talking to people. Now, what are we going to do first? Omelet flip or pizza dough?"

Once the audience was seated, Kennedy turned on her microphone and introduced Miles and Jordan to the audience. Miles began talking about the merits of hand-tossed dough while Jordan spun a circle of white dough in the background. "Jordan, are you ready?" he asked, and she took a few steps forward and tossed the dough to him. It landed gently on his outstretched hands to the delight and gasps of the audience. They threw the dough back and forth a few times, and then it was time for the audience to try. Art and Bert stayed busy capturing the comical faces the passengers made as they tried to toss the dough back and forth. Deuce, seated in the audience, nodded his head with approval.

"The next thing we will do is show you how to flip an egg. It will amaze anyone in your kitchen at breakfast," Miles said. He walked to the center of the stage, where Kennedy had placed a single electric burner and frying pan on a small table. He juggled three eggs while he waited for the pan to heat up. When it was ready, Miles pocketed two eggs into his chef's coat and cracked the third egg into the pan. He waited patiently for the egg to cook, and when it was time, he placed his hand on the handle and began to lift the frying pan. Suddenly the handle fell off, and the pan fell to the floor, clattering loudly. A collective groan came from the audience, and Kennedy kicked herself for not checking the pan. Miles doubled over with laughter. He held up a finger to the audience. "Rule number one. Check the handle first!" Jordan brought him another frying pan. The egg somersaulted through the air this time and landed expertly in the pan.

"Once you have mastered the pan flip, go one step further and flip from the pan to a plate. I wonder if we could ask our cruise director, Kennedy, to come and help us?" The audience applauded, and Kennedy stepped out on the stage. "Kennedy, stand there and catch the egg with the plate." Miles pointed at a spot a few feet away from him. He held up the remaining egg from his pocket and cracked it into the pan. "Let's do this one over easy," Miles said, and after a few minutes, he called out, "One, two, three," and flipped the egg into the air. It cartwheeled, making its way toward Kennedy. Art moved in closer to capture the footage, and Kennedy, sensing her movement, took her eyes from the egg. Kennedy looked up too late and saw the egg as it landed with a splat on her forehead. Miles looked at the audience and held up two fingers. "Rule number two, ensure the person holding the plate has their eyes on the ball, or should I say, egg."

Kennedy waved to the crowd and wiped the yellow yolk away. "I think it's time for our question-and-answer session while I get the egg off my face."

The passengers laughed and clapped as she stepped offstage, and Jordan and Miles walked over to sit in some chairs for the question-and-answer period. Someone had set two glasses of the ship's punch on the table between them, and Miles drank his glass in two gulps. "Thirsty work," he said. "Let's take our first question." Hands shot up as the passengers shouted their questions, and Miles and Jordan fielded them comfortably, bantering back and forth. Jordan had lost her nervousness and was beginning to enjoy herself.

"Chef Miles, you made fresh mayonnaise today. Could you please tell me how to make it? Is it hard?" a woman stood and asked.

Jordan, expecting to hear Miles's answer, only heard silence and a soft snore. She looked over in horror and realized his eyes were closed.

"I guess all of that pan-flipping made Miles tired," Jordan gave a nervous laugh and answered the woman's question. Miles let out a loud snort, and his microphone broadcast the noise through the speakers. She glanced uneasily at the audience. "Do we have another question?" Jordan asked and gently shoved Miles's knee.

Miles woke up with a start. "To make mayonnaise, you—" he tried to focus on the audience but felt like he was moving underwater in slow motion.

Jordan felt sweat pop out on her brow. "We have a question about searing steaks," Jordan said nervously. "Chef Miles, what do you recommend?"

"Butter," he slurred, "but if you don't have that, use canola or avocado oil," he waved his hand, "but don't use olive oil." And suddenly, he was asleep again.

The audience began to mumble to themselves. Jordan's eyes latched onto the spatula Miles had left on the table while he was cooking the egg. She took a deep breath. There were butterflies the size of pelicans in her stomach as she stood up and walked over to the table. "I have one more fun kitchen trick to show you. We did the pan flip, but you should also know how to do the spatula flip. Have you ever wanted to flip a piece of shrimp or a vegetable into someone's mouth?" The audience began to applaud. "I need a volunteer." She saw Bert kneeling, poised to take a photo. "Bert, would you be kind enough to help me out?" He began to edge away, but the audience began chanting his name.

"Bert, Bert, Bert."

Jordan looked around and spied the egg and broken pan that Miles had used earlier. She brought the pan over, placed it on the table, and cut a bite-sized piece of egg. "Bert, would you stand here?" Bert, pink with embarrassment, took his place six feet away from Jordan. She turned back to the passengers and began flipping the spatula back and forth between her hands. "The key is to keep the eyes of your audience on your hands. Open wide, Bert. One, two, three!" Jordan expertly lifted the piece of egg with her spatula and tossed it toward Bert's open mouth. He caught it, putting his hands up in victory. The audience burst out with cheering applause.

Kennedy, seeing an opportunity to end the show, walked out to stand beside Jordan and Bert. Simultaneously, Miles, hearing the cheers, woke with a start and scrambled to his feet, waving to the audience.

After the crowd left, Miles took off his chef's coat and folded it over his arm. He wanted to get away as quickly as possible. However, Tristan, who had been watching the show from the back, walked up and gave him a slow clap. "That was some show. First, you put an egg on the cruise director's head, and then you started snoring. Did you celebrate too hard after winning this afternoon?"

Miles smiled tightly. "An unfortunate incident. They happen. I'll see you later. I need to go to my cabin," he said quickly.

"Want to grab a beer to calm your nerves? You look a little jumpy."

Miles sighed heavily. He was embarrassed and angry that he had an episode during the cooking demonstration. After the competition, he celebrated his win with two cocktails, believing he could handle the alcohol. But when the handle on the saucepan broke and the egg landed on Kennedy's head, his brain shut down. He reasoned he could have one drink with Tristan and then slip away. "Let's go," he said to Tristan.

Bert was helping Art wind up her cables. "Art, would you like to have dinner again?" he asked hopefully.

Art looked at him with regret. "I would, but I have to edit both videos. I'll probably get a sandwich and eat in my room." Feeling foolish, Bert looked down at the floor as a flush began to creep up his neck. He was crestfallen and mumbled that it was just as well as he needed to edit the photos he had taken.

"Why don't we grab a drink later? You could show me the stills you took after you've edited them."

Bert was suddenly nervous at the thought of Art looking at his work.

"We could talk about tomorrow's competition and the shore excursion for the chefs. I could use your help. I think we work well together."

Bert squared his shoulders. "I-i-if you say you need me, I'll be there," he stammered. He could feel his face reddening, "I've got to get busy editing the photos and setting up for the dinner photos. Is it okay if I stop by around ten?" he asked.

Art smiled shyly at him. "See you then."

Omar knocked on the door of Emily Abbott's cabin to escort her to dinner. She opened it wearing a black long-sleeved caftan and gold earrings. "Good evening Mrs. Abbott. You look lovely again tonight."

"Omar, you are kind to an old woman. Keep the compliments coming," she winked. "I plan to repeat them word for word to Vera."

Omar laughed. "Where would you like to have dinner tonight? We can go to the—"

Emily interrupted him, "I want to dine in the Vantage Point Lounge. It's too bad I don't smoke. Vera went on and on about your chat in the smoker's lounge."

"Then let us go." He offered her his arm. When they reached the smoker's lounge, she looked at it critically and said it looked like a mammoth birdcage. Omar chuckled and shared that Vera had been of a similar opinion. They entered the Vantage Point Lounge, and Omar escorted her to the seating area by a wall of windows that looked out onto the ocean.

Luke approached the table. "Mrs. Abbott, welcome to the Vantage Point Lounge. I am Luke, the beverage manager."

"Are you *the* Luke?" Emily asked. "The one who has named a cocktail after Vera Jameson?"

Luke beamed. "I am."

Emily gave the two men an eye roll. "She's always such a snob and brags about her special cocktail. The stories I could tell you about Vera. She wasn't always so hoity-toity."

Luke grinned. "Mrs. Abbott, if I may, I have made a special cocktail in your honor." He left, and ten minutes later, Luke returned holding a tray behind his back. He placed a crystal glass in front of her with pineapples cut into the design. A purple orchid garnished the drink. "May I present to you the Smoky Abbott."

"Oh, my goodness," she said in awe and took a sip. "I taste so many things: smoke, bourbon, pineapples, and…" She paused and took another sip. "Do I taste maple syrup?" Luke nodded, and Emily grinned. "This is going to make Vera green with envy. So much more personal than an old fashioned in a champagne glass."

# THE SMOKY ABBOTT

3/4 OUNCE SIMPLE SYRUP

1 1/2 OUNCES BOURBON

1/2 OUNCE MEZCAL

3/4 OUNCE FRESH PINEAPPLE JUICE

MAPLE SYRUP TO TASTE

COMBINE ALL INGREDIENTS IN A COCKTAIL SHAKER. ADD ICE AND SHAKE. STRAIN INTO AN ICE-FILLED GLASS, AND GARNISH WITH ORCHID.

Luke smiled back at Emily. "Please don't make Vera mad at me. It has taken me years to make her like me." He turned to Omar. "How is your bourbon?"

"Excellent as always." He turned to Emily to explain, "I'm afraid Mrs. Jameson has turned me into a cigar and bourbon snob."

Emily chuckled. "If anyone could, it would be Vera." Luke left them, and they enjoyed their drinks in silence. Emily finally spoke up, "Vera often speaks of Kennedy."

"Vera and Kennedy have a long history." Omar shared the stories he knew about the two women. The last-minute requests, the unusual dishes Vera wanted the chefs to prepare, and the time Kennedy told Vera no.

"I've seen Vera make grown men hide at the mere thought of her being in their office. It would have been funny to see her bested. She doesn't get told no often."

Omar sat back in his chair, getting comfortable. "Tell me about yourself, Emily. We didn't get to speak much last night at dinner. You are a very well-traveled woman and know the history of the places you have been."

Emily blushed. "Only because my husband and I lived in Europe for many years." She told Omar how she and her husband, Alexander, met at a bistro in Paris. "When he died, I made a pilgrimage to every place we had visited." She sighed. "Now I fill my days with social engagements, attend board meetings, and vote the way I am told."

"What made you take this cruise?" Omar asked gently.

"Honestly? I wanted to be a part of something, and the competition was the answer. I feel terrible that I have never been on one of our ships, and even worse, I didn't realize the amount of work involved. But today's tour opened my eyes."

Omar gave her a low nod. "It would be good to have someone who understands our challenges." He changed the subject. "Mrs. Abbott, you are a gifted speaker. I have traveled and seen the places you spoke of, but you brought them to life for me and the others at the captain's table. You would be an excellent travel lecturer."

Emily playfully pushed Omar's hand. "I believe the bourbon is going straight to your head. But I intend to tell Vera about your compliment."

They sat quietly, each absorbed in their thoughts. Emily thought back on her past while Omar pondered his future.

Kennedy and Mila were in Mila's cabin, drinking a bottle of wine and catching up on the day. Kennedy was looking thoughtfully at her glass.

"Are you in there?" Mila knocked on Kennedy's temple.

"Just thinking. It's been a strange year," Kennedy said.

"How were things with Omar today?"

Kennedy shrugged. "Confusing. Flirty one moment and an iceberg the next. It makes navigating difficult." Mila gave her friend a comforting smile. Kennedy was an open book to those she trusted, and she was all in once she gave that trust. Omar, however, was a different kind of book. One with ripped-out pages, folded-down corners, and words in code handwritten in the margins. She hoped Kennedy had the perseverance to get through the current chapter.

"What do you think about the competition so far?" Mila asked deftly, changing the subject.

Kennedy stood up. "Cutthroat. Not at all what I expected. Lola and Tristan bicker like junior high rivals, and I don't know what happened, but Miles fell asleep or passed out during the cooking demonstration. Thank goodness for Jordan. She handled it like a champ." She grinned. "I think Ano and Michèle have taken a shine to her."

"Hmmm," Mila mused, drumming her fingers together. "Michèle likes someone other than his reflection in his knives."

"And on that note, I'm going to bed." Kennedy placed her wine glass on Mila's desk. "We dock in Punta Cana early tomorrow. I'll see you at the morning staff meeting."

While Kennedy was opening her cabin door, Omar was walking out of his. Luke had asked him to come to Longitudes on the lower level. There had been trouble with Chef Miles, and he needed to see how he could contain it.

Miles's evening started well. The high of winning today's round, the alcohol in his veins, and the sea breeze made him feel excited to be alive. As he got ready for dinner, his watch chimed, reminding him to take his medication, but he convinced himself he didn't need it. "You've got this under control, buddy. Maybe this is the change you needed."

He went to the disco after dinner and danced with several pretty passengers. Then, he left the disco for the casino. When he opened the door, the distinct music of the casino greeted him. Robotic melodies called out from the slot machines while the roulette wheel made a soft tick like a pendulum. Miles listened to the click of the chips on the rail and the muted thump of the dice as they hit the back wall at the craps table. He walked further and heard the welcome whisper of the cards as the dealer shuffled them.

A cocktail server walked by and asked if Miles would like a drink. He hesitated for only a second and nodded.

"Double scotch," he heard his mouth say before his brain could overrule. Deep down, he knew he had no business in the casino, but Miles promised himself he could handle it and would only play until his drink was gone. He settled in at an empty seat at one of the blackjack tables, losing money and winning it back until he had amassed a tidy pile. The cocktail server replaced the empty glass with a fresh one. He looked at his hand; a king lay on the bottom, and a three was on top. He pushed his chips to the betting area.

"Sir? Sir? Do you want to split?" the dealer asked Miles. "Sir, hello? Split, hit, or stand?" Miles still did not respond. Paulie and Karl waved their hands in front of his face.

"He's asleep!" Paulie said to everyone at the table, hearing a light snore.

"Sir?" the dealer asked a third time. He looked at the others around the table and shrugged his shoulders. He turned over his bottom card which showed an eight of diamonds. "House wins." He swept the chips and the cards from the table as Paulie and Karl threw their cards down in disgust.

"Sir, if you are not playing, I'm going to have to ask you to leave," the dealer said with some exasperation.

"W-w-what?" Miles looked puzzled at the dealer. "No, hit me."

"I'm sorry, sir, but that game ended. You will need to get more chips. You lost what you had when you fell asleep."

"I what?" Miles asked in confusion which quickly turned to embarrassment. "I wasn't asleep! I was thinking." His words began to slur together, and he felt like the room had turned sideways. Miles looked around in a panic. He saw the dealer's face become the mask of the grim reaper and let out a silent scream. The dealer motioned to the two guards in the center of the casino.

"Sir, you need to come with us," one of the security guards said gently, placing a beefy hand around Miles's arm to maneuver him away from the table.

"I'm not going anywhere with you!" Miles said, terrified, and tried to shake the man's hand off.

The other guard quickly came to his opposite side and wrapped a hand around Miles's upper arm. They pulled him from his seat and hustled him out of the casino. Miles stood outside the casino doors, shaking and disoriented. His heart was pounding. He ran a hand over his head and felt oily sweat. Paranoia seeped through his brain, and he wasn't sure why, but he knew he needed to get away. He jerkily ran down the corridor and bounced into one of the walls when he turned around to see if someone or something was following him. He found the elevator and mashed the call buttons at the same time. The doors opened, and he scrambled on, pressing buttons. When the doors opened, he exited quickly and stood outside of the entrance to Longitudes.

Longitudes Lounge had a unique feel to it. Wooden tribal masks hung on emerald green grasscloth walls. Fishing nets suspended from the ceiling held glass fishing floats, yellow buoys, and orange life preservers. Miles made his way through the bar, bumping noisily into tables and chairs. At last, he reached the long bar and grasped the counter with shaky hands. He sat heavily on one of the bright green leather barstools. The bartender turned around.

"What can I get you?" Luke asked the panting man. "Glass of water to start?" Luke was there tonight as the regular bartender had called off, not feeling well.

"Scotch, make it a double." Miles cast a nervous glance around the room.

"Hey, aren't you one of the chefs in the competition?" Luke asked and placed a rocks glass in front of Miles. He filled it with amber liquid and slid it toward Miles. "Cheers."

Miles looked at the drink. He had not touched a drop of alcohol in fifteen years, and today he wanted to drain every bottle on the ship. Miles shuffled off the barstool and tightly grasped the glass in his left hand. He sloshed his drink as he made his way to a banquette on the far wall and sat there for a long time, staring into the dark room, only moving to raise his hand with an empty glass. Later, when Luke looked over at the banquette and realized Miles was no longer sitting upright but had fallen over drunk, he radioed the security office. "I need a wheelchair in Longitudes for an intoxicated passenger, one of our VIPs. I'm calling Omar to let him know."

Omar walked into Longitudes fifteen minutes later. He had just closed his eyes when his telephone rang, and Luke quickly explained the situation. "Sorry, my friend," Luke said, motioning to the sleeping man. "He came in very jumpy and then got quiet when he sat over there. I honestly forgot about him. I had some good tippers down here and wasn't about to turn down their business." Two security guards pulled Miles into a sitting position and maneuvered him into the wheelchair.

"I understand," Omar clapped Luke on the back. "Officers, please take our friend here to Cabin 757. After you have tucked him in, please perform wellness checks on him every hour and log it."

One of the officers shook his head, looking at Miles. "Did you know he was kicked out of the casino earlier tonight? You should watch the footage, sir. He was a handful."

Omar stroked his chin. "In that case, let's make sure we have two officers perform the wellness checks on him."

He raised his hand to Luke, "Thanks for calling me. This situation could have been ugly."

The two security officers poured Miles into his bed and went to his cabin every hour to ensure he was breathing normally. Then, just before dawn, calls came into the security office from the cabins on either side of Miles to report a disturbance. When they arrived, they found him wild-eyed, beating on the bathroom door, screaming that he had to get out. The officers gently led him back to bed, and he was in a calm sleep before his head hit the pillow.

# Sunny Dayz Cruise Line

# THE HELIO

## DAY THREE

COSTA MAYA, MEXICO

ARRIVAL 8:00 A.M.

DEPARTURE 6:00 P.M.

Omar telephoned Kennedy, knowing she would be up early preparing for the day's port of call. "Kennedy, we had some problems last night with Chef Miles. I need to tell Deuce Dawson what happened, and I'd like you there as well. Can we meet in the conference room right away?"

Kennedy groaned. "Is he okay?"

Omar was silent for a moment as he rubbed his grainy eyes. Sleep had eluded him again last night. "Yes, but we need to discuss the situation." Kennedy quickly called Deuce Dawson's cabin and explained what she knew.

The occupants of the conference room were tense as Omar shared the security footage from the previous evening. "I'm genuinely concerned about the man. I can overlook what happened in Longitudes, but I worry that he is a danger to himself and others."

Deuce shook his head. "I can't remove him from the competition. We've launched the promotional materials and have sent back footage to the network." He washed his face with his hands and stood up. "I need to go for a walk and think about this." Omar and Kennedy watched the door close, and Omar pushed away from the table to leave.

"Omar, have you spoken with Dr. Craig?" Kennedy asked.

Omar looked at her curiously. "Why?"

Kennedy chewed her lower lip. "When he arrived, Miles asked that Dr. Craig come to his cabin."

"Do you know what it was about?"

Kennedy shook her head. "No"

"Unfortunately, I cannot ask him due to doctor-patient confidentiality."

"Oh," Kennedy said.

"However, if he does this again, I will have to confront him about it."

While Omar, Deuce, and Kennedy were in the conference room, Lola and her admirers were on the pool deck having breakfast. "Lola honey, you need to stay away from Miles," Eddie cautioned.

"It's not like I can avoid him. We have a schedule that we have to follow."

"We saw him get a little rambunctious last night, and we don't want to see you get hurt," Karl said gravely.

"Rambunctious?" she echoed. "Miles was probably letting off a little steam." She patted his arm lovingly. "I can take care of myself, sweetie. He's harmless."

Eddie shook his head, "Lola, it's not like a guy in a bar getting rowdy. He was, well, he was..."

Lola rolled her eyes at the five men. "Good grief, spit it out. I'm not a delicate flower."

"He was combative, hon," Paulie said quickly. "We watched them throw him out of the casino, and later, we saw him taken out of Longitudes in a wheelchair after he passed out."

"We just want you to be safe, Lola," Larry said gently. "He doesn't seem to be in his right mind when he drinks, and we don't want you to come to any harm if we aren't around."

Lola looked at their serious faces. "Wow," she said slowly. "I'll be careful, scout's honor." She gave them a beatific smile. "Will you guys be at the competition this morning? I'm hoping my cheerleading squad is there."

The five men looked uncomfortable, and Karl sighed. "Not exactly, honey," he put an arm around her shoulders. "We thought the competitions would be in the afternoon and booked an offroad adventure today." He looked at Lola's crestfallen face. "We can cancel if it would make you feel better."

"We are not canceling!" Marshall's reedy voice spoke up. He pointed at Lola with a shaky finger. "She cooks without us at Breezy Bayou, and I'm not giving up my adventure." He turned his head to face Lola, "Sorry, toots, but I'm looking forward to riding around the jungle in an ATV and not this thing," he pointed to his wheelchair. "I don't have much time left, and I need to have all the fun I can have before I'm dead."

Lola loved Marshall's honesty. She gave them a dazzling smile. "I'll be fine, guys, I promise, and when you get back, we'll celebrate my win!" She pointed to the harbor coming into view. "Look, we are arriving in Costa Maya. It's so beautiful." They went to the railing to watch the *Helio* pull up to the dock, and Lola pulled up the hood of her sweatshirt against the breeze.

The cruise terminal was a beehive of activity as the shops, restaurants, and water activities opened for the day. Larry pointed at the cruise terminal. "I'm going down to the lobby. As soon as we are allowed to leave the ship, I need to find a coffee shop and check my messages."

"Always the protective mama bear," Marshall laughed. "When are you going to let these people make their own mistakes? It's the only way they will learn."

"But that's the point, Marshall. I'm the restaurant fairy godmother. They only pay until they don't need me anymore. I pave the path, and they pay the bills." He looked at Lola. "Good luck! You are going to be great!" He turned and walked through the double doors.

"Any idea what today's challenge is?" Paulie asked. He ran a hand through his hair, a silent signal between them.

Lola shook her head. "Not a clue, we'll find out thirty minutes before the show, and it will be broadcast live today to the network's morning show. Maybe it's good that you guys will be gone so I won't get distracted." She gave Karl a wink.

"Well, Pop and I need to get ready for his jungle excursion," Karl said and squeezed Lola's arm. "Good luck today!"

"Knock'em dead, toots," Marshall said, putting his hands up like a boxer. Karl went to stand behind his father's wheelchair. "You know, back in my day—"

"Come on, Pop," Karl interrupted and began pushing toward the double doors. "We'll be here all day if we listen to your stories, and you won't get any bikini-watching time."

Paulie ran a hand through his hair again. "You guys go ahead. I'm going to get in my laps around the promenade deck," he patted his stomach. "I need to watch my girlish figure. I'll meet you in the lobby in an hour." Paulie climbed the stairs to the promenade deck and made one loop. He smiled when he came around the bend and saw Lola waiting for him.

"Oh, Paulie," she said, hugging him. "This has been torture. I've missed you," she said into his chest.

"I know, sweetie, but it was the only way. The guys would have suspected something if I had gone on a cruise alone at the last minute. So, I had to find a way to have everyone go." He gently pushed her away. "How are you doing, kid? Yesterday's competition was tough, and that Tristan guy is a jerk." He made a face. "I'll turn him into hamburger meat if you want. Just say the word."

"No, I'm okay, Paulie," she said quietly, looking down. "It's just, I just," she broke off. "Never mind."

"What is it, sweetheart? Tell me." He picked her chin up with his finger. "You can tell me anything. We don't have any secrets."

"Well, we have one," she sulked.

"We've talked about this, Lola. You know we can't tell anyone right now. I promise we'll find the right time," he said tenderly. "Now, you started to say something. What was it?"

Lola took a deep breath. "Well, this thing came up in such a hurry, and I had to buy all of these clothes, and I didn't have time to get to the bank, and well, that's just it." Her words came out in a rush. She put her hands on her hips. "I'm broke."

Paulie started to laugh and pulled her into a bear hug. "Is that all? How much do you need?" He pulled his money belt from the waist of his pants and unzipped it.

Lola saw the thick wad of money and licked her lips. "Just a couple of bucks to get me through the next few days. I'm so embarrassed."

He counted off some bills and handed them to her. "Put this somewhere safe. If you need more, let me know. I like to take care of my girl even if I can't do it in public." Paulie smiled. He wished his mother were alive; she would have loved Lola. "You'd better get going. I don't want to press our luck. I'll be thinking of you."

"Thank you, and thanks for this," she held the wad of money close to her chest and hugged him again, "I'll pay you back, I promise." She put her arms around his neck and kissed him.

"Go!" he chuckled.

Lola bounced away and passed Monique Patrick, who was taking a morning stroll to get herself organized. She had watched the passionate embrace between the tiny chef and one of her fan club members and wondered how the others felt about it. She recalled Tristan's comment from his interview when he wondered aloud if any of the men were Lola's sugar daddies. Now, Monique wondered as well.

Larry walked briskly down the long pier to the port. He scanned the directional signs and found what he was seeking: a coffee shop with Internet. Patiently waiting to place his order, Larry wondered which of his clients had sent messages. He had owned and managed restaurants for many years but was now a consultant and found he thrived on the work. Larry was currently consulting on four projects, each in a different stage. He was thankful none were ready to open yet, as it would keep the consulting fees coming in. He took his coffee, found an empty table, and began looking at his messages. Larry answered his clients quickly and set appointments to meet each of them when he returned from the cruise. The last note was from an old friend who lived two hours away.

Larry—

I'm getting engaged! Can you believe it? I found love in the grocery store, of all places! You might even know Lila. She's a chef, and you always tell me that everybody knows everyone. She doesn't work in a restaurant, so she isn't working those horrible hours you always talk about; she's a private chef. My biggest gripe is that she's constantly being called at the last minute to cook a fancy meal for one of her clients or cater one of their parties. I guess these people are so rich that they don't think about planning ahead. But you should see the planes they send for her and some of the kitchens. I'm not sure what she sees in me, but I'm the luckiest guy in the world! I hope you can attend our engagement party and meet my bride-to-be. I've attached a picture of the happy couple.

Larry clicked on the attachment and felt uneasy. The photo was blurry, but Larry could see his friend standing beside a petite brunette in front of a fountain. Thoughts raced through his head, and he scolded himself for his wild imagination. He figured it was because of the mystery novels he had been reading.

Kennedy was standing in the lobby bidding passengers goodbye as they hurried to port. After a full day at sea, most were anxious to leave the ship and walk on land. She spied Terri and Jones Butler and waved to them. "What fabulous excursion are you off to see today?" she asked as they walked up to her.

"Well, Jonesy wanted to see some old ruins, but I said no, we've got old ruins galore back home." She gave Jones the side eye. "I've seen every historical marker within a five-hundred-mile radius of the house. Instead, we have a private charter taking us to a lagoon that has seven colors of blue. We'll tour an old fort in the afternoon to make Jones happy."

Jones piped up, "I am sorry we will miss the cooking competition today. Yesterday was pretty wild." He motioned for Kennedy to come closer. "The casino was *pretty wild,* too, last night. Chef Miles got a little—" He made circles at his temple with his forefinger. Kennedy smiled tightly and held a finger to her lips. Jones winked. "Gotcha. Nothing about a B-O-D-Y or a C-R-A-Z-Y chef."

Thirty minutes before the competition, the four chefs waited for Deuce in the main dining room. "Chefs," he said briskly as he walked in, "as promised, I am here to tell you about today's competition. First, remember that we are on a live feed with our network's morning show," he looked at all of them, "I cannot begin to tell you how important this is. Millions of viewers will be watching, and I will remind you that this is a family show." He looked hard at Tristan and Lola. "Watch your language and no snide remarks or theatrics." Then, he began pacing. "Costa Maya is in the state of Quintana Roo which is known for its cocoa, and today's challenge will be to make a main dish using it. You will only have thirty minutes to complete today's challenge. After the competition, we will go to the town of Mahahual, where we will take a cooking class."

Tristan held up his hand. "Wait a minute. We have to go to a cooking class?" He put his hands on his hips. "What happened to us being able to have fun?"

Deuce glared at him. "Chef Colon, this was on the itinerary. I believe you have forgotten the reason for this competition, and I assure you it isn't to give you an all-expense paid vacation." He turned to the other three chefs. Sitting at a table, Miles was pale, clammy, and red-eyed. "Chef Miles, I would like to see you after the competition. We have a matter to discuss." Miles swallowed and looked down.

Tristan waited until Deuce had left the room before speaking. "Dude," he said, looking at Miles, "what happened to you? You look like a piece of roadkill."

"I didn't sleep well last night," Miles said dully.

"That's not what I heard," Lola said in a sing-song voice. "I heard grandpa's been banned from the casino, and he was so drunk in one of the bars last night that he had to be taken out in a wheelchair." Miles glared at her through bloodshot eyes. "So, how are we supposed to…I mean, what are you guys going to make with cocoa? It's a great little drink when you are cozy by the fire, but to use it in a recipe? In this heat?"

Miles winced and squeezed his eyes shut. The high-pitched twang of Lola's voice made him feel like there were tiny men behind his eyeballs using sledgehammers and picks. "I'm sure you'll come up with something, Lola," he said tiredly.

Tristan began to snicker. "Why don't you make your chocolate surprise again for Deuce? He was certainly surprised the last time."

Lola narrowed her eyes at Tristan. "I don't have to take this."

Tristan smirked, "Nope, but if I throw a stick, will you leave?"

"Tristan, you are such a big jerk," Lola said in exasperation and stalked over to a nearby table. She angrily threw herself into the chair, and the death glare she was giving Tristan should have turned him into charred meat.

"She makes it so easy," Tristan grinned as he sat down in a chair at Miles's table.

Miles put up his hands to stop him. "Tristan, I need to think."

Tristan wrote on a napkin and slid it to Miles. "Just follow me," the note said.

"Miles, I didn't want to say anything in front of Lola, but I don't know what to do. I've never used cocoa before," Tristan whispered loudly. "It's the thirty-minute time crunch that bothers me. I guess I could make chili or something easy like that."

Miles made a noncommittal grunt.

Lola heard Tristan's words and suddenly became excited. Chili was simple to make. All she needed to add was cocoa. She sat back in her chair, smiling to herself. This wasn't going to be too hard after all.

"Where is our audience?" Deuce hissed into his mic to Art, standing across the set from him. He scanned the empty seats. "We have an empty space where an audience is supposed to be."

"I don't know, Deuce," Art said. "Let me ask Bert." She motioned to Bert, and he walked over. She put her hand over her mic. "Deuce is freaking out because there is no audience."

"It happens after a sea day. Passengers get antsy to get off the ship. I can round up some of the staff and crew if that would help."

"Yes! Go! Go! Go! I'll see if I can grab some people around the pool deck." Then, she spoke into her mic, "Don't worry, boss, you'll have an audience momentarily."

"Hurry!" Deuce said. "We go live in twenty minutes." He paced the competition area and was relieved when Chef Michèle and Emily arrived to take their places at the judges' table.

"You look stressed, Deuce. Is everything okay?" Emily asked.

"Live feed jitters," he said, shaking his arms and hands. He felt a wave of relief wash over him when he saw people begin to sit in the chairs. He caught Art's eye, "Thank you," he mouthed. She saluted him and then tripped and fell into a chair. Deuce chuckled. If nothing else, her tripping had made him feel at home, it was a constant in their tapings over the years. "Are you ready for the chefs to take their positions?" Art nodded, and he motioned for them. "Please remember, this is a live feed," he said and turned on his mic. The chefs at their workstations looked ill at ease which amused Art. Competing on live television had removed some of their earlier bravado. She held up her hand in a fist and then pointed at Deuce. The large television screens on the sides of the set went from blue to suddenly showing the faces of the hosts of the network's morning show.

"Deuce, you are a lucky son of a gun. Are you enjoying your vacation?" the smiling male co-host asked jovially. "How did you get this gig? I'm jealous!"

"It's not all fun and games. This is a serious competition for us to find the chef for our new show, *Classic Flavors*. Have you seen the clips from yesterday's competition?" Deuce shot back.

"Yes," the female co-host said. "We just showed yesterday's footage, and it seems like the wild west out there, Deuce. We particularly enjoyed Chef Lola's race to the bar." Art zoomed her camera onto Lola, who smiled beatifically and curtsied. Then, she panned back to Deuce.

Deuce was holding up a large reddish-brown, pod-shaped fruit for the camera to see, turning it around. "The cacao seed, or as you may know it, cocoa, comes from this, the fruit of the cacao tree, and has played a part in history from its beginnings in Central America. The ancient Mayans used it for trade, money, and in their recipes. Today's competition will require that our chefs use a form of cocoa in their dish and make it in thirty minutes." He walked over to a table. "We have given them a variety of items to use today," he began pointing out items on a table, "cocoa beans, cocoa nibs, cocoa paste, cocoa powder, cocoa butter, and of course, chocolate." He looked at the four contestants and then at the monitor, which showed the countdown clock. "Chefs, are you ready?" They nodded. "You may begin."

Art panned her camera at the four chefs while the overhead cameras captured the cutting, mincing, and slicing happening at the individual stations. Deuce walked back and forth between the judges' table and the cooking stations, offering commentary as Art filmed him. At one point, he pointed out to Lola that her frying pan was smoking. She quickly pulled the pan off the burner, explaining that she was trying to get a smoky flavor for her dish.

Next, he visited with Tristan, who offered him a taste of the pesto he had prepared. When Deuce asked Tristan if he had tasted it, Tristan waved him off and said he made it every night and didn't need to taste it. Deuce walked back to the judges' table, running his tongue against the top of his teeth to scrape the taste away. He looked at both Emily and Michèle and shook his head. "Have your water close by." He turned to Emily, "Would you like to join us in Mahahual?" Emily shook her head and told him she had arranged a private tour to see some Mayan ruins. As time trickled down, the workstations became a flurry of activity. Jordan pulled a sheet pan out of the oven and smiled, smelling the aroma of what she had made. Lola had thrown off her hat and was feverishly stirring her large stockpot, flinging items into it. Tristan tasted his pesto and raced to the cooler, and, while gone, left his burner on. He let out a scream when he came back and saw smoke billowing from it. Miles was curiously standing still, his back to the audience.

Art was motioning to Deuce, her fingers counting down. They would be live in a few seconds. "And time," Deuce said into the microphone. Jordan, Tristan, and Lola walked to the front of their stations, but Miles stood unmoving with his back to the audience. "Chef Miles, please step away from your station," Deuce repeated louder this time, and when Miles turned around, Deuce saw the confusion on his face. Miles suddenly realized what had happened. He had fallen asleep again, and this time on live television. His chocolate-infused barbeque sauce had been made, and the grilled shrimp was on the plates, ready for the velvety mahogany sauce to be drizzled over them; however, he had not completed the presentation. He hung his head. The other three chefs stood awkwardly as Ano came to get each tasting plate to take to the judges.

"Chef Miles," Deuce said quietly. "I am sorry, but we will have to disqualify you from this round as you did not complete today's challenge." Miles, dejected, looked down at the ground.

Deuce saw Art make a fist telling him they were live, and he gave the camera a wide smile. "Welcome back to our competition. It's been a busy thirty minutes since we last saw you. Our chefs were tasked with making a main course dish using a form of cocoa. Let's see how they did."

The three chefs lined up near the judges' table. They started with Lola. Art zoomed in as Lola explained that her chocolate chili was a favorite among her clients and her secret ingredient was cocoa powder. Michèle casually asked Lola if she relied on tasting the dish as she added the cocoa powder or if she had a set measurement. When Art saw Emily pick up her spoon to taste the chili, she panned her camera over to capture Emily's reaction. Lola fluffed her hair and was about to answer as Emily grabbed a napkin to cover her lips.

"A cup?" Lola squeaked, seeing Emily's face, and then watched Michèle draw a zero on his notepad.

The judges then turned to Tristan's burnt steak with pesto sauce. Deuce was surprised when he tasted the pesto. Whatever Tristan had been searching for in the cooler had helped. Jordan's dish was the last to be tasted as Miles had been disqualified, and they swooned over the cocoa nib and harissa phyllo pizza topped with sausage and cheese. Emily remarked that the colors in the dish made it resemble an impressionist painting of a sunrise as it went from a golden yellow to dark red.

After tasting Jordan's dish, Deuce looked at the two judges. "I believe we have our winner for today's competition." Michèle and Emily nodded.

Joanna, the co-host of the morning show, broke in, "Deuce, aren't there four chefs competing? We've only seen the dishes from three contestants. Was there a problem with the fourth one?"

Deuce frowned into the camera. "Unfortunately, Chef Miles was disqualified as he did not complete his dish in time."

"Couldn't you at least taste it?" she pushed. "I know *I* am curious, and I am sure our viewers are too." The cameraman panned to show the studio audience at the network, who were nodding their heads enthusiastically and clapping. Deuce nodded to Miles, who miserably trotted to his station and quickly drizzled the rich chocolate barbeque sauce onto the fat pink shrimp. He came back to the judges' table carrying three plates.

Michèle was the first to speak. "Chef, I would like to have this recipe." Miles smiled sadly. Mike, the co-host, spoke up and asked Deuce to share the recipe with the viewers so they could try it for themselves. Surprised, Deuce said they would send Miles's and Jordan's recipes with the clips from the cooking class the chefs would be taking in Mahahual later in the day. Deuce smiled at the camera and waved as Art held her hand up in the air as the two co-hosts began to talk about backyard barbeques and then made a fist signaling that the live feed was over.

"And we are out," Art said. "Excellent job, everyone!"

Deuce then read out the scores for each chef. Tristan and Lola walked away quickly from the competition scene, embarrassed by their scores. Jordan and Miles were cleaning their knives and workstations. Deuce walked over to Miles. "We need to talk," he said quietly, and they stepped away and stood by the judges' table. After the two men spoke, Deuce reflected on the four chefs. He liked Miles. He was respectful, jovial, and connected with people, but a Jekyll and Hyde persona made Deuce, as a producer, nervous. Tristan was young and arrogant but had the needed sex appeal. Lola was cute but a complete disaster, and he wondered again how she had been selected, even as a last-minute replacement. Finally, his thoughts turned to Jordan. She had the qualities needed, but her timidness and shyness were detractors. Nevertheless, he decided to pay close attention during the cooking class to see if any of them had the spark he was searching for.

Kennedy was in the lobby waiting for the small group to gather for their excursion into Mahahual. She was surprised to see Bert as the first to arrive. He was wearing one of his favorite T-shirts. It showed a camera wearing a cape, and the caption read: *I can freeze time. What's your superpower?* "Bert, are you going to the cooking class? Do you have time?"

Bert smiled and straightened his shoulders. "Art requested I go, and you said I needed to help out."

The corners of Kennedy's lips went up. "Your helpfulness is to be commended, especially as it seemed such an *imposition* in the beginning."

"Well," Bert said, turning red, "I didn't realize she'd be so pretty and smart, and—"

"Art, how did it go this morning?" Kennedy blurted out, seeing the pretty redhead walking up to them with Deuce.

Deuce motioned for everyone to gather. "Today, we will travel to Mahahual to a friend's restaurant, where he will teach us the secrets of cooking foods native to this area. Then, we will prepare several dishes we will share at lunch.

It will be a good time for us all to open our minds and close our mouths," he said, looking pointedly at Tristan and Lola.

Kennedy waved them off and turned to go to the conference room for the morning staff meeting. "Sorry, I was seeing off the passengers," she said as she dropped into her chair.

"We've already gone through our lists, Kennedy," Franklin said. "I'm sorry we didn't wait for you, but there wasn't much to share. How is the competition going?"

"We've had a few hiccups, but nothing unsurmountable." She turned to Mila. "Can you fit Emily Abbott in tomorrow? I know it is last minute."

"I'll take care of her myself, so anytime she wants to come will be fine," Mila said, writing Emily's name down in her book.

Kennedy turned to Michèle. "Chef," she began.

"No, non, nein, nee," he said emphatically, crossing his arms and glaring at her.

"You forgot tak," Mila giggled.

"I'm not sure, Kennedy, but I think Michèle is saying no. Although we haven't heard the question," Franklin said dryly.

"She's going to ask me to allow that writer woman in my kitchen." He looked Kennedy in the eye. "The answer is no."

Kennedy held up her hands defensively. "Don't kill the messenger. I promised I would ask. And as I heard it, you were the one who suggested she see you 'conduct' in the kitchen."

"Who won this morning?" Luke asked.

Kennedy shook her head. "I didn't get to go," she turned her head, "Michèle?"

The dark man uncrossed his arms and rubbed his hands up and down his face. "Jordan, hands down. The others were a train wreck." He shared what had happened, and they listened in rapt attention.

"What are the plans for the rest of the day, Kennedy?" Omar asked, looking at his watch. He hoped he would have time to get off the boat for a little while to make a private call.

Kennedy shrugged her shoulders. "Everyone is in port, including Bert, who is taking photos of the chef's excursion. Art asked, and he couldn't say yes fast enough."

There were snickers around the room. Luke clapped Franklin on the back. "I guess it's time to have the big talk with him, Pops. Of course, if you need my assistance, let me know, as I am the resident ladies' man."

Omar turned his attention to Luke. "Speaking of being a ladies' man, I understand a certain writer has been seen frequently in the Vantage Point Lounge. Be careful, Luke," he said solemnly, "for all of our sakes, she may come across as friendly, but she's looking for things to write about."

"She's already latched onto the Butlers," Kennedy sighed, "and confirmed what happened earlier this year. I'm not sure how she found out about it." Luke looked down at the pile of papers in front of him. The room was uncomfortably silent, and Kennedy cleared her throat. "We pull anchor at six, followed by dinner and a show in the theater." She grinned. "Twenty musicals in one night."

"Twenty?" Franklin repeated. "I could stand in the back and see twenty musicals in one night?" He rubbed his hands together. "What time should I be there?"

Rosemary punched him in the arm. "Not so fast, big guy. You promised we would see some when we got off the ship."

"But, Rosemary, didn't you hear her? We can do all twenty," he trailed off when he saw Rosemary's glare, her arms crossed, and her mouth set. "I guess that's a hard no, huh," he said sheepishly. He hurriedly changed the subject. "What time should our teams be ready for Operation Elf?" he asked.

They went through the logistics of decorating the ship for the holidays. Billy would meet the maintenance and housekeeping teams at the storage lockers as soon as dinner was underway to begin bringing up the boxes and staging them in the back corridors. Michèle and Ano shared that they had plenty of snacks and cookies for those helping, and Luke would bring drinks.

"Just keep me away from the glitter," Franklin said grumpily.

"Why is that, Franklin? You always leave a little sparkle when you leave the room," Luke laughed.

"Ooh, Franklin, you should try less bitter, more glitter." Michèle chuckled and patted the big man on the back.

Franklin rose from the table and turned to leave, but then he stopped and turned around. He batted his eyelashes and outlined his body with his hands. "You can't handle all this sparkle." The group broke out in laughter, some clutching their sides, others wiping their eyes as tears fell down their faces. While the group was laughing, Omar quietly slipped out of the room.

"That was probably one of the best adventures I have ever had," Marshall sighed. He was reclining in a lounge chair under a cabana. "I haven't done anything like that since I was a young man."

"They didn't have automobiles back then, did they, Marshall? It must have been tough with your mule and cart," Paulie chortled.

"Uphill both ways in the snow," Eddie added, his voice muffled by the towel over his face.

Marshall shook his finger in the air, "Just wait until you two are as old as I am and have to hang out with a bunch of punks." He looked around. "Where's that pretty girl with the drinks? My pineapple is empty, and I need another one, and I hope she brings it with those little umbrellas."

"Easy there, Pop. You may not have tasted it, but there was a lot of alcohol in that drink. I don't want to push you back to the ship," Karl said, getting up. "I'll get us another round of drinks, but I'm having a virgin one made for you, Pop."

"Make it a regular one, son," Marshall said, "Either way, you will have to wheel me back to the boat, and on the upside, if I'm passed out, I won't be talking."

"Good point," Karl said, leaving to get another round of drinks.

Paulie motioned to Larry. "I'm going to take a walk on the beach; do you want to go? We might see some bikinis," he waggled his eyebrows.

"Sure," Larry said, "although if we meet anyone wearing one, I'm sure they will tell me I look just like their favorite toy: a soft, old, worn-out teddy bear.

They walked a while chatting about everyday things when Paulie asked, "What do you think about Lola?"

Larry looked at him, puzzled. "What do you mean? She's a nice girl, keeps us fed, and tolerates us on poker night. It was a great idea to come on the cruise to cheer her on."

Paulie interrupted him, "Let me go about this another way. What do you think of older guys like us dating younger women?"

Larry shrugged. "It doesn't bother me. I mean, it wouldn't happen to me, but…" He trailed off, realizing what Paulie was trying to say. "Oh."

The two men were silent. The only sound between them was the roar of the waves.

Larry swallowed hard. "I didn't know the two of you were involved."

Paulie cocked his head to the side and looked at Larry. "We've been keeping it quiet for the last few months. I have a feeling her business will dry up once everyone finds out, but then I could help out more financially. She wouldn't need to work."

Larry held his hand out to stop Paulie. "What do you mean more?"

Paulie shrugged. "I help her out here and there. Like this morning, she was so busy getting ready to come on the cruise; she forgot to stop at the bank to get money. I didn't want her going into port without any cash; she might want to buy something."

Larry's thoughts were bouncing like pinballs in his head. "Paulie, take some time to think about it before you ask her. Being out of our normal schedules sometimes makes us do crazy things. Did I ever tell you about the tiki bar I once bought after too many rum punches?"

The two men turned around to walk back to the cabana. "No, I don't think you have ever shared this greatest moment. This has to be a doozy."

When they returned to the cabana, they found Marshall snoring softly, a paper umbrella tucked behind his ear, and his hands wrapped around a pineapple. Larry picked up his things. "I'm going to head back to port," he announced. "I've been thinking about one of my clients today."

"All right, mama bear," Eddie waved to him. "We'll see you at dinner."

Larry returned to the café near the port and ordered another cup of coffee. While on the walk, he had composed the message he wanted to send in his head. He typed the note and hit send, hoping he was on a wild goose chase.

"Chef Jordan," Monique said softly, "first, thank you for your time this afternoon. I've watched you in the competitions and looked forward to our chat. You are a bit of a dark horse." Jordan shifted uncomfortably in her chair. "Let's start with some easy questions to get you comfortable." She noticed Jordan fidgeting with the sleeve of her shirt. She pointed at Jordan's arm. "Your tattoo is fascinating."

Jordan looked down at the long chef's knife made up of tiny flowers that ran along the scar on her arm. Jordan pulled her arm in and rested the tattoo against her stomach.

"It's just a tattoo," she said in a low tone, and Monique felt a door slam shut.

Monique bounced around, asking Jordan about the restaurant and if working in a male-dominated world was difficult. She wanted to show the kitchen as a sexist warzone. "Some of your colleagues in St. Augustine describe you as a badass. There is a rumor your workout routine involves lifting slabs of beef from the refrigerator to the counter."

Jordan rolled her eyes. "Good grief, it was a side of lamb. I'm just a chef, doing her job, working with a team to make memorable meals for people."

Monique switched gears, "Let's talk about the other competitors."

Jordan was taken aback. She did not feel it was right to speak about the others. "I'm not comfortable with this discussion."

Monique bent her head to the side and shrugged her shoulders. "The others had no problem sharing their thoughts. Tristan had quite a bit to say." She leafed through her notebook and read Tristan's words out loud. When she was finished, she saw Jordan rub the long scar on her face.

"Poor Chef Miles had a rough morning. I heard he fell asleep yesterday during your cooking demonstration. I hope it doesn't happen in his restaurant. It could be dangerous." Jordan remained silent, which perturbed Monique. The interview was not going the way she had planned. She touched her pencil to her forehead. "Just a few more questions. Where did you go to culinary school?"

For the first time during the interview, Jordan smiled at Monique. "I didn't go to culinary school. I learned on the job."

Monique looked down at her notepad. "In Oregon, right? You had some difficulties out there, didn't you?" Monique watched Jordan flinch.

An iron wall went up inside Jordan, and she stood up to leave. "If you would please excuse me," she said shakily. "I suddenly feel drained from the competition and the day in port."

Monique smiled. "Well, I hope you feel better soon." Before Jordan could take three steps, Monique spoke again. "Jordan, the choice is yours. Either I can piece together what happened in Oregon, or you can tell me your side of the story."

Kennedy had never seen something go as disastrously as the afternoon's cooking demonstration. She had heard from Art that things had gone relatively well at the cooking class in

Mahahual. Despite Tristan's sullenness at being forced to attend, the others had enjoyed their time as they cooked and sampled chicken pibil, grilled fish in banana leaves, and ceviche. After watching the events of the cooking demonstration unfold before her eyes, she was grateful it had been poorly attended, as many passengers had not returned from the port to see the demonstration. Deuce was so angry with Lola and Tristan that he told them to stay away from him until the following day.

As soon as she could leave, she went to Mila's office to share what had happened. Mila listened in fascination as Kennedy repeated the insults traded, how Lola became covered in avocado sauce after turning on a blender at Tristan's request, and the end of the show, which featured Tristan taking a large gulp from a plastic cup and then frantically searching for a trashcan.

"All of this happened in front of the passengers?" Mila asked.

"Yep," Kennedy answered slowly. "And a lucky few were also covered in avocado sauce."

"So, how did this end? What did the passengers think?"

Kennedy blew out a breath. "What could I do? I apologized to the audience and invited everyone to the pool bar for some complimentary SunRumbrellas. Ano found me and said the cup smelled like fish sauce." She looked at Mila and rolled her eyes. "Apparently, it's an old culinary trick." Kennedy began to giggle. "I wish you could have seen Lola standing there covered in green muck. She looked like a bowl of guacamole with false eyelashes."

Mila let out a dramatic sigh. "Great, now you have ruined taco night for me. Whenever I take a spoonful of guacamole, I'll see it blinking at me."

When the blender spewed its green contents all over Lola, she was mortified and crushed. She had hoped Deuce Dawson would see she had the stage presence he needed for the show. Getting the job would solve some problems that might soon explode. "I've been looking for you. I wasn't sure where you went," she heard a rough voice say.

Lola smiled crookedly. "Hi Eddie, I'm sorry you have to see me like this," she held out her green splotched chef's coat. "As you can see, Tristan made a fool out of me."

Eddie laughed. "He's trying to rattle you, kid. After you ran off, he drank something from a cup, and whatever it was must have been terrible. He puffed his cheeks out like a blowfish and ran for the trashcan. Now, go dry your eyes and take this." He placed a roll of money in her other hand. "Go to the shop downstairs and buy yourself something pretty to wear tonight. My mother always said looking good was the best revenge." He brushed a piece of avocado out of her hair. "Now, go buy something to knock everyone's socks off. That's an order."

She hugged him and saluted. "Aye-aye." She turned around after taking a few steps, rushed back, and kissed him on the cheek. "Thanks, Eddie. I promise I'll be the belle of the ball tonight."

"Well, well, well," Monique said, watching Lola and Eddie from where she sat, her face hidden by her wide-brimmed hat.

While the Tristan and Lola show was imploding, Miles was on his way to meet Monique Patrick for his interview when he saw Dr. Craig on the pool deck. "Miles, how are you today?" he asked with a tinge of concern. "I understand there have been some hiccups yesterday and today. And I also know you haven't been by to pick up your medication. You should remember—"

Miles cut him off. "Doc, I had a couple of setbacks, but I'm fine, and everything is under control," he said tersely.

"I don't need a mother hen telling me when to take my medicine. I had one of those until a few weeks ago. And I certainly don't need any of your psycho mumbo-jumbo. Now, if you'll excuse me, I'm late for an interview. I'll stop by your office in an hour and get the rest of my medication. After that, I won't require your assistance any further." He brushed past Dr. Craig and went quickly up the steps plastering a smile on his face.

Monique noticed Miles was flushed when they shook hands and sat down.

"Where do you want me to start?" he asked anxiously.

Monique blinked, and her face showed surprise. "I guess, just talk and I'll listen and try only to interrupt if I have a question."

"Great!" Miles said, and he began to speak animatedly, crediting his mother for his love of cooking, his education, and being her sous chef.

When Monique brought up the allegations about Miles's involvement in a Ponzi scheme, he laughed and explained it had been a misunderstanding between his bookkeeper and some potential investors." He waved his hand. "No big shocking story, I'm afraid. Just a mix-up." Monique's next question was about the fire that had destroyed a restaurant Miles had been on the brink of opening. Miles turned pale, and Monique saw sweat glisten on the top of his head. He caught her eye and ran his hand across his crown. "The sun is strong today. I should have worn my hat; I'll be as red as a tomato tonight," he laughed uncomfortably. "There's not much else to say, a rag caught fire, and the whole place burned to the ground. Old news, I'm afraid. So, if that's all," he said, rising from his chair.

Monique could tell she had hit a nerve, so she changed direction and held up her hand, "Just a few more questions, and I am sorry about those last two, but the rumors are out there, and I won't be the only person to ask you about them. You always need to know the direction of the bullets, don't you? Let's try something a little lighter. What's your favorite ingredient?" she asked.

Miles, caught off guard, slowly sat back down in his chair. "My favorite ingredient?" he repeated thoughtfully. "An onion." Monique burst out laughing and settled back in her chair as Miles told her about the magic of onions. "My mother made me practice my knife skills on onions. I have always believed she had ulterior motives for making me practice on them. It gave her an unlimited supply of prepped onions for the restaurant, and it also assured her that no girl in high school would go near me because I reeked."

Monique laughed as she scribbled, "Now *that* is a story I can write about. Let's talk about the other chefs in the competition. Have you formed any opinions?"

Miles let out a whistle. "I'm not sure I am comfortable with this question. It doesn't feel right."

Monique raised her eyebrow. "Miles, you are the most qualified of the four of you. You must have thoughts. What if you described them as types of people you might find in a kitchen? Would that work?"

Miles nodded his head. "I can do that and teach you some culinary lingo. Are you ready?" Monique gave him a quick nod as she held her pencil over her pad in anticipation. Thirty minutes later, Monique looked down and saw that she had filled several pages of her notebook. He looked at his watch. "And now I do have to go," he said with regret. "This was a pleasure, other than those very awkward questions."

Monique shrugged her shoulders slowly. "Unfortunately, it's a part of my job. I would be careful, though, Chef Miles. The skeletons in the closet always seem to come out when you least expect them."

"I'll try to remember that," he said and turned to walk away.

Monique wondered about Miles's statement about an apology but let it go. She paged through her notebook. It had been a productive day, and now it was time to seek out her handsome bartender to see if he had more to share.

Omar and Emily arrived at the captain's table, and he introduced her to David Stearns, who was sitting opposite her, explaining that in addition to being a travel writer, he was also a friend of Kennedy's. "The three of us can go for a walk later, Mrs. Abbot. I believe you may already be acquainted with some of David's friends through Vera," Omar smiled. "They have an unusual club, and one member has a company which caters to a very," he looked at David, "unique clientele?"

"Wait! Are they the—"

Omar held his finger to his lips and smiled.

Suddenly, the captain and David both gasped. "It appears that the Butlers have arrived," the captain pointed his head toward the entrance. Terri and Jones stood at the podium with a pale Tony. Jones's black jacket featured brightly colored embroidered flowers down the sides and across the back. While his outfit was bold, it was Terri who was stealing the show. The black bustier she wore under her satin bolero jacket was trimmed in yellow fringe, which danced with every move she made. Her long legs, encased in satin pants split to mid-thigh, were embellished with the same fringe, going from red at the hip to yellow at the cuff.

"She looks like a cross between a tassel and a mariachi band," Emily breathed. "I want to stop looking, but it's like when you pass a traffic accident. You can't help but stare."

The captain laughed good-naturedly. "That is generally the effect the Butlers have on people."

"Ah, it looks like our last guest has arrived," the captain stood as Tony escorted Monique Patrick to her seat at his table. "Ms. Patrick, welcome. We are delighted that you could join us."

"My apologies for being late. I found myself very engrossed in my work." She looked at David. "I learned something about you today."

David looked at her and smiled. "If it's that I am fabulous, it's true. And I have no secrets."

"No?" she pressed, arching an eyebrow

"None," he said evenly.

Realizing he would not rise to her bait, she turned to Emily. "Good evening, Mrs. Abbott. I must say I am looking forward to our interview tomorrow. There is so much for us to talk about."

Lola entered the dining room wearing a short orange sequined dress and strode purposefully past where Miles and Tristan were seated and stopped at the table where the Gents from Breezy Bayou sat. "I think it's high time I sat with my fan club," she called out loudly enough for Miles and Tristan to hear. "Do you have room for me?"

"If not, you can sit on my lap, toots," Marshall wheezed. He maneuvered his wheelchair out and patted to a spot for her on the banquette."

"That is a stunning dress, Lola," Karl said quietly.

"It is," Paulie said slowly. "It fits you like a glove." Both men were unable to take their eyes off her.

"Eddie? Larry? Anything to add?" Marshall asked. "Or are you both so tongue-tied you have forgotten how to compliment a lady." Eddie's face flushed scarlet, and he took a drink of water. "Larry? Earth to Larry, come in, Larry," Marshall wheezed. "You're staring at Lola as if she had two heads."

Larry had been scrutinizing Lola, trying to see if she resembled the woman in the photo. Because the picture was blurry and taken at a distance, he could only ascertain that both women were petite and had long brown hair.

He shook his head. "I'm just speechless in her presence."

"Where did you get the dress, Lola?" Paulie asked curiously. "It looks like one that was in the gift shop window."

Lola looked down at her dress. "Oh, this old thing?" she smiled, "No, it was in the back of my closet, just waiting for a special occasion."

Larry sat back in his seat. He could see the back of the dress and, barely peeking out from the top of the zipper, the price tag, with the name of the ship's store. He wondered why Lola would lie about it.

"She may not be able to cook her way out of a paper bag, but she certainly cleans up well," Tristan said, pointing at Lola.

Miles turned to look at Tristan. "Did I hear right? Your cooking demonstration had to be shut down?"

Tristan turned red. "That's not what happened."

"Then what did?" Jordan asked as she slid into her seat. "I heard Lola got a face full of pureed avocado, and you got a mouthful of fish sauce."

"Who told you that?" Tristan sputtered.

Miles began to laugh. "I haven't thought about the old fish sauce in the cup in years. We used to do things like that to whoever was slacking in the kitchen in culinary school."

Tears smarted his eyes, and he pinched the bridge of his nose. "Salt in the coffee, chocolate dipped garlic cloves, and my favorite, mayonnaise crème brûlée, oh, the good times."

"Frozen aprons and cayenne pepper on the back of the neck," Tristan added, snickering.

Jordan shook her head. She was glad she had missed the hazing which often took place in culinary school and larger kitchens. She watched Monique get up from the captain's table, "How did your interviews go with her?" she pointed her head at Monique.

"Fine," both men said simultaneously.

"Did she...was it…" Jordan groped for the words. "Does she remind you a bit of a spider?"

Miles understood what Jordan was asking. "She seemed to go back and forth in my interview. It started with easy questions: school, work, the restaurant, and then, out of nowhere, she hit me with some sensitive topics, trying to shake me up. When I pushed back, she changed the subject and wanted to know my favorite ingredient." He scratched his head. "I still can't figure out how she found out about some things."

Tristan puffed out his chest and put his hands behind his head. "She was pretty easy with me. But, then again, she was so busy checking me out that she forgot some of her questions." He lifted an eyebrow. "When we started the interview, I was changing out of my jacket into a T-shirt. All she could do was stare at my abs and these guns until I suggested she start asking her questions." He patted his stomach and flexed his biceps. "It's a good thing I kept her distracted, though; there are some stories that, as you said, are better left untold."

The Solstice Theater was packed, and the cast was backstage in a state of nervous excitement. As the opening music began, Kennedy placed her top hat on her head and strutted onto the stage. "Ladies and gentlemen," she said, spreading her arms wide, "we welcome you tonight to the Solstice Theater. Join us as we take you through twenty musicals in one night. So, sit back, relax, and sing along with us." She tipped her hat to them. "And Willkommen," she said in German and began to sing the famous song from *Cabaret*. The cast, dressed similarly to Kennedy in black vests, shorts, and bowler hats, joined her in the chorus as the curtains raised. When they finished, the audience rose to their feet, clapping. While the dancers ran offstage to change for the next song, Vitor, the pianist from the Lunar Lounge, and his piano were rolled out. Kennedy picked up the red feather boa lying on the lid and draped it around her neck as Vitor began to play the opening bars of a risqué tune from the musical *Chicago*.

"Excellent," Omar said quietly.

"Oh, my goodness," David whispered behind his hand. "John would die if he saw the opening number. This is very clever." He turned to Emily. "He's the owner of Club Diva and the absolute *queen* of the club." He turned his eyes back to the stage. "And if Phil ever sees Kennedy perform this song, he'll hide in his dressing room."

"Why would Phil hide in his dressing room?" Emily whispered back. "You haven't told me about your friends, and I only know the little bit Vera told me. But she's a bit of a prude and didn't go into any details. How long have you known Kennedy?"

David turned to her. "Tomorrow, when you go to the spa, I'll go at the same time. I'll tell Anna Marie to book us together, and while we are there, I will tell you stories you won't forget."

As Kennedy finished her song, she rushed off the stage, handing her hat and feather boa to Mila's assistant Anna Marie who was waiting for her. "I'll be back for these in a few minutes. I need to make sure things are going well with the holiday decor." She stopped for a second. "Are you okay? You look upset." Anna Marie shook her head and waved her hand at Kennedy.

She raced across the hall and into the dining room, which now looked like a cross between a holiday decoration store and a shipping warehouse. She would check on Anna Marie later. She spied Billy. "Is everything up from the storage lockers? Did you have any trouble with the freight elevator?"

Billy grinned. "We were lucky. Franklin keyed one of the elevators off so we could get everything up quickly. We need to make one more trip, but I've organized everything by outlet." He began pointing to different sections of the room. "I left the rolls of tape down there, so we know where they are when we pack everything back up in a few weeks. And I've told everyone to put the plastic wrapping around the trees back in the boxes so we can reuse it when we take everything down. Now I understand why nothing moved around inside. There is a ton of packing material in those boxes."

"Good idea," Kennedy said. "Hopefully, it won't be a pain to rewrap everything."

Billy saw Tony over Kennedy's shoulder. "Oh, and be warned, Tony is having a conniption fit, and he's coming this way."

Tony charged up to her. "I don't know what I was thinking when I agreed that you could use the dining room for the Christmas setup. The glitter and fake snow will be everywhere. The passengers can't see it this way." He began flapping the lapels of his suit coat.

Kennedy thought he looked like a chicken ruffling its feathers. "Tony, relax. Would you please show Ano the tables you want us to use for the food and drinks?"

"Yeah, yeah, of course, I can do that," he looked around distractedly, "I just need to figure out where." He left muttering, half walking and half running in a zigzag pattern.

"Wow, for a minute there, I was afraid I was going to have to go down to the shop and get some duct tape to strap Tony to a chair," Franklin said, walking up with Luke.

"What about Christmas lights?" Luke asked, setting down several boxes. "We could put him in his desk chair and spin it around and around."

Kennedy looked at her watch. She had thirty minutes before she had to get back to the show. "Okay, let's gather up," she called out to the group. "First, if you can't find me, ask Billy if you have any questions. He knows as much about the plan as I do."

Billy, hearing his name called out, straightened his shoulders.

"Rosemary, I need you, Franklin, and your teams to set up the lobby area. There is a lot to do, and you have the largest teams. Here are the pictures and the diagram of where everything goes."

Franklin squinted at the paper and then put on his reading glasses. "Is that really a giant Christmas ornament in the middle of the lobby?"

"It's not as bad as you think, Franklin," she said, handing him a diagram and the assembly instruction.

"Of course, you have a diagram," he growled.

"Two sides and a top, and it's pre-lit, so all you have to do is plug it in once you put it together. Then, Rosemary and her team will come behind you to fluff up the trees, add the snow, and set out the presents."

"Where do you want us?" Mila asked and wiped some glitter from Kennedy's forehead.

"Can you take a couple of the maintenance guys and set up the Vantage Point Lounge? I have a diagram for you, too." Kennedy handed Mila a sheet of paper.

Kennedy turned to go through the staff passageway door to return to the theater when she bumped into Anna Marie, who had just walked in with a worried look. Kennedy grabbed her hat and feather boa from Anna Marie's outstretched hands. "I was on my way to get her," Anna Marie said, relieved. "That girl…"

"I know," Mila watched Kennedy race out of the room, "she's a hot mess of make-it-happen, learn-on-the-fly kind of girl, isn't she?"

"That's the perfect definition of her," Franklin said. "She makes it happen. She makes me crazy half of the time, but she makes it happen." Then, he turned to Rosemary. "Ready, Rudolph?" he asked, noticing Rosemary's reindeer antlers and red nose.

"Ready, Santa," she grinned.

"Well, let's go," he said and let out a hearty, "ho-ho-ho."

"And he hasn't had any eggnog yet," Mila said to Anna Marie. "Heaven help us when that happens."

Kennedy had a few minutes to catch her breath before the last two numbers. When they had been mapping out the show, the team approached Kennedy and asked that she sing the song, *Thank You for the Music*. Her solo would allow them time to don their costumes for the finale.

Vitor returned to center stage again and bowed as his piano was pushed out to him. He sat down, and as soon as he did, Chris turned out every light in the theater except a small pool over the piano. Vitor began playing a light intro, and

Kennedy took her place beside the piano and set her hat on the lid. Omar sat forward in his chair. She began singing in a clear, controlled voice, and he was mesmerized.

"My God," David sighed, and the entire theater seemed to be holding their breath as she poured out her soul. When she finished, every passenger jumped to their feet in thunderous applause.

Emily caught Omar wiping his eye. "Dust," he said.

"Is there nothing that the girl can't do?" Emily asked over the din of applause.

Omar grinned. "Cook," he chuckled, "the girl can't boil water."

"Well, thank goodness she has a flaw."

Music came out of the speakers, and the cast came out in their outrageous costumes, clapping their hands over their heads to the beat. "Ladies and gentlemen," Kennedy said into her microphone, "we ask that you remain standing and dance with us as we close out this fantastic night."

When the confetti cannons exploded, showering the audience with colorful paper, Kennedy saw the captain off to the side, giving her a thumbs up. She walked over to him. "I don't know how you pull these things off," he said to her, "but I'm awfully glad you are on my ship."

Kennedy was euphoric, the show had been a success, but she knew she needed to calm down before entering the dining room. "Thank you, Captain. If you'll excuse me, I need to get some holiday decorations up before tomorrow morning."

He looked at her and grinned, making a sweeping gesture with his hands. "By all means," he said, "we can't keep Christmas from coming."

Bert knocked on Art's cabin door, and she opened it. "I'm sorry, Bert," she said, "I know I said we'd have a drink, but I'm not going to be able to make it." She looked over her shoulder at her computer screen and then back at him. "There's too much to do."

He grinned. "Come with me for a short walk, it will clear your head, and I promise you will see something magical."

Art looked at him quizzically. "*Magical*?"

"I'll have you back in less than fifteen minutes, but I can't promise you won't want to stay," he said mysteriously.

They began to walk down the corridor. "Wait," she said, "I forgot my video camera! I never leave without it."

Bert paused. "That's a great idea. Do you have a still camera I could use?"

Art was confused, but she grabbed both cameras from her cabin and followed Bert to the elevator. He pressed the lobby button, and she looked at him oddly. "Bert, I have a ton of work to do," she said impatiently and pressed the button to go back up to her cabin, but when the doors opened, her eyes widened, and she sucked in her breath. Standing in the middle of the lobby was the outline of a white and gold Christmas ball. "It's got to be ten feet tall," she said in awe. She walked toward the shimmering ornament. On each side, a forest of Christmas trees twinkled in a bed of glowing white fluffy snow.

"It's twelve feet tall," Franklin's deep voice boomed from the side. He strode over to stand beside Art and Bert. "Would you like to be the first to have your photo taken?" he gestured to the camera in Bert's hand.

"Really?" she turned to him, and her eyes were filled with wonder. She grabbed Bert's hand. "Come on," she said giddily.

Franklin looked through the viewfinder and smiled.

"Franklin, what are you doing?" Rosemary called out impatiently. "We have work to do. We don't have time for you to play photographer. That's Bert's job."

"Run while you can," Franklin whispered.

Omar, David, and Emily went straight to the Vantage Point Lounge for a nightcap after the show. Omar noticed the spa attendants straightening out the branches of a gathering of Christmas trees near the wall of windows. He pushed his glass back and slid off the barstool, holding his hand to Emily for her to get down. "I have something to show you. Remember how I said we all pitch in to help?" Emily nodded. They walked down the corridor to the elevator and descended. When the doors opened a few seconds later, Emily gasped.

"What on earth is going on?" She turned around open-mouthed.

Franklin cleared his throat. "Welcome to Operation Elf."

"But why are all of *you* doing it?"

Franklin looked uncomfortable. "As I understand, there were some budget cutbacks, and the holiday decorating labor allowance was struck. Kennedy has been working on it for a few weeks, and we were all drafted."

Omar's radio chirped. "Base to Mr. Meier, we have a situation in Longitudes, sir, and need your assistance."

Omar sighed. "Emily, I am so sorry. I must leave. Duty calls." He looked at David, "Would you escort Mrs. Abbott back to her cabin?"

"Nonsense!" Emily turned to Franklin. "I want to help. What can I do?"

"Are you sure?" Franklin asked. "It's glitter and sparkles and…" he trailed off, seeing Emily's face. "Just remember, you volunteered."

David grinned. "I'll pass on all this magic and return to my cabin. Club Diva gives me all the glitter and sparkles I need."

Omar took the back staircase and entered Longitudes from the staff entrance. "I didn't know what to do, sir," the security officer explained anxiously. He had been standing at the back door, keeping an eye on the intoxicated man to ensure he didn't endanger himself or anyone else. "I figured we should handle him differently since he was with the competition."

Omar nodded his head and sighed. They walked into the bar where a very intoxicated Tristan was half sitting and half standing on the barstool. "Hi there, officer," he slurred. "My friend, Miles, do you know Miles? He's an excellent chef, but he's got this problem: he's always falling asleep. He told me about this bar, but they won't serve me anything else to drink. What kind of place is this?" he asked drunkenly.

Omar got a hand around Tristan's arm. "The kind that stops serving when people get too drunk." They eased Tristan off the barstool, through the back area, and into the freight elevator. Tristan chattered aimlessly.

"Chef Tristan, have you ever played the quiet game?" Omar asked. "The three of us will see who can be the quietest, and whoever *is* will win a special prize."

"What sort of prize?" Tristan asked.

"Shhhh," Omar held up a finger to his lips and pressed the button for Tristan's floor.

The elevator doors opened, and they walked a stumbling Tristan down the corridor. "How am I doing in the game?" he whispered loudly as he bounced between the two men.

"Shhhh, almost there," Omar said.

"Ha-ha!" Tristan yelped in glee, shaking his finger drunkenly at Omar. "I made you talk. You lose!" He stopped for a second and then hung his head. "Uh, oh, I think I lost too because I talked." Omar was thankful they were near his cabin. The guard opened the door while Omar held Tristan upright and marched him inside. He let go for a moment to shut the door, and Tristan fell face-first into his bed, snoring.

"What is it with these guys, sir?" the guard asked.

"I wish I could tell you," Omar answered. "At least he was a friendly drunk." He looked at his hands which had something black on them. "What is this?" he asked, holding them out.

The guard shook his head. "I'm not sure, sir. It looks like a black plastic residue of some kind."

Omar brushed his hands off on his handkerchief and pointed at Tristan. "Hourly wellness checks, please. I'm going to make my rounds."

He entered the dining room and saw that the dining room was almost empty of décor, and people were playing games and eating. "Looks like Operation Elf was a success," he said, walking up behind Kennedy, and she whirled around.

"Where have you been, Private Meier? Didn't you offer to help?" she asked, her eyes glowing.

"Putting one of your chefs to bed," he answered and saw her look of apprehension. "Tristan this time, and he's a friendly drunk. We took him to his room, and he was asleep before we shut the cabin door." He turned to her. "Would you care to take a quick stroll? I'm not one to stick around for these kinds of things."

"Certainly," she said, her heart suddenly racing.

Suddenly, a large crash and a yell came from the kitchen area. Everyone stopped in their tracks, and a few rushed to the kitchen. "It's Chef Ano!"

Omar pushed the swinging door open, and Kennedy, Rosemary, and Franklin were steps behind him. Ano was lying on the floor, wincing, and holding his ankle. "I'm fine, guys," he said, embarrassed. "I landed on my foot wrong. I'll be fine if someone will help me up." Michèle extended his hand, and when Ano put his weight on it, he yelped.

"Kennedy," Omar said quietly, "would you please call for Dr. Craig?"

It took a few minutes for the doctor to arrive. He knelt beside Ano, lifted the bag of ice, and made a face. "I need a wheelchair," he said to Omar and turned his attention back to Ano. "I don't think it's broken, but you won't be on your feet until we get back to Port Canaveral."

"I could sit in the wheelchair and—"

Dr. Craig cut him off, "Let's find out what is wrong before we decide how you will work, okay?" He looked at Michèle and Omar. "I'm going to get things set up in the infirmary. I'll meet you there."

The wheelchair arrived, and Franklin and Michèle carefully lifted Ano into it and wheeled him out of the galley and into the dining room. He blushed as he received a kiss on each cheek from a housekeeper and one of the spa techs.

Kennedy saw Emily Abbott off to the side. She had been cleaning up the party debris. "I wasn't sure where the trashcan was, and I didn't want to bother you," she said.

"I am so sorry, Mrs. Abbott. I completely forgot that you were here. You shouldn't be doing this."

Emily waved her hand. "Kennedy, it's quite all right. Tonight has been incredibly exciting. I saw twenty musicals in one night, walked through a winter wonderland, and helped with the holiday decorating." She held her hand up to cover a yawn. "I will admit, I am a little tired and should probably go to my cabin. And don't worry, I can find it on my own. I don't need an escort."

"Give me just a moment," Kennedy said, and she raced over to Franklin and Rosemary. "Franklin, would you mind escorting Mrs. Abbott to her cabin? Rosemary and I can clean up."

"I like this kind of trade-off," he said. "I'd be happy to," and he pinched Rosemary on the nose. "Good night, Rudolph."

She smiled, looking up at him, "Good night, Santa."

Franklin walked over to Emily and extended his arm. "Your escort, my lady."

"OOOO, the silver fox escorting me to my room after midnight, just wait until I tell Vera about this," she giggled.

# Sunny Dayz Cruise Line

## THE HELIO

### DAY FOUR

COZUMEL, MEXICO

ARRIVAL 7:00 A.M.

DEPARTURE 4:00 P.M.

Kennedy was watching the sunrise on the pool deck when the *Helio* dropped anchor in Cozumel. She saw Franklin and his team already up early, dismantling the competition set so they could move it to the main theater.

"Can I do anything?" she asked Franklin, who was lying on his side loosening a bolt.

"Stop having great ideas?" he growled. "Somehow, your great ideas mean I get extra work."

"I think it's time for me to go."

"Wise idea," he said dryly.

She took the elevator down to the main dining room and saw Tony standing at the host stand.

"If you are going in the galley to get coffee be careful. He's a very active volcano this morning."

Kennedy entered the galley and saw the terrified looks on the culinary team. "Chef, may I get some coffee?" she asked. Michèle, distracted, waved his hand at her in disgust. "How's Ano?"

"Ano is fine. A badly sprained ankle, and now I have his job and mine to do." His eyes bulged, and his cheeks filled with air as he slammed a tray of pastries on the counter. "How am I supposed to oversee the kitchens, take care of the dinner service, and judge the competition?" he snarled.

Kennedy quickly poured her coffee into a paper cup and returned to the dining room.

"You aren't kidding," she said to Tony, who was shaking two antacid tablets into his palm. "I'd stay and try to diffuse the situation, but something tells me whatever I say will be wrong."

"Coward!" Tony whispered and went to console a server who had come out of the kitchen in tears.

Kennedy made her announcements about Cozumel and then stepped into the lobby. She looked forward to seeing the passengers' reactions when they saw the transformation. However, it was Kennedy who was surprised when she saw Bert taking photos of passengers inside the giant ornament.

Kennedy visited with the Gents from Breezy Bayou before they departed for the day. They were going on a tequila distillery tour, and Marshall was trying hard to get Kennedy to go with them.

"Come on, toots; they won't miss you for a few hours. I'm told I get more handsome with every cocktail." Marshall waggled his bushy white and brown eyebrows. "Just imagine how good I'll look after a couple of tequila shots."

Kennedy laughed, "Oh, Marshall, you are quite the card. Unfortunately, today is my day to mind the ship while we are in port." The others chuckled, and she looked at the group curiously. "Aren't you missing someone?"

Paulie explained that Larry had decided to stay behind as one of his clients was in crisis. "It's not like it can't wait two more days," Paulie snorted. "It's restaurant consulting, not brain surgery." He looked at the others. "All right, time to get moving, gentlemen," and they bid Kennedy goodbye.

Kennedy heard Terri Butler's squeal before she saw the couple. "Jonesy, do we have time for Bert to take pictures of me?" Jones nodded and walked over to Kennedy. "Quite the decorating job this morning, Kennedy. How did you get all of this done so quickly?"

"Oh, some elves stopped by for the night," she said.

"Think you can get any elves to come to Mississippi to finish up Tara? I could use them, and I pay in more than hot chocolate and candy."

Kennedy tilted her head and smiled, looking up at the enormous snowflakes above them. "Sorry, Jones, just like Santa, this was a one-night deal."

Terri bounced up breathlessly. She looked beautiful in a navy-blue top with a white sequined anchor and a blue and white long striped skirt. "Reporting for duty, sir," she saluted Jones.

"Ahoy, matey, are you ready for our next adventure?" he asked. Terri gave him a wide smile, and Jones explained they were going on a submarine tour. "It's the only one of its kind, and it takes you to one of the largest reefs in the area. Terri's hoping to see an octopus." He wiggled his fingers, imitating one. "She loves those crazy things." As they took their leave of Kennedy, Bert sauntered over.

"How's Ano?" he asked.

Kennedy sighed. "Badly sprained ankle. I left just as Michèle was deciding whether he would have a volcanic eruption or a pity party."

Bert looked at her and shrugged. "As long as Ano stays off it, he should be walking in a few days. It's a shame he can't just switch places with Chef Michèle and be the judge." He laughed. "Wouldn't it be funny if a sous chef was one of the judges? Especially as this is the Sous Cruise?"

Kennedy's eyes lit up, and she planted a huge kiss on Bert's cheek. "Bert, you are a genius! Why didn't I think of that?"

Bert began wiping the spot where Kennedy had kissed him. "I don't know what I said, but I don't need Art seeing any lipstick on my face, Kennedy. Why do you have to wear such a bright color?"

Kennedy began to talk a mile a minute to herself. "I need to clear it with Chef Michèle and Dr. Craig and get Deuce on board, but it might work. Oh, and Ano. I need to get him to agree, but that shouldn't be hard." She looked at Bert, who was staring at her uncertainly. "I'm so sorry. My mind is whirling. Thank you, thank you, thank you!"

Bert bowed. "My pleasure, and now I'm going to find a bathroom to scrape the rest of your lipstick off before Art sees it. There's no telling what she will think."

Kennedy raised her hand to him absently and was still scribbling on her clipboard when Emily Abbott walked up. Dressed impeccably in a pair of black capri pants, a black silk blouse, and several long strands of pearls around her neck, Emily looked regal. "Good morning, Kennedy. I trust all is well this morning."

"Yes, ma'am," Kennedy answered. "I was writing down some notes for a last-minute change to tonight's competition." She caught Emily's look of distress. "It's okay," she said quickly, and she shared Bert's idea with Emily. "What do you think?"

Emily clapped her hands. "I think it's a lovely idea and will give the competition a little punch. It should be an interesting competition tonight. Deuce shared that it is a mystery basket. That should put the chefs on edge. Do they know?"

Kennedy shook her head. "Don't forget you have the interview with Monique Patrick late this afternoon."

Emily let out an irritated sigh. "That woman is repulsive. She was at the captain's table last night and took over every conversation."

Kennedy gave her a wink. "I have come up with a plan to cut your interview short. I'm going to interrupt and say there is an important meeting about the competition and take you to the spa."

"Sneaky," Emily grinned. "I like it. Do you want me to bring you back anything from this pearl farm Vera talked me into being part owner of?"

"Good morning, Mrs. Abbott. I hope you are well," Omar said, walking up to the two women.

Kennedy looked at him strangely. "Good morning, Omar. I didn't expect to see you down here this morning."

"I need to bring you up to speed on some things before our morning meeting."

Emily looked at Omar and winked. "On that note, I'm going to learn about harvesting pearls."

"Is everything okay?" Kennedy asked after Emily left.

"All fine, I simply wanted to…" he paused, "I wanted to say good morning and tell you I enjoyed the show last night." He cleared his throat and looked at his watch. "I suppose we should go to the conference room for our meeting."

Kennedy was confused but didn't show it. She thought Omar was going to say something else. "Go on without me. I need to catch Deuce Dawson before they go into Cozumel. I want to see if he would be comfortable with Chef Ano filling in for Chef Michèle as a judge tonight and tomorrow. Michèle was torn on which role he would play this morning: tyrant or victim. I didn't stick around to find out which one he decided on."

"Ano as one of the judges is not a bad idea," Omar mused. "Although, will Chef Michèle be willing to give up the limelight? He has enjoyed being the celebrity."

Kennedy found Deuce waiting for the others. He had arranged for the chefs to go on a food tour of the city. She told him about the accident and the idea of having Ano fill in as a judge. "I don't know if it will cause issues with the network, but it will take some of the pressure off Chef Michèle."

Deuce beamed. "I think it's a splendid idea. Would you like a job with the network? I could use someone who is always thinking on their feet."

Kennedy laughed and pointed at Bert, who was walking up to them. "Actually, you have this man to thank. It was his idea."

Bert blushed. "It was just a thought. I'd hate to be judged by Michèle when he was stressed. It doesn't bring out the best in him," he gulped.

"Now, wait a minute, if Michèle could be really nasty," Deuce began.

"No," Bert and Kennedy said at the same time. Michèle's fiery temper was something Kennedy wanted to keep far from any live or television audience.

She left Deuce and walked quickly to the conference room. "I think this can be a quick meeting," she said, shutting the door and taking her seat. "Franklin won't be here. He's still moving equipment to the theater."

Michèle was making notes on a packet of papers in front of him. "I don't know how I will have time to do all this," he huffed.

"Michèle, with your permission, we have a solution," Kennedy said. "We'd like to ask Chef Ano to judge the remaining competitions."

Michèle looked up. "Ano?" He looked perplexed. "My Ano?" Kennedy gave him a hopeful look, and he turned her words around in his head. "I suppose," he agreed in his thick Haitian accent, "but he better remember he is *my* sous chef and not a celebrity when he returns to the kitchen. I don't need him having a big head."

Those sitting around the table fought to keep a straight face, and Kennedy was thankful Franklin was up on the pool deck. He would not have been able to resist needling Michèle about having a large head—or ego. "Chef, can you share with us what you know about tonight's competition?"

Michèle smiled widely, his white teeth gleaming against his dark skin, "Tonight will be exciting." He rubbed his hands together and explained that each chef would be given a wicker hamper filled with different ingredients. Their task would be to make a main dish from whatever was in the basket. He rocked in his chair and laughed heartily. "Oh, the things Ano, Deuce, and I have put in the baskets— let's just say they aren't for the faint of heart."

"Next item," Kennedy looked around the room, "please thank your staff for their help last night."

"I think everyone, except Tony, enjoyed themselves. It was nice to blow off a little steam," Luke replied.

"Speaking of blowing off steam," Omar began, "there have been a few overserved guests on this trip." He looked pointedly at Luke. "We've had two chefs so intoxicated they needed hourly wellness checks performed. Luke, I can't take my guys away from their security duties to babysit. Please speak with your bartenders."

Luke hung his head. "It's my fault. I'm sorry. I guess I've been distracted."

"Distracted? Maybe it's more that you are attracted to a certain nosy travel writer." Mila looked venomously at Luke. "I can't believe you would share personal information about a friend."

"I said I was sorry, Mila!" Luke shot back.

"What happened?" Kennedy asked, and Mila and Luke glared at each other while everyone else in the room looked uncomfortable. When Kennedy asked if anyone else had any information to share, she only received a collective shake of heads. "Mila, I'll stop by the spa in a little while. I need to update you on Mrs. Abbott."

Twenty minutes later, Kennedy walked into Oaza and waved to Anna Marie. She never tired of looking at the spa. The oasis Mila had created was stunning. She never tired of seeing the muted colors of the fabrics that complemented the rich woodwork, the shimmer of the mother-of-pearl mosaic tiles on the walls that danced off the ring chandelier, and the metallic flecks that gleamed like the night sky in the dark blue floor tiles. Smiling, Kennedy walked through the door that led to the hallway where Mila's office and the private treatment rooms were located.

Mila was standing by the coffee maker and immediately handed Kennedy a cup. "Do I look that bad?" Kennedy asked.

"Well, we could pretend you didn't wash off your eye makeup last night," Mila smirked, crossing her arms and leaning against her desk. "Or we could find some glitter and hide the dark circles that way. Then, of course, you'd look like a showgirl, but, honestly, anything would be an improvement."

Kennedy raised her eyebrow at Mila and blew on her coffee. "What happened this morning? I was afraid you were going to rip Luke's lips off."

Mila began walking back to her desk. "I should. It would serve him right." She sat down and began to pull her hair into a topknot. "Especially if it would prevent him from sharing anything else he shouldn't with his new love interest."

Kennedy swallowed the hot coffee in her mouth, scalding her throat. "What?" she rasped.

"Ms. Patrick came by the spa last night as we were closing. Anna Marie politely explained we were closing but asked if she could help Monique with anything." Mila closed her eyes. "Monique looked Anna Marie in the eye and said, 'I understand visits to the spa can be deadly, especially the sauna. I hear it's hot enough to kill someone.' " Mila blew a stray hair up in the air. "Anna Marie panicked and ran back here to get me."

Kennedy groaned and leaned forward to rest her elbows on Mila's desk. She covered her face with her hands. "Oh, no."

Mila continued. "I found Monique in the retail area and guided her to the private lounge. Thank goodness we were closed, and no one was in there. When she asked the question again, I explained that, due to company policy, I could not discuss the matter." Mila took a large sip of coffee. "I offered to give her an interview about the spa renovation as a peace offering, but she wasn't interested. Then she dropped her next bomb."

Kennedy opened her fingers and peeked at Mila. "What?"

"She said she had heard what an exciting life I had led. She wanted to know what it was like to grow up in a circus family, and then…she brought up my divorce from Stefan." Mila banged her head on her desk. "Even dead, he manages to cause me drama." Mila raised her head and looked at Kennedy. "Luke had to have told her. It's the only thing that makes sense. We've made comments about her always sitting at the bar when he's working, and last night when we were decorating in Vantage Point, there she was, perched on a barstool flirting with him, getting who knows what information about us. He only left her side to fix a drink for one of the servers. It had to have been Luke."

Kennedy sighed. "It may not have been all Luke. I'm afraid she got friendly with the Butlers at breakfast, and Mr. Butler told her about finding the body. And Winnifred in the corporate office mentioned your family."

"Great," Mila sighed. "But it still doesn't let Luke off the hook. He's aired my dirty laundry for some meaningless shipboard romance."

Kennedy sighed. "She played Luke like a violin."

Mila snorted. "More like an entire orchestra!"

The rest of the morning and afternoon went as smoothly as Kennedy could have hoped. She checked on Franklin and his team several times as they moved the four makeshift kitchens from the pool deck to the theater. After her third check of the setup, Franklin barked at her and told her not to come back. Kennedy decided to see if Ano was in the galley. He had reluctantly agreed to serve as a judge once Michèle had given the green light. She found the young sous chef, not in his wheelchair but hopping back and forth between the four wicker baskets sitting on the stainless-steel counter.

Ano blanched when he saw her. "I have ice on it." He lifted his checkered pant leg to show her the bag of ice taped to his ankle.

Kennedy shook her head slowly. "Are you excited about judging the competition?"

"Not really," he said morosely. "I'll do it, but Michèle is the personality, not me." He waved his hands around the massive kitchen. "I'm happy here, behind the scenes making sure things go smoothly."

"Ano!" Michèle bellowed, marching into the kitchen. "Oh, Kennedy," he softened his voice, "I didn't know you were here." He turned to Ano. "You promised to direct what went into the baskets and sit in the wheelchair." He pointed at Anno's wheelchair and brought over a bucket and a fifty-pound bag of rice. Ano sheepishly lifted his foot onto the bag of rice, which acted as a cushion on the overturned bucket. "You need to do what the doctor says, or you will be no good to me later. I'm counting on you to manage the kitchens when I go on vacation *if* I ever get one." He grinned widely, staring at the four wicker baskets. "Should we show Kennedy what is in store for tonight?" he asked Ano. Ano nodded his head with excitement. "You must keep this a secret. Only Ano, Deuce Dawson, and I know what is inside." He walked over and opened the first basket. "Prickly pears, jalapeños, and tomatoes."

"Cactus?" she echoed, looking at the green and pink pad Michèle was holding. "I didn't know you could cook cactus."

"If you are hungry enough, you will eat anything. Imagine how the first person who ever decided to try an oyster felt," he laughed. He told her what was in the next two baskets and then pointed to the last one. "My personal favorite," he said, pulling out a waxy yellow object with long, alien-like fingers. Kennedy shrank back.

"What is it?" she asked nervously.

"Buddha's-hand," Ano replied, looking reverently at the fruit. Michèle handed it to him, and Ano turned it back and forth. "It is a fruit from Asia and a symbol of good fortune."

"But the fingers," she shuddered and waved her own in the air, "are so long and creepy."

Ano laughed. "Sometimes the hand is open," he splayed his fingers and then closed his hand tightly. "And sometimes it is closed. It depends on the fruit."

Kennedy furrowed her brow. "But how do you use it? Other than as a Halloween decoration."

Michèle and Ano shared a smile. "That will depend upon the chef. If they are knowledgeable, they will know exactly what to do." Michèle held a finger to his lips. "Now, time to close up the baskets and remember, not a word to anyone."

"I'm glad this round is being taped," Kennedy said as she watched the alien-like fruit disappear into the basket. "Whoever gets that basket might scream."

Michèle smirked and raised his eyebrows. "They might. Now, I have many things to do," he looked at Ano, "and you need to rest before the show." Ano began to protest, but Michèle held up his palm. "Ano, in the eleven years we have known each other, have I ever told you to rest? Besides, you need to see if you can look as good as I did. This is your television debut!" He walked out of the galley laughing.

During the food tour excursion, Deuce and Monique decided it made more sense to do their interview at the last restaurant on the tour instead of going back on board the ship. Monique watched Tristan leave and blew on her coffee. "I don't believe Chef Colon has ever given an interview before. He behaved as if it was an opportunity to hit on me rather than an interview with a serious journalist. If he wins, you will need to spend time showing him the ropes."

Deuce chuckled. "*Whoever* wins the competition will be given a great deal of preparation for interviews. Unfortunately, I have had my fair share of some which veered off course."

Monique cleared her throat, and they danced around various subjects. She tried several times to get Deuce to tell her who he thought would win, and each time he parried, explaining that each chef had a unique set of skills that could be useful to the show. "That was a very polite deflection," she grinned, finally deciding to give up on the line of questioning. "But, wouldn't it have been easier for you to be the host? The concept was yours, and you *are* a chef." Monique picked up her coffee cup and looked over the rim at Deuce. "I read the article written about you. You were called one of the top ten chefs to watch, and a few months later, you disappeared from the face of the Earth."

Deuce folded his arms. "That was another time." He looked around the restaurant and then at Monique. "However, we are here to discuss our exciting new show *Classic Flavors*."

She put her coffee cup on the table and looked down at her notebook. "The network was kind enough to send over your bio, but in your own words, would you mind telling me a little about yourself and how you became a chef?"

Deuce hunched forward and leaned his arms on the table, spreading his fingers. He told her about working in the family restaurant and gravitating toward the kitchen, attending culinary school, bouncing around the United States at various restaurants, and then switching to join the network's food and beverage department. He explained how, on a whim, he had pitched the idea of adding a cooking segment to the morning show, and the idea had quickly morphed into a show with its own timeslot. However, they still needed a host chef, and Deuce explained to the network executives that he was still searching for one. Unbeknownst to Deuce, during this same time, the network and the cruise line had entered into a partnership and, shortly after, hatched a plan to have a competition on the ship to find the host chef.

Monique was bored. She already had this information from the network. She tapped her lip with her pencil. "What happened after the article was written? When you vanished."

Deuce's eyes snapped open. "I was exploring other avenues. Let's go onto another subject, shall we?" he said flatly. "As you said, the network gave you my bio, and we agreed this interview would be about the competition, not me."

"Okay," Monique said slowly. She was frustrated. Deuce kept blocking her questions and had been very defensive on a few of them. She looked down again at her notebook and then back at Deuce. "Let's talk about your favorite ingredient. I have had fun learning about everyone's favorite ingredient, and I must admit, I'm looking forward to figuring out what mine is when I get home. Chef Michèle loves oranges, and yogurt is Jordan's favorite. Lola told me ketchup is her secret weapon, Tristan, of course, loves butter, and Chef Miles's favorite ingredient is onions, which took me by surprise."

Deuce smiled, this was one of his favorite questions, and he had been asked it many times. Reporters always thought they had a new angle to uncover a secret. "Lemons," he said, "I love lemons. They are one of the most versatile fruits in any chef's kitchen." He spoke of using lemons to perk up the flavors of a dish, making limoncello with his grandfather as a boy, and using it as a household cleaner. "Did you know you can use them to scrub your grill?" Monique shook her head again, frantically writing as Deuce explained how a lemon and some salt could turn a greasy, dirty grill clean again.

"That's quite fascinating," Monique said and quickly changed the subject. "Which restaurant was your favorite to work at?"

"The Wicked Smokehouse," he said reflectively. "I was owner and chef."

"Was it difficult to wear both hats? That must have been a tremendous amount of pressure."

"It had its challenges," he said evasively.

She leaned forward and played with her coffee cup, trying hard to act casual. "What happened? It sounded like it was a successful place."

Deuce waved his hand. "The details aren't important. It ran its course, and something new came along."

Monique persisted, "But..."

"It ran its course," he said curtly. Then, he offered her a forced smile and ran his hand through his thick curls. "I've rambled on long enough about my glorious past, and I thought we agreed to use this time to talk about the new show and the competition."

Monique nodded; she knew she would not get anything more from him. "Then I suppose we should do that."

Deuce was thoughtful as he walked back to port. They had finished the interview on a high note, and he had given Monique a great deal of inside information about the show and hoped she would use it instead of dredging up any old news. The stories of his life's highest and lowest points had already played out in the headlines.

The Wicked Smokehouse had been a smashing success from the moment he opened the doors. As the face of one of the hottest restaurants in town, Deuce's face was frequently captured for the entertainment and social pages of the newspaper. Then, one night, it came to a crashing halt when blue lights appeared in his rearview mirror. The arresting officer stated Deuce had offered her a complimentary dinner at the restaurant if she wouldn't issue him a citation, assuring her he was only a few blocks from home. The officer declined and asked him to step out of the car for a field sobriety test which he failed. After the breathalyzer test at the police station, he was booked for driving under the influence. The spiral continued when the authorities discovered Deuce had received four previous warnings, but no charges had been pressed. Suddenly, questions were raised about bribery, and it was now Deuce's mugshot that was plastered all over the media. The story took on a life of its own and gave readers the juicy gossip they craved. Drawing a judge with little mercy, Deuce spent six months in jail, and The Wicked Smokehouse quickly folded.

He sighed, shoving his hands deep into his pockets. It had taken a while, but he was regaining ground. He hoped Monique would not use his sordid past to sensationalize the story of the competition and the new show. He quickly called the legal department at the network to alert them of a potential problem.

Kennedy was stationed in the lobby to help any of the returning passengers when Monique walked up to her. "Interesting day today," she said. "I assume we are still on for my interview with Mrs. Abbott at four o'clock?"

"I have it set up in the game room on deck eight. Few passengers go in there, and you shouldn't be disturbed."

"I should hope not," Monique said stiffly.

She gave Monique a tight smile and changed subjects. "How was the tour of Cancun's food scene with the chefs?"

Monique rolled her eyes. "It was like a terrible food tour I once took. There was no spice or bite to the dishes we tried, and the tour was as exciting as eating overcooked oatmeal. So, after that food tour, I made a point to always bring my own seasonings in case I need to spice things up." She winked at Kennedy. "Now, if you will excuse me, I need to prepare for my interview with Mrs. Abbott."

Twenty minutes later, Kennedy saw four very strained chefs making their way to the elevators. "Welcome back?" she asked slowly, taking in their faces. "Did you not have fun?"

Miles gave Kennedy a grim smile. "I think I can speak for everyone when I say that while we enjoyed our taste of Cozumel, Ms. Patrick gave us severe indigestion."

Kennedy's brow furrowed. "What did she do?"

The four chefs looked at each other warily. "Let's just say she would have been in high demand during the Spanish Inquisition," Miles offered.

Kennedy bit her lip. "I'm so sorry." She didn't know what else to say.

"Kennedy, do you want to see something funny?" Tristan asked and held up his camera. Kennedy leaned in and saw Lola's lips pursed, her face a cross between horror and disgust as she stared at a fish that had been fried whole with the tail, head, and fins still intact.

"I wasn't expecting it," Lola protested. "I'm used to fillets, not the whole fish." She looked at Art. "He's not allowed to post anything like that, is he? I mean, what if my fans on the network or my followers saw it?" she whined.

"He won't post it, I promise you," Art said, laughing and holding out her hand, making a motion for Tristan to hand over the camera. Tristan gingerly gave it to her and cracked his neck while Art removed the photo.

"I need to relax a little before the competition. I'm going to the gym to work out and then for a swim. Want to go, Miles?" asked Tristan.

Miles nodded. "That's a great idea. And a good way to clear my head before tonight. Jordan, do you want to join us?"

Jordan shook her head. "No, thank you. I'm going to sharpen my knives." She saw Kennedy's uneasy look. "It helps me relax," she laughed.

Kennedy was helping some passengers when she saw Emily Abbott come up the gangway. "Mrs. Abbott, welcome back. How was the pearl farm?"

"It is a long trip, but if you ever get the chance, you should go." She sighed. "I suppose I still have to give that dreadful woman an interview, don't I."

Kennedy smiled apologetically. "We are set for four o'clock in the game room. And as I promised, I will interrupt the interview and ask that you come with me. Then, I'll sneak you down to the spa."

Emily took a deep breath. "Very good. I think I can hold my own for fifteen minutes. Will you go with me? I don't think I've seen the game room." Kennedy agreed, and half an hour later, she knocked on Emily's door. "I feel like Marie Antoinette or Ann Boleyn on my way to meet my executioner," she said somberly.

"I'm sorry, Mrs. Abbott," Kennedy said. "I'll be there as quickly as I can." She tried to lighten the mood as they walked to the game room. "I'm glad you enjoyed your visit to the pearl farm."

"Did I show you what I bought?" Emily asked, and Kennedy shook her head. Emily held out her hand.

"It's beautiful," Kennedy said, admiring the large, irregularly shaped pearl ring sitting in a nest of gold wire.

"I just had to have it," Emily said with embarrassment. "When you are as tall as I am, wearing a dainty ring looks silly, but a piece like this," she held her hand out to admire the ring, "it makes a statement." Finally, they reached the game room doors and saw Monique sitting there. "I hope I make the right statements now. I need to remember she's a writer, not a monster," she said wryly.

Emily entered the room, and Monique stood, and as she did, she pressed a button on the recorder in her pocket. "Good afternoon Mrs. Abbott. I'm delighted you could find time for us to chat today."

"I didn't have much choice, but as I am here, let's get this over with."

Monique touched lightly on Emily's background, her position on the board of directors, and the company's history. "Have you been to the spa?" she asked. "What a beautiful space. It was forward thinking to spend the money in a time when most companies were pinching pennies."

"I am delighted we did it." Emily was beginning to let her guard down, believing the interview was going well. Her eyes darted to her watch and saw she only had a few more minutes until Kennedy would arrive. "With the ships out of commission, it was the perfect opportunity to do the work."

"Given the exorbitant amount of money spent on the renovation, how do you feel about the labor cutbacks? It seems that the staff and crew must work with fewer people and supplies but are still expected to make the passenger's experiences flawless."

"I was not aware of the cutbacks until recently," Emily said defensively.

"Surely the board discussed these issues at their meetings?" Monique persisted.

"It was, but I—"

Monique cut her off. "Did you vote for the cutbacks?"

"I voted the way I thought made the most sense," Emily answered defiantly.

"I wonder if your employees would think those reductions made sense, but then again, I'm sure it doesn't matter to you as long as you get your piece of the profits. I heard the company hired a consultant. What did they tell you after observing the people who work for you? Did they show ways to generate more profits off the backs of your employees? It would be interesting to read the report." Emily bristled at the suggestion, and Monique poised her pencil at her lips.

"Ms. Patrick, I assume you understand we are a private company, and how we choose to spend our money is *our* business," she said evenly.

The two women stared at each other. "I suppose that is why your actions are not questioned," Monique said with a sly smile. Emily broke eye contact and stole a glance at the glass doors hoping Kennedy was there. "I assume you know of the deadly accident in the spa?" Emily's eyes snapped back to look at Monique. "It happened on the first cruise if I'm not mistaken."

Emily was silent for a few moments. "I am," she said stiffly.

Monique smirked. "I would think a scandal about a deadly accident on this ship, especially one that involved someone from the corporate office, might make any traveler wonder if they would be safe on one of your ships. If information like that got out, it could jeopardize the partnership with the network, couldn't it?" Monique saw Emily blanch, and she touched her chin.

Kennedy knocked on the door and walked in. "Mrs. Abbott, I apologize. You are needed in the conference room regarding the competition." Emily threw Kennedy a grateful look and stood up.

Monique stood up at the same time and held out her hand. "Well, wasn't that convenient timing? Thank you for your time, Mrs. Abbott."

Emily ignored Monique's hand and walked to the door Kennedy was holding open. Knowing it was not the time to speak, Kennedy guided a silent and irate Emily to the staff staircase. When the doors closed behind them, Emily asked abruptly, "Are we paying that woman?"

"No, ma'am," Kennedy said quietly. "She is a well-connected travel writer with her own travel agency. She was on the VIP list from Winnifred Wallace in the corporate office. The information I received indicated they were friends. She's writing about the competition and a potential article on cruising."

"Travel writing," Emily huffed, "I assure you her intentions were not about travel writing or writing about the competition."

"Mrs. Abbott, what did she say to upset you?"

Emily shuddered. "Suffice it to say that if she twisted some of my answers, it could be disastrous."

Kennedy took Emily down the two flights of stairs and opened the door a few inches, peeking out. There was no one in the corridor. "It's safe," she said, guiding Emily through the spa doors.

Emily gasped as she walked in. "Why, it's breathtaking."

David was standing at the reception desk holding two glasses of champagne. "I told you, didn't I?"

Emily took the glass of champagne and turned around, her eyes darting in all directions. "Does anyone else know how lovely this is?" she asked breathlessly.

Kennedy shook her head. "Only by word of mouth from the passengers who have been on previous cruises and the photos Bert took for the corporate office several months ago."

Emily looked at David and grabbed his arm. "David—"

He patted her hand. "Don't worry, Emily, between Bert's photos and my melodious words, people will be flocking to the *Helio* simply to enjoy the spa. Now, come with me. Mila and I have a delightful afternoon set up for us." He looked at Kennedy. "Are there any instructions, ma'am?"

Kennedy shook her head. "Please make sure she gets to relax. She just came out of an interview with Monique Patrick."

"Ah, time with Cruella," David said, "It sounds positively dreadful." Anna Marie let out an unexpected giggle and then clapped her hands over her mouth.

Emily shuddered. "That woman would make a pit viper seem docile. And I will certainly speak with Winnifred in the corporate office to tell her how awful her 'friend' is." Emily closed her eyes, drew a deep breath, and slowly let it out. She looked kindly at Anna Marie. "I'm sorry, my dear; I didn't mean to be so rude. I'm here to experience this beautiful spa, which is precisely what I want to do."

Anna Marie came out from behind the desk smiling timidly. "Mrs. Abbott and David, if you will both follow me?"

David chattered as they followed Anna Marie. "Emily, I'm so glad you will get to feel these robes. I don't know where Mila found them, but you will think you are wearing a cloud."

"David," Anna Marie said, "you know the drill."

David smiled, "Yes, and I keep coming back because of *you*." Anna Marie turned bright pink. "She's in love with me," he sighed, making Anna Marie giggle again. Then, he turned to Emily, "I'll see you in a few minutes, and soon you'll feel like a new woman."

Emily changed and stepped into the waiting room. David waved her over, and she sat beside him, sinking into a soft overstuffed chair.

"This is absolute heaven," she sighed.

David smiled, "I love this space. It just begs you to feel peaceful." Emily looked around the room. Every detail had been well thought out. Anna Marie walked back in and asked if they would like more champagne or cucumber water. "Champagne, of course!" David said. "And let's leave the bottle. I need to stay hydrated." Anna Marie rolled her eyes and left the room.

"Now, how did you meet Kennedy?" Emily asked.

"Well," he began, "I think I should go a little further back," and he shared the story of how he, Phil, Steve, Robert, and John had met at Club Diva many years ago and then how the five of them had taken a very young and green assistant cruise director under their wings. "We've been her backstage mothers for so long that when we are on board, we forget we are passengers and not her family."

Mila opened the door. "Hello, you two. Are you ready?" she asked.

David held up the empty champagne bottle. "We are," he said, "but I'm afraid I've talked myself dry," he said playfully, "can we get a refill?"

Mila bit her lips to keep her laughter from coming out. When David drank champagne, he became as chatty as a magpie, and she could only imagine what he had already told Emily. "I'm sure I can find you some more bubbles. I went to the storeroom before you got on board to ensure I had enough. Let's get you settled in the treatment room for the hot stone facial. If David starts to talk too much, Mrs. Abbott, I'll put rocks across his lips."

Two hours later, Emily emerged from the locker room feeling refreshed.

"Well?" David asked.

"I feel positively radiant." She touched her face. "My skin feels so youthful and alive, and all of my tension is gone."

David nodded and patted his face. "I agree. I cannot wait to write this up. People will book reservations on the *Helio* just to try the facial."

The passengers began to trickle back on board, and Kennedy ran into Terri and Jones Butler, who raved about their submarine excursion. Terri described the submarine and the fish they had seen. "And I had time to do a little shopping for my outfit tonight." She held up a white bag.

Jones winked at Kennedy. "We *always* find time to buy jewelry, but she never has enough time to wear it."

As Terri dug into the bag, pieces of tissue paper floated onto the floor, and Kennedy bent down to pick them up. Coming up from the ground, she gasped as Terri dangled her necklace in Kennedy's face. At first, Kennedy was unable to understand what she was looking at.

"I just thought, after spending the day looking for one and seeing nothing but clownfish, eels, and sharks, I should have my very own," Terri said. "You know what it is, right?"

"It's an octopus." Kennedy shuddered inwardly. The necklace looked menacing. The eight metal tentacles seemed to writhe and intertwine around each other, and she pictured them sliding across Terri's collarbone.

"Wait until you see it on her tonight. My mermaid on land."

Terri yawned. "Speaking of which, this mermaid needs a nap by the pool before dinner. Kennedy, what is the show tonight in the theater?"

"Tonight, the chef's competition is our entertainment, and I hope Deuce doesn't have them making dishes with octopus," Kennedy said mischievously.

Terri looked perplexed. "Kennedy, you can't cook an octopus," she said huffily, putting her hand on her hip. "Can you?"

"Come on, Sweetsie," Jones put his arm around her, "let's get changed for the pool, and I'll explain what calamari is."

The four chefs arrived promptly at five o'clock in the Solstice Theater and inspected their cooking stations to ensure everything was how it had been on the putting green. Deuce turned around and clapped his hands to get their attention. "Chefs, you will each receive a mystery basket at the beginning of tonight's competition."

Lola was adjusting the cuff of her white ankle sock and echoed him, "Mystery basket?"

Deuce ignored her. "Inside your basket will be items you will use to produce a main dish. I will tell you now that some items you find may be unusual. You will have fifty minutes to complete the challenge."

"Fifty minutes?" Tristan gasped. "That's a weird amount of time."

Lola rolled her eyes. "Math is obviously not your strong suit. Five minutes to decide what to make and forty-five minutes to cook it." She turned to Deuce. "Am I right?"

Deuce quickly hid his smile behind his hand. Lola may not have been formally trained, but she could think on her feet. He motioned to the racks and mobile refrigerators. "As usual, extra ingredients and supplies will be available for your use." He looked at four very strained faces. "I'm sure this feels overwhelming, but it will show how versatile you can be."

"It will also give the audience top-grade kitchen drama," Lola said smartly. "I've watched these on television."

"Chef," Miles broke in, "are we expected to be on display again tonight in the dining room? After learning what tonight's competition is about, I need time to focus. Being in a noisy dining room with people coming up to me to pepper me with questions is going to make it hard to prepare."

"We thought about that," Deuce said, looking at Kennedy and then back at the four chefs. "If you sit at your regular table for a few minutes, Kennedy will announce that tonight's competition will be in the main dining room before the dinner service begins. You can stand, wave to the passengers, and then leave if you wish. Will that work?" The four chefs bobbed their heads in agreement. "Chefs, good luck. Please be at the theater's front doors at twenty minutes before eight."

The four chefs were quiet as they watched Deuce walk up the aisle. "What do you think will be in our baskets?" Tristan paced back and forth.

"Well, when I've watched these on television, it's just about anything," Lola replied. "I remember haggis being used on one show."

Miles nodded. "Squid ink, maple syrup, beer."

"Beer?" Tristan echoed and clasped his hands together. "Please let there be beer in my basket."

"You are supposed to cook with it, dumbbell," Lola chuckled. Then, she turned to Miles, "How will you decide what to do?" she asked sweetly.

Miles ran a hand against the back of his head and neck. "I'll open the basket, sort things out, and figure out a plan." They were all quiet for a while as they contemplated the upcoming challenge.

"Jordan, are you okay?" Miles asked.

Jordan didn't answer. She was breathing hard and rubbing the long scar on her arm.

"Jordan!" Lola yelled, and Jordan looked at her, startled.

"I-I-I'm sorry," she stammered as three faces stared at her.

"Where the heck were you? And who the heck is he if he is making you breathe so hard? I need to meet him," Lola snickered.

She shook her head. "Sorry, it was nothing—anxiety about tonight. What were you saying, Miles?" she cocked her head at him.

"I've got to get out of here," Tristan said in exasperation. "You guys are going to make yourselves nervous wrecks. I need to clear my head; I'll see you in a few hours." He walked up the aisle, throwing punches in the air.

"Good evening, Kennedy," the captain said, walking up to her as she stood by his table. "Are you sitting with us tonight?"

Kennedy smiled hesitantly. "No, sir, I wanted to make sure your table was situated before I went to the theater to make any last-minute adjustments for the competition." She craned her neck around.

"Are you looking for someone in particular?" he asked.

"No...yes..."

"Is that a no or a yes?" he asked patiently and began looking around the dining room. "Is there a problem I should be aware of?"

She let out a sigh of relief when she saw a laughing David enter with Emily Abbott on his arm. "Mrs. Abbott's interview with Monique Patrick was less than smooth," she shared. "I'm concerned Ms. Patrick will antagonize her at dinner."

"It appears our writer friend, David, has her well in hand. And I'll keep Mrs. Abbott occupied for the evening. I'll tell her my stories of the sea." He laughed. "They are so dull they will put her in a stupor, and she won't remember a thing about her interview with Ms. Patrick." He suddenly began coughing. "Good grief, what is Mrs. Butler wearing tonight?"

Kennedy whirled around, and as she did, she could see and hear the commotion at the podium. Terri Butler stood at the host stand wearing a dress that Kennedy thought was more befitting a prom than dinner on a cruise ship. Ocean blue sequins formed a strapless bodice that hugged her body to mid-thigh. Yards of tulle created the illusion that Terri was standing in a sea of ocean foam. While the dress gave the passengers in the dining room plenty to talk about, the necklace that rested across her collarbone would make them never forget her.

One of Tony's assistants was escorting them to their table when Jones veered away with Terri, making a beeline for the captain and Kennedy. "Captain," Jones said, "what do you think about my mermaid on land?"

The captain took Terri's hand and kissed it. "As usual, Mrs. Butler, you leave us speechless."

"Kennedy, do you know where we are sitting? I wasn't sure if Tony had changed our seat assignments tonight," Jones looked longingly at the captain's table. "We *are* VIPs."

"I believe you are at your regular table Mr. Butler," the captain said hurriedly. "Mrs. Butler should be seen by everyone in the dining room tonight, not tucked away at my stuffy table." Terri smiled and fluttered her eyelashes, and the captain held his arm out to her. "May I escort the beautiful mermaid to her table?" When he returned to the captain's table, he saw Kennedy trying to hold back a giggle. "Not one word, Kennedy," he said and stood near his seat. "Good evening Mrs. Abbott, David. How are you both?"

"To be honest, I'm a little envious of Mrs. Butler's dress, Captain," David said, stifling a giggle. "I'm only glad John and the others aren't here. There may have been a catfight."

"Please, let's sit down," the captain gestured. "David, why don't you sit on the other side of Mrs. Abbott." Then, he turned his attention to Emily. "How was your day today?"

Kennedy whispered to David, "Please have Mrs. Abbott in the theater a few minutes before eight." He gave her a quick nod, and Kennedy walked away, looking at her watch. She would wait outside of the dining room for the chefs. When she walked through the dining room doors, she scanned the corridor for any of the chefs and heard loud whispers from behind a grouping of Christmas trees near the entrance. "Please, I'm begging you, please leave the past where it is. What happened was a terrible accident."

"Have you considered what will happen if you win the competition? You can't hide forever."

Kennedy began muttering loudly as if to herself. "Good grief, where are those chefs? We are supposed to introduce them in a few minutes." She walked up the corridor opposite where Monique and Jordan stood and turned back toward the dining room doors.

"Monique, thank goodness you are here," she said with forced enthusiasm, noting Jordan's mottled face and swollen eyes. "I wanted to apologize. I have been so wrapped up with these competitions that I have completely neglected to make sure you have a good seat to watch them." She pretended to look at her watch. "Do you mind coming with me into the theater? You could see where you would have the best vantage spot, and I could reserve the seat for you." She turned to Jordan. "You don't mind if I steal her away, do you?" Jordan shook her head, unable to speak.

Monique was momentarily taken aback at Kennedy's offer. "That would be lovely, Kennedy," she said, "but I'm sure I need to get into the dining room soon, as I am at the captain's table again tonight."

Kennedy kept her eyes on Monique and asked Jordan to have the other chefs wait with her until Kennedy returned. "I need to announce them again," she explained to Monique. "I'll take you through the back passageway between the dining room and the theater. It may even give you another angle to write about: the secret doors of cruise ships." She gestured for Monique to follow her, and they made their way to the Solstice Theater. Kennedy opened the doors and said, "I also realized we haven't introduced you to the passengers." Kennedy could feel Monique begin to preen, and she rambled on, "Having someone of your travel and writing stature is a real coup. May I introduce you this evening?"

After Kennedy and Monique left, Jordan blew out the breath she had been holding and walked to the restroom. She had a feeling that Kennedy realized something was wrong, and she needed to get Monique away from Jordan as quickly as possible. Jordan looked at herself in the mirror and touched the jagged scar on her face.

Kennedy swiftly took Monique through the theater, and Monique chose where she would sit for the show. "I appreciate your taking care of me personally, Kennedy," she sniffed. "I felt you and I had started out on the wrong foot."

"And I do apologize for that, Ms. Patrick. Only a few hours before we met, I learned of my additional duties about the competition, as Winnifred would not be joining us. I'm afraid I was not initially told how important you were." Kennedy motioned to Monique. "Let's go this way," and she led Monique through the backstage area and down a corridor. "This is one of the passageways the staff uses to get around. It's not the most attractive area, but it gets us where we need to be quickly. We can pop out of a door and look like we appeared by magic."

Monique looked around and saw carts full of dishes, glassware, and linens. "Are there many of these passageways?" She looked at the scuffed walls and the dark industrial flooring and turned Kennedy's words around in her mind. Secret passageways could be an interesting angle.

"Plenty," Kennedy laughed. "I've been known to forget about some of them after I've been on a break." She turned a dial and pushed open the door. From the dining room side, no one would have known the wall was a hidden door. It looked like the other wall panels. "And here we are." She escorted Monique to the remaining seat at the far end of the captain's table, where the first officer and a few others sat. They stood, and one held out Monique's chair. "Captain, my apologies. I detained Ms. Patrick. I wanted to ensure she had a good seat for tonight's competition." The captain gave her a curt nod, trying to look stern. Kennedy turned to Monique and said loud enough for the captain and the others to hear, "As I said earlier, I'll introduce you after the chefs. I am so embarrassed I didn't do it sooner." Emily looked at Kennedy oddly. "You don't need to do anything but stand and wave from your seat. It will make it easier for people to find you during dinner." Kennedy turned back to the captain. "Sir, I am afraid you may experience some disruption during dinner as passengers will want to meet such a renowned travel writer."

David understood what Kennedy was doing. He leaned over and whispered to Emily. "You don't have to worry about dealing with Monique anymore. Making her feel like a celebrity and introducing her will keep her busy all night and all day tomorrow with the passengers."

"Ms. Patrick," Omar said after Kennedy had left the table, "your scarf is quite unusual, I have seen that print before, but I cannot place it."

Monique fingered the black and cream silk scarf wrapped around her shoulders. "It's a vintage Hermès scarf, a gift from a client I had arranged a safari for. I was unable to go with them due to another travel commitment, but the scarf was a token of their gratitude."

"It is lovely. May I see the pattern?" Omar asked, and Monique took the scarf off and held it out. "It's quite unusual with the leopards. My mother had one. She never wore it, but she would take it out to look at it."

"That is a terrible shame." Monique shook her head, and her ivory earrings swayed back and forth, "I believe things like this are meant to be shown off." Then, she turned her attention from the scarf to Omar, "Tell me, what is it that you do on the ship? You don't wear a uniform like the captain or his staff."

Omar smiled widely. "My apologies," he said, "I am Omar Meier, and I am the director of security."

Monique's eyebrows went up, "Oh, I have some questions for you. I was going to ask Kennedy, but having the director of security answer them will be much better."

Dinner in the main dining room had just gotten underway when Kennedy took the microphone to introduce the chefs again and talk about the competition, which would be held in the Solstice Theater that night. She had been a little concerned about the four chefs as she introduced them. They seemed very subdued, and she hoped it was nothing more than nervousness due to the theme and new location, as they would be in front of a larger crowd. "I hope you will attend tonight's competition," she said to the passengers, "as I am told it will be *mysterious*." Chatter suddenly filled the dining room as the passengers wondered what Kennedy's cryptic comment meant.

"Gentlemen!" Lola said enthusiastically after Kennedy had announced her, walking up to the table where her friends were sitting. She winked at Marshall. "How are my good luck charms tonight?" Lola looked stunning in a short navy-blue strapless dress.

"An outfit like that, they shouldn't even bother to show up!" Marshall wheezed.

"Oh, Marshall, you are too much sometimes!" Lola giggled. "I wish I could wear this onstage." She clicked her champagne-colored satin and rhinestone shoes together.

Marshall blew out a weak whistle as he looked at the shoes. "Wow," he said slowly, "those must have set you back a penny. I don't ever remember seeing them before. And believe me, I would have remembered those little rhinestones around your ankles. They are bright enough that even my old eyes can see them."

Lola rolled her eyes. "None of you ever pay attention to anything I'm wearing when I'm cooking. All you care about is the food." She put her hands on her hips. "So, am I going to get any good luck kisses from my fan club?" she asked.

"Of course!" Eddie immediately stood up and pecked her on the cheek.

"Bend down and let me lay one on you." Marshall pulled Lola into a tight embrace and puckered his lips.

Karl cleared his throat. "Pop," he said quietly, and then he spoke louder when Marshall was still hugging Lola and placing wet kisses all over her face, "Pop!"

"What? You heard her, she said she needed her good luck charms, and I'm covering her with good luck."

"Come on, you old coot," Paulie pulled Lola out of Marshall's arms, "it's time she had some good luck from a real man. Knock'em dead, kid." He hugged her and looked meaningfully into her eyes.

Karl, startled by Paulie and Lola's embrace, squeezed her upper arm and said quietly, "Good luck, Lola."

"Where's Larry?" Lola pouted. "It won't be good luck if I don't get it from all of you."

"He went into the business center to see if a message had come through," Eddie answered.

"Whoa, it must have been important if that tightwad was spending money to use the ship's computers," Paulie chuckled.

"It's probably a dire emergency, like what color napkin to use," Marshall rasped. "Those people won't make a decision without running it past him."

Lola put her hands on her hips. "Well, you can tell him I'm mad at him," she said in a petulant tone. "And if I don't win tonight, it's all his fault."

"Lola, would you like to join us for dinner?" Karl asked. "We aren't sure if Larry is going to show up."

"Gosh, I wish I could," she looked at him apologetically. "I've got to get changed for the competition. I'd hate to get anything on this dress. I just wanted all of you to see me in it."

"Maybe you could wear the shoes so these old eyes can follow you onstage." Marshall pointed a shaky finger at her shoes. "The stage lights would make them twinkle."

Lola gave Marshall a quick hug. "That's a perfect idea, Marshall! The judges will be so distracted by my shoes that they won't notice what any of us make!" She smiled and waved goodbye.

"She's something else, isn't she?" Marshall said reflectively. "If I were thirty years younger, I'd sweep her off her feet. No offense to your mother, son."

About halfway through the dinner service, a distracted Larry joined the group. "All okay with the bear cubs?" Eddie chuckled, seeing Larry's grim face.

"Fine," he said tightly, "just some information I need to sift through."

"Is there a china pattern that isn't perfect or a linen catastrophe? At some point, these people will need to learn how to make decisions on their own," Paulie chided.

Larry plastered a smile on his face. He needed to have a difficult conversation and wasn't sure how to do it. Did he have the discussion individually, embarrass one friend, and possibly lose their friendship? Or would it be better to share the information with the group? It would affect them all one way or another. Whichever way he did it, there would be hurt feelings, and what had started as a relaxing and fun cruise would become a bitter memory.

The four chefs were backstage. "Why are we so anxious tonight?" Lola peeked out into the audience. "I'm ten times jumpier than before the other competitions."

"Maybe because it's evening, and we are in the main theater?" Jordan offered as she shook out her arms. "The other two competitions were on deck, in the daylight, and with a much smaller crowd."

"What a bunch of drama queens." Tristan snickered and rubbed his hands back and forth quickly. "Why are you so nervous? I've told you since we met that this will come down to myself or Miles, and based on my television star looks and sex appeal, it will obviously be me."

"Good grief, Tristan," Lola said, rolling her eyes, "you need a ladder just to get over yourself!"

"Look on the bright side, Lola," Tristan smirked, "you'll always be able to tell your fancy clients you competed against me...and lost"

Emily Abbott, Ano, and Michèle joined the chefs while Kennedy and Deuce entered from the back dressing room area. "Are you ready for us to take our places?" Emily asked anxiously when Kennedy and Deuce joined them.

"Yes, it's time. First, I'll introduce the judges and then the chefs. When you hear me call your name, please walk across the stage and take your seat," she said.

"Before we do," Deuce held out four playing cards, "Chefs, please pick a card, do not look at it until I say so." The four chefs took a card. "Now turn them over. Your card matches your basket. When your number is called, you will take the basket with the coordinating number."

The house lights dimmed, and the spotlight came on. It followed Kennedy as she walked across the stage. "Ladies and Gentlemen, welcome to tonight's third competition for the search for Classic Style Network's new host chef," Kennedy said into the microphone. "Tonight's competition will have all of the elements of the theater." She pointed around the stage. "A little tragedy, a little comedy, and perhaps some choreography as our chefs dance back and forth preparing their dishes." Then, she turned to her right. "But first, let's introduce our judges." Emily, Deuce, and Chef Michèle, wheeling Ano, walked across the stage and waved to the audience. As he did, Kennedy explained that the ship's sous chef was making a guest appearance and would be judging in place of Chef Michèle.

Kennedy once again looked to her right. "Now, please put your hands together for our competitors: Chef Lola, Chef Tristan, Chef Jordan, and Chef Miles." The audience applauded wildly.

Michèle passed Miles, Tristan, and Lola as they walked across the stage. "Nerves are good," he said with a broad smile as he passed Jordan. "They tell you that you are alive."

She looked at him and bobbed her head quickly. "Thank you, Chef," she whispered.

Four members of the ship's culinary staff, dressed in black and white checked pants and black jackets, came across the stage, each holding a large picnic hamper with a playing card taped on the lid.

"Zoom in on the baskets," Art said into her headset to Chris and the others from the ship's audio-visual team.

"Chefs," Deuce said into the microphone, "you each pulled a playing card before you walked out here. Will the chef who pulled an ace please step forward and claim their basket."

Tristan came out from behind his station and flashed his playing card. "An ace for an ace," he said cockily and winked at the camera.

"Number two?" Lola curtsied to the audience and sashayed over to claim her basket.

"I'm glad she wore the shoes. Look at them sparkle," Marshall said, causing several people to turn around.

"Number three?" Miles stepped forward and took his basket. "And last but not least, number four."

"All cameras on each basket!" Art said excitedly into her headset. "I want to capture every moment of this. They have no idea what is inside!"

"But you do, don't you?" Chris said into his headset.

They could hear Art's grin through their earpieces. "I might."

"Ladies and gentlemen," Deuce said, "our chefs do not know what has been provided to them. They must prepare a main dish using everything inside the basket." He turned to look at Miles, Tristan, Lola, and Jordan and said excitedly, "GO!"

The audience gasped at the large screen televisions as the chefs unpacked their hampers. They murmured among themselves as cactus pads, jalapenos, a bottle of wine, and other items began to litter their countertops. Then, there was a loud gasp, and members of the audience started to point at the monitors when one of the chefs pulled something with alien-like yellow fingers out of a basket.

"What the heck is that?" Paulie whispered to Larry, pointing.

"Buddha's-hand, and I hope Lola didn't get it."

"Buddha's what? Hand? What kind of ingredient is that?"

Deuce went first to Miles's station. Art had the camera zoom in on the ingredients he had pulled out. "Chef Miles, what did you receive?"

"Well, it looks like I have pâté, an onion," he opened a plastic container, "pork belly, and a bottle of red wine." He held up the bottle. "Care to join me for a drink, Chef Dawson?"

Deuce and the audience laughed. "If I had those ingredients, I might need a drink first. Any ideas yet?"

Miles shrugged. "No idea, but the first thing I know I need to do is find a corkscrew."

Deuce walked over to Tristan's station. "Chef Tristan, can you describe what you have?"

Tristan looked blankly at the items on his table.

"Chef?" Deuce asked again.

Tristan came out of his fog when Deuce called his name the second time. He had been thinking about the handwritten note he had found under his door. He thought he knew who it was from. He shook his head to clear it and answered Deuce by rattling off the items that littered his counter. "But this, I have no idea what this is." He held up a grayish-brown square wrapped in plastic.

"Chef Ano," Deuce turned to the judges' table, "would you please explain to Chef Tristan what he is holding?"

Ano smiled and spoke into the microphone. "Scrapple, a mixture of minced pork—"

"Oh, that's right!" Tristan cut Ano off and tapped his head. "Temporary amnesia. It must be the sea air." He winked at the audience. "Don't worry, folks. I've got this!"

"Ladies and gentlemen, you heard the man. Let's see how Chef Lola is doing."

"Switching to Chef Lola," Art said into her headset.

Lola was beaming when Deuce reached her. "Chef Lola, what are you going to do with those?" He pointed at the green cactus pads.

She held one up for Deuce to see. "I'm not sure if I should cook this, cut it open and smear it on my face, or plant it." The audience laughed at her quip.

"Any idea what you will make?"

Lola flashed a toothy grin. "I have an idea."

Deuce made his way over to Jordan's table. "Chef Jordan, it looks like something alien landed on your table. Would you tell our audience what that is?" He held up the yellow tentacled item.

"It looks a little like your necklace, Terri," Jones chuckled, and she shivered.

"It's Buddha's-hand. I've never worked with it before, but I have read about it. So, I guess tonight is the night I'll figure out how to use it," Jordan said hesitantly.

Tristan confidently walked to the pantry and took a box of chicken broth. Then he went to where the fresh vegetables were kept and picked up some tomatillos, chilies, and cilantro. Finally, he strolled back to his station. He spread the tomatillos and chilis on a baking sheet and placed them in the broiler. He then turned his attention to the cilantro he needed to chop. As he cut up the leafy green herbs, the paper he had found under his door flashed in his mind.

*A recipe for disaster— Take five parts of sexual harassment and add equal amounts of lies and deceit. It's a wonder you kept your job as long as you did. When I write the article, I doubt you'll be able to get a job at a fast-food restaurant.*

After reading the note, Tristan had torn it up and thrown it in the trashcan. He had just been joking around. It only blew up when management got involved, and he remembered the words said that day.

"A joke?" the general manager said after listing the grievances filed against Tristan. "Your sense of humor is disgusting." He looked sternly at Tristan. "Chef Colon, your service with our restaurant has been terminated, and you are banned from ever stepping foot in here again."

Tristan stood up red-faced. "This place will fall down without me," he said belligerently. "I am the show and the after-party. Diners can't wait for my visits to their table. I am the only reason people come to this overpriced and overrated steakhouse because it certainly isn't for the food." The executive chef pinched the bridge of his nose, looked from the general manager to the human resources administrator, and shook his head. He made a motion with his hand, and a security guard materialized. The guard tried to pull Tristan away, but Tristan shook off his hand. "You'll see how your numbers and profits fall when I'm not here anymore," he spat out. "You need me, you'll see. I am the show! You'll be begging me to come back to bail you out!" Hours later, drunk, he had tried calling several of the cooks and bartenders. Each call went unanswered. "Screw all of them," he said to his empty apartment, "when I am the face of my own show, they'll be begging me for jobs."

Jordan stared at the yellow fruit in front of her. The long fingers made her shudder, reminding her of other long fingers that had clutched her throat and beaten her in drunken rages. "Shake it off, Jordan, concentrate," she muttered. She cut into the fruit, and the aroma of lemons assaulted her nose, and she instantly saw the many lemon-based desserts she had made while healing from her husband's fists. Never saying a word about the blackened eyes or the bruises on her throat, her boss at the diner, whose brother was the county sheriff and a frequent visitor in the small kitchen, would beg her with his eyes to file a domestic abuse report. Jordan couldn't. She was too ashamed to admit she didn't have the courage to leave her husband.

As she sliced into the fruit, she saw the note she had found under her door and replayed her run-in with Monique outside the dining room. *Concentrate,* she ordered herself and shook her head to clear it. She forced herself to look at the other items from her basket: truffles, cream cheese, and chicken stock. Her eyes slid once again to the yellow-fingered fruit. She closed her eyes and heard her mother's voice. *Take the fruit out of the equation. It is merely a flavor or a garnish. Look at the other items. What is the delicacy that becomes the centerpiece?* Jordan's eyes snapped open, and she walked to the pantry and took a bag of risotto off the shelf.

Miles had pondered over the items he had pulled out of his basket. There were so many ways to go. He felt a familiar lethargy settle over him and jogged in place for a moment to wake up. *Don't overcomplicate it. Keep it simple.*

Deuce decided it was time to check the chefs' progress. He walked over to Lola, holding a towel around one of the cactus pads and scraping it with a paring knife.

"Zoom in overhead on Lola, please," Art said and added, "Bert, get some closeups? Especially of her scraping the cactus."

"Chef Lola, what else was in your basket?" Deuce asked.

Lola gave him a million-watt smile. "Well, the best way to describe this basket is that someone went to the grocery store drunk, hungry, and without a list."

Deuce let out an unexpected laugh. "You seem to have gotten over your initial shock of finding the cactus. Have you decided what to do?" Deuce looked at the other items Lola had taken from the pantry.

She put her hand on her hip. "Well, it's a good thing I spent some time in Arizona because it's where I learned how to cook these things." She pointed to the cactus pad on her cutting board. "I had tons of these behind my house and didn't have two nickels to rub together. So, I learned very quickly how to use them." She pointed to the mahi-mahi she had taken. "Prickly pear salsa with mahi-mahi."

Deuce was stunned. He had not expected this level of creativity from Lola. "Chef Lola, we will leave you now. I am pleasantly surprised," he said in wonder, and the audience applauded politely.

"Maybe they'll take our girl more seriously now," Paulie whispered, crossing his arms as he sat back in his seat.

Deuce walked over to Tristan. "Chef Tristan, is everything under control over here?"

"Not only is it under control, Deuce, but I have a song to sing for my chef friends," he pointed at Lola, Miles, and Jordan with a wooden spoon. "I am the champion, my friends," he sang, and the audience laughed.

"Why would you think you are the champion tonight, Tristan?" Deuce asked with a laugh.

"Well," he pointed at the food simmering on the stove, "this recipe, like me, is versatile, creative," he leered at the camera, "and delicious!"

"Would you like to share with us what you are making?" Deuce prodded.

"I think it should be a surprise, Deuce. Unlike my tiny competitor," he pointed at Lola, who had stopped what she was doing to look at him, "I don't want to give it all away so quickly. I want to build some anticipation so the judges' tastebuds will dance when they take their first bite," Tristan said confidently.

"Okay, folks, I guess we will have to wait for the tasting. So, let's move on to see what Chef Jordan has decided to make."

"Zoom in on the creepy, yellow-fingered thing," Art said into her headset, and as the camera magnified the yellow fruit, the audience squirmed uncomfortably.

"Chef Jordan, how are you after your initial shock?"

"All is well, Chef." Jordan looked up, smiling. "I'm going to make something unusual for the judges to taste."

"I think we'll leave you on that note and see how our friend Chef Miles is doing." Miles had been waiting for Deuce and handed him a glass of wine. "Well, I shouldn't," Deuce said. He raised it to the audience in a toast. "To mysterious ingredients and what they will become." He turned back to Miles. "What are you making over here?" He pointed to the parmesan cheese Miles was grating. The smell was pungent.

"I don't have any secrets like our singing chef. I am making a ragu using the pâté I found in my basket. I wonder if it would be a good segment for the new show, how to use up party leftovers."

Deuce nodded. "Not a bad idea." He turned to the audience. "Who amongst us has never thrown away food after a party because we didn't know what to do with the leftovers." He clapped Miles on the upper arm. "We'll leave you and look forward to tasting what you have created from your leftovers." He walked back over to the judges' table. "Chefs, you have twenty minutes until serving. Ladies and gentlemen in our audience, please feel free to get up and stretch, but we ask you not to distract the chefs from their preparations. We will continue to film them and keep it up on the television screens."

Larry leaned over to the others. "I'm going to the Vantage Point Lounge. It's obvious that Lola is going to win this one. Meet me there?" he asked.

"Hey, maybe we should bring Lola for a celebratory drink," Paulie said happily.

Larry hesitated and then shrugged his shoulders. "Sure." He got up from his seat. "I'll see you in a bit."

Deuce called out the three-minute mark, and in what felt like a blink of an eye, the buzzer sounded. "And time," Deuce boomed. "Chefs, please step back from your stations and present your plates to the judges. Chef Miles, you may go first."

Miles walked over with two small plates, placed them in front of Emily and Deuce, and quickly hustled back to get the third for Ano. The pappardelle, coated with ragu, looked lovely with the freshly grated parmesan and parsley. Miles explained how he had made the dish using the ingredients in his basket. The passengers leaned forward as the three judges tasted the dish and smiled at each other.

"Intriguing choice using the pâté as your base. I will need to remember this after my annual New Year's Eve party, and the pasta will soak up any of the night's overindulgences," Deuce said. "Thank you, Chef Miles. You may step back." Emily and Ano scribbled on their scorecard. He looked at Jordan. "Chef Jordan, please come forward with your dish."

Jordan came over to the judges' table carrying three shallow bowls and placed one in front of each judge. She had topped the creamy risotto with a mixture of dark, thinly sliced truffles and shaved yellow curls.

"Chef Jordan, please tell us what you have brought for the judges to try."

Jordan took a deep breath. "Black truffle and mushroom risotto."

Ano took a bite of the risotto. The bright citrus of the Buddha's-hand quickly hit his tastebuds, and then moments later, the rich earthy flavor of the truffles slowly took over. He gave Deuce and Emily an enthusiastic nod.

"What was the most difficult part of your basket, Chef Jordan?" Emily asked.

Jordan was thoughtful for a moment. "Choosing which ingredient should be the focus of the dish."

"It appears you were able to use them both. Excellent job." Emily took another bite of the risotto, and Jordan gave a quick bob of her head to the judges and returned to her station.

Deuce then called Lola forward, and she walked across the stage, her shoes glittering in the spotlights.

"Chris, get behind the judges and zoom in on Lola's plates. Bert, get some stills. This is great footage!" The array of colors on the plates was dazzling, and the theater hummed as the passengers whispered to each other and pointed at the screens.

"I thought your shoes would have been the showstopper tonight, Chef Lola," Emily said, looking at the plate in front of her. "But whatever you have prepared for us appears to be more exciting than your sparkly shoes."

"Go on, try it!" Lola urged, and Emily began to pick up a fork. "It might be easier if you just dig in like this." She took a tortilla chip from the plate in front of Ano and loaded it with the mixture.

Emily looked at Ano, who grinned. "Here goes!" The audience laughed as a hesitant Emily imitated Lola and popped the chip into her mouth. "Oh, my goodness," Emily said, her hand going over her full mouth. She swallowed. "This is delicious!"

Ano took another bite. "The salsa is tart and bright and brings out the flavor of the mahi-mahi. Excellent job, Chef Lola," he said.

Deuce nodded. "This is exceptionally good. The roasted corn is an added plus and gives a delightful taste. You may step back." Lola curtsied to the judges and walked across the stage. When she reached her station, she curtsied again, and the audience applauded.

"Chef Tristan," Deuce said into the microphone, "we are ready for you to present your mystery dish." Tristan didn't answer. Instead, he looked at the three bowls in front of him. He wasn't sure what had gone wrong, but he knew he didn't want to walk over to the judges' table with what he had made. Deuce motioned for the culinary team members to bring over what Tristan had plated up, but Tristan waved him off, placing the bowls on a tray.

He threw back his shoulders. "I've got this, guys. There is only room for the star." He swaggered over to the judges and said to the audience. "Sorry, I was daydreaming of how I would celebrate tonight. After all, when you taste this dish, you will say it was unforgettable." He placed a bowl in front of each judge. The contents were gray with flecks of red, green, and black.

Emily put her spoon in the bowl, and the consistency and color reminded her of wet cement. She looked at Tristan questioningly, and he winked at her. "Brace yourself. When you taste it, it will be a moment you will never forget."

"Before we begin," Deuce interrupted, "would you like to tell us what you made?"

Tristan cocked his hip and placed a hand on it, grinning. "Scrapple chili," he said proudly.

Emily stirred her bowl hesitantly. "Scrapple?"

Tristan raised his hands, palms up. "Yeah, it's like pork."

Ano and Deuce shared a look. "Chef Tristan, would you like to tell us how you prepared the chili?" Deuce asked. "I understand you wanted to build some anticipation, but I'd like to hear about the preparation before your dish dances on my tastebuds."

"Well, I just made it, you know." He cocked his hip and flexed his bicep. "It just all sort of came together in my head."

Emily smiled warily at the audience and then looked at Ano and Deuce. "Well, gentlemen, on the count of three: one, two, three," and they each put a spoonful of the gray-flecked contents in their mouths. Emily quickly grabbed a napkin and put it to her mouth, Deuce took a large drink of water, and Ano swallowed hard. The audience began murmuring loudly.

Tristan was shocked. He had been so confident that substituting the scrapple for the pork would not cause much change to the dish that he had not bothered to taste it. Instead, his biggest concern had been the gray color and consistency of the chili.

Emily was the first to speak. "You are quite right," she pointed to the bowl, "this is a moment I will never forget," and she drew a zero on her scorecard.

Deuce looked at Tristan. "Chef Colon, you may step back." He waited until Tristan reached his station before standing up and facing the audience. "Ladies and gentlemen, our judges have rendered their decisions. Mrs. Abbott, would you please give us the scores?"

"Zoom in on the faces, everyone," Art said quickly.

Emily spoke into her microphone, "Chefs Miles and Jordan each receive seventeen points, Chef Tristan receives two points, and Chef Lola is our winner with twenty-five points."

"Keep the cameras on their faces. This is priceless," Art said urgently. "They are all in shock!"

The four chefs stood there dumbfounded, and suddenly there was a cry from the audience. "Way to go, Lola!" Marshall warbled.

It was then that Lola realized she had won, and she jumped up and down, her hands coming up to her mouth. "I won, I won! Oh my gosh, I won!" She ran over to kiss Deuce and knocked him down in the process. "I told you I was going to knock your socks off!" she hollered into Deuce's microphone. The audience, who had been as stunned as the contestants, began applauding as a red-faced Deuce scrambled to get up. Stunned that Lola had won and humiliated at his score, Tristan angrily wrenched his apron off and threw it on the floor. He shot the three judges a nasty look and stalked off the stage.

Kennedy, seeing the commotion, quickly walked onstage, thanked the audience for attending, and reminded them that the final battle would be the next day. As she was speaking, Lola's fan club raced to the stage to congratulate her. Kennedy watched as Lola left the theater sitting on Marshall's lap while Karl pushed the wheelchair up the aisle.

Miles and Jordan were quietly cleaning their stations. After a few minutes, Deuce, Ano, and Emily walked over to them. "It wasn't anything you did wrong," Deuce said quietly. "Your dishes were delicious and creative." He sighed. "But Lola's was…" he searched for the right word, "inspired."

Jordan picked up what was left of the yellow fruit. "She deserved to win. I blanked when I saw this and got overwhelmed."

Miles crossed his arms and looked at the ragu in the saucepot. "Let's face it; my dish was okay but pedestrian. We get so comfortable with our regular ingredients that we panic and go into safe mode when asked to use something out of the ordinary."

Deuce knocked on the cutting board at Miles's station. "We all do it," he said kindly. "And I will remember your ragu for my New Year's Day menu. It was a skillful use of the ingredients." He brightened. "Tomorrow is our last competition, and I'm sure you will both be back in fighting mode."

Miles looked at the three judges. "One question, just how bad was Tristan's chili."

Ano, Emily, and Deuce exchanged glances. "It was positively the most repulsive thing I have ever eaten," Emily shuddered, "and I have eaten hákarl." Deuce and Ano blanched, but the other two chefs looked at her with puzzled faces. "Fermented shark," she explained. "It's considered a delicacy in Iceland."

"I should go look for Tristan," Miles said worriedly. Jordan put a hand on his arm and shook her head. She had seen Tristan's angry face, which reminded her of darker times in her life. She told Miles that it might be best to allow Tristan time to lick his wounds, especially as he lost to Lola. Miles nodded slowly and picked up his knife kit. "I need to think about how to step up my game for tomorrow." He winked at Jordan. "I intend to win." She laughed and waved goodbye.

"Deuce," Art said, her voice coming through the speakers, "would you come up to the booth? I'd like you to see what I think we should send back to the network for tomorrow morning's show."

Deuce gave her a thumbs up. Then, he turned to the others. "I'd better go. I don't want her to send the footage of Lola kissing me and knocking me down." He turned and walked off the stage and up the aisle.

David stepped out of the wings and motioned for Emily. "I believe my date has arrived to take me out for a nightcap," she announced to Jordan and Ano, who remained. "Hopefully, he won't mind a stop at my cabin so I can brush my teeth. I can still taste Tristan's terrible chili."

Ano looked around. He and Jordan were the only ones still on the stage. "I think my boss forgot me," he said and began maneuvering his wheelchair toward the ramp.

"Can I at least get you to an elevator?" Jordan asked. "I'm not in a party mood, but I don't want to go back to my room yet."

"How about a cup of coffee in the galley? I bet we could find some dessert, too."

Jordan gave him a beatific smile. "As long as there is no chili involved, I'm game. We aren't doing well with that dish."

"Chef Tristan," Monique called out as he blew through the side doors of the theater. "Do you have a moment? It is urgent." She hurried after him and tried to grab his arm, but Tristan yanked it away quickly, and Monique's fingernails made a long scratch.

"Not now," he snapped and walked toward the elevators.

"Pitiful score tonight. Do you think the points you received were out of pity? It seems like things aren't going your way lately."

"What do you mean by that?" Tristan asked caustically, marching back to where Monique stood.

Monique cocked her head to the side and winked. "I think you know."

Tristan shook his finger in Monique's face. "Just leave me alone! You don't know what really happened!" He stormed off and hit a wall with his fist near the elevators. Monique smiled. She would add his temper tantrum to her notes. She had known what she would do since dinner. She would write a fluffy piece about the competition to keep both the network and the cruise line happy which would equal a nice paycheck. She was still toying with the idea of leaking information about the new host chef to whichever tabloid would pay the most. Each competitor had plenty of unsavory baggage they wouldn't want to be disclosed, but by her calculation of points, it was obvious that, short of a miracle, Tristan would not be the winner.

Miles came out of the theater deflated. He had been sure he would be named tonight's winner, especially after Deuce had complimented his ragu, and they had talked about a possible show topic. However, when the points were awarded, he was crushed. He walked past the casino, looking at the doors longingly. *I could go in for a minute, one hand of blackjack with a scotch and water, to take the edge off.* The entire day had been filled with stress. The pestering by Monique Patrick on the food tour, the handwritten note he had found in his room, and then losing the competition. *Just a hand or two of blackjack and a couple of cocktails, I can stop whenever I want.*

Dr. Craig saw the tall chef standing in front of the casino doors. He had watched the competition and had been disappointed that Miles had not won. "Is everything okay, Chef Miles?" he asked with concern.

Miles stiffened. His last interaction with the ship's doctor had not been pleasant, and he had gone to the infirmary after his interview and demanded his medication.

"I saw the show and wish I had been able to taste your ragu," the doctor said sincerely. "Using the pâté that way was genius. I tend to buy pâté when I'm trying to impress someone, and then it becomes the odd moldy thing in the back of the refrigerator I only discover when it begins to smell."

Miles smiled crookedly and hitched the knife kit hanging off his shoulder. "I wish you had been one of the judges, Doc. You would have certainly helped me win."

"Do you mind if I ask how you made the ragu? I saw how you did it, but how did it come together in your head?" the doctor asked. He was trying to keep Miles engaged. "I don't know that I could pull something like that together in front of an audience."

Miles chuckled. "It's nothing more than what you do every day, Doc. I had an emergency of sorts and bandaged it up."

Dr. Craig laughed along with Miles. "Except when people have emergencies and need me, it usually means their vacation has taken an awkward turn. Mostly I tell people to drink plenty of water and stay out of the sun. Don't sell your talent short. You make dishes that bring people joy."

The two men began to walk and talk about food for an hour, and during that time, Miles's brain began to settle down as he spoke about the foods he loved to cook. Finally, he put out his hand. "Thanks, Doc. I appreciated our talk and the walk. I think I was heading toward something that would have caused me more trouble."

"My pleasure, Miles. You know where I am if you need me. And thanks again for the cooking tips. I always forget to add pasta water to my sauce. Now I understand the importance of it."

They parted, and Miles made his way to his cabin. He opened his door and stopped as a strange feeling came over him. He looked around the room. Nothing was out of place, but he felt certain someone had been in his cabin. "I'm losing it," he said to himself. He looked at the note lying on the desk and, picking it up, tossed it into the trashcan. "I need to get out of here," he said and quickly stowed his knife kit in the closet and changed clothes. He decided he needed a long session in the gym. Making his body work hard, clearing his head, and taking a dose of medication would allow for a restful night's sleep.

Not knowing that Dr. Craig had waylaid Miles after the competition, Tristan had gone to Miles's cabin to complain about Monique's ambush. He winced when he pounded on the door, and it swung open as it had the first time he had knocked on Miles's cabin. He had hurt his hand when he smacked the wall, and the side of his fist was beginning to swell. "Miles, buddy, can you believe that Princess Know Nothing won? The sea gods are against us," he said as he walked in and realized he was talking to an empty room. "Hello?" He pulled the door shut and looked around the room, noticing the folded piece of paper on the desk. It looked the same as the one he had received. He opened the note and read the words, putting it back in the exact spot on the desk. Tristan opened the door noticing a couple walking down the corridor. "I'll see you at Longitudes in an hour, Miles. We can drown our sorrows," he said loudly to the empty cabin and shut the door behind him.

Monique had sought out Luke, hoping to pull another story from him. "Good evening Ms. Patrick," he said, looking up as she slid onto the barstool. "What may I get you?"

"A dirty martini and a matching story." She smiled coyly at him.

"I'm happy to get you the martini, but I'm all out of tales from the sea."

"Oh, Luke," she brushed his hand with her fingers, "don't be that way. You are a great storyteller."

He shook his head at her sadly. "I'll be back with your drink." He left to make her a martini which another bartender brought to her. Monique was disappointed. She had hoped to get a few more tidbits out of him. "Oh well," she said, taking a sip of her martini. "All good things must come to an end." She saw Lola and her entourage sitting nearby, celebrating her victory. She noticed that one of the men at the table looked unhappy and stared at Lola with hard eyes. *Is there trouble in paradise with one of the boyfriends?* Monique walked over to the table where Lola sat. "Chef Lola, congratulations. Could you spare some time for me tomorrow? I have a few follow-up questions."

"I'll be around," Lola giggled and downed the glass of champagne in her hand.

When Monique returned to her cabin a few hours later, she found a note under her door.

*Why waste time on things that are in the past? I found something bigger for you to write about. Meet me on deck six at 2:00 a.m. Come alone.*

"Curiouser and curiouser," she said, ripping up the note into tiny pieces and flushing it down the toilet.

Twenty minutes before two, Monique put on her shoes and tied the scarf she had worn to dinner around her neck. She looked at herself in the mirror, shut her cabin door, and walked down the corridor, curious to see who would be on deck six as they each had secrets to keep buried. She felt strongly that the person she was meeting was Jordan. She had the most to lose as an investigation could be reopened. It could also be the spa director, she reasoned. It was convenient that the director of security had been the one to clear her when the man was found dead in the spa. After hearing how the man had treated her, it was feasible. Deuce momentarily flashed through her mind; she had touched a nerve when she had pressed him on the missing years on his resume. There was the slight possibility that Tristan would be there, but she quickly decided he was too self-absorbed to understand the implication of a sexual harassment lawsuit. Finally, her mind entertained the possibility that Miles would be the person waiting for her. There were some curiosities about the fire. The private investigator she used would have the detailed information for her when she returned to Port Canaveral, and Miles had been very defensive when she brought the subject up. As far as Lola, she had a lot to lose socially, but it wouldn't do anything more than force the petite brunette to tell the truth or start over in a new town.

Monique sat at a small table, her scarf dancing around her face in the wind. She clawed it away and unwrapped it from her neck, tying it to the arm of her chair so the wind would not carry it away. She rubbed her arms and walked to the railing while she waited.

"I'm glad you showed up," a muffled voice said behind her. "I was afraid you wouldn't come." A hand held out a cup of coffee. "It's chilly out here, isn't it?" Speechless, Monique blinked and took the proffered cup of coffee. "I wasn't sure how you took it, but it's hot, and after I show you what I found, you will be up all night writing. The cruise line is serving expired food."

Monique was wide-eyed. "What do you mean?" she asked, finally finding her voice.

"Think about it," the voice said. "Feeding all these people day and night can't be cheap, and when we were on our behind-the-scenes tour, I saw something I shouldn't have seen. Come with me, and you can see for yourself."

"I don't know," Monique took a large gulp of coffee. "This seems strange. Why would you do this?" she asked the person in the hooded sweatshirt.

"Because, in exchange for giving you this information and showing you the evidence," the voice said, "you will write a nice story about the competition. No one gets hurt because of what you dug up." The person shrugged. "If you expose the cruise line, who cares? It will be a flash in the pan. It's a company, not a person."

"Just a company," she said slowly. She would still make the network happy, and she could take her time writing the story about the cruise line. She began to see a multi-part series in her head, *The Secrets of Sunny Dayz*. She could use the information she learned tonight, sensationalize the story about the spa director, sprinkle in some make-believe employees, and give them the scandalous stories she had learned when researching the competing chefs. No one would know the difference between fact and fiction. Luke said everyone on the ship had a past of some kind. She felt dizzy for a moment but shook it off, thinking it was adrenaline rushing to her head.

"Finish your coffee, we can't take it with us, and our window of opportunity is closing." Monique felt a tug on her arm. She swallowed the last of her coffee and placed the cup on the table. She was pulled inside to an unmarked door. "Staff staircase," the voice whispered, "it will take us down to the hold where the food is kept." As the door shut behind her, the cup she had placed on the table blew out to sea.

"That's right," Monique whispered, remembering Kennedy's comment about passageways they forgot about. She felt disoriented and thought it was because it was so dark. It took a while to get to the hold, and when they finally reached the bottom, Monique grabbed the railing. "Dizzy," she slurred. "I need to sit down."

"Just a little bit further," the voice urged from behind. Monique felt hands on her shoulders guiding her down the maze of chain-link cages. Finally, they stopped in front of one. "Shhhh," and the door was pulled open. "You can sit in here, and no one will see us. These are the lockers Kennedy uses for her holiday decorations. As soon as you feel better, I'll show you the expired food."

"Won't someone see us?" Monique whispered thickly.

"We were told there is no need for security down here when we went on our tour."

"I think I can get up," Monique said and struggled to get to her feet. "Nope, can't." She patted the floor. "I think I'm going to lie down here for a few seconds until my head stops spinning," she said dreamily and closed her eyes. A few seconds later, she was grabbed roughly under the arms and placed in one of the oversized boxes on the floor. Her hands and feet were tightly bound with plastic wrapping, and plastic and foam packaging was placed around her to form a tight cocoon, rendering her immobile. A hand went over her nose and mouth. She was breathing slowly. The two doses of the drug put in the decaffeinated coffee would keep her quiet for a while, but more would need to be administered. A sock, wet with the drug she had ingested in the coffee, was placed over her lips. Then, a wide piece of tape was stretched across her mouth to hold the sock in place. "I just need to keep you quiet until the ship docks in Florida."

# Sunny Dayz Cruise Line

## THE HELIO

### DAY FIVE

## AT SEA

The following day, a group of passengers out for their early morning coffee and stroll discovered Monique's scarf tied to the chair. The woman, untying it, held it out for her friends to see. "It looks expensive. I'll take it to the guest services desk. Surely someone is looking for it."

Omar had been at his desk early, the phone call he had taken on the day of their departure from Port Canaveral had weighed heavily on his mind, and sleep had eluded him again. His attempts to call the United States were met with no answer. He sat at his desk, hoping to finish the pile of paperwork in his basket. There were a few reports needing follow-up. One report, in particular, had to be dealt with some finesse as it pertained to a chef in the competition. The passengers in the adjacent cabins to Chef Miles had called security at two o'clock that morning. They stated that a fight was taking place in the cabin, but the corridor was quiet when security arrived. Having previously dealt with Chef Miles's behavior, the security guards decided it had simply been another one of his nightmares and chose not to knock on the cabin door. Instead, they would have Omar speak with him in the morning.

Omar rubbed his face. He didn't look forward to having another conversation with the chef about his behavior. The two male chefs had caused more security issues than Omar had expected. "One more day and night," he sighed and folded the report into thirds. He reached around for his suit coat and placed the folded papers in his inside jacket pocket for the discussion to come. He worked diligently through the early morning hours, significantly reducing the pile of paperwork.

"Boss," one of the guards knocked on his door and came in. "One of our early birds found this tied to a chair."

Omar looked at the black and cream-colored scarf. It looked familiar. "Open it up, please." The man did as instructed, and the scarf revealed two leopards. "Where was this found?" Omar asked sharply.

"Deck six. Do you know whose it is?"

Omar nodded. "I am sure she simply tied it on the chair and forgot about it." He motioned for the guard to hand over the scarf. "I'll take it. It's an expensive item, and I'm sure she will be worried." He ran a finger across the soft silk. "I don't know how someone could forget about a Hermès scarf."

"A what scarf?" his officer asked.

"Hermès, it's a designer. Some of them are quite valuable."

The guard shook his head. It was a scarf, not a muscle car or a watch. "Should I fill out a lost and found ticket since you know the owner?"

Omar paused for a moment. "A lost and found ticket…" he said slowly, remembering Monique Patrick's insinuations about lax security protocols. He handed the scarf back to the guard. "Yes, you should fill out a lost and found ticket and place it in one of the secure bins. We need to maintain our regular practices. In fact, we will discuss our need to follow protocol at our morning meeting. In the meantime, I'll check with who I believe is the owner of the scarf. If it is hers, she can come down and retrieve it."

His guard chuckled. "Good thing it's a sea day, huh, boss? No need to chase anyone around or wait until they return from the port. They can't just disappear."

Omar smiled back, his white teeth showing against his tanned skin. "Yes, but it always seems we have more drama on sea days than any other. It's as if some insanity comes over the passengers when they realize they can't get off the ship."

Kennedy was making her rounds. She checked the pool deck to ensure it was set up for the long day and saw the early morning risers already claiming their chaises by the pool. Late risers would have to stalk the area waiting for someone to leave so they could snatch one for themselves. She bumped into Omar as they were both walking into the dining room at the same time. "Have you seen Ms. Patrick this morning?" he asked, looking around the room for her.

"No, but it's early. With no port of call today, she may be sleeping in." She pointed her head toward the kitchen doors. "But if you peek through the door, you'll see Chef Jordan helping Michèle in the kitchen."

Omar stared at her. "That's surprising," he said slowly.

Kennedy grinned. "I think there was some wine and tall tales in the galley last night. I was as shocked as you are when I went in to get a cup of coffee and saw Jordan on the line." She looked at him. "Why the need to see Monique Patrick?" she asked curiously.

"Nothing, really. A scarf that I believe is hers was found on the deck by some early morning walkers, and I want to make sure to give it to her. It's rather expensive."

"Oh," Kennedy said quietly. "Do you want me to page her to the security office when I make my morning announcements?"

"That would be ideal." He looked at his watch. "You do them about twenty minutes from now, correct?"

"Yes, I'll plug it at the end."

"Kennedy," Omar began and shook his head. "Never mind, thank you for making the announcement." He walked into the galley to get a cup of coffee, and as he did, Michèle looked up and saw Omar trying to contain his grin.

"Out!" he pointed his meat cleaver at Omar and then at the door. "Out!"

Omar raised his coffee cup to Michèle. "And good morning to you as well, my friend. I see you have a new helper. Try not to run her off." He quickly ducked out of the room, chuckling, and walked back to his office.

A little while later, Kennedy's voice came through the speakers as she welcomed everyone to the last day of the cruise. She shared the day's activities, including holiday movies in the theater, a lecture by Emily Abbott in the Lunar Lounge on Mayan culture, and a mixology class at the pool bar.

Omar's ears perked up when he heard Emily Abbott was giving a lecture. When she had come to him with her plan, he had suggested she try one on the ship first.

At the end of the announcements, Kennedy paged Monique Patrick to the guest services desk in the main lobby. Omar stood there awaiting Monique's arrival, and fifteen minutes later, Kennedy made the announcements again. He stood there for thirty minutes, and when Monique still had not appeared, he returned to the security office. "I'm going to call this woman's room," he said irritably to one of the officers. "Would you please call her cabin for me?" The officer's fingers flew across the keyboard as he looked at his computer screen and punched the number into the telephone, handing Omar the handset. No one answered the ringing phone. Aggravated, Omar blew out a breath of air. "I'm going to knock on her door. Please radio me immediately if she comes here to collect the scarf."

The officer gave him a quick nod, and Omar took the elevator to deck seven and knocked on Monique's door several times with no answer. He was about to use his key to open the door when a sleepy head poked out of the cabin opposite Monique's.

"Is something wrong?" the man asked sleepily. His thin hair stood up on his head and resembled a spiderweb.

"No, sir, trying to check on a passenger. I'm sorry I disturbed you," Omar replied crisply.

"She went out around one thirty this morning." The man pointed at Monique's door. "Not sure where she would go, but I remember the time because I looked at my watch. We're usually in bed by ten," he said sheepishly.

"Who's out there?" a woman's voice called out from the cabin.

"Just someone from the ship looking for the lady across the hall," the man called over his shoulder.

"Oh, did you tell them we passed her when we came back to our cabin, and she was all dressed up?" Omar heard the woman say.

"Thank you," Omar said quickly. "Again, I apologize for the disruption." He knocked on Monique's door again and used his key to open it. He called out her name, but there was no answer. He realized he needed to find Luke. Given the time Monique was seen leaving by the couple, Omar reasoned she may have gone to meet Luke after he was done for the night. He walked quickly to the elevators and went back to his office. He dialed several numbers until he found the beverage manager. "He's there? I'll be right down. Please tell him not to leave." Omar went quickly down to Longitudes and found Luke restocking the coolers.

"What's up?" Luke asked.

"I need to ask you a delicate question. Is there a certain passenger in your cabin? I know the two of you have been very friendly on this cruise," Omar asked cautiously.

Luke leaned against the cooler and crossed his arms. "Nope, Ms. Patrick and I parted ways yesterday."

Omar's eyebrows shot up. "You did?"

Luke looked down at the boxes of beer in front of him. "She went a little too far, ambushing Mila. I feel awful. I told her last night I had no more stories to tell."

Omar clapped Luke on the back. "Luke, I am sorry for your trouble, but if you see Ms. Patrick, please call me. We found something of hers that is quite valuable, and I don't want her to search for it if she doesn't have to." Omar left Longitudes and went back to his office. An hour later, he radioed Kennedy explaining that he needed her to gather the senior team to meet with him in the conference room. He dreaded his next duty, which was to alert the captain of a potential issue.

Omar and the captain arrived at the conference room, followed by Safety Officer Tully and the first officer. The looks he received were curious.

"Omar, what's going on?" Kennedy asked. "It must be serious if you have all of us gathered."

Omar bit his lips together and looked down for a moment before raising his head. "I'm taking some precautions. One of our passengers, Ms. Monique Patrick, the writer, cannot be found. We need a thorough but quiet search of the ship." He paused. "Her scarf was found tied to a chair on deck five this morning. We have paged her over the public address system, called her room, and I performed a wellness check, but the room was empty."

"Did you check Luke's bed?" Mila said cattily.

Omar sighed and washed his face. "Ms. Patrick's ambush of you made Luke realize his mistake. He has not seen her since nine o'clock last night." He handed each of them a copy of Monique's passport photo. "If you find Ms. Patrick, please notify me at once. If she finally answers her page, I'll let you know you can stop searching."

The captain spoke up, "It goes without saying, but I will say it anyway, we need to keep this as quiet as possible. I am certain this is simply a case of Ms. Patrick not hearing the pages."

The group dispersed, but Franklin and Omar stayed back. Franklin ran a hand over his face. "Nothing on the cameras?"

Omar shook his head. "We've looked at all the footage we have, but as you know, some cameras are not working."

"Damn!" Franklin said and closed his eyes. "We'll find her, I'm sure she's sleeping soundly somewhere, and it happens to not be in her bed."

Ninety minutes later, the group reconvened. Omar looked haggard. "Captain, I'm afraid ..."

The captain held up his hand to stop him from saying more. "I'll take care of contacting the authorities. Do we know when she was last seen?"

"Approximately one thirty this morning, sir," Omar replied. "Two guests coming in from the evening saw her leaving her cabin."

The captain frowned. "That's a long time. Are we sure we have checked all known areas?"

Safety Officer Tully spoke up, "Yes, sir, we've looked in every area a guest would have access to."

The captain let out a sigh and looked at the group. "I'll be on the bridge. Please continue to scour the ship. I cannot believe that someone like Monique Patrick would jump." He turned to Kennedy. "I'm assuming you have planned a full day of activities for our guests?" She nodded her head. "I don't think we need anything dramatic," he winked at her, "but you may need to pull a few more tricks out of your bag."

"Captain," Omar spoke up, "with your permission, I'd like to ask Kennedy to go through Ms. Patrick's room to see if she sees anything of importance. Kennedy has a keen eye that I trust."

The captain was thoughtful. "I suppose, but you will need to accompany her." Omar hesitated. "Is there a reason you can't, Mr. Meier? Are you two still fighting? I might be on the bridge, but I see and hear everything."

Omar turned red. "I need to have a conversation with one of our chefs. There were noise complaints again from his room—sounds of a struggle near the time Ms. Patrick was seen leaving her cabin. I want to interview him informally to see if Ms. Patrick's disappearance and the noise complaints are connected."

The captain sighed. "As usual, you are two steps ahead of me."

Kennedy told Omar she could be at Monique's cabin in ten minutes. She needed to get her clipboard from her cabin to make some changes to the day's events.

"Captain, we *should* alert Mrs. Abbott about Monique's disappearance," Kennedy said. "With your permission, I'd like to invite her to our morning staff meeting."

"I was thinking the same thing but was dreading telling her. If you tell her, I would be grateful. For some reason, people take news like this better from you than they do from me. I hear my foghorn-like voice can be frightening." He gave her a half smile. "Please update me after you have completed your search."

Kennedy went to her cabin, retrieved her clipboard, and walked quickly to Monique's stateroom. One of Omar's team members was waiting for her holding a folded plastic bag. "In case there is evidence," he said a little louder than was necessary.

Kennedy put her finger to her lips, thankful there was no one in the corridor. "Let's not alert the neighborhood."

Monique's cabin was a disaster, and the security guard whistled softly as he looked around. "This looks like the sign of a struggle. I'm going to call Omar," he said, putting the radio to his lips, but Kennedy stopped him.

"Stop, not yet." She surveyed the living area and then went into the bedroom. Undergarments, accessories, shoes, and other articles of clothing were strewn across every surface. It looked as if Monique's suitcases had burst open, and the contents had landed haphazardly throughout the room. "This is simply a woman who is very messy."

"Are you sure?" he asked, and Kennedy nodded. "Okay, what are we looking for?" He bent down to pick up a robe from the floor and placed it on the bed.

"I'm not sure," Kennedy said thoughtfully, her eyes darting over the spaces. She walked back into the living area. "I know she was gathering information for several articles she was writing." She saw a notebook on the desk and a pen lying across the open pages. Kennedy bent over and began to read the words on the page. She sucked in a little breath and, picking up the book, quickly thumbed back through the pages, realizing the first section of the notebook held a running written commentary of her trip. The rest of the notebook was divided into sections for each person she interviewed on the cruise. Monique's room may have been a disorganized mess, but it was clear her interview notes were not. Each section had observations, questions to ask during the interviews, commentary on interactions, and notes about how the discussions went. Beside many of the questions was a reference that said, "SEE FOLIO." Kennedy looked around the desk and saw a black leather folio peeking out from underneath a tote bag. She eased it out and untied the red band around it. Inside were files with the names of each competing chef and Deuce Dawson written on them. Kennedy spied a folder that read 'Jones and Terri Butler: Chicken Hillbillies', which contained Monique's notes and observations about the couple. The last file was thicker, and Monique had written '*Helio*' across the top. Curious, Kennedy flipped through and found paper-clipped packets for key members of the ship's staff and crew. She looked at the one with her name written across it and found a few photos from the ship's website. Other packets, including Mila's, contained police reports, photos, and newspaper articles. She turned to the security guard. "I need to take these two items," she pointed at the notebook and the folio, "for the captain and Omar to see. Is there something special we should do?"

He pointed at the desk. "I need to take a photo exactly the way you found them on the desk, and I'll write down a description of each of them for the file." He poked his head into the bedroom again. "Are you sure there wasn't an altercation in here? I can't see someone living this way. I'm going to take some photos of the rooms for Omar."

Kennedy shook her head. "Go ahead and take some photographs, but some people just live this way."

"If you say so," he said. When he was finished, he handed Kennedy the notebook and folio.

"Is this all you are taking?" he asked, and Kennedy nodded. "Let's put it in the bag." He opened the yellow plastic bag he had been holding earlier, and Kennedy placed them inside. "I'll have maintenance come back and rekey her door to a high-level security key."

Kennedy looked at her watch, "I need to find a few people. Please let Omar know I have some things to discuss with him after our staff meeting."

"Of course," he said and motioned for the notebook and folio. "But since you aren't going straight to see Omar, I'll take these back with me to the security office. It's not that

I don't trust you. It's protocol. Omar reminded us this morning about following procedures."

Kennedy handed him the yellow bag and left the cabin. She walked up a flight of stairs and knocked on Emily Abbott's door. When Emily opened it, she smiled, seeing Kennedy standing there. "Hello, my dear," she said warmly, "what brings you to my cabin?"

"There are a few changes to the schedule, and it will be easier to explain everything to the group together."

"That sounds fine." She furrowed her brow. "Kennedy, is everything okay? You look worried."

"Yes and no," Kennedy let out a small sigh and stepped into Emily's stateroom, closing the door. "A small issue with Monique Patrick."

Emily snorted with disgust. "Ugh, that woman, if she would fall overboard, it wouldn't hurt my feelings."

Kennedy had to stop herself from saying anything else. She looked at her watch. "We'll meet in an hour in the conference room, the same one we met in previously on deck five. If you will excuse me, I need to find Mr. Dawson." Kennedy walked down the corridor to the stairs and took them two at a time. When she reached Deuce's cabin, she knocked on the door but didn't receive an answer. Disappointed, she went out to the pool deck, hoping she might see him. Instead, she saw the long faces of Lola's fan club as they sat at one of the large round tables. Kennedy was torn. She needed to find Deuce, but the looks on the five faces made her feel she should check on them. Karl was sitting at the table, staring off into space. Paulie, wearing sunglasses, had his arms and legs crossed and a scowl on his face. "Tell me that you didn't lose all of your money at the casino last night?" she smiled at them warmly.

"No, toots, we lost our girl last night," Marshall wiped a tear from his eye.

"You lost your girl?" Kennedy was confused. As far as she knew, the Gents from Breezy Bayou had never met Monique Patrick. "I'm sure she's okay."

"That no good hussy, she's been, she's been—" Marshall pulled out his handkerchief and blew his nose.

Larry got up from the table and motioned to her. They stepped away from the table toward the railing. "I have a friend who lives north of us in another retiree community. He emailed me on the trip to tell me he was engaged and wanted me to meet his fiancé, a private chef. He sent a photo, but it was fuzzy. All I could tell was that the woman in the photo was petite with long brown hair. He wrote that she traveled a lot as a private chef for her VIP clients, which struck me odd because Lola tells us periodically the same thing. So, I asked him to send another photo so I could see his new bride-to-be." He looked out onto the ocean. "It was Lola."

Kennedy looked at Larry in shock, and he continued his tale, "To make matters worse, both Paulie and Karl came to me during the trip and shared that they were each going to propose to Lola after the competition." He shook his head. "After Paulie and Karl told me about their plans and getting the new photo with Lola and my other friend, I had to tell everyone the truth. They're now trying to decide whether they want to confront Lola. Paulie is so angry that he won't speak, and Karl has done nothing but look mournfully off into the distance. I have also learned that everyone but me has given her a great deal of money. It's just a mess," he said sadly. "And now I wonder if she has other gentlemen friends in other places." He looked back over at the table. "I feel terrible for telling them, but I couldn't let it continue."

Kennedy put her hand on Larry's, which was resting on the railing. "Telling a friend the truth is hard. We don't want to cause them pain, but not telling them is an even greater disservice."

Larry looked up at her with mournful eyes. "I'm sorry. I didn't mean to unload on you."

Kennedy gave him a comforting smile. "Listening is just another service we offer here on the *Helio*. Is there anything I can do in the meantime?"

Larry shook his head. "Thanks, Kennedy."

She left him at the railing and went up to the promenade deck. Unfortunately, time was running out, and she still needed to update the reader boards. If Kennedy didn't find Deuce quickly, she would have him paged to the conference room. Thankfully, as she was leaving the pool deck, she caught him out of the corner of her eye at the elevator.

"Deuce," she called out. "You are a hard man to find sometimes. I need to speak with you," she said when she finally reached him.

They got on the elevator. Deuce pressed the number for deck four, and Kennedy pressed deck five. "I'm hiding from the chefs and Art," he explained. "Everyone seems a little manic today. So, I thought I would go to Longitudes and get a little paperwork done."

"Before you get comfortable down there, I need to ask that you attend our morning staff meeting. There are some changes to the schedule, and I thought it would be best to do it with everyone in the room."

Deuce looked at her strangely. "Do I need to bring the chefs and Art? Does her friend Bert know? Those two have become thick as thieves. I'm not looking forward to leaving the ship tomorrow. I may have a watery-eyed young lady on my hands."

Kennedy shook her head. "I think it would be best for you to come to the conference room alone."

He looked at her seriously and ran a hand through his iron-gray curls. "This is more than a mere change to the schedule, isn't it?"

Kennedy took in a breath and gave him a long look. She got off when the elevator doors opened, leaving a mystified Deuce in the cab going to deck four.

Twenty minutes later, she had updated the reader boards and printed a few copies of the new schedule for the staff meeting. She walked quickly to the conference room and opened the door. Everyone looked up expectantly. Making her way to her seat, she bit her lips together and shook her head quickly. A few moments later, Omar and the captain arrived, and a hush fell over the room.

The captain cleared his throat. "What I am about to say does not leave this room. Monique Patrick, the writer, has gone missing as of one thirty this morning." Emily gasped, and Deuce's eyes snapped open.

Omar stood up. "Some early morning walkers found the scarf Ms. Patrick was wearing last night at dinner tied to a chair on one of the decks. Because I knew the scarf was hers from a conversation at dinner, I had her paged to the security office. When she didn't come down, we telephoned her room, performed a thorough search of the ship, and finally checked her room which we found empty. We are doing another full search of the ship as we speak, leaving no area unchecked." He sat back down.

"In the meantime," the captain said, "we don't want to alarm the passengers or cause undue gossip. The ship becomes ridiculously small on a sea day. Kennedy?"

Kennedy stood up and passed out the pieces of paper she had brought. "To keep the passengers busy, we'll have a ship-wide competition to win the Sun Trophy."

"A trophy?" Emily echoed disbelievingly. "At a time like this, we are going to have a contest for that ridiculous thing I saw in Alfred's office?"

Kennedy smiled and turned to Emily, "It's quite popular. The corporate office had asked me to have you present one to the winner. Fortunately, or unfortunately, I forgot about planning something when I took over the reins of the chef's competition. I hope everyone will be so focused on winning the trophy that they won't have time to gossip." Kennedy turned to Mila and Tony. "Would you two gather every deck of cards we have and bring them to the pool bar? Check the crew bar and recreation room. I have some down in my storage locker that I will get after the meeting."

"How can I help?" Deuce asked.

Kennedy turned to him. "We need to move the chef's competition up a few hours. To keep people busy, we need to have it before dinner. You can announce the new host chef at the end of the holiday show after Mrs. Abbott presents the Sun Trophy."

"What do I tell the chefs?"

"I'll go with you to talk to them. We can tell them that you moved up the time because the total points are so close, and the judges need time to deliberate."

The captain stood up. "Unless you need anything further from me, I will return to the bridge."

"Captain," Kennedy said with a hint of urgency in her voice, "I need to speak with you and Omar together."

"Let's meet in my office in thirty minutes. I should have an update on the sweeps of the ship and an update from the authorities." He nodded at everyone around the table and left the room.

Kennedy looked around at the faces staring back at her. The room was uncomfortably silent while they each thought of what may have happened to the woman. "Mrs. Abbott, would you come with me down to the lower hold to get the cards? I could use an extra hand."

Emily, pale from what she had just learned about Monique Patrick, stood up. "Of course."

Kennedy guided Emily to the freight elevator, and they descended to the provisions area. Ali looked up when he saw the elevator doors open, and Kennedy waved a hand at him. "I don't know if you remember from the tour. I have lockers where I keep things in case we run into foul weather or have an extra day at sea." They walked through the maze of lockers. "Here we are," Kennedy said. "My lockers are here," and then she pointed her finger down the hallway, "and the holiday decorations I showed all of you on the tour are down there." Kennedy pulled out her key and unlocked the lock. She walked over to a stack of small boxes and handed one to Emily.

"May I?" Emily asked and peered inside. She pulled out a golden cruise ship on a small wooden base sitting on a bed of blue acrylic waves. Emily suddenly cocked her head to the left. "Did you hear that?" she asked.

"Hear what?" Kennedy was rummaging noisily through some boxes. "Ah ha! Playing cards! I found them," she said triumphantly.

Emily walked out of the storage unit and stood in the hallway. "I thought I heard something rustling." She turned her head from one side to the other, straining to hear the noise. Kennedy joined Emily in the corridor and began to pull the door closed. It screeched as she shut it. Emily held up her hand to stop her. "There it is again."

Kennedy cocked her head to listen, and at that moment, they felt the ship move. She gave Emily a reassuring smile. "Just like an airplane, things shift with a little turbulence. And the *Helio* is a little older, so like some of us, she creaks, pops, and groans. You may have heard a box shifting with the movement." She closed the lock. "Ready to show off the trophy?" she asked, and they walked to the service elevator, taking it up to the pool deck.

Emily turned to Kennedy as they rode up. "Please forgive a foolish old lady. I honestly thought I heard something when we were down there. I have so much to learn about our ships." She held out the trophy looking at it strangely. "I still can't believe people will try to win this thing."

"Good morning, *Helio* cruisers. We hope you are enjoying your morning at sea. We have a little surprise for you today. As you know, today is a sea day, and we have no ports of call, but we thought it would be the perfect day to see who would win the coveted Sun Trophy," Kennedy said into her microphone.

Terry Butler sat upright in her chaise and squealed. "Jones, I want that trophy!"

Kennedy explained how the contest would work. At each event, players would receive a playing card for participating. Passengers would turn in their cards at the guest services desk to be tallied before dinner, and the person with the highest score would be the winner. "Don't forget that you can get a card when you attend the chef's competition, which will take place at four o'clock in the main theater. So, I encourage you to look at the list of activities and map out your day. Good luck!" She turned off the microphone and stepped back. Kennedy handed out packs of cards to the cast, Luke, and then to Emily. "You are giving a lecture today," she said, smiling.

"Oh, goodness," Emily said. "I suppose people may attend now."

Kennedy left the pool deck and walked quickly to the captain's office. She knocked on the door.

"Come in," the captain said, and she entered and sat down in the empty chair. "This brings back an unpleasant memory."

Omar turned to Kennedy. "I understand you thoroughly searched Ms. Patrick's cabin and found these items." He pushed the yellow plastic bag toward Kennedy. She pulled the notebook out and opened it.

"When we went in, I found the notebook on her desk opened to this page," and she pushed it across the table so they could read what was written.

> L— Do you kiss all the members of your fan club that way? Or do the ones that give you money get special perks? What an intriguing tidbit for my article. Will it hurt your social media page when I expose you?

> M— Was the fire at the new restaurant really an accident? Remember what I said about skeletons in the closet coming out? They might make your dear mother's restaurant their new favorite place to eat.

> T— A recipe for disaster. Take five parts of sexual harassment and add equal amounts of lies and deceit. It's a wonder you kept your job as long as you did. When I write the article, I doubt you'll be able to get a job at a fast-food restaurant.

> J— Did you decide it was the last time he would hit you? Wouldn't it have been easier to poison him? Working for the brother of the sheriff may have the district attorney decide to reopen the case after

reading about you. I'll make sure to send him a copy of the article.

D— I found out what happened during your lost years. Did you wear a chef's coat over your striped jumpsuit? The viewers will love this juicy tidbit when they read it. Should you reconsider the theme and do a show about tips and tricks for cooking in jail?

M— What did happen to your ex-husband? Curiously, he disappeared during the divorce proceedings. Did it make things go quicker? What a riveting spin this will put on my article about the *Helio*.

E— I learned a dead body was found on the *Helio* on the first cruise. Ironic that it was the same cruise the consultant was on. I hear whoever died was some corporate bigwig. I can keep my mouth shut about this little death by misadventure if I get free cruises whenever I want. I understand the cruise line has fallen all over itself to keep the Butlers quiet.

Omar looked at the list. "I assume the E stands for Emily Abbott with the demand for the free cruise. One of the M's stands for Mila."

Kennedy looked at him, surprised. "You know?"

"I've known for a long time."

"Well, it looks like we all know," the captain said. "Let's call her and see if she got one of Monique's notes. It could help us figure out what happened." He dialed the spa extension, and Anna Marie answered.

"Y-y-yes s-s-sir," she stammered. The captain could hear her as she put her hand over the phone. "Mila, it's the captain," she hissed. "He wants to talk to you!"

A few moments later, Mila's throaty voice came over the phone. "Yes, sir? How can I help you? Your usual? A haircut and manicure? On the bridge, or would you like me to come to the office?" Her low-pitched laugh came across the speaker.

He cleared his throat, embarrassed. "I have you on speaker with Kennedy and Omar, and I'm afraid this is serious. Did you receive a note in the last few days asking about your ex-husband?"

Kennedy heard Mila let out a slow chuckle. "I did. When I opened the spa, I found it under the door. I assumed it came from Monique Patrick. She made some innuendos about what happened a few months ago and some veiled references to my past, but I didn't budge. Why?"

"What did you do with it?" Omar asked in a clipped tone.

"I threw it away. I may have family members with ties to questionable people, and I made some bad choices in men, but that's it. I've got nothing to hide."

"Thank you, Mila," the captain said.

"Don't forget to call me later for the haircut. We don't want you looking grizzled."

"I'll give you a call soon." His face was pink as he pressed the button to disconnect the phone. Then, he looked sternly at Omar and pointed at the notebook. "That's one off your list. I believe you need to have some heart-to-heart talks with others to see if they also received a note. My guess is they did, and," he paused, washing his face with his hands, "and one of them could have pushed Ms. Patrick overboard. Although I seriously doubt it was Mrs. Abbott." He stood, and Kennedy and Omar stood as well. "I'll check with the bridge and see if there are any updates from Tully or the authorities."

Kennedy and Omar were silent as they walked down the corridor. "Were you able to have your conversation with Chef Miles?" she asked.

He shook his head. "No, I didn't find him in his cabin this morning. I'll have him paged."

Omar's radio chirped, interrupting their conversation. "Omar, Dr. Craig called; he needs to speak with you immediately in the infirmary."

"That's odd," Kennedy furrowed her brow, "what do you think he wants?"

"I have no idea," Omar said, equally surprised.

Two chefs, Deuce, Art, Bert, and Kennedy were standing in a group talking in the lobby. "Has anyone seen Miles or Tristan?" Deuce asked. There was a collective shaking of heads.

"I can catch up with Miles later," Kennedy said brightly, "and I guess we can find Tristan. Oh, wait, here he is."

Tristan shuffled to the group wearing checkered chef pants and a hooded sweatshirt. He stood beside Lola, and she wrinkled her nose. "You look and smell like an alley behind a bar. Did the shower in your cabin stop working? Or did you decide to bathe in whatever you drank last night?"

"Sorry," he yawned, "I was about to get in the shower when I got the call, and I came as quickly as possible." He tossed his head back and then lowered his sunglasses revealing bloodshot eyes. "A little party last night with a young lady." He cocked his hip. "I was legendary as usual."

Lola rolled her eyes and sidestepped away. "A legend in your own mind. Keep downwind, Romeo."

Kennedy cleared her throat and looked at Deuce, who bobbed his head. "We have moved up the time of the competition. We've reviewed the scores and have found that we will need additional time for the judges to deliberate. It will also allow us to build some suspense between today's competition and the announcement of the winner, which we will do after the holiday show in the theater."

Jordan piped up, "Any chance we'll find out now what today's competition will be?"

"Didn't like your freaky yellow fingers last night, Jordan?" Tristan waved a hand in Jordan's face.

Deuce cleared his throat. "I will meet you in the main dining room at three o'clock to give you the details. I'll see you then."

As they began to depart, Lola asked, "Has anyone seen that woman, Monique? The writer?"

"Ugh, why would you want to find her?" Tristan asked. "Didn't you get enough of her yesterday? I know I did." Jordan nodded her head in agreement.

Lola shrugged. "She caught me last night in the lounge after congratulating me on my epic win and said she had some follow-up questions for me."

Tristan pulled down his sunglasses. "It's not that I don't want to hear a rehash of the only time you have won something, Lola, but I need to make sure the young lady I shared company with found her way out."

Lola rolled her eyes as they watched Tristan leave. "That poor, poor pillow," she whispered to Jordan and snickered.

"That's enough," Deuce said and let out a breath. He had caught the odor Lola had mentioned and agreed that Tristan had probably spent the evening drinking away his sorrows instead of in the company of a woman.

"I'll see everyone later," Jordan said and yawned. "I was up early helping in the galley this morning and left my knife kit."

Art turned to Kennedy. "Can I speak to you for a minute in private?" The two women stepped away. "This will come out completely wrong, but I need help. I want to take Bert to dinner in the main dining room. Can you help me get a table for two?"

Kennedy smacked her forehead. "Oh wow, I completely forgot. Bert had asked me to speak to the captain two days ago. I'll set it up, but will you let Bert ask you? He was a nervous wreck when he came to me for help." Art nodded, blushing.

While Kennedy and Art were talking, Deuce turned to Bert and held out his hand. "I haven't said thank you yet for being our photographer. The network has been uploading your photos to our social media pages, and your shots are receiving some great comments. I can guarantee you a job if you ever want to return to land."

Bert looked down at the floor, embarrassed. He was not used to receiving compliments. On the contrary, a horrible episode years before had landed him in legal trouble and unable to find work in his field as a newspaper photographer. He had begrudgingly taken the job on the *Helio*, promising himself it was only for a short time until things blew over. Now he wondered if it was time to move on.

"Thanks, I'll think about it."

"You will always have a place with me, Bert," Lola trilled. "I'll need an official photographer when I become the show's host. I think I will make sparkly shoes my trademark on the show. What do you think, Deuce?"

There was an awkward silence as neither Bert nor Deuce knew what to say. Deuce swallowed and rubbed his hands together. "Well, I should be going. I'll see everyone this afternoon."

"I've got to go as well," Kennedy said. "There's a ship full of people trying to win a trophy."

"Looks like that leaves us, Bert. Want to take some shots of me?" Lola batted her eyelashes.

Art grabbed Bert's arm. "Sorry, Lola. Bert and I have work to do," and she pulled him away from the pretty, petite brunette.

"Huh," Lola huffed, looking around at the empty lobby, "that's never happened before."

Omar knocked on the infirmary door. "Come in," he heard, and when he entered the room, he saw Dr. Craig and Chef Miles in conversation.

"I'm sorry I didn't know you were with someone," he said quickly, trying not to look at the chef, who he noticed was pale, and his head was slick with sweat despite the hooded sweatshirt he wore.

"No, we called you here, Omar. We need to share some information with you."

Miles swallowed hard. "My narcolepsy medication has gone missing from my room. I didn't notice it until late last night."

"You called me here to take a report for missing medication?" Omar snapped and looked at each man intently.

"Not exactly, Omar," Dr. Craig interjected. "Miles is on a medication that is a controlled substance called sodium oxybate. You would more commonly know it as GHB."

"GHB as in…" Omar said slowly.

"Exactly," Dr. Craig answered.

"Actually, I'm glad you are here, Chef Miles. I was going to have you paged. We received complaints from the cabins on either side of yours at two this morning. They said that it sounded like a fight was taking place." He looked hard at Miles. "Was there a problem?"

"No, but—"

"Was anyone in your room?" Omar asked sternly.

Miles looked apprehensive and looked at Dr. Craig for reassurance. "No, absolutely not. I had a series of violent dreams last night; it's a side effect of my condition when I don't take my medication and stick to my routine."

"How is the drug dispensed, and why was it just sitting out in the room?" Omar asked in a clipped manner.

Miles looked uncomfortable. "At home, I don't worry about it. I live alone, and I don't advertise my condition. On the cruise, I arranged for Doctor Craig to hold onto it, but I got angry with him and demanded to take it back."

Omar was quiet. "As the drugs are a controlled substance and have gone missing, we'll need to open an investigation and file a report. But, first, we'll do a lock interrogation on your door. You haven't given an additional key to anyone or shared yours, have you?"

Miles held up his key. "This is the only one, and it hasn't left me. But—"

Omar cut him off. "Have you allowed anyone in your room?"

Miles shook his head. "Chef Tristan was in there with me the other day, and," he looked down at his shoes, "your guards who made sure I didn't hurt myself when I got drunk."

Omar remembered how Miles had behaved the night he had been found in Longitudes. "No one else?"

Miles shook his head again.

"I'll send a security team member to your cabin to take a full report and check the lock." Omar paused. "I have another question not pertaining to this matter, but I need to ask Doctor Craig to step out."

Miles held up his hand. "Doc can stay. I have nothing to hide."

"Did you happen to find a note under your door yesterday?" Omar asked; he was paying close attention to Miles's body language.

"Yes, I did, and I believe it was from Monique Patrick," Miles answered, looking Omar squarely in the eye.

"Why?" Omar asked quickly.

Miles crossed his arms. "Just a feeling. She mentioned some rumors she had heard while getting background information on me and made mention of skeletons in the closet. And yesterday in Cozumel, she kept picking away at them."

"Why?"

Miles threw up his hands. "Who knows?" he said, exasperated. "She's been needling all of us. She ran Jordan out of a restaurant yesterday with her insinuations."

Omar counted to sixty in his head. It was a technique he had learned many years ago as a police detective. Someone with something to hide would try to fill in the silence. When Miles said nothing more, he pulled on the cuffs of his jacket and put out his hand. "Chef Miles, thank you again for your time. I'll have one of my team members meet you at the cabin shortly.

Miles nodded at Omar and then looked at Doctor Craig. "Thanks, Doc."

"My pleasure, Chef," he said, and the two men shook hands. "I'm here anytime you want to walk and trade recipes." Dr. Craig turned to Omar when the door closed. "A little insensitive there, weren't you, Omar? Did you have to interrogate him? I know it is serious that the medication is missing, but I'm sure this is a case of an overzealous housekeeper who thought it was trash."

Omar sighed. "I'm not so sure." He paused; he needed to take the doctor into his confidence. "This is confidential. We have a passenger, Monique Patrick, the same one Miles mentioned, who has gone missing.

"You don't think—"

Omar held up his hand. "I'm not sure what to think. I have a missing person and a missing controlled substance that causes unconsciousness. It doesn't help that the cabins on either side of Chef Miles said it sounded like fighting in his room. And I don't think it is a coincidence that all of this happened last night."

Omar left the infirmary and walked back to the security office. He pondered what he had just learned and was equally troubled by what Kennedy had found in

Monique's cabin. Two words kept chanting in his head—means and motive.

"Well, if it isn't the most handsome men I've ever seen in my life," Lola drawled. "I've looked all over the ship for you."

"Look, Lola now is not a good time." Larry stood up to steer her away from the group.

"Why not? It's not like we have to rush off the ship to go somewhere," she said wryly. "I just came by to tell you they've moved up the time of the competition. I'm hoping my favorite guys are there rooting for me. You know—"

Eddie interrupted her, "Lola, it's not a good time." He stood up and walked to stand beside Larry.

"What's wrong, Marshall? Don't you love me anymore?" Lola asked sweetly, but her voice held a tinge of panic.

Marshall crossed his arms and glared at her. "I have no love for a two-bit, two-timing trollop." He looked at Eddie and Larry. "I'm going for a lap around the deck," he snorted and looked daggers at Lola. "Suddenly, the view around looks like a toxic waste dump." He shook Karl's arm. "Son," he said gently, "come with me. A change of scenery would do you good."

Karl stood and looked at Lola. His eyes were full of grief and sadness. "Sure, Pop," he said quietly and began to push his father.

"I think I'll join them." Paulie got up from where he was sitting. It was the first thing Eddie or Larry had heard him say in hours.

Lola wrinkled her brow as she watched Paulie leave. He had not given her their signal. "What the heck was that all about?" She looked from Larry to Eddie.

Larry stared at her. She was so self-absorbed that she was oblivious. "They know, Lola," he said coolly.

"Know? Know what?"

"About your other life," Eddie said lifelessly. "You know the one you have when you aren't around us."

The color drained from Lola's face, but she faked a smile. "What are you talking about, silly? My life is with you boys at Breezy Bayou," she playfully punched his shoulder.

Eddie stood up. "I think I'll join Paulie on that walk." Lola looked bewildered as Eddie brushed past her.

Larry let out a sad chuckle. He had to give Lola credit; she played the game well. He gestured for her to sit. "Larry, I don't know what's going on, but it isn't funny." She took the dark sweatshirt she had draped over her shoulders and placed it behind her as a cushion against the chair.

"Lola, I'm not laughing because anything is funny. You broke the hearts of three, possibly four men, and when we get back to Florida, there will be a fifth." Larry took a sip of coffee and placed his mug on the table. "I know about your scams, Lola." She narrowed her eyes at him. Larry hunched over the table and continued, "When you land in a new town, you figure out where the retiree villages are, target the ones near the higher-end grocery stores, and make yourself a regular. Then you market yourself as a personal chef targeting the older single male community. With your looks, southern charm, ability to make tasty meals," Larry rolled his eyes, "and willingness to listen to us prattle on, you are a shoo-in for the lonely. But you aren't a real chef, are you, Lola? What I have deduced is that you go to big box stores and buy pre-made items that only need to be heated up. Then, you divide the meals at home, put them in nice containers, and add a garnish. You use hotel restaurants if you have to offer something more complicated."

Lola stood. "I don't have to listen to this. You don't know what you are talking about. I am a chef and a highly regarded one!"

"Oh? Then why is it not a single person in any one of my professional circles has heard of you? The culinary world is tiny, Lola." He pinched his thumb and forefinger together and gestured for her to sit back down. "You should stay and hear the other things I learned so you don't make the same mistakes in the next town."

Lola sat down, glowering, and crossed her arms and legs. Larry smiled at her indignation. "Let's talk about the other side of your scam." Lola rolled her eyes. "You become romantically involved with one of your clients and then find another lonely heart an hour or so away in another retirement community where you provide the same meal delivery services. You keep your stories simple and have plenty of photos for backup. I don't remember you mentioning living in Arizona until last night during the competition, which got me thinking. Something tells me you have been doing this for a while across the country. Did something happen in Arizona that made you need to leave and move to Florida?" He took a sip of coffee. "You tell both men that in addition to being a personal chef, you are also a private chef for several VIP clients all over the United States. They don't need you often, but when they do, you have to jump to keep their business. You have even gone so far as to take photos of yourself inside a private jet to show your lovers what the very wealthy and needy client sent. I haven't quite figured out how you took the photos in the kitchens, but I compliment you on your attention to detail."

Lola wiggled in her seat uncomfortably. The table near them was straining to hear their conversation. They had watched four of the men get up and leave soon after the pretty brunette chef had walked up. "Could you say this a little louder?" she hissed. "I don't think they heard you at the next table."

Larry smiled sadly at her. "You keep your relationship up with both men and flip-flop between them. When you need a break, you tell one of them you've been called to cater an event. He's sad but proud that you are a career girl. At some point, you pretend to be overwhelmed and explain that you need to buy supplies but don't have time to get to the bank. Being the gallant knight, he offers to help. You promise to pay back the loan but somehow never remember to. Your shining knight then presents you with an engagement ring. He begs to show you off to his friends, which you have put off from the beginning telling him you want to stay in your little cocoon. How many engagement rings have you received, Lola?"

Lola began to drum her fingers on the table in irritation. "You decide to end the relationship with one of the men. So, you share that you've been offered a job as a full-time private chef in another state and have to leave. It's a tearful time, and you tell him you need to do this to further your career, but you promise you will find a way to make the relationship work. Then, you begin to duck his calls. He begs to visit, but you tell him you are swamped. Finally, there is the breakup call. You call your knight in shining armor in tears and tell him you need to make a sacrifice, and unfortunately, it's love. Do you offer the ring back? My guess is no. You probably take them to a pawn shop. Then you repeat the entire scenario with the other man and move on to your next town." Larry sat up straight. His eyes bored into Lola's. "How did I do?"

Lola clapped her hands slowly. "Bravo. I wondered who had slipped the note under my door."

Tristan went back to his cabin after the meeting in the lobby. He looked at himself in the mirror. Lola was right; he did look like he had slept in the gutter. He took off his sweatshirt and flexed his muscles, admiring his reflection. Even though he knew he didn't have the points, he was sure he would be named host chef. It would be stupid of Deuce not to choose him. He had the looks and the sex appeal they needed to get viewers. As far as his culinary skills, he had faked his way in the kitchen long enough to know just how much he needed to do. He reasoned there would be underlings to handle the tedious or complicated parts. After all, the network wouldn't expect the star to do it. And as their newest and hottest celebrity, their legal team could make Monique go away with a signature and a tidy check. They would want to protect their new face.

He practiced his signature pose, crossing one arm across his waist and cupping his chin with the other. He noticed the long scratch Monique had left when she grabbed his arm last night outside of the theater and the flaking from the temporary tattoo sleeves. *I'll wear a long sleeve shirt under my chef's coat today, but before I start as host chef, I'll need to get real ones.* He flexed his biceps again and grinned at himself in the mirror. *Yeah, it's time; chicks dig ink.*

An hour later, he heard a knock on his door and opened it. Mer, the cabin steward, was standing outside. "All good in here, Mr. Chef?" Mer asked. "Do you need me to straighten up your cabin? Do you want turn down service tonight?"

Tristan shook his head. "All good, my man, and no need for you tonight. I'm sure I'll have a lady friend to help me celebrate my new job as host chef after the competition tonight." Tristan could hear voices down the hall. He looked over Mer's shoulder and noticed two security officers outside Miles's room. "What's going on down there?" he tilted his head toward the cabin.

Mer shrugged. "I don't know. Probably redoing the lock on the door. Sometimes the batteries go dead. So, nothing for you?" he asked again. "Mr. Chef?" Mer repeated himself, trying again to get Tristan's attention.

Tristan shook his head. "Sorry, little dude, I was in a trance for a minute. My lady friend kept me up last night." He yawned. "I should take a nap or go to the gym before the competition. Thanks for checking on me."

Mer turned to walk down the corridor, and as Tristan was about to shut the door, he heard one of the men in front of Miles's door speak, "Hey, this door doesn't latch all the way." He pushed it open and then allowed it to swing shut. "Look, it doesn't engage the lock. We need to call this into maintenance." He pulled his radio off the clip on his pants.

The other man put a hand up to stop him. "Wait, shouldn't we call Omar?"

"About what?"

"About the fact this door doesn't shut all the way. Someone could have gotten into the cabin if they had just pushed the door."

The other guard rolled his eyes. "Oh, yeah, right. A random person walks down this corridor and pushes all the doors to see which ones aren't closed all the way, and they just happen to find this one." He shook his head. "I forget, you're new. After you've been on the ship for as long as I have and seen what I have seen, you'll understand." He patted the small handheld computer. "We got what we came for, and I'm going to call this into maintenance." He looked at his coworker meaningfully. "If you think you need to tell Omar about it, go ahead, but I doubt it's anything."

Terri Butler was determined to win the Sun Trophy, and when Terri set her mind on something, she was like a hungry dog who had caught the scent of a bone and was now trying to find it. "Jonesy, I'm not leaving this ship without that trophy." She got up from the chaise lounge and put on her coverup.

"Sweetsie, I can buy you one of those trophies." Jones patted the chaise she had been sitting on. "When we get home, I'll email Kennedy and just have her—"

"Jones!" Terri stamped her foot and interrupted him. "I want to win this trophy and need your help."

Jones took a deep breath. The look on Terri's face made him realize she was serious. "Well, Sweetsie, it's like those poker runs we went on when I had the motorcycle. For each stop, you get a card, but to win this trophy, you need the highest number of points instead of having the best poker hand. So, I think you want to find out how many things there are to do and see how long they each take."

"I'll be right back." She raced to the pool bar and was back moments later. "Okay, here's the list." She thrust the piece of paper at him with a glint in her eye. "Let's make a plan."

Jones realized that if Terri were on an all-day scavenger hunt of activities, he would be able to relax by the pool. He told her to go back to their cabin and get dressed, and while she was gone, he would work up a plan for her to hit every event, allowing her to get as many points as possible.

Terri squealed and hugged him. "Oh, Jonesy, you are the best husband ever!"

"Go, my little shark!"

Omar walked into the galley to get a cup of coffee and found Jordan wiping down the stainless-steel countertop. Her knife bag and a hooded sweatshirt were sitting on the corner of the counter. "Chef Jordan, I'm glad I ran into you." He poured the dark brew into a paper cup. "May I get you some?"

Jordan nodded as she continued to wipe the counter in front of her. "Yes, please, it was an early morning, but I was happy to lend a hand. It helped calm me down."

Omar had his back to her as he poured the second cup of coffee. "Was something wrong?" He turned back around. "Cream or sugar?"

"Just black, thank you." She took the coffee from him and leaned against the stainless-steel counter.

"You said you needed to calm down. What was wrong? Is there anything I can do to help?" he asked with concern.

"It's just, it's just…" she bit her lips together, "it's okay, it's nothing."

Omar looked at her. "I think whatever *it is*, has upset you." He looked around the galley. "Especially if you volunteered to work the breakfast shift. Michèle is not exactly Prince Charming in the morning." He paused and said wryly, "or any time, for that matter."

A laugh escaped from Jordan's lips. "I actually find him quite charming."

Omar looked surprised. "I've heard cantankerous, belligerent, irritable, and disagreeable, but I have never heard Michèle called charming. But now, what was bothering you so much that you needed to work in the galley to feel better?"

Jordan opened her mouth to speak and quickly closed it when she saw three of the cooks coming through chattering. They clammed up when they saw Omar and

Jordan and walked through the space speedily, their eyes downcast.

"That was odd," Jordan said.

Omar tilted his head to the side. "Not exactly. As the person in charge of security, everyone thinks I am stealthily searching for criminal activity when usually," he lifted his cup of coffee, "I'm just searching for this." Omar watched Jordan's face. "You were about to say something."

She sighed and waved her hand. "It's nothing more than a nuisance, and I can deal with it. It caught me off guard and was upsetting." A tense silence came over the galley, and Jordan finally broke it, speaking anxiously. "Before dinner, I found a handwritten note under my door. I knew it was from Monique Patrick because she's been badgering me." She took a ragged breath. "It's something I have tried to bury, and now it will come out again because of her." She took a few steps, picked up the sweatshirt on the counter, and put it down again. "I just wanted to start a new life."

"Why?" Omar asked quietly.

"Because I couldn't stay there anymore. People were always staring and wondering and whispering." She slammed her hand down violently on the counter. "I couldn't stay because even though it wasn't my fault, people thought I had killed my husband!"

Now it was Omar's turn to be surprised. "Your husband?"

"Yes!" Jordan's eyes had a look of defiance in them, and she looked down at her hand on the countertop. "My husband," she said quietly. She began to pace again, and with each footstep, her story poured out. The whirlwind romance and quick move to Oregon, the alienation from her family, and the horrible discovery that her new world was, in reality, a living hell as the man Jordan thought she loved used harsh words and fists to make his point. She recounted the last horrible night— the one that had given her the long, deep scars on her arm and face. She looked up at him with a tear-stained face. "I didn't mean to kill him. I was only trying to get away."

Omar took a deep breath. The raw pain that had come out of Jordan as she told her story was heart-wrenching. "But you were cleared," he said. "You said the sheriff ruled it as an accidental death."

Jordan nodded and wiped her eyes with the back of her hand. "But people still talked, it was a small town, *his town*, full of *his* family and friends, and I was the foreign stranger. The fact that I worked for the sheriff's brother didn't help matters." She looked at him earnestly. "But I didn't kill him. It was just a terrible, terrible accident." She looked far away and took another ragged breath. "Somehow,

Monique discovered it and brought it up during my interview. I told her the subject was not something I wanted to discuss. When we were in Cozumel, she kept coming over to me, whispering that it would all come out anyway when she wrote the article and that I should tell her my side of the story. Then, just before dinner, I found a note under my door." She rubbed the scar on her arm. "I waited for her outside the main dining room and begged her to leave what happened in the past. I think Kennedy heard a part of our conversation because she asked Monique to go with her into the theater for something." She took a shaky breath. "So, that's it. That's why I've been so upset."

Omar pursed his lips together. He didn't want to ask the question he was compelled to ask, but with Monique's disappearance, he had to know.

"Jordan, where were you last night?" he asked gravely. "Can you account for your whereabouts? Specifically, between midnight and six."

"I can," a deep male voice with a French accent answered. "She was with me all night," Michèle said. Three of his cooks had found him and told him Jordan and Omar were talking in the front galley. He went to jokingly give Omar a hard time about being in his kitchen, but as he heard Jordan's story for the second time, he stopped in his tracks to prevent anyone else from walking in and overhearing her tale. Then, when he heard Omar speak, he walked in.

Omar was startled. "She was with you?" Suddenly he remembered Jordan's comment about Michèle being charming.

"Is that so hard to believe, Omar?" Michèle asked, not taking his eyes from Jordan's.

"Michèle, on your word as a senior leader, she was with you all night?"

Michèle smiled broadly, still looking at Jordan. "Yes." He turned to Omar. "Is there anything else?"

Omar took a breath. "I think I'll take my coffee and go to my office. Thank you both," he said quietly and walked out of the galley. He needed to look at Monique's notebook. He was sure whatever was in there would point to what had happened to the woman.

An hour later, a troubled Kennedy knocked on Omar's door. "Mind if I come in?"

"Please," he gestured to the chair opposite his desk. They had flirted many times in this room, but now, she looked uneasy.

"I hate to ask this, but is there any word?" she asked.

Omar shook his head. "I spoke with Emily Abbott this morning," Omar said. "She showed me the note she had received. She assumed it was from Monique Patrick and planned to take it to the corporate office's legal team when she returned so they could deal with the situation. However, now…" He raised his hands and let them drop to his desk.

Kennedy sighed. "I've never had anything like this happen before. We practice it; we talk about protocol…" she trailed off, not finishing her sentence. Omar was silent as well, lost in his thoughts. "Omar," she said, getting his attention, "I have something else I need to share with you about one of the chefs." She pointed a finger at the yellow plastic bag sitting on his desk. Omar listened while Kennedy shared what Larry had told her about Lola.

"She hasn't technically done anything against the law, but what a piece of work." He shook his head. "Those poor men."

There was a knock on his door. "Boss, sorry, I've got the information for you on the lock interrogation."

"Why didn't I have it sooner? I've been waiting for it," he snapped.

"Sorry, boss, we were dealing with an altercation on the pool deck. Two of the passengers got into a fistfight."

"A fistfight?"

The officer grinned. "Yeah, two old guys were trying to pummel each other, and one in a wheelchair was egging them on. It was pretty—" he stopped when he saw Omar's glowering face. "Sorry, boss, here it is." Omar snatched the paper from his hands and read the printout. "You can go," he said to the guard.

Kennedy stood up. "I should leave as well. It sounds like I need to do some triage. I have an idea of who our boxers are."

Omar stood as well. "I need to find Mer."

"Mer?" Kennedy questioned. "Rosemary's Mer?"

"Yes," Omar said quickly.

"Omar, what does that have to do with Monique Patrick?"

Omar sighed. "Because in addition to having a missing passenger, someone supposedly stole a controlled substance out of Miles's cabin. A drug that forces unconsciousness. Mer's key was used to open Chef Miles's door sometime yesterday."

"What?!"

"Not a word of this to anyone," Omar said. "Now, I need to find Mer. Excuse me," and he left a bewildered Kennedy standing in his office.

It only took Omar ten minutes to find Rosemary and Mer in the housekeeping offices. "Omar, this is ridiculous! My nephew has never done anything wrong," Rosemary said in her thick Filipino accent. "Mer, you tell him." However, before either Mer or Omar could say another word, Rosemary went into a rant.

Omar finally had enough. "Rosemary! I need to talk to Mer. You are here as his boss, not his aunt. Now be quiet," he said sternly, "please." Rosemary crossed her arms and glared at Omar. "Mer, did you see any medication on the desk in Chef Miles's room?"

Mer closed his eyes as he pictured the cabin. "There was a bottle and a needle thing without the needle on the desk, but I didn't touch it. When I introduced myself on the first day of the cruise, the chef told me never to come into his room unless he specifically asked."

"Then why were you in there?" Rosemary and Omar asked at the same time. Omar held his hand up to Rosemary to silence her. "Mer, why were you in there?" he asked again.

"He wanted new linens. He said he had a bad night and would sleep better if he had fresh sheets on the bed, but he told me he would make the bed himself."

"So, you put the sheets in the room?" Omar pressed.

Mer nodded. "I placed them on the bed and left."

Rosemary shook her finger at Mer. "Why didn't you make the bed, Mer? I trained you better."

"Auntie, you've told me a million times to do exactly what the guest requests, so that's what I did."

"How do you remember what was on the desk, Mer?" Omar asked flatly. "You take care of many rooms. Why do you remember what was on the desk in his cabin?"

Mer shrugged his shoulders. "Auntie assigned me only to the VIPs on this trip. So, after I took care of their rooms, I worked in the public spaces."

Rosemary gave a curt nod of her head. "That's true," she said smiling, "only VIPs and public space."

"Mer, I'm going to have to search your quarters," Omar said gravely.

Mer shrugged his shoulders. "Okay with me."

Omar, Rosemary, and Mer walked down to the crew cabins. Mer shared a room with three other men, and the space was cramped. After searching the room, Omar found nothing.

"See, I told you this was a wild goose chase," Rosemary said triumphantly, her arms crossed. "Are you happy now?"

"Rosemary," Omar said tiredly, "I meant no disrespect to you or Mer. Mer's key was the last one used before Chef Miles went in for the night."

"Hmph!" Rosemary snorted and then looked at Mer. "Why are you still here? Don't you have a lobby to clean? I'm sure it's a disaster."

Mer looked at Omar questioningly. "Yes, Mer, you are excused. Thank you for your time and for allowing me into your cabin." Mer bobbed his head and quickly scurried away before his aunt could find more for him to do.

Terri Butler was a machine as she tackled the events Kennedy had set out. Jones had looked over the list while she was changing clothes and mapped out a plan to make sure Terri would hit every station. He sighed, watching her from his lounge chair as she furiously played a game of ping pong. When she set her mind to something, there was no stopping her, and he only hoped she would pull playing cards that would total up to enough points to win the trophy she coveted. He pulled his hat low across his forehead and opened his book. If nothing else, he'd have time to catch up on his reading.

Omar returned from the bridge, having shared his updates with the captain, and the captain reported that no ships or planes in the area had found anything. "And there is nothing from the last sweep of the ship, according to Tully," the captain said soberly.

"It's perplexing, sir," Omar said. "It's like she vanished into thin air."

The captain nodded. "I agree. Something does not seem right. You've interviewed everyone from the notebook?"

Omar shook his head and looked at his watch. "I need to speak with: Deuce Dawson, Chef Tristan, and Chef Lola. I've spoken with everyone else. Mrs. Abbott has decided to turn her note over to the company's legal team."

The captain cocked his head. "Did I hear things right? She's giving a lecture today?"

Omar smiled. "Yes, on Mayan culture. Her knowledge of history is astonishing."

"Hmmm," the captain said quietly. "Perhaps we should float the idea of a guest lecturer on the ships." Omar then explained Emily's desire to become more involved in the company but less in the boardroom and more on the ships. "That could be a good thing and a bad thing," the captain chuckled. "There are some things the board and the family don't need to know about."

Omar left the bridge and headed for the spa and gym. His team had been trying to locate Chef Tristan and had radioed Omar when he was found in the gym. He wanted to observe the chef for a few minutes before speaking with him, and the two-way glass in the spa service hallway would make that possible. Mila had requested the unusual setup when she renovated the spa, as it would allow the staff to check on the gym without being obtrusive. It had proved valuable a few months ago when Kennedy had confronted a killer.

He walked past Anna Marie, pointing to the door marked private, and she waved to acknowledge him. He went through the door, down the hallway past the men's locker room and private treatment rooms, and took a right at the short service hallway. Tristan was using one of the weight machines and staring at himself in the mirror. For a moment, Omar remembered another person who had also been mesmerized by his reflection. After a few minutes, he entered the gym and grabbed a bottle of water from the refrigerator. "Chef Tristan," he said with a friendly smile holding out the bottle of water, "I wondered if I could have a word with you. I am Omar Meier, the director of security. I don't know if you remember me from the other night."

Tristan, who had been concentrating on his reps, looked startled. "Yeah, I remember you vaguely. Was it the night I was drunk?"

"That was the night." Tristan picked up a hand towel from the pile of items on the floor and mopped his head and neck. Omar noticed he was wearing a long sleeve shirt and was drenched in sweat.

Tristan flexed his bicep, felt the muscle, and then did the same to the other arm. "Got to keep this up so I look good for the ladies." He gave Omar a knowing smile. "What can I do for you? A recipe or a question about the competitions? Some workout tips?" He took a long pull on the water.

Omar smiled. "Not exactly. I wanted to see how your interactions have been with Ms. Monique Patrick. I've had a few complaints about her."

Tristan choked on the water as it went down his throat, and he began coughing. "I'm sorry, that took me off guard." He coughed again. "She's been a pain, but I handled her."

"Handled her?" Omar questioned.

"She tried to dig around for some dirt during our interview." He extended one arm over his head and leaned over. "Sorry, I've got to stretch after the workout." He stretched the other side, and when he did, Omar noticed the bruising on the side of his hand. "I turned the tables on her, though, and offered her a date when we got back to Florida. I figured she probably didn't get asked out by younger guys because she was older. You know what I mean?"

Omar crossed his arms. "You said she tried to dig around for some dirt. I don't understand. I thought she was here to write an article about the competition."

Tristan pulled one leg behind him with his hand. "Hamstrings," he said. "Stuff that happened a long time ago." He lowered his leg and picked up the other one. "It was a misunderstanding that got blown out of proportion. A guy like me wouldn't be into someone like her."

"Into whom?" Omar asked.

"Oh, sorry, dude." He chuckled and lowered his leg. "You know, for a security guard, you talk like my English teacher in high school. Yeah, so back to Monique. My former business partner thought I had the hots for his wife. I mean, yeah, I flirted with her, but it didn't mean anything. When she told me she wanted to leave her husband for me, I was like, no way." He held his hands out as if to stop someone. "Monique talked to this guy, and he said all sorts of stuff, and she brought it up in my interview."

Omar nodded his head. "Has anyone else had trouble with Monique?"

Tristan rolled his eyes. "We all did, dude! Even Jordan, the ice princess." He sat down on the floor, extended his legs, and reached for his toes with his fingers. "Is something going on?" he asked, keeping his eyes on his feet.

Omar shook his head. "We've received a few complaints, and I wanted to check with you and the others before we had any discussion with Ms. Patrick. Before I leave you, I have one last question, did you find a note under your door yesterday?"

Tristan hesitated for a split second and then shook his head. "Not that I know of, but then again, the little guy that takes care of my cabin, I can't remember his name; he would have picked it up if it was there. He's been picking up my clothes for the whole cruise." He looked up at Omar and grinned. "I wish I had someone like him at home to clean up after me."

Omar smiled tightly. "Mer is a fine young man who takes immense pride in his job. But to confirm, you didn't find a note under your door."

Tristan shook his head again. "Like I said, if something were on the floor, the little dude would have found it and thrown it away." Tristan went into his next stretch. "Anything else? I kind of need to finish my workout. It gets me pumped for the competition."

Omar put his hands behind his back. "No, thank you for your time. Good luck today."

Tristan pushed a lock of hair back. "No luck needed. I'm a sure winner. Miles falls asleep at the drop of a hat, Jordan is scared of her own shadow, and Lola's only culinary skill is using a can opener. It's good that those men who follow her around the ship are old." He pointed at his tongue. "No tastebuds left for them. No, I've got this in the bag. The looks," he flexed his bicep, "the physique, the sex appeal, and I'm young. And besides, the host doesn't actually cook on those shows. They have people to do the hard work. The host's job is to sell it to the camera. And that's something I do well. I can sell anything to anybody." He grinned and lowered himself quickly to the ground and began doing pushups. Omar stared at Tristan as he bobbed up and down.

"Well, thank you again for your time," Omar said, leaving the gym. He stopped in Mila's office and pointed at her coffee maker. "Spare a cup of your magic brew for an old friend?"

Mila looked up from the papers on her desk and smiled, gesturing for him to come in. "I just made a fresh pot, but it comes at a price." He looked at her questioningly. "What exactly is, or shall I say, *isn't* going on between you and Kennedy." She walked over to the coffee maker and began pouring coffee into a mug.

Omar sighed as he sat down. "It will sort itself out when I get back to town. I only wish I knew what happened to Monique Patrick."

"No word from search and rescue?" She handed him the mug.

Omar stared into the cup's inky darkness. "No, and it's a large footprint to cover. It's like looking for a needle in a haystack."

Mila sat down in her chair. "She wasn't well-liked, that's for sure."

"So, I am learning," Omar said. "Every interview I have had has shown that repeatedly. I'll admit she needled me at dinner last night with her questions about security protocols."

The two friends sat in the quiet. "So, you aren't going to tell me anything about you and Kennedy?"

Omar looked down at his shoes. "Nothing to tell."

"May I give you a small piece of advice, my old friend?" she asked. "Don't keep her in the dark. For Kennedy, talking is like air. It keeps her alive."

They were both quiet as they drank their coffee. Finally, Omar stood and placed his mug on the desk. "Thank you for the coffee and the words of wisdom."

"Ah, but will you heed them?" Mila laughed softly as he stood in the doorway, "Be careful, Omar. Trying to be noble has killed more knights than slayed dragons."

"Jonesy, take these," Terri Butler said as she threw more playing cards onto her husband's lap. "What's next?" she asked, bending over and panting.

Jones looked at the list. "Go attend the lecture in the Lunar Lounge. Sit at the back where the tall cocktail tables and barstools are so you can get out first. They'll be handing out the playing cards by the door. After that, hurry back out here for a line dance class." He saw her make a face. "I know you already know how to do line dancing, but it will get you another playing card, and it's quicker than watching the movie in the theater." He looked back at the list. "After dance lessons, go straight to the pool bar for the cocktail class with Luke. I'll even take that one with you. Sitting out here watching you scurry around has made me thirsty. I'll even have a SunRumbrella waiting for you."

"And maybe give me your poker card?" she asked slyly.

Jones shook his head vigorously. "Nope, if you are going to win this trophy, you are going to do it fair and square." He made a shooing motion with his hands. "Now go. You need to hustle to get your seat for the lecture."

She kissed his cheek. "What would I do without you, Jonesy?"

"I don't ever want to find out, Sweetsie." She began trotting away, and he hollered, "Don't fall asleep during the lecture. It will be dark and cool. Stand up if you feel yourself nodding off."

She gave him a thumbs up and trotted away to the theater.

## SUNNY DAYZ SUNRUMBRELLA

2 PARTS PINEAPPLE JUICE

2 PARTS ORANGE JUICE

1 1/2 PARTS RUM

LIME JUICE

GRENADINE SYRUP

CITRUS SLICES

CRUSHED ICE

COMBINE ALL INGREDIENTS IN A LARGE CONTAINER. POUR OVER CRUSHED ICE. GARNISH WITH CITRUS SLICES AND PAPER UMBRELLAS.

"I'm so nervous!" Emily said to Kennedy. They were standing to the side of the small circular stage. Whenever someone walked into the room, Emily felt another three-hundred-pound butterfly land in her stomach. She fanned herself. "It's cold in here, but I'm sweating. How do you do this every single day?"

Kennedy gave Emily a warm smile. "I'm always nervous until I start, and then I'm fine. You are going to be great, don't worry."

"Maybe this wasn't such a good idea."

Kennedy looked at Emily. "It's a great idea, and I've seen the slides you put together. You'll have the attendees on the edge of their seats. You have the clicker, right?" Emily patted her pocket. "I want you to take deep breaths while I introduce you, then walk over to me at the podium." She squeezed Emily's hand. "Let's see if this is your new career."

After Kennedy introduced Emily, she walked to the back of the room and saw Terri Butler standing with her back against the wall. "Terri," she whispered, "there are plenty of chairs if you want to sit down."

"No, I'm good," Terri whispered back. "Trying to stay alert. After the lecture, it's up to the pool deck for line dancing and the cocktail class. I'm determined to win the trophy," she said fiercely.

"I'll leave you to it," Kennedy whispered. "Good luck!"

Kennedy went down the back steps to the Solstice Theater to check on the last cooking competition. Ano was checking the refrigerators and pantries. She looked around. "Where's Michèle? Don't tell me he left you to do this alone?" she asked.

"It's all under control. He was all weird and smiley this morning. He kept complimenting people and was even nice to Franklin and Tony. He didn't yell once during the breakfast rush."

Kennedy looked strangely at Ano. "Michèle, our chef, was smiling and handing out compliments?"

Ano closed the door to the refrigerator and turned the wheelchair around to face Kennedy. "I know, it's strange, and last night after the competition, he, Jordan, and I hung out in the galley telling stories, and this morning she was on the line helping, and he was all smiles." He looked up at Kennedy, suddenly stricken. "You don't think he's going to get rid of me because of this," he pointed at his leg, "and hire her to take my job, do you?"

Kennedy bit back a smile. "I don't think you have anything to worry about, my friend," she said and walked backstage. She went into the costume room. The clothing rack on the back wall was full of outfits for tonight's show: hats, gloves, scarves, and antlers. She fingered the hangers and found the dress she was supposed to wear tonight. Her heart swelled as she bent to smell the fabric. The gold velvet dress had been her grandmother's and carried the faintest scent of her perfume.

"Is everything okay?" she heard Omar's voice.

Kennedy whipped around, startled, "Yes, just taking a trip down memory lane," she smiled softly.

Omar walked over to her and saw the dress in her hand. He whistled and touched the velvet material. "Elegant and unusual, like you." He gave Kennedy a long look, and her heart melted. "It reminds me of the glow early in the morning when the sun is rising, and the clouds capture the light." Kennedy blinked, terrified that any sound might burst the moment. "Are you okay?" he asked. "You are not normally this quiet."

She bit her lip. "Was there something you needed?"

He straightened his shoulders. "Yes, could you help me find Chef Lola and Deuce Dawson?" he said brusquely.

Kennedy looked at her watch. "Check the dining room. They should be getting ready for the competition."

"Thank you," he said. He turned quickly and left the dressing room, leaving Kennedy puzzled. One minute, he was complimenting her, and the next, he was reserved.

"I can't worry about this," she said, hanging the dress back on the rack. She walked around the backstage area. The scenery pieces and large props were there, and tonight was the first time the cast would perform the holiday show. She felt something was missing but couldn't put her finger on it. Finally, she sighed, giving up. She hoped she would figure it out before the show started.

Omar shook Deuce's hand. "Thank you for your time, sir. I appreciate your willingness to speak about the situation."

Deuce looked grave. "I hope this does not reflect badly on the show; so much work has gone into it."

The doors at the back of the dining room opened, and they could hear a flurry of voices. "I'm sure your network and our corporate office will manage it appropriately," Omar said. "I'll get out of your way so you may prepare your chefs for the competition. I still need to speak with Chef Lola. May I do so after you finish?"

Deuce shrugged his shoulders. "Be my guest, but please, don't shake her up too much. She was impressive last night, and I honestly didn't expect her to win. She now has a real shot at becoming the host chef. She may not be by the book, but she does think on her feet, which has its merits." Omar gave him a tight smile and left the dining room via the galley doors.

Miles, Lola, and Jordan stood before Deuce. "Chefs, good afternoon. We are one hour away from the competition, and I want to share today's theme."

"Sorry I'm late," Tristan called out loudly as he strutted through the dining room. "I had to take care of something, or should I say, someone," he leered, taking off his sunglasses.

"So nice of you to join us, Tristan, and showered," Deuce said dryly. "As I was saying, we are one hour away from the competition. Today's theme—"

"Another mystery basket full of things to trip us up?" Tristan asked snidely.

"Aw, bless your heart, Tristan," Lola held up a spoon and smiled into it. "You tried your best." She used a finger to wipe off a smear of lipstick on her tooth. "But it wasn't good enough to beat me," she cackled.

"Some of us would like to hear what Deuce has to say," Miles said in an exasperated tone.

"Thank you," Deuce glared at Lola and Tristan. "This afternoon's competition is a little easier than the others, and there will be no surprise foods. Today's theme is holiday dinners, but…" he held up a finger.

"Ah, there it is," Tristan tossed his head, "there is always a catch."

Deuce talked over Tristan, "…but, I'm not going to give you any other information until you get onstage. You will have forty-five minutes to complete your task."

"But we can use whatever we want?" Jordan asked.

Deuce nodded. "We have stocked the pantries and the refrigerators with all manner of items. However," he held up his hand, "as with all the other rounds, you may need to improvise." He looked sternly at Lola. "As a reminder, you may not leave the theater once the competition starts. You are welcome to stay here or leave. I will be back in forty-five minutes to collect you. I wish you all good luck." He left the room through the galley doors.

"I wish you all good luck," Tristan mimicked Deuce's voice. "As if he wants one of us to win." He blew out a breath and threw himself onto a chair. "He wants us to lose so he can swoop in and be the star of the show." Jordan,

Lola, and Miles exchanged looks. Tristan snorted. "You haven't figured that out yet? It's pretty obvious!"

Bert walked into the room as if in a daze.

"Why Bert, I didn't see you there," Lola drawled. "Are you here to take my picture?" She began to pose for him. "Which one of my poses do you want to start with? This one?"

"Bert?" Miles asked. "Are you okay? You seem a little shell-shocked."

"I'm-I'm-I'm fine," Bert said slowly, then shook his head quickly. "I'm here to get some group shots and a few of you as you contemplate what you will do for this last competition."

Tristan snorted and pointed at Lola. "You want to get a picture of her thinking?" He laughed. "Good luck. I don't think it's been captured on film before."

"Shut up, Tristan," Lola spat out. "I'd give you a nasty look, but I see you already have one. Oh wait, it's your face."

"Enough!" Miles roared. "This afternoon is our last chance to become the host chef of a new cooking show, and none of us have enough points to be the clear winner, so whatever we do out there today is do or die." He pointed at Lola and Tristan. "You two bicker so much that I can't decide if you hate each other or if this is some sick mating ritual."

"Dude, turn your burner down. Your pot is boiling over," Tristan chuckled, and Lola and Jordan began to snicker, and soon all four chefs were laughing hard.

"So," Bert began hesitantly as they began to settle down, "could I get those photos?"

"Sure, sorry guys, I'm just a little nervous about this afternoon. A lot is riding on it," Miles apologized. He put his arms around Tristan and Jordan. "Come on, Lola, get in here."

Lola walked over, grinning, and gave Tristan the side eye as she stood beside him. "Well, at least you don't smell like a gutter now. Just the town dump." Bert snapped several photos as the group chatted and laughed. Miles's outburst had somehow taken away the tension of the last competition.

While Bert was taking the last of the group photos, Omar walked in. "Bert, do you have many more shots to take?" he asked.

"Just a few individual ones as the chefs contemplate what they will make."

"Could you take Lola's first? I have a matter to discuss with her."

Lola suddenly lost all color in her face as she wondered if Larry had gone to the security director and then reasoned there was nothing he could do about it. She fluffed her hair and pulled her compact out of her pocket, giving her reflection a wide grin. "Come on, handsome," she said to Bert, "you can tell your friends you took this before I became a famous television chef."

Bert looked around the room for Art as he answered Lola. It was strange that she wasn't there as she always chatted with the chefs and Deuce before any of the competitions. "Sure," he said distractedly and motioned for Lola to sit at one of the tables. He looked around again for Art and then began snapping photos of Lola. He hadn't seen Art since they had been in the theater earlier in the day when he had asked her, quite awkwardly, if she would like to go to dinner and sit at the captain's table. "I mean, if you want to," he blushed. "If you have work to do, I understand."

"It's perfect timing," Art had said. "I'll be able to enjoy dinner because the competition will be over. I'll ask Chris and the AV team to film the announcement of who wins tonight, and we can edit the video later. I'll meet you in front of the dining room." Bert could only nod. He was afraid to say anything. He had a date, and he was terrified.

Leaving the theater in a daze, Bert walked toward the main dining room to take the group shots that Art and Deuce had requested. When he walked in, Tony was standing at the podium, perusing the seating chart. "Are you okay, Bert?" Tony had asked.

"I think so. I don't know," Bert said, bewildered. "I have a date," he blurted out.

"A date?" Tony asked in surprise. "Congratulations, my friend!" He clapped him on the shoulder.

"I'm taking Art to dinner tonight," Bert explained and then looked up at Tony wild-eyed, shaking his head violently. "Why did I ask her? I can't do this. I have to take the photos for dinner tonight, break everything down, and put it away. I don't even have a jacket to wear. No, Tony, would you find her and tell her I can't do it."

Tony chuckled. For once, he was not the nervous wreck his colleagues typically saw. "I am going to help you, Bert," and he put his arm around Bert's shoulders. "First, don't worry about a jacket. I have several in the closet that we use for guests who forgot to pack one. Now, we need to figure out where to store your gear. What will you have?"

"The backdrop screens, my tripod, my bag," he patted his camera, "and my friend here. After dinner, I have to go to the Solstice Theater for the holiday show. Kennedy wants some photos, and they will announce the winner at the end of the show, so I'll need my camera." He shook his head. "Why in the world did I ask her to dinner and at the captain's table?"

Tony snapped his fingers. "I know what to do. We'll store everything but the camera in security. Their office is across the hallway, and someone is always there." He began to get excited. "Don't worry about breaking anything down. My team and I will take care of it during dinner. You will wait outside the dining room for her, and when you are ready to come in, hand me your camera." He smiled widely, opened his jacket pocket, and began to unwrap a roll of antacids.

"Are you okay, Tony?" Bert looked at the antacids that were in Tony's palm.

Tony grinned. "I'm fine, but you look like you could use these."

"All right, chefs, we are fifteen minutes from showtime." Deuce clapped his hands together to get their attention. "Has anyone seen Art?" he anxiously looked around the dining room.

The four chefs shook their heads. "She's fine," Kennedy said quickly. "She's already up in the AV booth."

"It's not like her not to check in with me," Deuce said impatiently. "We always go over things before I go on camera."

"Do you need to *see* her? Could you talk over the headset when we get into the theater?"

"That will be fine," Deuce said, perturbed. "Is everything ready onstage?" Kennedy gave him a thumbs up.

She turned to the four chefs. "Okay, we'll do what we've done before. But this time, when I announce you, go to the center of the stage, take a bow, and then go to your station. We want to get the audience excited. So, now is your chance to have some flair. After the four of you are in place, I'll announce the judges and turn the show over to Deuce."

"Is that Monique chick around anywhere?" Tristan asked. "I don't want her coming backstage and pestering us with questions before the show."

Deuce gave Kennedy a quick look. "I haven't seen her, but I am sure she's already seated in the audience, ready to write about the last competition," he said. "If she shows up, Kennedy or I will turn her away."

Kennedy took the group through the back hallway to the theater and left them backstage as she went out to greet the audience. "Ladies and gentlemen, thank you so much for attending the final contest between our four chefs. We at

Sunny Dayz have never hosted a competition like this, and we look forward to meeting the host chef for *Classic Flavors* on the Classic Style Network."

Kennedy announced each chef, starting with Jordan, who surprisingly waved enthusiastically to the crowd. Miles was next and doffed his Panama hat to the audience. Not to be outdone, Tristan did his hat trick again and ended with his signature pose cupping his chin, and Lola paraded across the stage in her sparkling high heels and waved like a beauty pageant contestant. After Lola took her place, Kennedy turned the microphone back on and introduced the three judges again.

"Good afternoon, everyone, and welcome to our last competition," Deuce said as he walked to center stage. "This has been an interesting time as we search for the face of our new show, *Classic Flavors*. Today's competition is the fourth and final event. After today's winner is announced, the judges will spend some time deliberating, and we will announce the name of our new host after tonight's holiday show." He turned to the four chefs. "Chefs, you are tasked today with making a holiday meal consisting of a starter, a main dish, and at least one accompaniment. You will have forty-five minutes to complete this task." He paused dramatically. "You must also incorporate red and green in your dishes." The audience gasped and applauded. Deuce held up his stopwatch. "Chefs, you may begin!"

There was a definite air of excitement as, once again, the four chefs raced to the refrigerators. The audience immediately began laughing as they watched Lola jump up and down in frustration. Standing in front of the refrigerator doors, Tristan blocked her way as he decided on his ingredients. Then, to the audience's delight, Lola went under him and stood up. Now, *she* was in front of the doors. She took the items she needed and was gone before Tristan realized what had happened. Lola raced back to her station and dumped everything on her table. Miles walked over to the storage racks and took several bouquets of herbs, tomatoes, a jalapeno, and a bottle of champagne. He pulled the foil off the bottle while he trotted to his station. Ano and Emily exchanged looks as they saw his ingredients. Then, as Jordan returned from the refrigerator, she saw Lola coming toward her. Not wanting to get hit by the tiny tornado, Jordan stood still and held the fish she had taken up high in the air as she felt the wind blow past her.

"Ladies and gentlemen, we usually visit with our chefs while they are cooking, but today, we will allow them to prepare their dishes without interruption. Our overhead cameras will capture what they are making." He pointed to the screens above him. "In the meantime, let's remember some of the best and worst moments of the competitions and our excursions." The house lights dimmed, leaving only the four spotlights on the mini-kitchens, and Art began to play the video clip on the center screen.

"We've had chefs going rogue," Deuce said into the microphone, and the audience laughed and pointed at the video of Lola running barefoot down the aisle to the pool bar as it flashed above. "And chefs with dough on their face." A photo of Jordan wearing a pizza dough mask popped up. "There have also been moments we'd like to forget," and the screen showed Emily's face as she tasted the chili Tristan had made. The audience continued to roar with laughter, and Deuce didn't understand why until he turned and looked up at the screen. Art had put up the video of Lola knocking Deuce down as she planted a kiss on his face. As the slideshow continued, laughter broke out again and again: Lola covered in avocado sauce, Miles's face when the handle on the pan flew off, Tristan's red-faced reaction to drinking fish sauce, and Kennedy's head dripping with egg yolk.

Lola smiled and checked her reflection in her spatula. "Wow, I'm looking good today. The avocado masque was wonderful for my skin," she said. Then, she put her hand on her hip. "Sometimes I look in the mirror, and even my reflection is jealous of how good I look."

Tristan could not allow the comment to sit there. "Well, mirrors don't lie, but they can't laugh either." Several audience members heard him and chuckled.

"Fight nicely, children," Miles said, not looking up from his cutting board as he minced parsley.

Terri and Jones were sitting in the back of the theater. She had been counting her cards. "Jones," she whispered, "do you think I have enough?"

Jones looked at her cards once again and smiled. Today, she had had the focus of a shark searching for prey. "We won't know until you get your card from here, but I sure hope so. I don't want to go home with you if you don't win that trophy."

"Chefs, you are at the two-minute mark," Deuce said into the microphone. With those words, an electrical current went through the theater, and the audience sat up straighter as the four chefs went into hyper mode, and their workstations became scenes of frantic movement.

Deuce looked down at his watch. "And time," he exclaimed. "Chefs, please step back from your stations." As they did, members of the ship's culinary team stepped forward and placed the tasting dishes on carts to take to the judges.

"Chef Lola, as you won yesterday's competition, we will start with you."

Lola paraded across the stage. She gave the audience a curtsey and stood behind the cart which held her dishes.

Deuce looked up at her and cleared his throat. "Could you please share with us and the audience what you have made?" The camera zoomed in on her plates as they were placed in front of each judge.

"Well, Deuce, as the holidays are my absolute favorite time of the year, I made some traditional favorites. Mini cheese balls, green beans wrapped in bacon, and barbequed chicken."

"That certainly sounds like a unique menu," Emily said.

Deuce, Ano, and Emily took a knife and smeared some of the cheeseballs onto the crackers on their plate.

"A bit heavy on the Worcestershire sauce and onion powder," Deuce sighed as he drank heavily from his water glass.

The green bean bundles on the plates were bright and looked lovely. Deuce took the first bite. "They are a bit crunchy, and the bacon is undercooked." He looked at Emily and Ano. "Try the green beans but avoid the bacon." Lola bit her lip as Emily used the side of her fork to try to cut a green bean, and it skittered across the table. Deuce rubbed his hands together and looked down at his plate. "I must admit, I am looking forward to the barbequed chicken. I haven't eaten it in a while, and I must compliment you on an interesting choice." Lola beamed. Ano began to cut into the chicken, placed his fork and knife down, and put his hand over Emily's. He tipped the plate for Deuce to see. "Chef Lola, what temperature did you cook the chicken at?"

"Three hundred and fifty degrees, silly. Everyone knows it is the best temperature to cook everything," Lola fluffed her hair as she answered him.

"Chef Lola, this chicken is so raw, I'm surprised it isn't dancing on the stage." He tilted his plate to the camera to show the raw chicken, and the audience groaned and gasped.

"But it's got the barbequed crust on it!" she whined. "That should count for something."

"Chef Lola, you may return to your station."

"But..."

"Chef Lola," he said with emphasis, "please return to your station." Then, he sighed and looked at the other chefs. "Chef Miles, please present your items."

Miles stood before the judges' table. "I have prepared a beet salad over baby greens with goat cheese and walnuts, champagne risotto, and Christmas steak."

"The salad and risotto are fine," Deuce said arrogantly. "Let's talk about your Christmas steak." He pointed to the porterhouse steak Miles had cut to resemble a Christmas tree. One side of the steak had an emerald green sauce, while the other was bright red. Deuce used his knife to expertly cut six pieces from the steak, placing two pieces on plates for Ano and Emily. Deuce dipped his finger in the red sauce, and his face brightened. "Salsa roja and fresh chimichurri?" He paused and smiled. "Someone was paying attention on our excursion to Mahahual. Well done, Chef." Miles nodded and walked back to his station as the audience applauded.

"Chef Tristan, perhaps you can dazzle us with something," Deuce said dryly. Tristan strolled to the judges' table and flexed his biceps for the audience. Then, he stood behind the cart with his dishes. Deuce pointed at the plates and bowls in front of them. "Please explain what you have prepared."

"In front of you are crab and cheese stuffed mini peppers and cioppino," he said proudly.

Deuce looked at the bowl in front of him. "I see a lot of red here, no green. And where is the accompaniment? Did you not understand the rules for today's event?"

Tristan swallowed. "The stuffed peppers are green, and the stew is red. There are even fresh herbs in the stew, which would be green," he protested. "And it is a traditional Italian holiday dish. My grandmother makes it every year."

Ano picked up his spoon and brought it to his mouth. "Too much salt," he whispered and took a drink of water.

Deuce washed his face with his hands and then looked at Tristan, who glared at Ano. The theater was painfully silent. "You may return to your station," he said with disgust.

"Chef Jordan," Emily said brightly, "you are our last contestant tonight. Would you please come over and present us with your dishes."

Jordan walked over. "Good afternoon, chefs, Mrs. Abbott. I prepared two kinds of hummus, one using basil and the other using roasted red peppers and artichokes. Red and green grilled snapper with two homemade salsas and," she uncovered the foil packet on one of the plates, "warm tortillas."

"The presentation is lovely, dear," Emily said.

Deuce took a quick bite of the snapper. "Is this something that members of our audience could easily make?"

Jordan nodded. "Yes, it is. The hummus and salsas can be made ahead of time, and as for the fish, fillets could be used instead of a whole piece of snapper." She looked at the large piece of fish. "It would be easier to serve, although not as dramatic."

"Thank you," Deuce said curtly. "You may return to your station." He rose from his chair and looked at the audience. "Ladies and gentlemen, if you will excuse us, the judges must confer for a moment." Emily, Ano, and Deuce formed a tight circle.

"I think Miles should win this competition, his dishes made for a perfect holiday dinner," Emily said.

Ano agreed. "His sauces were perfect, and slicing the steak to look like a Christmas tree made for a terrific presentation."

"I agree with you both. Miles for top honors and then Jordan." He sighed. "I'm not sure what to do about Tristan and Lola. The cioppino tasted like brine, and there is no excuse for Lola's items. Serving raw chicken is unacceptable. Anyone who took home economics in high school would know the basics of making that dish. Are we all in agreement?" Emily and Ano nodded quickly and returned to the judges' table. Deuce picked up the microphone and walked to center stage. "Ladies and gentlemen, thank you for your patience. We are ready to announce the winner of today's fourth and final event. Chefs, please stand in front of your stations." Spotlights fell on each chef.

"Chefs Tristan and Lola." Lola beamed at him. "Your meals were inedible. Chef Tristan, as you incorporated a traditional holiday dish, you will be awarded points;

however, your grandmother's fish stew tasted more like a mixture of seawater and tomato juice. Chef Lola, I would encourage you to attend a basic home economics class before you attempt to make barbecued chicken again." The spotlights turned off Tristan and Lola. "Chef Jordan, a very nice job." The audience clapped, and the spotlight on Jordan winked off. The applause from the audience got louder as Chef Miles stood alone in the spotlight. "And now there is one," Deuce said slowly, "Chef Miles, congratulations on winning today's competition."

Kennedy walked back onto the stage. "Ladies and gentlemen, thank you for coming this afternoon. If you are collecting playing cards for the Sun Trophy, we have them at the back doors. We hope you will return for our holiday show and the announcement of Classic Style Network's new host chef."

Jones and Terri slipped out of the theater, and Terri looked at the fan of cards one of the cast members was holding. She pulled one and turned it over. "An ace!" she hollered and ran to the guest services desk to have her cards tallied. The agent printed her name, cabin number, and the total number of points on a card and complimented her on her score.

Karl was pushing Marshall up the aisle of the theater. "I need a drink," Marshall wheezed. "That was rough."

"I agree," Eddie said, "but we only have an hour until dinner."

"I just hope chicken isn't on the menu. I don't think I can look at a piece of poultry for a long time," Paulie said.

They went down to Longitudes. "You know, I like this bar," Eddie remarked. "It's a little seedy. A good place to drown one's sorrows."

"Well, this place should be packed!" Karl chuckled for the first time all day. "We can't be the only losers on the boat." They began to laugh.

Larry cleared his throat. "I need to apologize to all of you. I feel terrible about what has happened, but I had to tell you the truth."

"Thank goodness you did. You kept these two bozos from making a huge mistake," Marshall said. "But we're on our own now for cooking, and this one," he pointed a finger at Karl, "can't do anything more than make a sandwich."

"That's not true, Pop," Karl protested. "I make an excellent frozen pizza." Paulie shuddered.

"I've been thinking about our new problem," Larry said. "What if we made a menu of things we liked to eat and did the shopping together? We could divide up the chores and split up the meals. It would save us a lot of money."

"What about poker night?" Paulie asked and crossed his arms. "We've built a reputation for our poker nights based on our dinners."

Larry smiled. "That food came from a big box store and was reheated. We can do the same thing, and no one will be the wiser. Lola was pretty but let's face it. She wasn't a rocket scientist."

Paulie bent over, looking under the table.

"What are you doing?" Marshall asked.

"I'm checking out his legs. Lola had amazing legs. Larry's are not so bad. He could pull it off with the right shorts and a tan."

Larry looked down at his legs in surprise. Eddie began to laugh and was soon joined by Karl. Marshall started to snicker and wheeze, and Paulie wiped tears from his face. Karl's shoulders shook with laughter. "I needed that. Thank you, friend." He clapped Paulie on the shoulder.

"Boys, it's our last night, and I want to people-watch." Marshall maneuvered his wheelchair away from the table. "That one lady wears some strange outfits, but those legs," he sighed deeply. Then, he looked up quickly at Larry. "No offense, son. Paulie may think you have great legs, but the jury is still out until I see a tan on yours."

As soon as the cooking competition ended, the maintenance, housekeeping, and culinary teams began dismantling the stage setup. Kennedy walked around the backstage area, looking once again at the props. She felt strongly that something important was missing.

"Everything okay, Kennedy?" Kyle, one of the cast members, asked as he put on a pair of rhinestone-embedded sunglasses and placed a black pompadour wig on his head. "You look puzzled."

"Yes, I'm fine," she said distractedly, looking at her clipboard. "The question is, are you…" She tried to stifle a giggle. "Oh, good grief, what are you wearing?"

"I'm the king of rock and roll." He wiggled his hips. "I'm a hunka hunka holiday love," he said and whipped off his sunglasses in a practiced move.

She heard banging and a loud curse. "I wonder what that was," she said with some alarm and walked quickly to the stage and pulled the heavy velvet curtain back. "Is everything okay?" she yelled over the din.

Franklin wiped a bead of sweat from his forehead as he walked over to her. "Everything's fine. Noise means work, remember? Now, do you have a diagram of what goes where? My guys and I can help set the stage with the cast.”

“Really? Oh, thank you!” She hugged him and began sketching the stage, making a rough drawing to show him where the various props went. “There is one more piece, but I’m drawing a blank.”

Franklin looked at the drawing. “Can I make a suggestion?” She looked at him questioningly. “I know you are the most organized person in the world, but have you thought about writing down the songs in order and what props are involved with them?”

She blinked. “Why didn’t I think of that?”

He smiled at her and tapped her temple. “Because your brain runs like a hummingbird’s wings, and an old one like mine moves like a tortoise, just plodding along.” He looked over at his team. “And looking at my guys, they appear to be trying to imitate turtles, and I need to get them to step it up a little. And don’t worry,” he called out as he walked away, “Santa will be here to help if you need anything.”

Kennedy watched his retreating back, puzzled by his comment. She shrugged her shoulders, took a fresh sheet of paper from her clipboard, and began to draw the stage setup again when her radio chirped. She was needed in the conference room. Kennedy put her pencil down and put the piece of paper back into her clipboard, putting a fresh sheet on top.

She left the theater, and as she passed the guest services desk, one of the agents called her name.

"Kennedy," she said, holding up a piece of paper, "we have a clear winner for the trophy." Kennedy took the folded slip of paper and smiled when she opened it. Then, she entered the conference room, where she found Deuce and Emily deep in discussion. They looked up when they saw her.

"We have a problem," Deuce said in a defeated tone as Kennedy took her seat. He stood up and ran a hand through his hair, making his curls bounce back and forth. He held up his hand and extended his index finger. "First, I have a contestant pretending to be a chef." He raised his middle finger. "Next, I have a chef who falls asleep while cooking on live television." His ring finger went up. "I have one who is a complete bonehead." And then he held up his pinkie finger. "And finally, the one chef I thought I could count on is sleeping with your executive chef, who happens to be one of the competition's judges. If this information got out, the public could construe he had undue influence over the replacement judge, his sous chef, and possibly Mrs. Abbott." He fell into his chair and began massaging his temples. "We can't announce a winner because not one of them is suitable," he said miserably. "Oh, and then there is the small matter of Monique Patrick, who was writing about the competition, jumping overboard. This is a colossal mess."

Kennedy took a deep breath. "Deuce," she said quietly, "we can't do anything about the Monique situation, and we've done well to keep it under wraps. If we are lucky, we will continue to keep it contained, and hopefully, it will not attach itself to the network's reputation. But we have a ship full of passengers expecting to hear who the new host chef will be. They have watched the competition and interacted with you and the four contestants during the cruise. Many have already formed attachments to their favorite and hope that person will be the winner; however, if you don't announce a host chef, they might feel that this was all a scam. After this afternoon's competition, who would have been your choice?"

"Jordan," they said in unison.

"But it would be unethical to name her the winning chef now," Deuce said, washing his face with his hands.

"The points make Miles the runner-up, followed by Lola and then Tristan," Emily said. The room was silent as they searched for an answer. "Deuce, would there be any harm in extending your search?" Emily asked.

Deuce looked at her strangely. "You mean not announce a winner tonight? She," he pointed at Kennedy, "just said we had to have a winner."

"Not necessarily," Emily said thoughtfully. "You could say the total number of points is too close, and to be fair, you want to bring each of them on as a guest chef. But, in the meantime, you would be the show's host."

Deuce shook his head back and forth. "But I'm the producer of the show. It wouldn't be right."

Kennedy spoke up, "I don't think Mrs. Abbott means forever, just for a few weeks while you decide what to do. If you didn't have a host chef by then, you could take the show on the road. I'm sure you have other companies like ours you are in partnerships with, right?" Deuce nodded. "Maybe you could invite the chef at every location you visit to join a large-scale competition. But at the network," she added quickly, "not on the ship."

Deuce began to slowly nod his head at the solution the two women were offering. "We could go to the various resorts and towns that spend their advertising dollars with us, which would get more viewers as they tuned in to see their chef on television." His eyes brightened with excitement. "There could be a showdown at the end of next year and launch the new host chef then!" He looked at both women.

"This could work, but it would be a monumental undertaking."

"I think it's your best solution for now, and whatever assistance our company can offer is available to you," Emily said. "Especially due to our part in this," she cleared her throat, and her eyes sparkled merrily, "cooking conundrum."

The atmosphere in the dining room was festive. Bert had been taking photographs of the passengers as they entered the dining room for their final dinner at sea. He kept looking around between shots, searching for Art. Tony came out to his photo area to check on him. "Are you okay, my friend?"

Bert was pulling on the collar of his shirt. "I think this tie is too tight," he said. "How do you wear one of these every day?"

Tony grinned and straightened Bert's tie. "I've been wearing one since elementary school. Relax, my friend, this is dinner. You aren't walking down the aisle to get married."

"And this coat is hideous, Tony," Bert complained. It was a grey and red plaid double-breasted sportscoat and was two sizes too big on Bert.

"You can take it off as soon as you sit down," Tony offered.

"That's not the point! She's going to see me in it!" Bert said, exasperated.

Omar came around from behind the background screen. He had a navy blue sportscoat draped across his arm. "I think this will help, may I?" He helped Bert into the jacket while Tony nodded at his servers, who began taking down the screen and tripod.

"Please throw this thing in the trash," Omar said, handing Tony the jacket Bert had been wearing. "It's hideous."

"Bert, you look positively handsome tonight," Kennedy said, coming up to him. She frowned. "You need something…ah, this will do nicely," and she plucked Omar's pocket square from his jacket and stuffed it into Bert's.

"Now, remember to offer her your arm and pull out her chair for her," Franklin's deep voice said as he walked up with Luke, Mila, and Rosemary.

"And always open the door. They love that!" Luke offered.

"How did you? What?" Bert looked at his friends.

Tony laughed and slapped Bert on the back. "Did you think you would go on this date without all of us showing up? We feel like parents on prom night."

Franklin sniffled and pretended to wipe away a tear. "My little boy is growing up," he said in a falsetto voice.

"Bert, don't pay attention to them," Mila's melodious voice whispered in his ear as she kissed his cheek. "They are jealous old men." She stood back and looked at him. "You look perfect." She looked at the others and clapped her hands. "Okay, everybody, back to work. Showtime's over."

"Hey, Bert, come by the lounge tonight after the show in the theater, and I'll set you guys up," Luke said.

"Uh, sure," Bert gulped and turned to Kennedy. "I don't think…" He suddenly stopped speaking as he saw Art over Kennedy's shoulder. He walked toward her, and the others fell back. "Good evening," he said, not sure it was his voice coming out of his mouth, "you look stunning." He held his arm out to Art.

Mila had tamed Art's typically wild red hair into a chignon, and a simple black strapless dress, high heels, and earrings replaced her traditional flak jacket, T-shirt, and cargo pants uniform.

"Nice job, fairy godmother," Kennedy whispered to Mila.

"Just waved my magic wand," Mila whispered back.

Bert and Art began to walk up the three steps to the dining room's entrance, and suddenly Art tripped, landing on her hands and knees. Kennedy and the others gasped. Bert held out his hand, and Art, laughing hysterically, took it. She pointed at her shoes. "How women walk in these escapes me. It's like walking on stilts. Give me a good pair of sneakers any day."

Emily was speaking with the captain when she saw Bert and Art walking behind Tony. She pointed her head toward the couple. "That is nice to see."

The captain nodded. "Ah yes, I was asked if Bert and the young woman who works for Mr. Dawson could join us tonight."

"Who?" Deuce asked, taking a drink of water. He turned his head to follow Emily's nod and began spluttering and choking. "Art?" He stood up so quickly that his chair fell over. Tony and Bert both moved to hold out Art's chair; however, Bert was quicker, and she beamed at him as she sat down.

"Good evening, Deuce," she smiled as he tried clumsily to right his chair.

"Wow, y-y-you look—"

"You look absolutely lovely tonight," Emily quickly interjected. "I'm sorry Deuce's brain is not functioning. He must be nervous about his big announcement." She kicked him under the table. "Right?"

"Uh, yeah," he said, "it's just that you—" Emily kicked him again.

"Don't normally look like this?" Art finished his sentence. "No, but it's good to shake things up now and then."

"May I propose a toast," the captain stood up, holding his drink. "To strong, smart, beautiful women, may we be lucky enough to know them," and then he added, "And wise enough to stay out of their way."

Kennedy flitted around the dining room, making sure the passengers enjoyed their last night on the ship. She stopped to visit with the Gents from Breezy Bayou, Lola's former fan club. "All well tonight, gentlemen?" she asked.

"We'd be better if you were sitting with us, toots," Marshall said and then looked away as something caught his eye. His finger shook as he pointed at the dining room entry. "Could you get Mrs. Claus to come over here? I have been a *very* naughty boy."

"Pop!" Karl clapped a hand over Marshall's mouth before he could get another word out. Karl and the others followed Marshall's pointing finger to see what he was talking about. They watched as the Butlers were led to their table. Terri held the room's attention in a dark red velvet dress trimmed in white fur.

"That woman would make Marilyn Monroe hide in a closet," Paulie breathed.

"I saw her first boys," Marshall wheezed.

Once Terri and Jones were seated, their server brought a glass of champagne and a bourbon to their table. He cleared his throat and picked up his glass. "To the most beautiful woman in the room." He gently touched her glass with his. "Terri, I have something for you tonight, a new tradition for us."

"Jones, you are always buying me such beautiful things, and I feel terrible I don't wear them as often as I should," she said breathlessly.

"It's funny you should say that. I always want you to have a memento from our trips, and I found a way for you to have your memories together all the time." Terri gave Jones a puzzled look. Then, reaching into his pocket, he pulled out a small velvet box and opened it. Inside was a gold link bracelet with a shark fin charm on it. "From now on, on our special occasions, I'm going to give you a charm for your bracelet. This one," he pointed to the single charm on the bracelet, "is a shark fin to remind you of your hunt for points to win the Sun Trophy. I bought it today in the ship's boutique while you were running around collecting cards."

"Oh, Jonesy," Terri said breathlessly, holding out her wrist for Jones to fasten the bracelet, "it's perfect, and I can wear it all of the time."

"So, I was thinking about the house. First of all, you were right about the bathroom." Terri gave him a knowing smile. "Second, what do you think about a safari theme for my office? You know, animal heads, masks, pith helmets, spears."

"But you wanted a rustic hunting theme, remember?" she said. "The designer and I have selected everything."

Jones sighed and explained to her that the zebra print rug in their stateroom and their conversation with Monique had inspired him. "We might also need to go on a safari," he grinned. "Maybe we could talk to that Monique lady about helping us."

"Really?" She smirked. "If you are changing the office because of being back in our cabin, can I order the round settee and the crystal chandelier for my dressing room?"

He smiled. "Well, while we are talking about it…" Then, the two discussed more plans for their home that they had each thought of during the cruise.

Kennedy left the dining room through the staff passageway and walked into the back of the theater to check on the stage. No one would have ever known it had been home to a cooking competition a few hours earlier. The set reminded her of the snow globes her grandmother had brought out each Christmas. Groupings of oversized ornaments sat on either side of the stage, flanked by gigantic red and white candy canes. A majestic Christmas tree stood quietly in the back. Its lights had yet to be turned on. When the cast rolled it out during the last song, the lights on the tree would magically turn on. She made a face. "Everything is here. I'm overthinking this," she muttered and walked up the aisle to return to the dining room. She had almost reached the doors when she heard her name called out.

"Kennedy." Omar was quickly walking up to her. "I was on my way to update the captain." He shook his head at her unanswered question.

She swallowed. "I'm not sure what to say or think." She looked at her watch. "I hope we can keep things under wraps until we reach Port Canaveral."

He nodded grimly. "Only a few more hours. Speaking of which, we need to talk when we get back to port. Please excuse me. I need to find the captain." he brushed past her and walked into the dining room.

"Eighty-six the short ribs," Chef Michèle barked. "Jordan," he shoved a plate at her, "garnish this and take it to Mrs. Abbott at the captain's table. I don't need a dead plate for the great-granddaughter of our founder."

"Offline for expo," Jordan shouted and quickly took the plate of salmon that he had handed to her. She spooned some gremolata on the fish and took it to the dining room.

Emily had been speaking with Deuce, who suddenly stopped talking when he saw Jordan's ear-to-ear grin. She placed the plate of salmon in front of Emily, and as Emily turned to say thank you, her words stopped in her mouth. "My dear, what are you doing bringing me my dinner?"

Jordan beamed. "I'd love to chat, but I'm helping Chef Michèle, and I'm on cloud nine!" She hustled back to the kitchen and walked through the swinging doors. The orchestra of the galley was reaching a crescendo as stockpots hissed, and saucepans sizzled on the burners. The china plates on the stainless-steel counters rattled as knives beat out a staccato beat while chopping what was in front of them. She smiled, hearing the lyrics that accompanied the symphony which played around her. "Stretch it," she heard; "done swimming," another voice called out as they dumped a pot of pasta into a colander. They worked at a furious pace, riding the wave until Ano suddenly called out. "The board is clear." They took a collective breath; another night in the galley had come to a close, and the adrenaline rush was over until the next cruise.

"Jordan, fantastic job tonight," Ano said as he wheeled over to her. "No one would ever know you had not worked in a large kitchen before."

"Thank you," she said breathlessly. "It was amazing, and I don't know if I can go back to my tiny restaurant kitchen in Florida." She looked around at the others who were now cleaning their areas. "What are the chances of getting on with a ship?"

Ano's eyes were full of mirth. "One cruise and you are ready to jump on board. There are always openings." He looked at her solemnly. "It's a hard life, Jordan. The short cruises are not so bad. The longer ones are tough. But what about the show? And your restaurant?"

Jordan inclined her head toward Michèle. "I think I may have been disqualified. As for the restaurant, I don't know; it's safe and comfortable, but I wonder if I am ready for the next step." Ano nodded. Life on board was not for everyone, but then again, life on land also had challenges.

"Jordan," Michèle barked. "You should be in the theater in fifteen minutes." He gave her a wink and then looked at Ano. "And if *you* have time to gab, you must need something to do." He thrust a clipboard at him. "There are req forms to be filled out, menus to look at for the next cruise..." he was still talking as he walked toward his office.

Ano grinned at Jordan. "Back to my glamorous life," and he began wheeling himself after the tall chef.

Jordan looked at her watch. She knew she wouldn't have time to change after helping with dinner and had brought a fresh chef's jacket to put on. She was on her way into the theater when she saw Miles and Lola at the doors. "Good grief, you look awful," Lola said, taking in Jordan's outfit and damp hair.

"I was helping in the kitchen," Jordan replied. "There was no time to change."

"I wondered where you were," Miles said. "What's it like?" he asked. His eyes were bright with excitement.

Jordan's eyes lit up. "It's like riding a roller coaster. You slowly creep up the hill as dinner service starts, and then suddenly, you are flying down the rails, and your stomach drops as the orders begin to come in all at once. It was exhilarating."

"Excuse me," Lola snapped her fingers. "Has anyone seen Tristan? He wasn't at dinner, and I got stuck eating with Grandpa," she pointed at Miles with her thumb, "who surprisingly managed to stay awake through dinner. We are all supposed to sit together so they can bring us up onstage. They have seats for us on the front row."

Miles looked around, searching the area for Tristan. "Why don't the two of you go inside? I'll wait for Tristan out here. Or do you have to wait for your entourage, Lola? I didn't see your friends with you today, and they were strangely silent during the competition."

"They weren't feeling well," Lola quickly snapped. "A few too many drinks the other night after my big win. Like you, Grandpa, they can't handle their alcohol."

The two women went inside, and Miles waited in the lobby for Tristan. It was unusual that Tristan had missed dinner, and Miles was concerned. He took the steps up two flights and knocked on Tristan's door. "Tristan, we need to be in the theater." The door opened violently, and Miles looked at the man in front of him. Tristan's eyes were red, and he was sweating profusely. "I was coming to see if you were okay. You disappeared after the competition, and you missed dinner. They need us in the theater to announce the winner."

Tristan sniffed. "I don't know if I'm going. The man insulted my grandmother's cioppino. He said it tasted like seawater on camera, which I'm sure will be shown on the morning show, and my entire family will see it. He has purposefully found a way to humiliate me during this entire competition, and I think it's because he's intimidated by me," Tristan blustered. "I have *everything* this show needs, and he knows it! He's jealous."

"Tristan, swallow your pride," Miles said exasperatedly. "You owe some professionalism to the rest of us." Tristan glared at Miles. "For someone so concerned about their image, you aren't thinking ahead. Have you thought about the people that are watching the takes? Maybe someone watching needs a front-of-the-house chef like you, someone to be the face of their restaurant. You don't want to stay in Jacksonville at Swank forever, do you? Think bigger. New York, Chicago, New Orleans, or Los Angeles."

Tristan ran a hand through his unruly hair. "I didn't think about it that way."

"That's the thing, Tristan. You are so wrapped up in winning that you haven't considered what this competition could do for you in the long run. I knew I was out when I fell asleep the second time, but I hope my being in the competition drives people to my restaurant."

"Well, you did snore pretty loudly," Tristan snickered. "I'm glad they didn't make us share cabins. Your snoring would have made it hard to sleep. I would have needed a sleeping pill or some of your medication to knock me out. Look," he said fidgety, "I hear what you are saying, and you are right. I need to look at the big picture. I'll get cleaned up and slide into the theater during the show. They won't announce us until the end. Just hold me a seat."

"We're on the front row, don't take too long," Miles said and left Tristan. As he made his way to the theater, one of Tristan's comments kept turning around in his head.

Kennedy was backstage directing the organized chaos of a new show. Everyone was in their costumes for the first few numbers, and several crew members were there to help move props around as needed. Kennedy was surprised to see Franklin carrying a suit bag. "Ho-ho-ho," he bellowed, walking up to her. "Where is the dressing room for the star of this show?"

"The star?" Kennedy asked blankly, echoing his words.

"In the lobby, you asked me to do it." He held his fingers up in the air, making quotation marks, and mimicked her. "All you have to do is sit in the sleigh. You don't have to say anything—just wave. The reindeer dance and then pull you across the stage."

"Reindeer dancing, sleigh, Santa, oh my goodness," she said breathlessly and smacked her forehead. "I know what is missing! Can I borrow your radio?" He looked at her strangely and took it off his belt, and she motioned for him to follow her. As they were walking, she radioed the ship's operator and asked to have Billy Higgins paged to the theater's backstage area immediately. She opened a door with a star on it. "Here you go, a star for the star. Just put on your pants and boots for now. We need to go down to the hold to get your sleigh. I'll be back as soon as I welcome everyone to the show. I knew I forgot something." She smiled radiantly and handed him back the radio. "I'm not crazy."

"Well…that's debatable, but why do you need Billy? I can send a couple of my guys down—" Franklin put his radio up to his lips.

Kennedy shook her head. "Billy will know exactly where it will be because he loaded everything into the locker. But it will take the three of us to get it out. It's not heavy, just large and awkward."

"A little like me, you're saying." Franklin patted his stomach.

"I'll be right back."

Moments later, Franklin heard her through the speakers. "Good evening, everyone, and welcome to our last show of the cruise." The audience applauded politely, saddened by the thought that they were returning to reality the next day.

"She looks like Grace Kelly up there," Marshall whispered to his son. "What a knockout!" Kennedy did look lovely. The vintage golden dress fit her like a second skin. Rhinestone combs twinkled in the lights as they held back her dark hair. Omar stood at the back of the darkened theater; he could not take his eyes off the brunette beauty commanding the stage. He felt a flicker of worry at the thought of returning to Port Canaveral.

The curtains rose, and the cast took their places for the first set of holiday show tunes. Kennedy saw Billy bent over at the waist, catching his breath. "What's wrong?" he panted. "I took the staff steps two at a time when I heard the page. Is everything okay?"

"Yes," she replied and motioned for him to follow her. She knocked on a dressing room door and opened it. "Let's go." She walked quickly to the service elevator and pushed the down button. Billy looked strangely at Franklin, who was wearing red pants with red suspenders, a white T-shirt, and black boots.

"Not a word," Franklin growled.

Kennedy turned to Billy. "We need to find the sleigh. It's in one of the large boxes we left in the storage locker. It's one of the stage props."

Billy nodded his head in the affirmative. "I think it's the one I brought up when we were putting out the holiday decorations, but when I realized it wasn't supposed to go out, I put it back."

They got on the elevator, and Kennedy fanned herself. "Gosh, it's hot."

"Try wearing these pants," Franklin said. He looked sternly at both of them. "Neither of you will ever breathe a word of this. The minute I am offstage, I go back into my dressing room, and this," he pointed to the red pants he was wearing, "goes to the costume room."

"So, did a woman really—"

"No comment," he barked as the elevator doors opened.

"This way." Billy jogged down the maze and finally reached the lockers that housed the holiday decorations. He opened the first locker, scanning the boxes. "No," he shook his head, "this was the one with the stage props. It's the other one."

"I thought you knew where it was," Franklin said, annoyed.

"Trust me, after your fourth load of boxes going up and down the elevator, they begin to blur together. I've moved these twice already."

"I'm just going to double-check," Kennedy said and walked into the cage that Billy had just vacated. Franklin stood in the hallway, waiting for her to come out.

Billy opened the locker door in front of him. The hinge squealed loudly as he pulled on the door. "Kennedy," he said, his voice rising nervously, "w-w-why is that box moving?"

"Moving?" she called out and walked past Franklin to the locker where Billy was standing. "It's probably just sliding with the—" But before she could finish her sentence, the box on the floor began to buck violently.

"Franklin!" she shouted. "I need you now!" She wrenched open the two long flaps of the box on the floor and found a panicked Monique Patrick lying inside a cocoon of packing material. Her mouth had been taped shut.

Franklin lumbered in. "What's wrong? Oh my—" He did not finish his sentence and ran down the hallway. Kennedy could hear him throwing his weight against a door. The small office across from the two jail cells in the hold had a phone and a radio.

Kennedy and Billy were bent over Monique, frantically digging the packing materials out of the box. When she saw Monique's hands and feet bound with packing tape, she whipped her head around to face Billy. "Go to Ali's office and bring back some scissors or something to cut her hands and feet loose." Billy spun around and took off running. "And some water," she yelled out. Then she knelt beside Monique. "This is going to hurt," she said, and Monique nodded frantically, her eyes not leaving Kennedy.

Monique gasped as Kennedy pulled the duct tape and a sock away from her lips. "Tristan," she said weakly, her eyes rolling, "it was Tristan," and she fainted.

Franklin ran back to the locker. "I got Omar, and he's on his way down. I can't believe I left my radio in the dressing room. Where's Billy?"

"Looking for scissors or a knife or something. We need to cut her loose."

Franklin patted his pants. "Of all the times I don't have my regular clothes on," he grumbled.

Billy ran back into the locker, out of breath. "H-h-here," he panted, handing Kennedy a bottle of water and Franklin the scissors. He stared at Monique Patrick, lying in the box, packing material surrounding her.

"Billy," Kennedy said calmly. "Billy! Look at me. I need you to find the sleigh. It's going to get busy down here, but you, Franklin, and I still have to get the sleigh upstairs and finish the show. Can I count on you?" she asked.

Billy, visibly shaken, nodded. He looked around and pointed at a large rectangular box perpendicular to the others. "I think it's that one, but I should get a ladder to look inside and make sure."

"There is a chair in the office down the hallway," Franklin said, pulling the last of the plastic wrap from Monique's wrists.

"Where is Omar?" Kennedy said worriedly. "She said a name."

Franklin looked startled. "He'll be here soon with the calvary." No sooner had the words come out of Franklin's mouth than the staccato of shoes on the polished concrete floor echoed down the corridor.

"Kennedy, Franklin!" Omar called out.

"Over here," Franklin yelled and stood up. He stepped out of the locker and waved his arms. Monique's eyes fluttered at the sound of Franklin's loud baritone voice.

"Where am I?" she whispered hoarsely.

Kennedy patted her shoulder. "Safe." Monique's eyes closed again.

Billy was standing by the locker with a chair and watched as Omar and Dr. Craig walked into where Kennedy was crouched. The doctor knelt beside Monique. "She roused a few times but kept fainting," Kennedy said. "Will she be okay?"

Doctor Craig took Monique's wrist in his hand to check her pulse. "She'll be fine. Will you help me sit her up, and may I have that water?" he asked, and they gently helped Monique into a sitting position. "I think I know what kept her sedated until now."

Omar looked at Kennedy, Franklin, and Billy standing in the hallway. "How on earth did you find her? We turned the ship upside down."

"I forgot one of the props," Kennedy pointed to the box above them, "and we came down to get it. She must have heard us and made the box move around, and thank goodness she did because Billy saw it. Omar, I need to tell you what she told me before she fainted, and then we have to get upstairs," she said with some urgency. They walked a few steps away, and she told him the name Monique had whispered.

Omar walked back into the locker and knelt beside Monique. Dr. Craig and the captain had lifted her out of the box, and Franklin pushed it into the hallway. The captain suddenly noticed Franklin's red pants, suspenders, and black boots. He raised an eyebrow. "Lounging attire, Mr. Blaas?" A smile turned up at the corners of his mouth.

"No, sir, just another one of the many uniforms I wear around here," Franklin answered and glared at Kennedy as she tried to stifle a snicker behind her hand. She pointed at the box above Monique's head. "Is there a way we can get that box?" She looked at her watch. "We are on a bit of a time crunch and could get out of your way."

Dr. Craig helped Monique move over while the captain, Franklin, and Billy lifted the large box from its spot and carried it into the hallway.

"Guys, we've got to hurry. We only have ten minutes before the song starts, and our star is down here." They walked quickly to the freight elevator carrying the enormous box. Kennedy pressed the up button and looked at her watch. "Hurry, hurry, hurry," she whispered to herself. When the doors opened, they were happy to see it was Safety Officer Tully with a wheelchair and not a dozen linen carts. Kennedy pressed the button for deck five, and Franklin reached over and punched the button a second time. She turned to him. "You realize I just pushed the button, right? Do you think it will go faster if *you* push it?"

"I'm Santa," he growled, "and this thing better know I'm on it and need it to go as fast as my reindeer on Christmas night."

Kennedy rolled her eyes, and as if the elevator had heard him, it made a quick ascent to the theater's back doors.

She cocked an ear at the music playing and turned to Franklin. "Go get into the rest of your costume and meet us at stage right." Franklin jogged to his dressing room, and the captain, Kennedy, and Billy pulled the sleigh out of the box and walked it over to the side of the stage. Several cast members dressed in brown velvet jackets and bowler hats, which had sprouted reindeer antlers, walked by. If they were surprised to see the captain helping unload the sleigh with Kennedy and Billy, they did not show it. Kennedy had a way of getting people to do things.

"Kennedy, you find yourself in some of the most interesting predicaments, don't you," the captain said as he set his end of the sleigh down. "I cannot begin to tell you how thankful I am that the world's most organized woman forgot something, which led to Ms. Patrick being found. If you will excuse me, I need to radio the authorities to tell them we do not have a man overboard situation."

Several of the dancers dressed in reindeer costumes lined up by Kennedy and Billy in front of the sleigh. The next number was a fast-paced rock and roll piece with high kicks and acrobatics and was sure to wow the audience. When Kennedy put the show together, she envisioned Santa being pushed in his sleigh across the stage by his reindeer at the end of the song. "Hey, Kennedy," Franklin walked up to her, and he looked like the perfect Santa Claus. "What if I come through the entry doors when the song starts and walk through the audience?" he grinned.

Kennedy blinked and shrugged her shoulders at the cast members dressed like reindeer. "Whatever Santa wants, he gets. I'm not going on the naughty list."

"Your name is at the top of that list! Right there beside Mila and Rosemary!" Franklin roared over his shoulder. He began to make his way toward the side exit.

Kennedy had an idea. "Franklin! Give me one moment."

He waited, curious to see what she needed, and chuckled when he saw the Sunny Dayz trophy in her hands. "Terri Butler is in the audience sitting halfway down on the left side aisle. I'll have Chris put a spotlight on her when you are close. Will you give her the trophy? She won today's contest, and it's on her wish list, Santa."

Franklin left carrying the trophy, and Kennedy picked up the phone to tell the audio-visual team about the change. The music began, and the reindeer-dressed cast members began to dance. Suddenly the doors to the theater were thrown open, and Franklin bellowed out a hearty "ho-ho-ho." The audience turned in surprise, roaring their approval. As he made his way down the aisle, a spotlight fell on Terri Butler. He walked up to her and pretended to rummage in his bag.

He pulled out the gold award and gently placed it in her hands. Terri sat utterly still, her eyes watering. She hugged the trophy to her chest like a child who had been given a long-awaited toy.

The last song of the evening was the Christmas classic, "There's No Place Like Home for the Holidays" by Perry Como. Kennedy had asked the crew, cast, and staff for photos of themselves celebrating Christmas with their families and on the ship over the years. She received so many pictures that the audio-visual team could show different scenes on the four monitors. Then, the lights dimmed as the orchestral intro began, and holiday pictures filled the screens.

Kennedy walked out onto the darkened stage and began singing the song's first stanza as the lights slowly rose. "Ladies and gentlemen," she said into her microphone, "we feel like you are a part of our family too, and we ask you to join us in this song." Then, the curtain raised, and members of the cast, crew, and staff rolled out a large Christmas tree with twinkling lights. When the song was over, Kennedy once again took center stage. "Thank you all so much for sharing in our holiday show tunes showcase, and now I'd like to ask Mr. Deuce Dawson from Classic Style Network and our four competing chefs to come up on stage."

Deuce walked purposefully up the steps and took his place in front of the microphone at the center of the stage while Lola, Jordan, Tristan, and Miles stood off to the side in eager anticipation.

Deuce took a deep breath and looked first at the four chefs and then at the audience. "The moment we have all been waiting for is going to have to wait a little longer," Deuce said. There was a collective groan from the crowd. Deuce shook his head. "The scores are too close to determine a winner." Deuce held up a finger, "I know you are disappointed. I am disappointed, too but stay tuned to our morning show as each of our competitors will guest host a cooking segment over the next few weeks." He turned to face the four chefs who stood there dumbfounded. "Let's give them a round of applause." He and the audience began to clap enthusiastically. Not fully comprehending what Deuce had said, Lola, Jordan, Miles, and Tristan smiled and clapped along with him. One of Santa's reindeer came out from the wings and escorted them offstage as the house lights came up and the passengers began to leave the theater. No longer stunned but frustrated, they came back on stage to wait for Deuce. They had questions that only he could answer.

When Deuce finally arrived, Emily Abbott was with him, and the chefs began peppering him with questions.

"Chef, don't punish them for what I did," Jordan said. Miles, Lola, and Tristan turned their eyes to her.

"Oh my gosh, the Ice Princess screwed up. What did you do?" Tristan asked snottily. "I thought you could do no wrong. Please, tell us your big sin."

Emily gave Jordan a brief shake of her head.

"So, let me get this right, none of us won?" Lola interrupted loudly, putting her hands on her hips.

"Well, yes and no," Deuce replied. "The morning show has had great ratings during the competition, and they want to bring each of you on as a host chef for our cooking segment."

"This is so unfair," Lola whined.

"Life isn't always fair, Lola," Deuce said flatly. "On another note, there will be no article at this time. Ms. Patrick said the competition lacked excitement."

"Lacked excitement?" Miles echoed. "Did she watch the competitions? So, she interviews us, pries into our private life, pesters us about our dirty laundry, makes false accusations, badgers us in Cozumel, and suddenly we aren't interesting? That is rather unprofessional of her."

"I know it is unfair, but it was what she communicated." Deuce held his hands up in supplication. "She offered to do the article, and she can rescind that offer."

"I'm ready to get off this boat," Tristan said disgustedly. "This competition has been nothing more than a joke. I'm going to my room to pack." He took off his apron and looked at Jordan, Lola, and Miles. "No offense, but I hope I never see any of you again." He balled up the apron and threw it at Deuce. "And you can be sure I won't be watching your stupid show. You don't need to call me for the guest appearance. I have plenty of real fans at my restaurant."

Seeing Omar on the opposite side of the stage, Tristan began to make his way toward the steps to leave.

"Chef Colon, we need to speak with you," Omar called out, and Tristan stopped for a split second but resumed his quick pace as if he hadn't heard Omar.

"CHEF COLON!" Omar barked loudly this time. "I have some questions for you. We can discuss them in my office or here in front of everyone." The others watched, unsure of what was happening.

Tristan whirled around and crossed his arms in defiance. The others could see that his face was pale, and his eyes were wide with fear. Then he raised his hand in the air as if bidding them farewell and began walking. "So long, losers!"

He had almost reached the steps to the stage when Omar spoke again, "Monique Patrick had quite a bit to say."

Omar's voice carried through the empty theater as he slowly walked toward Tristan, who had stopped halfway down the steps.

Deuce and Emily looked at Omar in astonishment, and the other three chefs looked at him in curiosity.

"She's alive?" Deuce whispered, and Emily's body visibly sagged in relief.

Omar gave them a quick nod and then turned back to Tristan. "Chef Colon, you need to come with me. There are some allegations Ms. Patrick has made against you."

Five sets of eyes turned from Omar to Tristan.

Tristan rocked back and forth on the step. His right fist beat on the wall beside him. The room was silent, and Tristan's heavy breathing and the staccato of his fist on the wall was the only thing to be heard.

The silence and stares he felt suddenly overwhelmed him, and he turned to face the group. "She sidled up to me in Cozumel and threatened to expose me," he said in a rush. "I just needed her to be out of the way for a little while. The interview and her threats would have made sure I wouldn't be the host chef. None of us would have." He looked wildly at the three chefs. "You all got a note slipped under your door, didn't you? Notes threatening to expose your darkest secrets? She was going to print that information in her article, plus anything she had asked about during our interviews. So, I made a deal with her not to expose any of us."

"I don't think she would see it that way," Omar said dryly.

Tristan turned his eyes back to Omar. "It wasn't like I killed her," he said flippantly, rolling his eyes. "I just knocked her out and stashed her in the lower hold. I was going to make an anonymous call as soon as we reached Port Canaveral so someone could find her."

Omar made a motion for his two security guards to step forward. "Chef Tristan, we will need to hold you for questioning by the authorities in Port Canaveral. Officers, please take him down to the hold."

Tristan was led from the stage while the others looked on in shock. "How did he do it?" Miles asked, horrified by what he had just heard.

"What I have pieced together is that Tristan swiped your medication, Miles, and used it to keep her in an unconscious state. Did you have trouble with your cabin door? One of my officers said it wouldn't engage the lock."

Miles looked at Omar in surprise. "Yeah, I had to pull it hard, or it would suddenly open on its own."

Omar looked grim. "That explains how he got into your room." He looked back at the group. "Somehow, he got her down to the lower hold and into one of the storage lockers you saw on your tour. He kept her there drugged and in a box until she was found. We'll learn more, I'm sure, in the next few hours."

Suddenly Tristan's comment from earlier in the evening about taking Miles's medication to sleep if they had shared a cabin made sense to him.

"How dumb can you be?" Lola said disgustedly.

"About as dumb as a woman who passes herself off as a chef so she can swindle money and jewelry out of vulnerable men," Deuce said sharply. He looked at Omar, who had a surprised look on his face. "Her fan club stopped me outside of the theater tonight and told me everything," he said and then looked back at Lola. "You've cut a wide swath in Breezy Bayou and Sunny Acres. I'm sure you've done it elsewhere." He folded his arms. "We will not need you as a guest chef, Ms. Cobb." Lola looked at him murderously. Then, she turned on her heel and stalked through the heavy velvet curtains that led to the backstage area.

Omar cleared his throat. "I don't have anything for the rest of you, and as you heard, Ms. Patrick will not be writing her article. She turned these over to me." He handed them each a packet with their names on it. "She has promised not to write anything about any of you. Her time in the cardboard box has made her reassess her interviewing style."

# Sunny Dayz Cruise Line

## THE HELIO

### DAY SIX

ARRIVAL IN PORT CANAVERAL, FLORIDA, USA

DISEMBARKATION BEGINS AT 9:00AM

The following day started early for the *Helio* team. The passengers had left their luggage outside their cabins at midnight, and it was already waiting for them in the cruise terminal.

Kennedy stood in the lobby wishing everyone goodbye. Emily Abbott came up to her, "Kennedy, I don't know what to say. This has been a riveting cruise."

"Much more than any Mrs. Jameson has been on," Kennedy grinned. "We didn't get to talk after your lecture. Did you enjoy giving it?"

"My dear, it was simply marvelous! I was up all night thinking. I want to investigate taking our cruises up a notch: guest lecturers, cooking classes, and port discussions. And I think we can do it with our partnership with the Classic Style Network. Make a niche for ourselves." She paused. "What do you think about Chef Jordan?" she asked.

"Jordan is an incredibly talented chef. It's a shame I rarely get to St. Augustine because I would love to visit her restaurant."

"I agree," Emily said with a sparkle in her eye. "I'd hate to think that kind of talent was being swept out to sea on a technicality." She smiled mischievously. "I might have a plan for Jordan, but I need to speak with some people first and see if she is interested."

"Have you seen my friend Omar? I wanted to say goodbye and thank him for giving me things to taunt Vera with."

Kennedy shook her head. "I'm afraid he is tied up with the authorities all morning. Chef Tristan is in a cell in the lower hold while Monique gives her formal statement to the authorities."

Emily made a face. "Dreadful woman, I don't want to say she deserved what she got, but the way she went about her business was quite distasteful. I will have a stern discussion with Winnifred about her so-called friend and ensure our legal team is aware of her tactics."

Kennedy waved goodbye to a few other guests and smiled when she saw Deuce Dawson. He put out his hand. "Thanks for everything, Kennedy. I'm sorry we had such a bumpy start."

"All is well. Didn't someone say something about cooking being the art of adjustment?" Kennedy asked.

Deuce looked at her, surprised. "That was the great Jacques Pépin. I was led to believe that you didn't know anything about cooking, and here you are quoting a famous culinarian."

Kennedy gave him a grin. "His quote, and putting milk and cereal in a bowl, is the extent of my culinary skills."

"Have you seen Art?" Deuce asked, and Kennedy shook her head. She knew Bert and Art were on the promenade deck saying goodbye and didn't want anyone to disturb them. "Well, if you do, would you tell her I went straight to the office? I spoke with my bosses this morning to explain why we didn't have a winner, and the idea you and Mrs. Abbott came up with has knocked their socks off."

Kennedy stuck out her hand. "Good luck, Mr. Dawson. We look forward to seeing what happens on your show."

The next familiar face Kennedy saw was her friend David. "What happened to you?" she asked anxiously. "You went to dinner, and I never saw you again."

David smiled and held up his notebook. "Inspiration, my darling girl. I watched your holiday show and had an insane idea for Club Diva. I've been up all night writing out the show. John is going to scream over this. There is so much to do to get this done quickly. I promise I'll call you later, doll!" He jogged down the gangway. Kennedy shook her head. Whatever he was working on would be fabulous. David and the Club Diva Boys didn't know any other way.

Chef Miles walked up behind her and said in a deep voice, "Good morning, Ms. Reeves. Are you still having perfect strangers tell you that you are beautiful? Because I'm still perfect, and you are still beautiful."

Kennedy turned around. "Ah, but Chef Miles, we are no longer strangers, are we?"

"I suppose not," he chuckled.

"Tell me you didn't use that line on her, Miles!" Jordan said, shaking her head and looking at the two of them. "Tell me he didn't, Kennedy."

Kennedy rolled her eyes and grinned. "So, what's next for you both?"

Miles spoke up first, "I'm going back to my restaurant to give it a jumpstart. Mom's gone, and I need to stop riding on her coattails. She left me a legacy, and now it's my turn to stand on my own two feet."

Kennedy smiled and shook his hand. "Best of luck to you." Miles waved and walked down the gangway.

"And for you?" Kennedy smiled mischievously. "Is Chef Michèle disguising his tears by chopping onions?"

Jordan's eyes danced. "I'm not sure what is next. I've invited him to visit me when he has some time off. So, we'll see what happens."

"He'll be knocking on your door soon. I'm sure of it. Good luck, Jordan. I am sorry things didn't work out with the competition."

Jordan shrugged her shoulders. "Crossroads show up unexpectedly, and we need to decide what we will do. This cruise allowed me to find some happiness, courage, and a possibility I had never thought about, so I don't count it as a loss at all."

Kennedy hugged her and watched as she disappeared out of the lobby. She hoped she would cross paths again with Jordan. Kennedy spoke with a few more passengers, thanking them for coming on the cruise and helping them understand how to get their luggage from the terminal when she heard squabbling. The Gents from Breezy Bayou were coming toward her.

"Last chance, toots," Marshall wheezed as he wheeled up to her. "Last chance to run away with me. Once I go down the gangway, I'm back in the arms of a swarm of women."

Kennedy bent down and kissed Marshall on the cheek. "Our unrequited love story will be one of my greatest losses." Then, she straightened up. "It was a pleasure meeting all of you. I have some friends I think you would like to meet. They take our cruises quite often."

"Are they hot?" Marshall asked. "I only want to go out with hot women, my days are numbered, and I can't waste them."

Karl turned red and began choking while the others laughed. "Pop, you are either going to obedience or reform school when we get home. I haven't decided which, but we might stop at the pet store and get a muzzle first." He waved to the others. "We'll see you guys back at Breezy Bayou."

"I'm going to take off too." Paulie held out his hand to shake Kennedy's. "Thank you for taking care of us." He looked around the lobby wistfully. "She's got good bones."

Kennedy watched as Larry, Eddie, and Paulie left the ship. She hoped they would be back.

Kennedy did not see Terri and Jones Butler depart. After the holiday show, Kennedy stayed outside the theater doors mingling with the passengers. She had watched Omar go in through the side entrance and decided to stay in the lobby to ensure no one went back inside. Jones and Terri came up to tell her goodbye, and when she looked at them quizzically, Terri, hugging her trophy tightly, explained to Kennedy that they would be off the ship early. As soon as they got off the ship, they were going to try to meet with their decorator, the same woman who had designed the Owner's Suite, to discuss the changes they wanted to make.

A busy but relaxed quietness descended upon the ship. Crew and staff members went about their duties as they enjoyed having the ship to themselves once again. There was a staff meeting with Alfred in an hour. Kennedy looked over her clipboard. She could do everything on her list a little later. She decided she would find Mila for a quick catch-up. Kennedy stopped first at the spa, only to be informed by Anna Marie that Mila was on the pier accepting a delivery.

"They wiped us out of products. This new look makes people want to take home a piece of the spa, even if it's shampoo."

Kennedy walked quickly down the stairs and through the lobby. She was at the top of the gangway and saw Omar at the bottom. She was about to call out to him, but something stopped her. A woman was walking purposefully toward him.

"What are you doing here?" Kennedy heard him shout over the wind. "I tried to call you, but you didn't answer. I had some urgent matters that I needed to address this morning. You were always so very impatient, even as a little girl."

"Matters more important than this?" the dark-haired woman said and held out a sheaf of papers wrapped in pale blue. "Omar," she said passionately, "would you please sign these divorce papers?"

# AUTHORS NOTE

You didn't see that coming, did you? Now you *have to* read book three to find out what happens next! Thank you for reading *A Cruise for Sous*, the second in the Kennedy Reeves series. If this is the first time you've read a Kennedy Reeves Mystery, I hope you enjoyed meeting Kennedy and her friends as much as I loved bringing them to life. If you read the previous book, *A Boat for a Goat*, I hope you had fun reconnecting with the gang and meeting a few new people.

Book three in the series, *A Heist on the Ice*, finds Kennedy and her friends Bert and Mila helping on a VIP test cruise for their sister ship, the *Malina*, as she returns to her Alaskan waters. Things start out rocky when the welcome they receive is as icy as Alaska's waters. And while Kennedy and the passengers are taking in Alaska's dazzling beauty, someone else is busy pocketing other sparkling things.

—MJ Mac

✉ mjmacauthor@gmail.com

Facebook – MJ Mac

Linked In—MJ Mac

Instagram – MJ_Mac_Author

www.amazon.com/author/mjmac

www.goodreads.com/author/show/22910684.MJ_Mac

# OTHER BOOKS BY MJ MAC

## A BOAT FOR A GOAT
### Kennedy Reeves Mystery Series Book 1

Kennedy Reeves, cruise director for the *Helio*, has been called back to work after being on land for the last year. She looks forward to greeting her passengers: the business world's newest mega-millionaire couple, the Club Diva Boys, the Ladies from Harmony Lakes, and Vera Jameson (a businesswoman who could make a drill sergeant cry). Everything looks shipshape until the consultant hired by the corporate office arrives, and he has a very different course charted. Join Kennedy, her friends, and their zany passengers as they navigate the turbulent waters of their first cruise in *A Boat for a Goat*.

Available in paperback and e-book on Amazon, Barnes & Noble, Books a Million, and Indigo

# A HEIST ON THE ICE
## Kennedy Reeves Mystery Series Book 3
COMING SOON – SPRING 2023

*A Heist on the Ice* finds cruise director Kennedy Reeves helping on a VIP test cruise as the *Malina* returns to her Alaskan waters. Things start out rocky when the welcome she receives is as icy as Alaska's waters. And who does Kennedy see on the manifest? None other than the formidable Vera Jameson and the last passenger Kennedy ever wanted to see again—LaVonda Taylor, the woman who tried to have her fired years ago. Things don't get any better when the *Malina's* cruise director, J. Mitchell Templeton, threatened by Kennedy's presence on the ship, decides to treat her like his lackey. When he's not dumping his duties on Kennedy, he's finding ways to thwart her. And while Kennedy and the passengers are taking in Alaska's dazzling beauty, someone else is busy pocketing other sparkling things.

# <u>ACKNOWLEDGEMENTS</u>

The author gratefully acknowledges the assistance of many, many people who helped bring this dream alive: Dan McCarragher, for his patience, love, and support as I continue on this journey; Elvis for her patience on the late nights writing; my beta reader team (Kristy, Denise, Orson, Kathy, Marcia, Ann, and Paula) as they patiently read the first draft and offered *loving* critique; Chef Mike Putnam and Chef Kendall Linhart for sharing what really happens in the kitchen; Chris Gordon for answering my countless audio-visual questions; David Oetken for sharing the Galt House Hotel's dining room book, Michelle Krueger, my fabulous editor who polished another very rough diamond. The author also acknowledges Gettys Images, iStock Photos, Weape Studio, and Dharma Type for the use of images and fonts.

# **ABOUT THE AUTHOR**

Before embarking on a writing career, MJ Mac was a "Jill of all trades" in corporate America for forty years. MJ was a master juggler in her three-inch heels and lipstick, pulling the ropes from behind the curtain to seamlessly make magic happen. In 2021, a story about a cruise director, her coworkers, and their zany passengers began to formulate in her head. She traded in the corporate world of useless meetings, meetings about meetings, high heels, and suits for the sand, flip flops, and a sarong to pursue writing full-time and hasn't looked back. MJ and her husband Dan (her biggest supporter next to their adorable albeit scruffy dog Elvis) are living their best life on the beach, where she spends her time plotting what drama Kennedy and her friends will find next.